BLOOD LINES

BLOOD LINES

A Novel

NELSON DEMILLE
ALEX DEMILLE

THORNDIKE PRESS
A part of Gale, a Cengage Company

Copyright © 2023 by Nelson DeMille and Alex DeMille.
Scott Brodie Series.
Thorndike Press, a part of Gale, a Cengage Company.

Thorndike Press® Large Print Top Shelf.
The text of this Large Print edition is unabridged.
Other aspects of the book may vary from the original edition.
Set in 16 pt. Plantin.

LIBRARY OF CONGRESS CIP DATA ON FILE.
CATALOGUING IN PUBLICATION FOR THIS BOOK
IS AVAILABLE FROM THE LIBRARY OF CONGRESS.

ISBN-13: 979-8-88579-252-3 (hardcover alk. paper)

Published in 2023 by arrangement with Scribner, a division of Simon & Schuster, Inc.

Printed in the United States of America
1 2 3 4 5 6 7 27 26 25 24 23

For Dagmar,
who made this all possible

The old world is dying,
And the new world struggles to be born;
Now is the time of monsters.

ANTONIO GRAMSCI

PART I

CHAPTER 1

Harry Vance finished dressing in the dark bedroom, using his cell phone to find a pair of matching socks. It was past two in the morning and he was trying to leave without waking Anna, so he shouldn't have been so particular. But at the age of fifty-three, Vance had learned to accept and embrace his own bullshit. And he knew his steps felt a little less sure when his socks didn't match.

He walked to the tall window and parted the curtains. The dark streets below were lined with turn-of-the-century apartment buildings and shuttered storefronts, and the day's rain had turned the curbside snowbanks into rivers of gray slush. The sidewalks were barren on this cold January night, but the bars and clubs tucked away in this trendy corner of Berlin were still open, their music and laughter echoing down the dark street.

Vance turned and looked at Anna, asleep under a thick blanket. A space heater hummed at the far end of the room. These

11

old buildings were nice to look at, but they weren't insulated, and nothing worked. Anna thought the building had "character," a word that made Vance want to step into traffic. Well, that's what he got for becoming involved with a younger woman.

He approached the bed and took a closer look at her by the dim light coming through the window. She didn't look like herself when she slept. Her face was relaxed, soft. So different from who she was.

Vance reached his hand out to . . . what? Touch her? Try to wake her? Tell her where he was going? Why would he do something like that? *Because you're an idiot.* Which is another way of saying you're in love.

He withdrew his hand. The point was to not tell her anything. She didn't like that, of course. And neither did the brass back at headquarters when he froze them out of his investigations until it was time to make arrests. But this was how Army CID Agent Harry Vance had always approached his work. Just do it. Only amateurs and cowards needed outside opinions before the job was done.

So he hadn't told her about tonight's rendezvous, and he'd be back in bed before sunrise. They'd wake up together, maybe a morning roll in the sack, then fried eggs with black bread and coffee, watch the news. Sunday stuff.

Anna rolled over, muttering something in

German that he couldn't make out. Her arm flopped onto the empty side of the mattress, which still contained his impression in the cheap memory foam.

He pictured her waking up in the night to use the bathroom or get some water and seeing that he was gone. She'd freak out.

He took out his phone and typed her a text: *Couldn't sleep. Going for a walk. Back by dawn.* He hesitated, then added: *I love you.*

Every word of that was true, though he might have left out a few things. He hit Send and heard her phone vibrate on the bedside table.

He walked to the foyer, where he put on his scarf and wool cap. He eyed a small table piled with yesterday's mail, then slid open a drawer to reveal his Beretta M9 inside a pancake holster.

Vance stared at the pistol. He wasn't doing anything dangerous. Unless, of course, he was closer to the truth than he realized. And you never know you're there until you're there.

He clipped the holster on his belt, then put on his camel-hair topcoat. He unbolted the heavy door and stepped onto the dimly lit landing, closing the door quietly behind him.

Vance descended two flights of stairs, then stepped out into the winter night and felt the sharp snap of cold air on his face. He lit a cigarette and walked north to the Prenzlauer Allee S-Bahn train station, a handsome turn-of-the-century brick building that — like Anna's street and much of the neighborhood of Prenzlauer Berg — appeared to have somehow survived the war intact. Though in Berlin you didn't always know what was original and what got pieced back together from the rubble.

He walked down a set of icy stairs to the tracks, which ran along a trench below street level. He checked his watch as he waited on the platform: 2:27 A.M. It was the weekend, so the S-Bahn ran all night. He watched a young couple huddled inside a glass-paneled shelter as a cold north wind whipped down the platform.

On a typical case, he'd have his partner, Mark Jenkins, with him. But this wasn't a typical case. In fact, it wasn't a CID case at all. He was moonlighting here in Berlin, hundreds of miles from the headquarters of the U.S. Army's 5th Military Police Battalion in Kaiserslautern, a small city near Frankfurt where Vance lived and worked. His colleagues knew he came to Berlin whenever he had time off. They assumed it was for a woman, and they made their jokes. But they were only half right.

He thought about his wife, Julie, back in Kaiserslautern, soon to be ex if the papers ever went through. German efficiency, he'd found out, did not extend to divorce proceedings. She was a good woman and didn't

14

deserve half the crap he put her through. Then again, she'd chosen to stay in the marriage. We all make our own prisons.

Vance spotted the train approaching and took a last drag on his cigarette. He flicked the butt onto the tracks, then took out his cell and texted: *Ich bin unterwegs.* I'm on my way.

After a few seconds he received a reply: *Ich werde da sein.* I'll be there.

The train eased into the station and Vance boarded. He took a seat and looked around as the train pulled out. His car was mostly empty, as was the entire train, the length of which he could see due to the open gangways. He spotted a group of hyperactive twentysomethings at the far end, probably clubhopping until dawn. He'd done that once with Anna, which was one time too many. She thought she was keeping him young, but she was actually just reminding him of the gulf between them.

The city slid by out the grimy window. He was heading southeast to Neukölln, a neighborhood with a large Turkish and Arab immigrant population, made larger in the last few years thanks to Germany's generous asylum policy toward Syrian refugees. It was a policy that made many Germans proud — and enraged and frightened just as many.

Vance tried to stay out of his host country's internal politics, though as a Chief Warrant

Officer in the CID's Terrorism and Criminal Investigation Unit, or TCIU, this rapid influx of refugees had affected his caseload. There were dozens of U.S. Army installations across Europe, and Vance and his colleagues in the TCIU were responsible for investigating perceived terrorist threats against all of them, as well as threats against any U.S. Army personnel located on the European continent or North Africa, which was his command's area of responsibility.

In truth, most of the flood of refugees arriving in Germany came here to escape the ravages of war and create a better life, and even the criminal element among them largely restricted their activities to nonpolitical felonies. But it was the potential ISIS or al Qaeda operatives who managed to slip through, and also the jobless and isolated young men who became radicalized once in Germany, who kept Vance and his colleagues busy. As they say in counterterrorism, the good guys need to succeed every time; the bad guys need to succeed only once.

Vance looked out the window as the train crossed over the Spree River, and then passed from the former East Berlin into the West. What had once been a fortified wall of concrete, razor wire, dogs, soldiers, and searchlights was now a phantom border crisscrossed by twenty-four-hour train lines and rejoined streets, and you'd have to have a sightseeing guide to find the few shards of the Wall still standing. Vance figured that was probably a good thing. Berlin, more than most places, had to navigate remembering the past without becoming a shrine to its horrors.

He remembered watching the Wall come down on TV. The cheering crowds as people took sledgehammers to the hated structure. East German police and soldiers standing impotent as Germans from East and West defiantly held hands atop the Wall, one people again.

He had been in his first semester of his senior year at Johns Hopkins, thinking about a military career and what his role might be in helping to contain the Soviet menace. And then, in the blink of an eye, the forty-year Cold War was over. The Iron Curtain parted. The nuclear threat lifted. A new world had dawned overnight, and no one knew what to do about it. It turned out the new world was more complicated than the old, and thirty years later Vance was still trying to figure it out.

In a few minutes the train arrived at the Neukölln station and Vance got out. He walked along the elevated train platform, which was covered in graffiti and smelled vaguely of urine. He descended the stairs and exited onto Karl-Marx Straße, a street that mocked its namesake with a McDonald's.

He walked north along Karl-Marx, passing a number of closed halal groceries, Turkish coffee shops, and Middle Eastern restaurants. Up ahead an Arab teenager in a winter parka leaned against a lamp pole, watching him. Vance wondered if he was a dealer or maybe a corner boy for one of the Arab crime syndicates that operated in this area. Vance — with his barrel chest and a healthy paunch due to his love affair with dark German lagers — didn't fit the profile of a heroin junkie looking for a fix. In fact, he probably looked to this kid to be exactly what he was — a plainclothes cop. As Vance got closer, the boy averted his eyes.

After a couple of blocks, he found the place he was looking for — a five-story apartment building with a hookah lounge on the ground floor called Ember Berlin. There were only a few customers sitting in the dim smoky lounge amidst Turkish tapestries, garish blue lighting, and thumping Arabic pop music.

Vance entered through the glass doors and looked around the lounge. A group of Turkish thirty-something guys were in one corner smoking and laughing, and a couple of old Arab men in tracksuits were sitting near the front door quietly sharing a hookah. The tracksuits scanned him and one of them let out a huge puff of apple-scented smoke.

Vance walked to the back where upholstered vinyl seating ran along the rear wall behind small tables and chairs. He took a seat facing the door and placed his hat on the table. He kept his coat on to make sure no one caught sight of his holstered M9.

A young Turkish waiter walked over and dropped a menu on the table. "Guten Abend. Huka? Kaffee?"

"Türkischer Kaffee, bitte."

The young man nodded and walked off.

Vance checked his watch: 3:05 A.M. He pulled his phone out and looked at the text thread he'd exchanged with the man he was there to meet, Abbas al-Hamdani. He'd received the man's number from a local guy with connections. Hamdani wasn't known to CID, and Vance hadn't done much to verify al-Hamdani's identity other than to request the man send a current photo of himself. Vance looked at the picture. Hamdani was a heavyset man in his seventies with a bushy gray mustache and large, sad eyes.

He looked at Hamdani's last message: *Ich werde da sein.* I'll be there.

The waiter returned with his coffee and he sipped it as he watched the door. The street outside was empty except for an occasional car or Vespa. After a few more minutes, he sent a text: *Ich bin da.* I'm here.

No response. Vance drank his coffee and began to wonder why he'd left a hot woman and a warm bed for this crap. Then again, the woman — Anna — was the reason he was here in the first place.

His wife used to tell him he had a savior complex. He became overly involved in other people's problems instead of keeping his own house in order. She was right, of course. It was probably why he was a good investigator and a bad husband. After twenty-five years together, he and Julie had each other pretty well figured out. Which was the problem. Marriages, like criminal investigations, tend to be over when there's no more mystery.

His phone vibrated. He checked it and saw a message that said in German: *I can no longer meet there.*

Vance tapped out a reply: *We had an arrangement.*

The reply came quickly: *I cannot be seen with you.*

Vance wrote: *No one knows who I am.*

No response for a moment. Then: *Come to Thomashöhe Park. Up the road. Inside the park by the eastern entrance. This is better security for us both.*

Vance waited to reply. He eyed the two old Arab guys in tracksuits and wondered if they knew Hamdani. Like a lot of immigrant and refugee communities, this place was insular, with complex alliances and resentments that dated back to their native lands, and probably to the beginning of time. Maybe Hamdani got tipped to these guys' presence and didn't want to be seen talking to a white guy at three in the morning. Too many questions.

Vance had insisted on a public place, and Hamdani could have picked anywhere, in any neighborhood. Why here, in his own back-yard, if he was concerned about being seen? Something wasn't adding up.

He looked at the map on his phone and saw that Thomashöhe Park was only a few blocks away. His CID training told him that meeting an unknown informant in a park in the middle of the night was a bad idea, but his ego and his Beretta assured him it would be fine. He decided to split the difference and practice some minimal operational secu-rity. He spotted another park due south of Thomashöhe, called Körnerpark, and wrote back: *Meet me in Körnerpark. Near the northern entrance off Jonasstraße. Fifteen minutes.* He'd enter the park at the southern entrance and be there in five. If Hamdani balked, Vance would abort.

After a moment he received a response: *Ok. See you there.*

Vance knocked back the rest of the sludgy sweet Turkish coffee, put on his hat, then dropped some euros on the table and left.

He continued north along Karl-Marx Straße and after a few blocks made a left onto a side street. He walked a block and saw the entrance to Körnerpark, which was sunk

21

about twenty feet below street level and ringed with stone balustrades. A staircase led down into the park, with a chain stretched across it to indicate it was closed.

Vance walked up to the balustrade and looked into the park, which was lit by scattered lampposts. Gridded paths, manicured hedges, and white stone statues gave the impression of a palace garden. The place was nice to look at, but turned out to be a bad tactical choice — a lot of open spaces, and anyone observing him from a distance could easily have the high ground.

He walked to the stairway and paused. A chill wind shook the bare branches of the trees around him, and the fat crescent moon cast a spectral pall over the frozen stone figures in the park.

I want to tell you what happened to my father.

He remembered just how Anna had said it, in her crisp German accent, and how she'd looked at the time — her stark features barely revealed through the dim light of the nightclub where she had taken him on one of their first dates, some trendy spot located in a former East Berlin brick factory. It was a real Anna kind of place — cool and hip but also heavy with the weight of history, where in the gloom beyond the dancers and club lights you could almost imagine the poor bastards in the sweltering brickworks, laboring toward a new world that would never come.

22

"He was betrayed," Anna had said between blasts of industrial techno. "And then he was murdered."

That's when it had truly begun, this obsession of his. And it was why Vance was standing here now, knee-deep in an investigation of a cold case that he had no jurisdiction over, and which had occurred in a country that no longer existed. Leaving his wife for a younger woman might have seemed like the obvious sign of a midlife crisis. But maybe the real crisis was here, in the freezing night, looking for justice in all the wrong places.

He slid his M9 out of the holster and held it inside the pocket of his topcoat, then ducked under the chain and descended the stairs into the park.

PART II

CHAPTER 2

Chief Warrant Officer Scott Brodie drove his Army-issue Chevy Impala down the narrow back road. Thick growths of Virginia pine crowded the shoulders between dirt driveways leading to dilapidated houses and shanties. It was a bright and frigid day in the middle of January, and yesterday's snow still clung to the pine needles and patchy lawns.

Brad Evans sat in the front passenger seat. He cracked his window and lit a cigarette. "Hate these off-base busts."

Brodie did not reply.

"A soldier won't resist arrest in the barracks. But once he's got his own roof over his head, even one of these little shitboxes . . . his thinking is different. It's instinct. A man defends his castle."

Brodie preferred his partner in the morning, when he was hungover and didn't talk much. But it was 4 P.M., and by now Evans had had his Irish coffee for lunch, followed by two or three more, and he was all jaw.

27

Brodie, age thirty-nine, was a Special Agent in the United States Army Criminal Investigation Division, more commonly known as CID, which was responsible for investigating major felony crimes and violations of the Uniform Code of Military Justice within the Army. Brad Evans was his partner and, like many of Brodie's partners over the course of his thirteen-year career, Evans was an asshole.

Evans continued talking between drags. "These new enlisteds think they can get away with anything. Remember that jerkoff in Norfolk? Growing enough weed to smoke out a brigade? Just heard, they docked his pay, no reduction in rank, no confinement. Bullshit. What the hell kind of message . . . ?"

Brodie let Evans ramble and focused on the road. Brodie and Evans shared an office at CID Headquarters, which was within Marine Corps Base Quantico, a large complex in northeastern Virginia that also housed the Marine Officer Candidates School and Basic School, as well as the Marine Corps University, the FBI Academy, the Drug Enforcement Administration Training Academy, and the Naval Criminal Investigative Service — NCIS — which was the Navy equivalent of Army CID, but with bigger egos thanks to the hit TV show.

Brodie lived in a rented house close to base, though until recently he'd been a nomad, traveling the country and the world on challenging assignments. But that was back when his life was interesting. Before his wings got clipped. Now he could actually spend time in his office. He even got around to checking his mail and doing paperwork, the ultimate indignity.

He eyed the rearview, where the Virginia state trooper was following close behind. Since they were conducting a search outside of a military installation, civilian law enforcement had to ride along. Brodie also had to get the search warrant from a civilian judge. The military had its own ways of doing things, of course, and its own parallel justice system. But in America the civilians still ruled the realm, and intruded when they felt like it, which Brodie guessed meant it was still a free country. But it didn't make his job any easier.

Brodie glanced at his partner as the man kept smoking and yammering. Although CID was full of motivated professionals, Scott Brodie seemed to get stuck with the duds. He'd chosen to not read too much into this, despite his commanding officer Colonel Stanley Dombroski telling him on more than one occasion: "If everyone you work with is an asshole, the asshole is you."

Dombroski was a commissioned officer. Brodie and Evans were officers of a different stripe: warrant officers, which put them above all enlisted soldiers in the Army chain of command, including NCOs, but below the lowest-ranked commissioned officer, meaning a rookie lieutenant just out of ROTC, OCS, or The Point. Within the warrant officer rank there were five grades. Brodie was a CW4. Evans was five years older than Brodie and had served longer, but was still a CW3, which said a few things about Brad Evans.

Scott Brodie, despite his time in service and his time in grade, was fairly sure he'd never get that final promotion to CW5. And the reason for that was his tendency to buck authority when the authority was being stupid. But Brodie could close tough cases, and at the end of the day that's what the brass wanted to see — points on the board. Brodie had a lot of points, which partly made up for his bad attitude and other personality defects. He recalled another Dombroski-ism directed his way: "The only thing worse than a useless idiot you can't work with is an effective pain in the ass you can't fire." Brodie wondered how much of this wisdom the colonel had picked up at Officer Candidates School.

Warrant officers, while technically considered commissioned officers, differed from regular commissioned officers in a few ways that made sense only to the Army. They didn't have formal officer titles and were simply referred to as Mr. or Ms. — or occasionally the gender-neutral Chief — and as CID agents they usually wore civilian clothing and drove civilian unmarked cars. Today Brodie and Evans were both dressed in slacks, dress shirts, and dark-blue windbreakers with the words "CID FEDERAL AGENT" emblazoned on the front and back in big yellow letters. When you're smashing down a suspect's door, you don't want any confusion. And in case there was, Brodie and Evans were packing their M9s.

Evans flicked his cigarette out the window and punched the power on the car radio. A rock song came on, something awful that Brodie half remembered from his college days. Evans started tapping the glove box along with the riffs. "These guys rock. Saw them last summer at the Birchmere. They still got it."

Brodie suggested, "Keep an eye out for the turn."

"Shoulda let the state cracker lead."

"Not when you're with me, Mr. Evans."

This should be a simple bust. But sometimes the cases that looked straightforward ended up going sideways and screwing up your whole day. Still, it beat parking your ass behind a desk all day like some of Brodie's colleagues at Quantico.

Within the CID were experts in a host of fields such as cybercrime, procurement fraud, forensic analysis, polygraph administration, criminal records processing — the desk jockeys — as well as specialists in counterterrorism, protective services, and, in special circumstances, war crimes and treason.

Brodie and Evans were not in a specialized unit, but general criminal investigators — the equivalent of police detectives — working felonies that fell outside the skills and purview of the specialists. They spent much of their day out on the beat gathering evidence, conducting interviews, and — on a good day — locating and arresting the bad guys. Lately the bad guys seemed to be getting stupider and easier to catch, though in reality it was Brodie's cases that were getting stupider, and smaller. And this afternoon's assignment was a perfect example: searching for stolen goods at the home of Private First Class Eric Hinckley, who was suspected of involvement in a larceny ring operating out of Fort A.P. Hill, an Army base near Fredericksburg. Someone was stealing MREs — meals ready to eat — the canned and dehydrated rations that kept America's fighting men and women satiated and constipated while deployed in the field. Private Hinckley worked as a guard at a warehouse that stored MREs, and he was suspected of supplying a third party who was running an online store that had so far done about sixty thousand dollars' worth of business. That was more than enough for a felony charge, though not generally enough to get Scott Brodie out of bed in the morning.

He used to work big cases. Homicides,

narcotics, weapons theft. High-stakes stuff. Often overseas. Evans had too, before he sabotaged his career with an assist from Johnnie Walker. Scott Brodie, on the other hand, hadn't drunk himself into career oblivion. In fact, he'd done his job *too* well on his last major assignment, investigating beyond his mandate, pissing off several Intel agencies, and discovering a few things that were well above his pay grade, and way beyond his need to know. So he got saddled with a deadbeat partner and a bullshit case-load not befitting his experience or skills. Brodie wasn't sure if this was temporary punishment or an attempt to drive him into early retirement. Either way, the Army's aggression toward its maverick officers was often passive but never subtle.

The case that had gotten him on everyone's shit list was from five months back, and had involved tracking down an infamous deserter, Captain Kyle Mercer of the Army's elite Delta Force, who had apparently abandoned his remote post in Afghanistan and been captured by the Taliban. Captain Mercer eventually escaped his captors and turned up in — of all places — Caracas, Venezuela. It would have been more pleasant for everyone if Kyle Mercer had instead decamped to, say, Tahiti, or the Côte d'Azur, but Mercer had chosen the armpit of the Western Hemisphere for very specific reasons that dated back to some wet stuff he'd gotten into while commanding a Black Ops team in Afghanistan. It was a complicated, messy, sensitive, and ultimately sad case, and more than one person who should have stood in front of a court-martial instead came home in a body bag. And people like Brodie and his former partner Maggie Taylor, and their boss, Colonel Dombroski, should have gotten promotions — but got a ton of shit instead. Shit happens.

Evans pointed to a roadside mailbox. "Two-five-six. Right here."

Brodie turned off the road onto a dirt driveway that led to an aluminum-sided ranch house. He parked his car fifty yards from the house and the Virginia state trooper pulled in behind them.

Brodie noticed a Toyota compact parked in front of the detached garage. Brodie, Evans, and the trooper got out without slamming their doors shut.

The Virginia trooper, a pale and lanky redhead in his late twenties named Dave Finley, walked up to them with a crowbar in his hands. Brodie had interacted with Finley before in executing a search warrant, and the guy was a straight arrow. Trooper Finley nodded to the door. "How do you want to do this?"

Brodie looked at the house. The front bay window had heavy curtains drawn. He said to Evans, "Cover the back."

"Copy."

Evans headed around back as Brodie and Finley approached the front door. Brodie noticed there was no doorbell. He could hear something playing loudly on the TV — explosions, gunfire, demonic screams. Probably a video game.

Brodie waited a moment to give Evans time to get to the back door, then he knocked loudly and dialed up his Virginia accent. "Delivery! Need y'all to sign."

They waited. After a few seconds the sound from the TV cut out. They heard footsteps approaching the door. Brodie put his thumb over the door's peephole as he pulled his M9 from its holster and held it at his side.

The footsteps stopped.

Brodie said, "Need a signature or I can't leave it."

All was quiet for a moment; then a face peeked out from behind the window curtains, and disappeared.

Finley shoved the crowbar into the doorjamb and began to pry it open.

The door splintered and Brodie kicked it open as he raised his M9 and caught sight of a male figure running toward the back of the house.

"CID! Halt!" Which is military for "Stop, asshole."

But the asshole kept running.

Brodie took off after him, and the guy ran into a small kitchen, kicked open a metal storm door, and sprinted through the doorway, where he collided with Brad Evans, who didn't seem ready for what was coming and got knocked on his ass.

The guy bolted across the backyard and Brodie chased after him, past a scrawny black Lab that was barking and howling and pulling on the end of a chain.

Brodie cut wide of the dog and headed for the man he assumed was PFC Hinckley, a pasty young guy with a military buzz cut in a tank top and jeans running barefoot. Hinckley was a few yards from a high chain-link fence that marked the edge of his property. Brodie yelled, "Halt! Or I shoot!"

The guy knew that was bullshit and jumped onto the fence and started to scramble up. Brodie holstered his pistol as he caught up to him, grabbed him by his belt, and threw him face down onto the lawn. Hinckley, possibly recalling his Basic Training hand-to-hand combat class, tried to flip, but Brodie jumped on the guy's back and pressed his face into a patch of snow. "Say uncle, asshole!" Hinckley didn't, but he stopped resisting. Brodie grabbed the man's wrists and cuffed his hands behind his back.

"Private Eric Hinckley, I presume?"

"Fuck you."

"I will take that as an affirmative response."

Evans had recovered from his knockdown and was rushing toward them. "Guy came out of nowhere."

"Actually, he came out of the house. Get in there and check for other occupants."

Evans muttered something as he jogged toward the open storm door, gun at his side.

Brodie pulled Hinckley to his feet and spun him around. He flashed his badge and said, "I'm Warrant Officer Scott Brodie, a Special Agent in the U.S. Army Criminal Investigation Command. I am investigating the alleged offense of larceny, of which you are suspected. I advise you that under the provisions of Article Thirty-One of the Uniform Code of Military Justice, you have the right to remain silent."

Hinckley looked at Brodie, and they made eye contact.

"Yes, sir, I was —"

"Shut up."

Hinckley shut up.

Brodie continued, "Any statements you make, oral or written, may be used as evidence against you in a trial by court-martial or in other judicial or administrative proceedings." He continued to inform Hinckley of his Article 31 rights, essentially the military version of Miranda rights. Brodie had rattled this off hundreds of times over the course of his career, and most suspects were too scared, stupid, or belligerent to absorb what you were saying. But the inevitable lawyers sure as hell wanted to know that you said the magic words.

Brodie wrapped up his spiel with, "Do you understand your rights?"

"Yes, sir."

"Good. Now listen closely and answer yes or no. Do you want a lawyer? Do you want to see my search warrant? Do you want a kick in the balls?"

"No."

"Good." Brodie pushed Hinckley against the chain-link fence, patted him down, then pushed him toward the house. "Let's see how much trouble you're in."

They walked past the barking black Lab. Brodie now noticed the dog's rib cage pushing through its mangy black hair.

Hinckley said, "It's all right, girl."

The dog growled at him.

"I don't think she likes you, Private."

Hinckley didn't respond. Brodie led him through the open door and into a small, filthy kitchen. About two dozen cardboard crates labeled Meals Ready to Eat, featuring the Department of Defense seal, were stacked against one wall. Brodie said to Hinckley, "Don't they feed you enough in the mess hall, soldier?"

No reply.

"You want to tell me where the rest is before I turn this place inside out?"

Hinckley stared at the floor, silent. Brodie wondered if the guy understood that his Army days were over, except for the time he'd spend in a military prison.

Brodie led him into the living room, where Officer Finley was taking photos with his cell phone. Finley said, "Did a sweep. No one else here."

"Copy."

Brodie pushed Hinckley onto the couch. "Don't move."

Brodie heard Evans rummaging around in a room off the living room and entered a small, cluttered bedroom. Evans, wearing latex gloves, was closing a dresser drawer and slipping a small baggie of white powder into his jacket pocket.

Evans looked up at him. "About six cases under the bed." He gestured to the open closet. "Few more in there. And you saw the ones in the kitchen."

Brodie stared at his partner for a moment. "Check the garage. Then circle back for a thorough search of the house."

Evans nodded and walked out. Brodie reopened the drawer, which was full of civilian and Army socks, along with a wad of cash.

Brodie walked back into the living room and sat down on the coffee table opposite the handcuffed Hinckley, who was staring at the pause screen of his video game on the big flat-screen across the room. A voluptuous woman in a Nazi uniform with bloody chain-saws for hands was standing in some sort of bunker.

Brodie asked, "Why did you run?"

Hinckley shrugged, looked down at the floor. "I freaked."

"I didn't need the cardio, Private."

He looked at Brodie. "I'm sorry, sir."

"And you knocked down my partner. That's assault of a law enforcement officer, plus evading arrest in addition to the larceny charge. But maybe those additional charges won't show up in my report."

Hinckley looked at Brodie and nodded. "I certainly would appreciate that, sir."

"Is my partner going to find anything in the garage?"

Hinckley nodded.

"How much?"

"Fifty, sixty cases."

"You've got about ninety grand in stolen government property here, Private. And that's not counting what you've already moved. Who's helping you?"

Hinckley didn't reply.

"Someone at the base? Who's running the shop? They military?"

No reply. Brodie could still hear the dog barking in the backyard.

"We're going to call Animal Control about your dog."

Hinckley looked at him. "I don't want her

to go to a pound."

"What do you care?"

He was silent for a moment. "My sister can take her. She lives in Charlottesville."

"Maybe." Brodie asked, "Whose bright idea was this?"

Hinckley hesitated. "The seller. I don't know his name. He's not active-duty, maybe retired. Some kinda prepper dude. He heard from . . . someone that we had a big stash that had been ordered by DOD but wasn't going nowhere because of the drawdowns in Afghanistan. So, easy pickings. And demand's through the roof for this shit. Everyone's getting ready. You know?"

"Ready for what?"

Hinckley shrugged. "Things to go from bad to worse, I guess."

"I'd say it's already headed that way for you. Who linked you with the seller?"

Hinckley didn't reply.

"I might be able to keep you out of prison."

Hinckley looked at Brodie, maybe trying to read if this was bullshit.

CID agents had a reputation for playing the good cop to a T, empathizing with the suspect and promising the moon for cooperation, when half the time they were just giving the perp the rope to hang himself. There was no rule that you couldn't lie through your teeth when trying to extract information from a bad soldier. Brodie had

41

no idea what kind of deal PFC Hinckley could get, nor did he care. But over the years he'd learned to play the part, and play the perp.

Hinckley said, "I think . . . I need to talk to a lawyer."

Well, when the suspect said that, you were supposed to stop asking questions, but Brodie said, "Speak up, Private. I can't hear you."

Hinckley didn't respond and stared at the flat-screen.

Brodie regarded PFC Eric Hinckley. He knew from the man's file that he was nineteen years old, though he looked even younger. Probably a low-achieving student who got recruited in his high school on career day. Promised a steady paycheck, three hots and a cot, maybe some adventure, plus brotherhood and a meaningful career to boot. And that's not a lie. The Army can provide all those things if you're getting in for the right reasons.

Some guys, however, lost their way and went crooked, like Brad Evans, who was bored, burned out, and looking to start trouble if it didn't naturally present itself. But nineteen-year-old Private Hinckley hadn't lost his way. He never knew where he was going to begin with.

Well, the kid had asked for a lawyer, so the questions needed to stop. But Brodie still had something to say.

"Look at me, soldier."

Hinckley turned to him.

"You are a disgrace to your uniform and your country. You took an oath."

Hinckley averted his eyes.

"You made a bad choice, and you will face the consequences. And you better figure out why you made that bad choice, to prevent yourself from screwing up even more of your life. Do you understand me, Private?"

Hinckley looked back at him. "Yes, sir. I . . . wasn't thinking."

"This is a good time to start, Eric."

"Yes, sir."

Brodie got up and noticed Officer Finley looking at him. The man had probably listened to that interaction with some interest. There was no analog in the civilian world for what had just transpired. Cops don't usually dress down the perps they're arresting. But the Army was one big semi-functional family, and a criminal act within that family was a violation of something beyond and perhaps greater than the law.

Brodie went to the kitchen and opened the fridge. It was mostly bare except for a bottle of ketchup, a few cans of beer, and a couple of hot dogs.

He grabbed the hot dogs and walked out to the backyard. The dog was lying in the grass, lethargic. Her ears perked up as Brodie approached and tossed the hot dogs to her.

43

His cell rang. It was his boss, Colonel Dombroski. He picked up. "Brodie."

"Mr. Brodie. Where are you?"

Brodie watched as the Lab inhaled both hot dogs. "Executing an off-base search warrant."

"We need to meet."

"Is this business or pleasure?"

"I occasionally enjoy your company, Scott, but it's always business."

"Yes, sir. O Club?"

The Officers' Club was an on-base bar and restaurant that, as the name suggested, was restricted to military officers and their guests. Dombroski liked the Quantico O Club and often held his meetings there. At the age of fifty-five, he was on the old end of colonel, and he had something of a chip on his shoulder in place of the general's star he might never get. The O Club reminded Colonel Dombroski that he was still in the exclusive fraternity that is the military officers corps. Also, the club had a decent twelve-dollar sirloin.

Dombroski replied, "A little farther afield this time. Annie's Junction. Sports bar just off Ninety-Five, past the Lowe's."

"Is it ten-cent wing night?"

"Can you be there in twenty?"

"I'm working outside of Fredericksburg, Colonel. The Hinckley larceny case."

"Evans can handle that."

"Can I get that in writing?"

"It's urgent, Scott. Thirty minutes."

"Yes, sir."

Dombroski hung up.

Brodie put his phone back in his pocket as he saw Evans exit the detached garage and walk across the lawn toward Brodie. "The mother lode's in there."

Brodie nodded.

"Chili mac 'n' cheese. Beef brisket. Doesn't sound bad. You eat that shit in Iraq?"

Brodie had served as an infantry sergeant in Iraq in 2003 and 2004. He didn't like to talk about it much, but Evans, who had never seen combat, was always asking him stupid questions. "I ate snakes."

Evans laughed. "Hard-core." He stopped walking and stared at the black Lab looking up at Brodie, tail wagging. "You feed it?"

"Someone had to."

"This guy's a real prick."

"I need to head out. Call the evidence team and catch a ride back with them to HQ once they wrap up. Have the MPs send a patrol car to collect Hinckley and let him call his sister to collect the dog."

"Where you going?"

"Something came up."

Evans didn't seem sure what to make of that, but he nodded. "Okay." He walked past Brodie toward the house.

Brodie watched him walk away for a moment, then said, "And don't remove any more evidence."

Evans turned around. "What?"

"You heard me."

"I don't know what you're talking about."

Brodie stared into the man's eyes for a moment. "How does it feel to be everyone's hardship duty?"

Evans glared at him. "You think you're better than me?"

Brodie didn't reply.

"It was less than an eight ball."

"Great."

"A nice Saturday night for me and the boys, or a year in prison for our young private on top of everything else he's facing. What do you think?"

"You're a saint, Evans. A real class act."

"If I go back in there and find a kilo in the toilet tank, we got possession with intent to distribute. Until then, let's keep it in the family."

"Get out of my face."

"No one told me you were a fucking narc."

"Everyone told me you were a useless burnout."

"Eat shit." Evans walked back into the house.

Well, that had gone well. Brodie had been looking for the right reason to terminate this particular relationship. He wasn't going to rat the guy out to Dombroski, but this gave him all the justification he needed in his own mind to demand a new partner and maybe reassignment. Evans would second the motion.

Brodie looked down at the dog, which was whining for more food. He crouched and scratched behind her ears.

He'd never had a dog, or a cat, or any pet higher on the food chain than a goldfish. He also couldn't imagine himself with kids, and he had never stayed in a relationship longer than six months. He told himself that he needed the freedom to do his job and live his life the way he wanted.

But what good was that freedom now? He was tooling around the Eastern Seaboard arresting petty crooks and wife beaters, and solving blockbuster crimes like the curious case of the missing chili. And for the first time in his career, he had a partner who was even more screwed up than he was. This didn't work for him. This sucked in a whole new way.

Brodie walked around the house to his parked Impala. He climbed in, pulled out of the driveway, and navigated the narrow roads that led back to the highway.

It was past five and dusk was settling in. He noticed string lights and other holiday decorations on a few of the houses he passed.

Christmas was three weeks ago. Brodie was supposed to have gone back to his folks' place in upstate New York, but he hadn't. He wasn't sure why. He'd lied and said he was spending the holidays with a friend, which he allowed them to interpret to mean his girl-friend, whom he'd dumped a month earlier. So he spent the holiday alone, eating takeout and watching alien abduction documentaries on Netflix. He'd actually enjoyed himself, which worried him.

Whether in the infantry or the CID, his Army career had always required him to exist outside the rhythms of the civilian world. He'd spent Christmases in Riyadh and Tokyo and in South Korea a few miles from the DMZ. He recalled his first and most notable Christmas away from home — Baghdad in 2003, manning the mounted .50-caliber machine gun of an armored Stryker vehicle protecting a Christian quarter of the city from insurgents and car bombs.

He remembered rolling down the narrow streets at dusk. No lights or decorations, no music. Just the quiet air, thick with fear. He recalled passing an old church where he could faintly hear prayers, beautiful and solemn, in a language he did not recognize as Arabic and would later learn was ancient Aramaic.

He didn't miss being home. Who needed a ticky-tacky holiday when a place like this existed? A place full of history and meaning and consequence. A place where he had a mission and a purpose.

That same feeling carried him through his career. At some point he realized he'd structured his life so he didn't have things to miss. And that was fine. It was nice to be a lone wolf. Except once you're defanged, you're just alone.

He thought about his last partner before Brad Evans. Maggie Taylor. Despite her lack of experience on the job, she was one of the smartest and most capable people he'd ever worked with. She was also a knockout blonde, but that had nothing to do with his high opinion of her. Except that he had sort of tried to sleep with her in Caracas. But he blamed that on the stress of the mission and the strength of the Venezuelan rum. Also, she'd sent mixed signals. But they all do.

He'd struck out, which in retrospect would have been good for their continued professional relationship had there been one. But after the Mercer case she was transferred to Fort Campbell, Kentucky, where she was assigned a new partner along with — as Brodie had heard through the grapevine — a new rank of CW2. She and Brodie hadn't spoken since, despite Brodie's half dozen attempts to contact her. He assumed she was under orders to have no contact with him, and that those orders had come from either the Pentagon, who didn't like how the mission had turned out, or from the spooks at Langley, who were nervous about the classified Intel that Brodie and Taylor both now possessed. Or maybe her Army shrink had advised her to rid herself of toxic relationships. Or perhaps Maggie Taylor figured out all by herself that Scott Brodie was hazardous to her continued well-being.

Brodie got on the northbound ramp for I-95 and slipped into a stream of slow-moving taillights. He'd probably be a few minutes late, which in the Army was a crime close to desertion.

Dombroski had said it was urgent. Maybe Warrant Officer Brodie was being promoted. Maybe he was being relieved of duty. Maybe Colonel Dombroski was in cahoots with the CIA, who were going to put ricin in Brodie's happy hour nachos.

Well, it had been a while since anyone tried to kill him. That would at least be interesting.

CHAPTER 3

Annie's Junction was in a strip mall just off the highway, between a Panera Bread and a T.J. Maxx. Brodie parked his Impala near the entrance and locked his M9 in the gun safe he'd installed in his center console. He left his CID jacket in the car, threw on a thermal vest, and walked in.

Annie's had a typical sports bar vibe, with lots of flat-screens, a big horseshoe bar, and crap all over the walls. It was still early on a Sunday, and the bar was pretty busy.

Brodie didn't see anyone who looked familiar. There were plenty of military hangouts in the area, but Annie's wasn't one of them, which was probably why Dombroski had picked it. Which raised the question of what this was all about.

Brodie spotted Dombroski tucked into a booth along the wall. On the table in front of him were baskets of fried food and a couple of pints of beer. Brodie was used to seeing the colonel in full uniform, but this evening he was dressed in jeans and a maroon sweater.

Brodie approached the booth. "Evening, sir."

Dombroski looked up at him. "Scott." He gestured at the seat across from him, and Brodie slid into the booth.

"You're late," said Dombroski.

"Yes, sir."

Dombroski nodded at a basket of fried things in front of him. "I hope you're not watching your cholesterol."

Brodie took a fried ball from the basket and bit into it. A glob of scalding-hot cheese shot into his mouth, followed by a spicy kick. A jalapeño popper, one of the modern marvels of American food engineering.

Brodie washed it down with the pilsner in front of him and regarded his boss. A lot of senior officers looked out of sorts in casual civilian clothing, but Stanley Dombroski, stocky and overweight with hangdog features and a seemingly permanent five o'clock shadow, looked more in his element now than when he squeezed into any of his service uniforms.

Army officers didn't have the same physical training requirements and testing as enlisted men. Colonel Dombroski probably hadn't subjected himself to a PT test since the Obama administration, and his favorite machine in the gym was the vending machine. But officers were still expected to keep themselves in top shape, as both a symbol of self-discipline and a positive example to their men. Having a paunch was bad for your health — and your career.

Brodie wasn't sure if Dombroski's physical appearance was the reason he was still a colonel at the age of fifty-five. Maybe it happened the other way around, and after being passed over for promotion too many times he'd simply given up and reached for the corn dogs. Regardless, Brodie had a lot of respect for his boss, even if the idiots in the upper echelons would never grace him with a general's star.

Dombroski asked, "How's the Lansing case going?"

"The guy beat his girlfriend. Three witnesses on two occasions. So I guess it's going."

Dombroski nodded, took a drink. "And Hinckley?"

"We found what we expected to find. He'll spend the night in a cell, have a long talk with himself. We'll have the names of his co-conspirators by the morning."

"Good. You and Evans are batting about nine hundred."

"Keep lobbing softballs and I'll look like Babe Ruth."

Dombroski gave him a look. "You are administering justice, Mr. Brodie. I'd hate to think you were bringing your ego into this."

Brodie didn't respond, and Dombroski asked, "What do you want?"

"A cheeseburger."

"What do you want *from me*?"

Brodie looked him in the eyes. "I want my career back, Colonel."

Dombroski had no response. He finished his beer and waved over a young male waiter. He ordered two burgers, some onion rings, and another round of beers, then turned back to Brodie and lowered his voice. "Has anyone been in touch with you?"

Brodie understood what he was asking. While working the Mercer case in Venezuela, Brodie and Taylor had stumbled onto a Black Ops program in Afghanistan that was run by the Central Intelligence Agency along with some involvement from the Defense Intelligence Agency, Joint Special Operations Command, and other practitioners of the dark arts. The CIA didn't like individuals outside of their trusted circles to know about the things they did in the shadows, and Army criminal investigators Scott Brodie and Maggie Taylor were definitely not in that circle of trust.

There were a few ways to deal with that. One was to stick Brodie and Taylor in a windowless room in the bowels of the Pentagon to be reminded by threatening bureaucrats of the oaths they'd taken and their obligations not to divulge classified information. The other way was to perform unscheduled maintenance on the brakes of Brodie's Chevy.

Brodie and Taylor were given some version of the former within hours of their return from Venezuela — a very uncomfortable sit-down with General Stephen Hackett, the Provost Marshal General of the United States Army. It was a carrot-and-stick kind of meeting — they were both informed that they were getting letters of commendation in their files for the successful conclusion of a dangerous mission, along with a modest pay bump. They were also told, in an indirect way, that they could each expect to spend the rest of their lives in the Federal Penitentiary at Fort Leavenworth if they ever attempted to make public what they had learned about clandestine and top secret operations in the course of their investigation. The operations in question were also illegal — war crimes, actually — but why mention that?

Colonel Dombroski wasn't present for this Pentagon meeting, which was highly unusual; he instead met later with his two CID agents for an official debrief. After Dombroski listened to Brodie and Taylor's version of events, he informed them of the Pentagon's version, which bore little resemblance to the truth but did have the benefit of not embarrassing individuals in the CIA, DIA, or JSOC. Brodie and Taylor were expected to parrot this line of bullshit in their official report, and Colonel Dombroski didn't have to trouble himself making the threats already communicated by his Pentagon superiors.

Dombroski was an honest man by nature and it was clear that it pained him to strong-arm his agents into a cover-up, but it was indicative of just how big a rock they'd turned over in the course of their mission. Brodie and Taylor could not prove what they'd seen and heard in Venezuela, so they played ball and submitted a work of fiction to close the case file on Captain Kyle Mercer. Brodie was still troubled by all this, and while he and Dombroski had not spoken of the mission since, it seemed the colonel was still waiting for the other shoe to drop.

"Scott?"

"No visits, no phone calls, no bricks through my window or dead animals in my mailbox." He added, "My life has been very boring. Thanks to you."

Dombroski looked at him. "I'm just follow-ing orders. And so will you."

The waiter delivered their beers and onion rings, promising their burgers would be out shortly.

Dombroski pushed the basket of onion rings toward Brodie, who pushed them back. "You first, Colonel. Just in case the line cook is on the Agency's payroll."

"This is all a joke to you."

"Life's a joke. And death is the punchline."

"Sometimes I think you're too eager to get to the punchline."

Brodie didn't reply, and Dombroski said, "One of the great mysteries of life is why kamikaze pilots wore helmets."

Brodie smiled politely and took a swig of beer. He wondered when his boss would get to the point of this urgent meeting.

Perhaps sensing this, Dombroski cleared his throat and lowered his voice as he said, "Early this morning I received some disturbing news from our colleagues in Germany. We lost one of our own. Special Agent Harry Vance, based out of Kaiserslautern with the Fifth MP Battalion. Murdered in Berlin."

That took Brodie by surprise, and he had no response.

Dombroski continued, "I met Vance a few times over the years. You may have as well. He was a good man. A good agent."

Brodie did remember Harry Vance. He was one of Brodie's instructors at the U.S. Army Military Police School in 2005, where he taught a class on counterterrorism. Brodie said, "I took his class during the Special Agent Course. I remember being impressed."

Dombroski nodded. "He was one of the best."

Kaiserslautern was the headquarters for the CID's operations in Europe, and Brodie recalled that the agents of the 5th MP Battalion were nicknamed "The Professionals" for, well, their professionalism. Germany was considered a plum overseas posting, reserved for the best of the best — men and women who could hold their own with the Germans, who were natural-born policemen.

Dombroski said, "His body was found early this morning by a woman walking her dog in a city park. Single gunshot to the temple."

Dog walkers and joggers always find the dead bodies. Best to avoid both activities. No one had ever discovered a stiff while watching football on their couch.

Dombroski continued, "The woman contacted the Berlin Police, who in turn contacted the Bundeskriminalamt — the German Feds — once the police realized who the victim was. The BKA are taking the lead on the case and handling forensics, witness interviews, and so forth."

"How did they ID the victim?"

"His wallet was still in his pocket." He added, unnecessarily, "So this was not a robbery."

Brodie nodded. "Was Vance still working counterterrorism?"

"He was. A senior agent on the TCIU team. And the park where he was found is in a neighborhood called Neukölln, which is the center of the Arab immigrant and refugee community in Berlin. This is going to be a political and diplomatic shit-show." He added, "General Hackett has handed me this case."

"I hope you find the right sucker to take the assignment."

"I'm looking at him."

Brodie did not reply.

"Everyone's going to want a piece of this. German Feds, Berlin Police, FBI, State Department, and, of course, the U.S. military."

"And you thought to yourself, who works well with others?"

"I thought about who is loyal to the Army and who will keep the Army's interests in mind while dealing with the alphabet soup of agencies who will have a finger in this. As for the Germans, it might be their country, but he was our man, Scott. *Our* brother." He added, "And possibly killed by Islamic terrorists. So this is a biggie."

Brodie nodded.

Dombroski looked him in the eyes. "Whoever did this needs to pay. To be made an example of."

Brodie nodded again. Clearly this murder had affected Colonel Dombroski. And if Brodie was being honest with himself, it was affecting him too. As in any police force, every murder is taken seriously, but a murder of one of your own is also taken personally. Brodie asked, "Why isn't the Fifth MP Battalion handling this case?"

"They're a tight-knit group," said Dombroski. "And Vance was a much loved and respected senior agent. His murder has hit them hard and they are motivated to find the son of a bitch who did this. But General Hackett made the determination that they might be *too* motivated, and that we should bring in an outside team."

As Provost Marshal General, Hackett was in charge of all matters involving criminal justice in the Army, and he would usually delegate these kinds of personnel decisions to someone further down the chain of command. But this was no ordinary case. General Hackett was also a by-the-book guy who did not particularly appreciate Scott Brodie's approach to investigations. "Does General Hackett know that you are discussing this with me?"

"Of course."

"I'm sure I am not his first choice."

"He took some convincing." Dombroski added, "I stuck my neck out for you."

Brodie nodded, but did not say "Thank you."

Dombroski continued, "This mission requires someone who will show initiative and creativity in gathering information. And when it comes to sharing Intel, the Germans are tighter than a clam's ass. FBI's not much better. As you know."

Brodie nodded, remembering that Colonel

Dombroski's waistline wasn't the real reason he would never be a general. It was because deep down he thought like a cop, which made him good at his job but not particularly good at the politicking involved in advancing through the officer corps. To a different kind of man, "looking out for the Army's interests" would mean not tarnishing the Army's image, putting on a good show of displaying interagency cooperation, and other PR bullshit. To Dombroski, it only meant finding the bastard who'd killed one of their own.

That aligned with Scott Brodie's own philosophy, which was why the colonel had not relieved him for insubordination a long time ago. Dombroski had decided he needed a pit bull on this case, not a bloodhound, and he knew who that pit bull was.

The question was, was Scott Brodie ready to fill that role again? It had sidelined his career last time. Then again, was he really suited for anything else?

Brodie asked, "Do you have any information about the case or cases that Vance was working in Berlin?"

"Well, that's the strange thing. He wasn't working a case in Berlin, and none of his colleagues know what he was doing there. I spoke with his CO in Kaiserslautern, Colonel William Trask, who said Vance made frequent trips to Berlin when he wasn't on a case."

"Sounds like there is a fräulein in Berlin."

61

"The colonel didn't know and didn't speculate."

"Was Vance married?"

"In the process of a divorce. So, yes, there could be a woman in Berlin. If so, hopefully she'll come forward."

Brodie wondered if the divorce came before the girlfriend. But that's not usually how it worked. "His wife had him whacked."

"That's the kind of out-of-the-box thinking I've come to expect from you, Scott. But please keep that theory to yourself for now."

"Yes, sir." He added, "Colonel Trask needs to supply us with information on the terrorism cases that Vance was working in the past few years."

"Some of that will be classified. I will put in a request, but prepare to be disappointed."

"I need to know who his enemies were, Colonel."

"He's been a counterterrorism investigator for over twenty years, Scott. I'm sure it's a long list." He added, "I will request the records."

"What about Vance's partner?"

"Warrant Officer Mark Jenkins. Colonel Trask said Jenkins was en route to Berlin and is already in touch with the BKA and our embassy people."

"I would like his direct contact information."

"Does this mean you're taking the case?"

"Maybe. But I would need a new partner."

"You don't think Evans can handle this?"

"He's uniquely unqualified. And if I have to be on an eight-hour flight with him, there's going to be another murder."

Dombroski smiled.

Brodie knew that Dombroski already agreed that Evans was a dick, or else this briefing would have occurred at Quantico with Evans present.

Dombroski assured him, "You will have a new partner."

"Who?"

The colonel ignored the question. He looked Brodie in the eyes and asked in a low voice, "Do you have any concerns about being overseas?"

Back to spook talk. If the CIA really did want him dead because of what he knew, they would be happy to have their target on foreign soil in the middle of investigating a potentially terrorism-inspired murder. Another victim of Islamic extremists.

"Scott?"

Brodie refocused and looked at his boss. "I appreciate *your* concern, Colonel. But there comes a time when a man must not run from his fate." He asked, "Can I bring my gun?"

"You cannot. You'll be flying commercial and we have made no arrangements with the State Department — who we don't want to owe favors to — to transfer anything via diplomatic pouch. You can, however, be issued a sidearm by our defense attaché in the unlikely event that the need arises." He added, "You understand that, officially and legally, you will not have investigative powers in Germany. You cannot gather evidence. You cannot question witnesses. You cannot make arrests."

"Colonel, I don't have to tell you the number of investigations I have conducted overseas."

"This is different. You're not hunting down a perp who committed the act stateside and fled to a foreign country. And you are not investigating a crime committed on the grounds of an overseas American military installation or within a combat zone. You are also not conducting your investigation in a third world shithole with a corrupt police force that doesn't know its ass from its elbow. This is a murder on German soil. They are very capable, and they are extremely protective of their turf."

"The Germans tend to exaggerate which turf is theirs. Historically speaking."

"You will leave that joke at home."

"Yes, sir."

"This murder is also very possibly linked to Islamic terrorism, which the Germans are already up to their eyeballs in dealing with, on top of the white nationalist and neo-Nazi crazies who hate the Muslims in their country and are feeling nostalgic for a time that Germans should not feel nostalgic for. The German government will have their own internal security concerns at the top of their mind when seeking to resolve this."

Brodie absorbed all that. It was true that Harry Vance's murder presented a unique challenge. In fact, Colonel Dombroski was handing his star agent a shit sandwich and telling him to eat up. Well, he hadn't said yes to this assignment yet. He returned to the question that the colonel had ignored: "Who would be my partner on this case?"

"Maggie Taylor."

Brodie didn't reply.

"She's a good agent, and you two have a good prior working relationship. Plus, she's fluent in Arabic and can probably teach herself German on the flight over."

Maggie Taylor *was* a good agent. She was a sponge for knowledge and had an obsessive work ethic. She was also brave and had earned a Silver Star as a Civil Affairs officer for her actions in Afghanistan during a roadside ambush a few years before joining CID. And her language skills would be invaluable when navigating an investigation in an Arab immigrant neighborhood. On the other hand, she was crazy in a different way than Scott Brodie was crazy, which had caused some friction on their last case together in Venezuela. She had also committed a major act of betrayal on their last assignment, and Brodie had returned the favor by almost getting them both killed on one or two occasions. Maybe three. Also, Brodie harbored feelings for her, which were probably only lust but maybe something more, and she might not share those feelings, which was why she'd never returned his phone calls. On the other hand, before she'd gone silent, she'd dropped a few hints herself that the feelings were mutual. At least, he thought she had. Scott Brodie was a lot better at deciphering crime scenes than deciphering women.

"Scott?"

Brodie said, as if to himself, "No."

Dombroski looked at him quizzically. "No?"

"There are many qualified agents right here at Quantico who would jump at this opportunity. I'll take the assignment without the baggage."

"Have you spoken with Ms. Taylor since she left for Fort Campbell?"

"No." He added, "She hasn't returned my messages."

"Do you generally have that effect on women?"

"Depends on the woman."

"Well, to make you feel better, you ought to know that she has been under orders to have no contact with you."

"By whom?"

"By me." He added, "And by the Pentagon."

"Why?"

"The same reason she was sent to Kentucky and you've been benched with Brad Evans for the last five months. Damage control."

"Why wasn't I given the same order?"

"Because I'm smart enough not to give you an order you won't follow." He paused. "Listen, Scott, a lot of things went sideways in the Mercer case, but as far as I'm concerned you successfully completed your mission, and you both almost paid with your lives in the process. That's not lost on me, and that's not something I forget. You — and Taylor — also made me look good, and I don't forget that either. But you discovered things you shouldn't know, and there are a lot of people still nervous about that. So for your own good, and for good optics and for other good reasons, I suggested to those who were worried that you and Ms. Taylor should be separated."

Which, thought Brodie, was better than being terminated with extreme prejudice. He asked, "And now?"

"And now I need you. Both of you. And you need this."

Brodie processed that. He and Taylor knew the CIA's dirty secrets, and spies have long memories. Was the heat off them? Was five months enough? Not even close.

Then again, what difference did it make? He should have been KIA in Fallujah in 2004. The time since then was bonus. An Army psychologist had once told him that bad attitude was a form of survivor's guilt, and who was he to argue with a PhD? But it didn't feel like guilt to him. It felt like a rationalization to keep looking in the face of death and giving the guy the finger, which he enjoyed.

Dombroski, who was watching the gears turning in his agent's head, added, "If I had sent Taylor to Venezuela with someone else, they would have come home empty-handed. And if I had sent *you* with a different partner, you would both be dead."

Brodie didn't reply. The colonel might have a point.

Dombroski said, "Look at me, Mr. Brodie."

Brodie looked at him.

"Do you accept this mission?"

"Berlin in January. Sounds like shit."

"It's a step up from Caracas in August."

Or Quantico with Brad Evans any time of year. Brodie said, "Business class."

"Think of the American taxpayer."

"Extra legroom. Free drinks."

"Talk to the travel office."

"I assume you still need to convince Taylor to take this difficult assignment as my junior partner."

Dombroski confessed, "I actually spoke to

her this afternoon. She's catching a flight to Dulles tomorrow, and you'll meet her there for a night flight to Berlin."

Many of Brodie's professional and personal relationships had ended badly, and he'd never been granted an opportunity for a do-over. This could be interesting. Or it could be a disaster. Though disasters are also interesting. He asked, "Has she been briefed?"

"She knows what you know."

"Actually, I now know what she knew several hours ago."

"I had the easy conversation first, Scott. The one that didn't require beer."

Well, as often happened in the Army, a lot of big decisions had already been made before the guy being asked to put his ass on the line was asked to put his ass on the line. As it stood, Scott Brodie didn't have too many choices. He wasn't going to stay on the JV team with Brad Evans. And he wasn't going to decline the mission to investigate the murder of a fellow agent, a tragedy that had struck the CID only a handful of times in its hundred-year history. And if Maggie Taylor was willing to put the past behind her, maybe Scott Brodie could do the same. Sex, lies, and betrayal notwithstanding, they made a pretty good team.

Brodie asked, "Who would be our contact in-country?"

"You will be working with the embassy legal

69

attaché, an FBI agent by the name of Sharon Whitmore. She will be in regular contact with German law enforcement and will be arranging briefings from the embassy."

Legal attachés — legats in Fed speak — were FBI agents who maintained offices in every major American embassy in the world and were responsible for coordinating with local law enforcement on any investigations that concerned both countries. Brodie had worked with legal attachés on a number of his overseas assignments and understood they had a tough job — a legat was part investigator and part ambassador, hunting the bad guys while also glad-handing the local law enforcement, who in some of these countries were worse than the criminals.

Dombroski continued, "You will also be coordinating with our defense attaché, Brigadier General Frank Kiernan. I know Frank personally. We were in OCS together."

Brodie was certain that Kiernan was not the only OCS contemporary of Dombroski's who was now a general. Well, maybe this case would put a star on the colonel's shoulder. Or, Dombroski, Brodie, and Taylor would be reassigned to Alaska.

"General Kiernan will be your ally in this," Dombroski assured him. "He's no bullshit."

Brodie nodded. The Defense Attaché System was an arm of the Defense Intelligence Agency, the military's primary intelligence arm, and as such the attachés were sometimes Intel officers with espionage duties in addition to their official roles as liaisons to the host country's military. Dombroski was saying that General Kiernan was not an Intel guy, engaged in espionage. But if Kiernan was any good at his job, Dombroski wouldn't know.

Dombroski added, "Agent Whitmore and General Kiernan both have your contact information and will have an embassy briefing scheduled for you by the time you are wheels-down in Berlin."

"It sounds like you knew I'd say yes to this."

"You always say yes to challenging assignments."

Brodie had the distinct feeling of being jerked around and manipulated. He'd been cast out into the wilderness for five months so he'd agree to anything to get back on a big case. And he'd been separated from the best partner of his career only to have her forced back on him. He had the sudden urge to tell Colonel Dombroski to go to hell, turn in his badge and gun right there, hop in his car, and keep driving south until he reached somewhere with palm trees where he could get a jerkoff job and live a jerkoff life.

But he'd only just started on his second pint and the burgers hadn't come yet. More to the point, someone had killed one of their own, and that was not so easy to walk away from. So Brodie lifted his beer and said, "To Harry Vance."

Dombroski nodded and lifted his glass. "To Harry." He looked Brodie in the eyes. "Find the son of a bitch who killed him."

"You just told me I have no investigative authority."

"That's what German law says. The CID motto says, 'Do What Has to Be Done.'"

"I always do."

They clinked glasses and drank.

CHAPTER 4

Brodie sat with Dombroski, eating pub grub and listening to his boss talk about his ex-wife. Apparently the guy she'd moved in with after leaving the colonel had knocked her around a few times, and she'd since moved out and filed a restraining order. "And this is the asshole she leaves me for," said Dombroski. "I should pay the guy a visit."

Brodie nodded attentively. Commissioned officers of that rank rarely, if ever, poured out their personal life to lower-ranking officers, but Brodie sensed that the colonel needed someone to talk to, so he listened. Rank aside, they were both bachelors with no one waiting for them at home. After about half an hour, and before his boss could later regret the beery monologue, Brodie made an excuse to leave.

Dombroski handed him a gray folder with a few briefing notes and announced that he was staying to see if he could score at the bar, where he'd spotted a couple of cougars.

"I'm not much to look at, but the officer-and-gentleman thing tends to work."

"Right," Brodie agreed, though he knew that scoring in a military neighborhood had less to do with exalted status or an important job than it had to do with pay grade. Colonel Dombroski's pay grade was O-6, and with time in service and time in grade, he made about $140,000 a year, which was more attractive than his face. Brodie thought that Dombroski should have a baseball cap made with "O-6" on it. Brodie asked, "Can I split the bill with you?"

Dombroski waved away the offer. "On me."

"Thanks." He added, "Good hunting."

Brodie left Annie's Junction and got in his car, thinking about stopping at a CVS for Pepto Bismol, but instead he drove straight home to his rented bungalow near base. The small wood-shingled place hadn't been touched by skilled labor since the seventies, and it was, in fact, a dump. But the price was right. And the lease had the standard escape clause allowing Brodie to leave on short notice if he presented the slumlord with his military orders showing he'd been transferred to another duty station. Landlords didn't like that, but if they rented to military, that's what they had to agree to. Brodie wondered if the escape clause was good if he resigned — or if he was court-martialed and sent to prison. He'd have to reread the lease. In any case, he never used to care where he lived because he was always on the road. But lately his world had gotten smaller.

And now, suddenly, it had gotten bigger again. Murder. Berlin. Politics and media attention. This case would be a classic career booster — or a career buster.

And, of course, there was Maggie Taylor. Professionally, this was a good thing. Personally . . . he had mixed feelings. And he was sure she did too.

He parked his Chevy on the cracked concrete driveway and stepped out. A cold wind was blowing in from the Potomac a few miles to the east.

Brodie walked across the frozen lawn to the front door and went inside. He set his gun and holster on a side table near the couch, then tossed the briefing folder on his desk in the living room. He grabbed a beer from the fridge in the narrow galley kitchen, then went back to the living room and sat on the sagging floral-print couch.

This place had come fully furnished, probably sourced from a yard sale after someone's grandma died. It actually reminded him of his parents' upstate New York farmhouse where he grew up, which was full of thrift store finds and curbside crap thrown into the family Volkswagen van during weekend treasure hunts.

He smiled to himself as he thought about

75

Arthur and Clara Brodie, two college-educated counterculture refugees from Greenwich Village who'd decided they preferred wide-open spaces and starry nights to their illegal three-room walk-up on Bleecker Street. His dad became a local handyman, and his mom used their sizable plot of land to grow fruits and vegetables that she sold to local grocers. Neither endeavor brought in much money, but it was enough for the mortgage and taxes and enough to take care of one kid getting a perfectly mediocre public school education. His parents didn't ask too much of life, and they were never disappointed.

As a teenager Brodie began to resent his folks for being intelligent people who had wasted their potential. His decision to return to the city that his parents had fled and to attend NYU, in their old neighborhood of Greenwich Village, and then after 9/11 to join the Army and enter a world of discipline and rigor, was in some obvious ways a reaction to that resentment.

Miraculously, his parents were still married, which beat the statistical odds. Not only that, but they were *happily* married. In that respect, they were role models, though Brodie never understood what made them happy. Someday he should ask. Maybe it was the marijuana.

Brodie also thought about his last girlfriend,

Theresa, who was a civilian instructor at Quantico's Marine Corps War College. She taught a class on strategic thinking and had offered Brodie a few thoughts on how the guy she was sleeping with should approach the grand strategy of his career and his life.

Brodie stared at his dull reflection in the fifty-five-inch flat-screen, one of his few contributions to the décor. This shithole was starting to get to him. This overseas assignment had come at the right time.

Brodie got up from the couch and sat down at his desk, where he opened his laptop and ran a Google search for Harry Vance. He didn't find anything about the murder, which was strange considering the body had been discovered that morning in Berlin, which was six hours ahead of the East Coast. Next of kin had undoubtedly been notified by now, and maybe an autopsy already performed. The only reason he could think of for the press silence was that there was some inter-agency disagreement about what to report. The medical examiner can be as vague as necessary in an initial assessment and not mention cause of death. In this case, apparent homicide. But if that *had* been in the autopsy report, maybe the German government was concerned about public reaction from their own people if cause of death was murder, and place of death was the center of Berlin's Arab refugee community. That would be red meat for the anti-immigration press, politicians, and public, not to mention the neo-Nazis. But in an open society you can only keep a lid on a homicide for so long.

His web search did pull up information on other Harry Vances, including a personal injury lawyer in Tampa and an orthopedic surgeon in St. Louis, and it wasn't until far down in the search that he found something on Chief Warrant Officer Harry Vance of the Army Criminal Investigation Division — a 2006 article from CBS News entitled, "GITMO INTERROGATORS DEBATED OVER TACTICS," in which Vance was quoted. The article was about the Criminal Investigation Task Force, an organization created in 2002 by the Defense Department to conduct investigations of detainees captured in Afghanistan and other countries in the War on Terror.

Brodie knew about the CITF, which was a military-wide task force bringing Army CID together with the parallel criminal investigative outfits in the Navy, Air Force, and Marines. According to the article, members of the CITF were present at Guantanamo Bay alongside "separate intelligence investigators" — i.e., CIA and Special Ops — and the military had raised concerns about the interrogation tactics being employed by their Intel brethren, including waterboarding, stress positions, and other "enhanced interrogation

78

techniques." The CITF members had sounded alarms with Pentagon officials that these tactics were illegal, immoral, and unlikely to produce reliable intelligence. The CITF guys had been rebuffed by their superiors.

Brodie hadn't heard about this internal battle, but it didn't surprise him. It was a classic example of the clashing cultures of the military and Intel worlds. Military investigators were trained to build a rapport with the people they were interrogating as a way to get the most reliable and salient information. It was a method that relied on diligence and discipline. Whereas a lot of the Intel and Special Ops guys were cowboys who made it up as they went along, often with disastrous results. Vance himself summed up this difference perfectly halfway through the article:

Among the CITF investigators raising alarms at the time was Army CID Special Agent Harry Vance, who was present for some of the initial interrogations of detainees at the Guantanamo Bay facility. Vance said, "After 9/11 everyone was scrambling to prevent another attack, but these Intel guys were going about it all wrong. You don't make people talk. You make people want to talk."

Brodie finished the article. Vance and his colleagues weren't whistleblowers. They hadn't spoken to the press until 2006, when much of what had gone down at Guantanamo and also at Abu Ghraib prison in Iraq had already become public knowledge. Brodie wondered if Vance had any regrets about his initial public silence. Brodie, who had agreed to remain silent about what he'd seen and heard in Venezuela, was familiar with that feeling. Regardless, by raising concerns internally to his superiors at the Pentagon, Vance had made enemies in the Intel world. And now he was dead. Coincidence? Maybe. Or was Scott Brodie just projecting his own situation onto Vance? Probably.

Brodie opened the gray folder from Dombroski. Clipped to a short stack of pages was an official color photo portrait of Chief Warrant Officer Harry Vance in full dress uniform. He had been, as Brodie remembered him, a good-looking guy — square-jawed, pale-blue eyes, and close-cropped salt-and-pepper hair. Brodie figured this photo was a few years old because Vance was wearing the CW4 rank insignia on his epaulettes — the same rank as Brodie — but by the time of his death Vance was a CW5.

The first page of the briefing material was a short bio. Vance was born and raised in Ann Arbor, Michigan. He graduated magna cum laude with a degree in international studies from Johns Hopkins, then spent a year as a State Department staffer in DC before enlisting in and attending the Military Police School, followed by Army CID Special Agent training. He was stationed for a few years at Fort Benning, Georgia, before being transferred to the 5th MP Battalion in Germany where he worked in the Field Investigative Unit and then in the Terrorism and Criminal Investigation Unit. His first major terrorism case was investigating the 1998 al Qaeda bombing of the U.S. Embassy in Nairobi. There was no mention of his experiences at Guantanamo, which wasn't surprising.

The next page was a brief report prepared by the Legal Attaché Office at the American Embassy in Berlin that described the circumstances around the discovery of Vance's body. A dog walker — unnamed in the report — had found the body at 6:15 A.M. local time in a park called Körnerpark in the Neukölln neighborhood. Vance was found face up in the grass with a single gunshot wound to his right temple. No signs of struggle. His wallet was in the pocket of his slacks containing more than two hundred euros in cash as well as credit cards, a German driver's license, and his CID badge. He was wearing a watch. No other jewelry. His right hand was in the pocket of his topcoat, holding his Army-issue Beretta M9 pistol. The embassy was still waiting on ballistics results from the German police to learn whether the pistol had recently been fired. The deceased also wore his empty pancake holster, and he had no cell phone on his person. No bullet casings were found in the immediate vicinity of the body. Initial blood splatter analysis and other forensic evidence indicated that he was shot and died where the body was found.

The only other document in the folder was a photocopy of a typewritten report by the Berlin Polizei — the city police who were the first to be contacted after the discovery of the body. Brodie couldn't read a word of it but assumed the information was the same as what was included in the embassy's report.

Well, not much to start with. But there was more to learn in Berlin. He closed the folder. Brodie expected that ballistics would come back indicating the murder weapon was a long gun that could be fitted with a scope. Otherwise, he saw no way that a trained agent who was wary enough to have his weapon unholstered and in his grip would not have been alerted to a danger right in front of him.

Obviously, this wasn't a robbery, nor did the killer feel the need to even make it look like one. It would have been easy enough to steal his wallet, or at least the cash, along with his pistol and wristwatch if the killer wanted to stage a robbery.

As for his cell phone, no agent would leave home without it. So his phone was *taken*. The killer — or an accomplice — had searched the body and wanted the phone, which would contain GPS tracking information on where Vance had been in the hours and days before his murder. The phone could also contain any communications that had culminated in his presence at that park in the middle of the night. Clearly, someone needed to cover their tracks.

Brodie ran a web search for Körnerpark. It was a small park, about the size of a city block, right in the middle of Neukölln. He pulled up some pictures and saw that it featured paved paths and formal landscaping, lots of open spaces and not much natural cover. Interestingly, the park was sunken below street level. On the one hand, this layout allowed Vance to see someone approaching from any angle. But a shooter looking to snipe him from a distance couldn't have asked for a better perch. Vance had been a sitting duck.

If this was an act of terrorism, Harry Vance was a prime target due to his work. A terrorist could have posed as an informant to lure Vance to a location where it would be easy to take him out. There was plenty of precedent for that in cases of murdered journalists and investigators — people who met unknown people in strange places. And that was one of many reasons why agents were supposed to have backup in the form of their partners.

And that was the other mystery. If Vance was working a case in Berlin, why keep it secret from his colleagues and commanding officer? If there was a woman in Berlin, and he was worried about appearances because he was still married, official CID business could only help to justify his presence there, and he could have stayed for longer stretches. This wasn't adding up.

Brodie switched gears to think about Harry Vance the man, not Harry Vance the murder victim. Usually the first time a homicide investigator sees the victim, he or she is a corpse at the scene of the crime — or at the morgue. But Brodie could close his eyes and remember the guy. How Harry Vance carried himself, the sound of his voice. When Brodie took the Special Agent Course in 2005, Vance's counterterrorism class was one of the most popular. Morale around the War on Terror was still high, and every CID recruit fantasized that they might be the one to end up in an interrogation room with bin Laden or one of his lieutenants, putting their nuts in a vise.

But Vance was something of an eccentric — a serious and somewhat reserved guy who did not feed into the rah-rah military mentality and who refused to play to his student audience. He told the class that what they needed above all to be successful interrogators was empathy. The relationship between an investigator and a suspect is inherently adversarial, he'd said, but the job of the CID agent is to undermine that dynamic as quickly and effectively as possible. Show them that you see them as human beings. Respect their motives and desires. Do whatever you can to get them to lower their guard and talk.

This wasn't kumbaya bullshit from a guy who didn't understand the stakes. On the contrary, as Vance made clear in class, in the world of counterterrorism getting the right intelligence at the right time could mean the difference between thousands of people living or dying. Brodie didn't know it at the time, but Vance must have been recalling his experiences at Gitmo.

In retrospect, Brodie wondered if Vance was bitter. At the time of the 9/11 attacks, his career had been on the rise, and his expertise in counterterrorism was needed like never before in modern American history. Then he and his military brethren got sidelined for criticizing the controversial interrogation tactics of their supposed colleagues in the Intel community. Brodie wondered what that had done to him.

What were you doing in Berlin, Harry?

The answer to that question might answer all the others.

Brodie was eager to get to work, but he also knew it was a waste of time and effort to play desktop detective. He was about to close his computer when he saw a new e-mail come in.

It was from the Quantico travel office, an older woman named Joyce whom Brodie had become friendly with over the years: HI SCOTT. I'M THRILLED TO SEE YOU ARE GETTING OUT MORE. AT-TACHED IS YOUR FLIGHT AND LODG-ING INFO. THE HOTEL WAS SPECIFI-CALLY REQUESTED BY MS. TAYLOR, AND I AM SURE YOU WILL LET HER KNOW WHAT YOU THINK OF IT. PLEASE LET ME KNOW IF YOU HAVE ANY QUESTIONS OR CONCERNS. She added, as the military and their friends often do, GODSPEED.

That line about the hotel sounded ominous. He opened up the lodging info and saw that they were staying at a place called "Art Hotel." He pulled up a map of Berlin and searched for the hotel, and was not surprised to find that it was in the center of the dicey neighborhood of Neukölln, and actually across the street from Körnerpark where Vance's body had been found. *Specifically requested by Ms. Taylor.* Of course.

He checked out photos of the hotel on Google. It appeared to be a barebones crash pad one step above a youth hostel. Reviewers remarked on "the hospitality of the owner Mustafa" and "the smell of old socks in the hallway."

If the travel office had handled it on their own, they would have booked some standard

86

spot in central Berlin near the embassy. But Maggie Taylor was no doubt acting on experience from her days in Civil Affairs in Afghanistan, where she had to have her nose to the ground and be among the local populace negotiating with tribal leaders and farmers. She probably thought it was psychologically and tactically smart to begin and end each day walking the same streets that Harry Vance did in the last moments of his life. Also, given all the agencies involved in this investigation — and its political sensitivity — Brodie and Taylor were going to be kept on a tight leash, so staying in Neukölln was a good way to stay below the radar and maybe locate and interview witnesses without hassle from the FBI or the German police. It was good to be back with a partner who wasn't an idiot and who cared about her job. On the other hand, she hadn't consulted Brodie, her senior, on the choice of hotels. Good initiative? Yes. Poor judgment? For sure.

Brodie checked the flight itinerary, which included Taylor's flight to DC out of Nashville International, the closest major airport to Fort Campbell. She landed at 3:00 P.M. tomorrow, and then they were flying Lufthansa, 5:20 P.M. departure, landing at Berlin Tegel Airport at 7:15 A.M. the following morning. There was also contact information for the car and driver that would be picking them up at the airport and, he saw, bringing them directly to the embassy, which meant that he and Taylor would be briefed, probably by the legal attaché, FBI Agent Whitmore, and possibly someone from the Berlin Police Department. They weren't wasting any time on this.

Brodie had been to Berlin only once, in April 2000 during his junior year at NYU. His roommate, Adam Kogan, was doing a study abroad semester and invited Brodie to crash at his apartment for a couple of weeks during spring break. Kogan was a European history major but seemed to be mostly studying the local women. He was Jewish, and had explained to Brodie how Jewish culture had become trendy among young Berliners, maybe as a way to deal with generational guilt. Kogan said he had never had an easier time getting laid, and Brodie managed to benefit by association. It was a good couple of weeks.

Kogan's apartment had been somewhere in the former East Berlin, not far from where the Wall once stood. Brodie had been surprised to see all the open land where the massive structure used to be — stretches of overgrown grass in the middle of a bustling city. Construction cranes rose everywhere, as if everyone was working overtime to cover up the ugly scar that ran through their city and their psyches.

Brodie closed his computer, threw on a

coat, and brought his beer out to the front porch. He sat on a wicker chair and stared out at the quiet suburban night. The cold wind had picked up. Streetlamps threw sharp circles of light on the empty blacktop roads.

Brodie felt as though the past five months had been a shadow play of his old life, familiar forms and movements with no substance. He still had his badge, his gun, and his rank, and he'd pretended to still care about his job. But he wasn't sure he did. He wasn't even sure why he broke up with Theresa, whom he had liked. He'd told her it all felt wrong. But the thing that was wrong was him.

He thought about calling Maggie Taylor, but that was the beer thinking. He didn't know how that particular reunion was going to go, and best to reconnect in person.

He thought again about Harry Vance, whose death had set Brodie's life back in motion. In one of his lectures, Vance had discussed how a terrorist is different from other criminals. If you are hunting a murderer or a thief, they don't want to be caught by you, but their crime otherwise has nothing to do with you. The terrorist, on the other hand — the true believer — seeks the destruction not only of his victims but also of the entire world order that seeks justice for the dead. "And if you want to catch the bastard," Vance had said, "you must be as invested in his downfall as he is in yours. Don't bother pretending it's not personal."

Brodie had no idea who had killed Harry Vance, or why, but he had a premonition that Vance's advice would prove valuable. And making things personal was one of Scott Brodie's specialties.

CHAPTER 5

Brodie rose before dawn and went for a jog in the cold morning air, determined not to look like Stanley Dombroski. The neighborhood was safe enough, but he had his Beretta tucked into a belly band in case his last overseas assignment was following him.

He jogged along the cracked sidewalks past rows of modest split-levels and ranch houses that stood amidst towering sycamores. This was one of the older suburbs in the area, developed before the DC-area building boom that created endless sprawls of McMansions. He preferred it here, where the trees were bigger and the houses and egos were smaller.

He covered three miles along his usual route, returned home, showered, and put on his robe, then had a heart-healthy breakfast of black coffee and gas station sushi that he'd picked up yesterday. Maybe the day before.

Pieces of his conversation with Dombroski came back to him in no particular order. Regarding his gun, he hadn't been on assignment without a weapon in a while. Dombro-ski had said he could be issued a firearm if he needed it. Well, when do you know if you need a gun? Usually not until you're staring down the barrel of someone else's.

Germany, like most of Western Europe, was relatively safe. But Berlin, like all big cities, had its problems. Brodie got his laptop and did some Internet reading on Neukölln, which seemed to be a hard neighborhood to categorize — a hodgepodge of pensioners and young families drawn by the cheap rent, longtime Turkish and Arab residents, recent Libyan and Syrian refugees, and a wave of white gentrifiers. A number of Arab crime families operated in the area, dealing in drugs and human trafficking, and there was the oc-casional gang-related murder of another gang member that bothered no one except the murder victim. There were also a fair number of trendy and edgy clubs, bars, and coffee shops, which attracted Berliners and adven-turous tourists.

So, like a lot of urban neighborhoods undergoing change, Neukölln was divided by precarious barriers of race, culture, wealth, and, in this case, religion. He wondered if the murder of an American in a community park would shake up the neighborhood when it hit the news.

On that subject, Brodie ran another search on Harry Vance to see if the murder had been reported yet. It had. Top stories in the *New York Times,* the *Washington Post, USA Today,* and London's *Times,* as well as all the German-language dailies such as *Bild* and *Die Zeit.* The *WaPo* headline read: "AMERICAN ARMY INVESTIGATOR MURDERED IN BERLIN PARK." The London paper declared: "AMERICAN ARMY OFFICER FOUND DEAD IN HEART OF BERLIN'S REFUGEE COMMUNITY." He did a quick scan of the articles, all of which had miraculously managed not to bury the lede.

Brodie turned on the TV and switched to a morning news show. The chyron read: "AMERICAN ARMY INVESTIGATOR MURDERED IN BERLIN'S REFUGEE HAVEN." Three news anchors with the combined IQ of a smart chimp discussed the murder, sharing the screen with a superimposed portrait of Special Agent Vance — the same photo included in Brodie's briefing folder.

The anchors posed questions: Did this have the hallmarks of an ISIS operation? Are terrorist cells active in this part of Berlin? Did the victim have knowledge of an impending attack? How well does the German government vet refugees from Syria? Instead of finding an expert or even a legitimate journalist to direct these questions toward, they asked themselves, and then listened intently to each other's bullshit, running down the clock until the next prescription drug commercial.

Brodie turned off the TV. He got dressed in jeans, a button-down dress shirt, and a sports jacket, and called for an Uber.

The drive to Dulles International Airport took a little under an hour, and by the time he checked his bag and got through security, it was three-thirty. He went to the arrival board to check on Taylor's flight from Nashville. It had landed about thirty minutes prior at a different terminal, so she would probably be on the AeroTrain by now. He tried to guess how this reunion was going to play out. No way of knowing. But he was looking forward to seeing her.

The gate for their five-twenty flight to Berlin was posted, so he headed in that direction and spotted a pub in the concourse. He entered and sat on a stool at the bar. A few other travelers were seated with suitcases at their feet and their noses in their phones.

The bartender, a tall, ruddy-faced guy in his late forties, approached. "What can I get-cha?"

"A German pilsner."

"Radeberger?"

"Sure."

The bartender walked over to the taps.

Brodie took out his phone and texted Taylor: *I'm at a bar called The Clover near our gate having a German beer as part of my cultural immersion training.* He didn't invite her to join him, though it was implicit, given that he was the senior officer.

The bartender returned with the Radeberger. Brodie drank it and watched the NFL playoff game on the TV above the bar. The guys who had sucked all through the regular season were actually playing a strong game, which was encouraging. Sports, like life, allowed room for redemption.

After a few minutes his phone vibrated in his pocket. He took it out and saw a text from Taylor: *Don't get too immersed. See you in a few.*

Brodie flagged the bartender and ordered another beer as he waited for his partner to arrive.

He thought about the last time he'd seen her, as they'd walked to their cars outside of the Quantico CID headquarters following the intense and unpleasant back-to-back meetings with General Hackett and Colonel Dombroski.

They had both been silent, their postmission adrenaline having given way to exhaustion and then to something approaching despair. It could have been a moment for coming together. Two soldiers back from the field who had risked it all, getting screwed by the rear-echelon higher-ups who had risked nothing. A story as old as armies.

But that's not how it had felt — because it wasn't just that their superiors had failed them. In going along with the cover-up, they had failed themselves and each other, and it was hard to move on with someone who reminds you of what you're trying to forget. As they had both driven away from headquarters, Brodie had a feeling he would never see her again.

"Scott."

Brodie turned around to see Maggie Taylor standing in front of him. She was dressed smartly in a blouse, slacks, and a sweater-vest. She had wireless headphones around her neck and a leather satchel slung over her shoulders.

Brodie slid off the barstool, forgetting the cool and clever lines he'd rehearsed.

"Hi." She said with a smile, "Reporting for duty."

They stared at each other for an awkward moment.

Brodie said, "You look great."

"You too." Then, "I'm sorry I never returned your messages."

"Don't be."

"Dombroski told you why?"

"He got around to it yesterday."

"That's cruel."

"It's fine." Brodie gestured toward the barstools, and they both sat. Taylor threw her headphones in her satchel and put the bag by her feet.

For a moment they just looked at each

other. And Maggie Taylor did look great. Big brown eyes, shoulder-length flaxen-blond hair, perfect features. But something about her looked different to Brodie. Something in her eyes. Added confidence, maybe. Brodie assumed her last five months had been better than his.

He asked, "How was it being back at Fort Campbell?" Which was their last assignment together before the Mercer case sent them to Venezuela. They'd been at Campbell operating undercover as clerks in the adjutant general's office while they worked to expose a methamphetamine ring.

"It was all right," said Taylor. "My partner was great. Steve Lassiter. Know him?"

"I don't think so."

"He knows you."

Well, every CID agent at Fort Campbell knew about Scott Brodie after the meth case, mostly because it culminated in Brodie accidentally shooting a mule in the ass in the back hills of eastern Kentucky. But that was another story.

Taylor added, "Steve's also a CW2. So we were a junior team. We did some petty larceny. Occasional domestic violence. One case where a PFC blew his buddy's toe off with his service weapon while they were both too drunk to see straight."

Brodie nodded. Taylor might have ended up with a better partner than he did, but it

97

sounded like her caseload was the same JV crap as his.

Taylor eyed the beer sitting in front of her. It wasn't her preferred drink, he knew. She liked wine and knew more about it than fermented grape juice really warranted. She was also a sour mash whiskey drinker, a result of her upbringing in the Appalachian Mountains of eastern Tennessee — not too far, in fact, from where Brodie had plugged the mule.

Wine and whiskey. The two sides of Magnolia Annabelle Taylor, a girl from Appalachia who'd graduated at the top of her class at Georgetown, was fluent in multiple languages, was a decorated combat veteran — and whose family tree was a stump. Well, maybe that last part wasn't fair.

Brodie asked, "Did you get a chance to see family?"

She shook her head. "All the family that I care about are dead or in jail."

"Right." Taylor's father had been murdered when she was three years old. And her mother was in jail because she was the one who had done it — along with killing his girlfriend — after finding them in bed together. Two blasts from a double-barreled shotgun, which was at least more sporting than a five-shot pump-action. Divorce, Appalachia-style.

So Taylor had been raised by her grand-

98

parents, who had both died of natural causes a few years ago. Not much reason to go home for Thanksgiving.

She asked, "How about you?"

"Didn't get up to see my parents. But the old man's started growing weed, so that might be worth a trip."

"I'm asking how you're doing, Scott. How have the last few months been?"

"Right. Well . . . bad partner, bad cases. A waste of my God-given talents."

She looked at him. "We agreed to play their game. And the deal was that in return we could keep our jobs. But it was no longer the same job."

Actually, it was more than their jobs that was in peril if they didn't toe the line. It was also their freedom. And maybe their lives.

Taylor added, "They buried us, Scott."

"Right. And now we're resurrected to find justice for Harry Vance." He added, "I knew him."

She looked at him again. "How?"

Brodie recounted how Vance had been his counterterrorism instructor during CID training. He also shared what he'd learned about the clash between the Criminal Investigation Task Force and intelligence interrogators at Gitmo, and how Vance had publicly expressed his low opinion of the Special Ops people and their tactics to a reporter in a newspaper article. Which was not how Army officers were supposed to give their opinions, First Amendment notwithstanding.

Taylor, unsurprisingly, had done her own Google sleuthing and already knew about the Gitmo business. "He sounded like a man with a good moral compass."

"That was my impression," said Brodie. "But maybe not good judgment."

Taylor agreed, "Talking to the press is not good judgment, as we've been reminded."

Brodie lowered his voice. "Neither is being alone in a park in a remote and not altogether safe neighborhood in the middle of the night. Vance was surrounded by high ground, no natural cover or concealment, no backup. He was clearly aware of the danger since he was found holding his Beretta in his pocket. If he was investigating something, he apparently hid it from his partner and his commanding officer, meaning that whoever pulled the trigger succeeded in ending the investigation by ending Harry Vance. Altogether irresponsible behavior and shoddy operational security."

"So you're saying he was unnecessarily secretive and reckless. Reminds me of someone I used to work with."

He forced a smile. "This isn't about me."

"No, it isn't. But if we're trying to get inside the victim's head —"

"Then you can stay out of mine, thank you."

She didn't respond.

He changed the subject. "Good thinking on our accommodations."

"I can't tell if you're being sarcastic."

"I can't either. But the location is good, and I'll remember that when I'm treating my fungal infection."

"Have you gone soft, Mr. Brodie? I thought you spent a year in a war zone."

"Thirteen months and five days."

"You can handle the Art Hotel."

"Consult me going forward on all matters, large or small." He added, "That's a standing order." Meaning, does not need to be repeated.

"I will consult you. And I ask you to trust my judgment and encourage my initiative."

That seemed almost mutually exclusive, but he replied, "I will." He hesitated, then asked, "Did you take this assignment to get your career restarted? Or to work with me again?"

"I took this assignment to get justice for Harry Vance." She added, "I have no personal or professional motives."

"My bullshit detector just went off."

"Okay, one-third justice, one-third career, and one-third you."

"Good enough."

She didn't respond and they sat in silence, contemplating the math.

The bartender approached. "Do you want to see a menu?"

Taylor replied, "No thanks," and grabbed

her satchel. "Let's sit somewhere more private."

Brodie left a twenty on the bar and they brought their bags and beers to the sitting area, where they found a high-top table.

They sat, and Taylor said, "I understand why I was asked to be on this case. But I'm not sure about you."

"Excuse me?"

Taylor leaned forward in her chair. "C'mon, Scott. Working under the supervision of a foreign government, with no real investigative power, dealing with the FBI and State Department dips and whoever else. This isn't exactly playing to your strengths."

"I appreciate your candor."

"No you don't." She smiled. "But you and I . . . almost slept together and almost died together. So the least we can do is be honest with each other."

Or at least, almost honest. And should he remind Ms. Taylor that her commitment to honesty was a recent development? Maybe not. They'd both been guilty of BSing each other in Venezuela. Now they were reunited, and they had a homicide to solve. Together.

Brodie said, "I'm sure General Hackett wanted to send a team that would play nice with the Germans and take a back seat on this case. But the colonel had a different idea and so do I."

"Did Dombroski say that?"

"Not in so many words." He added, "One of our brothers is dead. We have a personal interest in seeing this case done right."

She asked, "When you reviewed the briefing materials, did you get the Berlin Police report translated?"

"No, but I bet you did."

"I translated what I could myself. And there appears to be a detail missing from the embassy report. About how the body was found." She paused. "Vance's left eye was missing."

"Missing?"

"It was . . . scooped out."

Brodie didn't respond.

"Based on the lack of any signs of struggle, we can assume this mutilation was postmortem."

"That's a fair assumption." And hopefully an accurate one for the sake of poor Harry Vance.

"And I've been thinking," said Taylor, "why leave that information out of the legat report? Maybe you don't tell the press, but for an internal embassy report . . ."

"Either the embassy omitted it, or the German Feds — the BKA who took over from the Berlin Police — decided to omit it. Why? Because the more people who know this detail, and the sooner they know it, the more likely it will be disseminated."

"Okay . . . and . . . ?"

"An American military officer has been murdered in what many people will conclude was an act of Islamic terrorism. And whether or not that's true, everyone from ISIS to the brigade of armchair jihadis living in their parents' basements will want to take credit."

Maggie nodded. "And if they know about the mutilation . . ."

"It's a calling card." Something else clicked in Brodie's head. "Which is the same reason the German authorities delayed reporting the murder to the press. To see if anyone would announce it before they did."

"Right."

Brodie's experience with terrorism cases was limited, but he was already beginning to see how that factor altered the rules of the game. Most murderers want to evade responsibility for their crimes. Terrorists don't. They just want to evade capture.

But this might have nothing to do with terrorism. This kind of postmortem mutilation sounded almost ritualistic, a more typical hallmark of a serial killer. Or an organized crime outfit looking to send a message. Brodie said, "An eye for an eye."

Taylor thought about that. "Revenge. For what?"

"For putting someone away for life, maybe. I'm sure Harry had his share of vengeful enemies."

They sat in silence for a moment; then Taylor said, "I didn't ask to be transferred to Campbell." She looked at him. "I want you to know that."

"Okay. Good to know."

"But I did tell you that I'd never work with you again."

"You did? When was that?"

"At the end of our last mission. Stranded, losing sunlight, dead bodies around us. Remember that?"

"A little. But I don't think I believed you."

"*I* believed me."

"I'm sure."

"But . . . after we got home, and I was transferred . . . I realized . . . I knew I could trust you with my life. And you had saved it more than once."

True, though his reckless behavior might have been responsible for her life being in danger in the first place. But why mention it? He said, "I'm glad we're working together again, Maggie." He thought it was time to leave Venezuela behind, so he asked, "Do you remember that I promised you a trip to Germany?"

Taylor smiled. "You said Oktoberfest in Munich. But I guess January in Berlin will have to do. Can't be worse than my last trip to Germany."

By which she meant Landstuhl Regional Medical Center, where Taylor underwent hours of surgery to extract the shrapnel from her leg after her convoy was ambushed by the Taliban and she was medevaced out of Afghanistan. She had large scars on her thigh to memorialize the IED blast, which Scott Brodie had seen in person once in Venezuela when she wore a bikini in the Caracas hotel pool. He didn't think the Art Hotel in Neukölln had a pool, and he doubted Taylor had packed a bikini for this trip, but maybe . . .

"Scott . . ."

Brodie refocused. Taylor was looking at a television at the far end of the bar that was tuned to the news. The chyron read: "FAR-RIGHT PROTEST IN BERLIN IN RESPONSE TO MURDER OF AMERICAN." A throng of mostly young men carrying German flags and signs were chanting slogans from behind a barricade in front of the American Embassy. One woman was holding a blown-up poster of Harry Vance's military portrait. A man nearby waved a sign that said: MUSLIME RAUS. Muslims out.

Brodie said, "They weren't about to let a tragedy go to waste."

"It looks like we're walking into a political shitstorm."

Brodie replied, "I see it as an enriching career opportunity."

"Shitstorm."

"Right. That too." He reminded her, "We're there to solve a murder and see that justice is done. We're not there to solve the problems of Europe or the refugee crisis."

"I think they're interconnected, Scott. And you know that."

"We're cops. Leave the other shit to other people. I'm sure you remember what happened on our last case when we got outside our lane and over our pay grade." He assured her, "That won't happen again."

She looked at him. "Can I hold you to that in Berlin?"

He didn't reply.

CHAPTER 6

Warrant Officers Scott Brodie and Maggie Taylor boarded the Lufthansa Airbus A350 and found their adjoining seats. The travel office had booked them in Premium Economy, a two-seat row, as per SOP so they could talk privately without a third seat companion to stifle their conversation.

On that subject, Brodie asked, "How do you feel about being naked?"

"Excuse me?"

"About being unarmed."

"Oh . . . well, I'd rather be carrying. But . . . we'll see if we need a gun when we get there." She added, "Dombroski said we may be able to pick up some hardware from the defense attaché at the embassy."

"Right. What if there's only one gun available? Who gets it? You or me?"

"You."

"Why?"

"You're older. You need a gun."

Brodie smiled, then got serious. "This is a

murder investigation. We need to be armed."

"Harry Vance was armed." She reminded him, "He's dead."

Brodie had no response.

"He wasn't using his head. And maybe he relied too much on his gun. We see this all the time." She added, "A smart detective doesn't need a gun."

"That's a stupid statement."

"I know. But it sounds good."

"We'll ask for guns."

"Let me ask." She explained, "I won't seem as psycho as you."

They both got a laugh at that. So far, so good.

The preflight safety demonstration sounded more authoritative in German than it did in English. Takeoff was on time, and within five minutes of reaching cruising altitude Brodie had a scotch and soda in his hands, a nice intro to German efficiency.

Taylor had ordered a Riesling that the in-flight menu promised was "crisp with a stone fruit aroma and a luxurious palate." Maybe there was something lost in the translation.

Taylor sipped her wine and said, "I'm dying of curiosity, Scott."

"About?"

"Your female companionship. Or lack thereof."

He replied, "I am currently unattached."

"And before currently?"

This, thought Brodie, would be a normal topic of conversation with a male partner, even if the guy was an a-hole. But this topic with a female partner, or a past or present lover, had no upside. Maggie Taylor, aside from being his current female partner, had also been a near-miss in the bedroom.

"Scott? Anyone special?"

"They all start out special."

She didn't reply to that, and they sat in silence for a moment. Then Brodie said, "There was one. She taught at the Marine Corps University. She was interesting. We had a good time."

"What happened?"

"I stopped having a good time."

"Okay."

Brodie hesitated, then asked, "What about you? Were you able to fight them off at Fort Campbell?"

She suppressed a smile. "Barely. But I decided I wouldn't date anyone in the military. Create some boundaries for once."

Well, that was a welcome change for Maggie Taylor. They made eye contact and Brodie asked, "Any old exes darken your doorway?"

Taylor took a long sip of her wine. "I heard from him. Within two days of being at Fort Campbell."

The "him" in question was a CIA officer by the name of Trent Chilcott with whom Maggie Taylor had had an unhealthy relation-

110

ship during and after her Civil Affairs training at Fort Bragg before deploying to Afghanistan. Trent had taken advantage of his role as one of Ms. Taylor's intelligence instructors, regaling his young student with war stories, including his time as a paramilitary fighter in the CIA's Special Operations Group tasked with hunting down Osama bin Laden in the mountains of Tora Bora in the early days of the Afghan war. If Brodie ever had the displeasure of meeting Mr. Chilcott, he'd be sure to remind him that he and his CIA buddies had allowed bin Laden to escape into Pakistan for another decade, and that it took the Navy SEALs to finally send the asshole to Paradise.

Getting involved with a CIA operative was not necessarily a great move at the beginning of a military career, but a young Maggie Taylor could hardly be blamed for falling for Trent's act. Once she returned from a few months in Afghanistan with her innocence lost and her worldview broadened, she'd tried to break things off with him. At which point Ms. Taylor learned the hard lesson that once you get into bed with a spy, it's not so easy to get out. Especially if the spy thinks you can be useful to him in other ways. And their continued relationship, as it were, had compromised the rest of her service in Afghanistan — as well as Brodie and Taylor's mission in Venezuela.

Brodie asked, "Did you see him?"

"He sent me flowers."

"Pretty thoughtful for a sociopath."

"He included a note congratulating me on my new assignment." She added, "He wanted me to know that he knew where I was."

"Anything else?"

"Why do I have the impression I'm being interrogated?"

"If I was interrogating you, I'd be much more charming."

Taylor set her glass down and turned toward Brodie. "I told you I trusted you, and I've noticed that you have not said the same to me. Do you trust me? If the answer is no, I will get a flight back to the States as soon as we land in Berlin."

"That sounds like a big waste of jet fuel. Think about your carbon footprint."

Taylor did not respond. Her big brown eyes stared at him, unblinking.

Brodie sometimes wondered how much of Mama Taylor's murderous temperament had passed down to her daughter, who was a cool customer on the outside but definitely had something smoldering on the inside. In fact, Brodie had the distinct feeling that he was one wiseass comment away from a punch in the face.

He said, "I trust you. If I didn't, you wouldn't be on this plane right now."

"Dombroski gave *me* this case before *you,*

Mr. Brodie, even knew about it. I was going to Berlin regardless of whether you joined me."

Well, someone had gotten a bit cocky since their last assignment together. A promotion will do that to you. But she might also be right. Was he the expendable partner on this mission?

He said, "It doesn't matter. I trust you, you trust me, and together we can play Spot the Spook once we get to the embassy."

"You think Langley's going to have someone on this?"

"Let's assume they're interested in the murder of a U.S. Army CID counterterrorism officer. Also, I have a feeling the Agency is not done with either of us."

Taylor was quiet for a moment. Then she lowered her voice and said, "We should assume our phone calls and electronic communications will be surveilled when we are within a one-mile radius of the embassy."

"That's interestingly specific."

Taylor reached into her satchel and pulled out a manila folder, then opened it and produced a map of central Berlin. The American Embassy had an X over it in yellow highlighter, and a circle was drawn in a wide radius around it. "Remember that scandal from a few years back, where Angela Merkel claimed that the U.S. had been tapping her cell phone?"

Brodie did remember the German Chancellor complaining about that, and doing it publicly, which embarrassed both nations.

Taylor continued, "It was a big story at the time, 2013, and then it kind of went away. Edward Snowden had released a slew of classified NSA surveillance documents, one of which revealed that the National Security Agency had been eavesdropping on Merkel's private communications since shortly after 9/11. And that they did it from the U.S. Embassy."

Taylor produced a printed satellite image from the folder, this one a tight three-quarters perspective on the U.S. Embassy building. She'd highlighted a small structure on the roof. Taylor continued, "The SCS, or Special Collection Service, is a joint NSA-CIA operation tasked with electronic eavesdropping on sensitive and difficult-to-access targets. Intelligence experts believe that the SCS operates out of this rooftop structure." She pointed to two beige rectangles on the walls of the structure that were a slightly different color than the rest of the outer walls. "These are concealed windows that have lines of sight toward major government and business centers in the heart of the city. It's believed that the SCS eavesdropping equipment has a range of up to a mile in any direction." She flipped back to the larger map and pointed to various buildings within the circled radius. "Look how much is within that range. The Reichstag. The Chancellery. Here's the offices of *Der Spiegel.* Also, lots of foreign embassies, and the Adlon Hotel, where important people stay." She pointed to an expanse of green. "And the Tiergarten, where spies, diplomats, and politicians go for private phone conversations. You couldn't ask for a better perch for electronic espionage."

Brodie looked at the map. The American Embassy was truly in the heart of Berlin, less than a block away from the Reichstag and mere steps from where the Berlin Wall once bisected the city in front of the Brandenburg Gate. "This is all public knowledge?"

Taylor nodded. "To anyone who cares to know it. Which means most people don't."

Right. The Internet was an incredible resource, and the information revolution was supposed to have brought a new breadth of knowledge, and therefore power, to the average citizen. Unfortunately — or fortunately — most people were lazy and stupid, and to the extent that they even bothered to try to learn things, they had a hard time discerning truth from bullshit. But Taylor was discerning, and she'd clearly done her homework.

Brodie asked, "If the existence of this listening station is known, why would the SCS still use it?"

Taylor shrugged. "It's probably hard to give it up. Also, there wasn't much fallout when the German Chancellor learned that the Americans had been intercepting her and her inner circle's phone calls and text messages for the better part of a decade. That tells me that there was some sort of deal struck between the two governments. The Americans could continue their illegal surveillance program in the interests of counterterrorism if they stopped eavesdropping on German government officials, and in return we would share intelligence with the Germans that pertained to any security threats against their government."

Brodie nodded. "The SCS will be combing their signals intelligence for anything related to the Vance murder."

"I'm sure of it."

And Brodie was sure the SCS would be monitoring the communications of every American official involved with the Vance investigation — including the communications of Mr. Brodie and Ms. Taylor. Why? Because they could. That's the problem with the surveillance state. It's built to suck up vast quantities of information, and that power becomes addictive and self-perpetuating.

This was disturbing to Brodie from a civil liberties standpoint. More importantly, it could also become a personal problem if the CIA decided that this was a good opportunity to get rid of two nosy warrant officers who knew too much. It's not paranoia if someone

116

really wants you dead. At the very least, the CIA would know if Brodie and Taylor were violating their narrow mandate and use that knowledge to blackmail them into continued silence about what they had stumbled on in Venezuela. So they'd have to watch what they said in and around the embassy. The Art Hotel in Neukölln was looking better.

Aside from all that, how would the existence of a spy den within the embassy materially affect their investigation? Maybe it wouldn't. Maybe it would actually prove useful. Assuming all the players on this case stayed on the same team and shared information. Miracles do happen.

Yet justice is a story that society tells itself to maintain order, and if those in power don't like how the story is going, they will rewrite it. Brodie and Taylor had found that out the hard way on their last case.

Harry Vance had found that out too, all those years ago at Guantanamo Bay. He was witness to interrogation by torture that he tried to stop. But he failed. And his objections were not even a footnote in history.

"Where'd you go?"

He turned to Taylor. "Venezuela."

She didn't respond.

"We uncovered American war crimes. Then we played ball with the devil. But I am never doing that again."

Taylor processed that. "Are you anticipating we will be asked to?"

"I don't know. I'm just telling you if it ever comes to that again . . . I'm burning it all down."

She looked at him. "All right."

"All right?"

"I'm with you, Scott."

Well, that was settled. Or was it? He recalled being given similar assurances by Ms. Taylor on their last assignment that turned out to be lies. But if he only judged people on their worst moments, he'd never trust anyone.

He watched as Taylor put her research materials back in her satchel. She turned and looked out the window as they glided over a thick sheet of clouds.

They were on their way to the land of Nietzsche, who had famously said that what does not kill you makes you stronger. They'd both narrowly survived their last mission, and before that, the battlefields of Iraq and Afghanistan. And they had gotten stronger. And through her own mistakes and naïveté, Ms. Taylor seemed to have learned the hard lesson that Scott Brodie had known for a while: A good soldier must know the enemy, and sometimes that enemy flies the same flag as you do. And while you might get screwed and betrayed, the least you can do is not be surprised.

Or as he used to tell his troops in Iraq: Those who stay alert stay alive.

118

CHAPTER 7

Brodie and Taylor got through passport control quickly and proceeded to baggage claim.

They passed through a small, crowded food court lit by fluorescent bulbs hanging from a low ceiling. Brodie vaguely remembered Tegel from his visit in 2000, and he was surprised that a world-class city like Berlin still didn't have a better airport. "This place is kind of a dump."

"You're not off to a good start, Scott."

"With what?"

"Your attitude." She added, "It's an f-ing airport. You did this in Caracas."

"I'm trained in situational awareness. Did you miss that class?"

She rolled her eyes, probably remembering one of the reasons she'd said she'd never work with him again.

They got their luggage from baggage claim, sailed through customs, and entered the small arrivals hall, which had a glass ceiling offering a view of the bright-blue winter sky. Brodie checked his phone: No messages. Local time, 7:50 A.M.

Up ahead was a line of dark-suited drivers holding handwritten signs and tablets with the names of their expected passengers.

Brodie spotted a burly guy in his mid-sixties in a suit and tie under a long black topcoat holding up a card that said <u>BRODIE/TAYLOR</u>. If the guy were a sausage, he'd be a knockwurst with a weisswurst complexion. He also had thinning gray hair and a bushy gray mustache.

Brodie signaled to the man, who walked over as he extended his hand and said in barely accented English, "Mr. Brodie. Ms. Taylor. My name is Ulrich. Welcome to Berlin."

They all shook hands and Ulrich took Taylor's rolling suitcase. "This way, please."

He led them to a bank of elevators and pressed the call button. "How was your flight?"

"Uneventful," said Brodie. "I believe we're going straight to the embassy."

"Yes, sir."

Brodie always wanted to know who was driving him, so he asked, "Are you employed by the embassy or a car service?"

"I am an embassy employee, sir."

"Good." Meaning fully vetted and not likely to have been bribed to drive them somewhere to be kidnapped.

They took the elevator down to a covered parking area, and Ulrich led them to a black Mercedes sedan and Brodie noted the diplomatic plates. Brodie and Taylor climbed in the back seat as Ulrich loaded their luggage into the trunk; then he got in and pulled out of the parking lot onto an airport road.

Brodie asked, "How long to the embassy?"

"At this time of day, maybe twenty minutes. I am told you have a nine o'clock meeting." Ulrich assured them, "Plenty of time." He added, as if he'd said this before, "Tegel isn't pretty, but it's close to the center. It will be too bad when they shut it down."

Taylor asked, "When will that be?"

Ulrich shrugged. "They've been talking about it for years. They built a big new airport just south of the city, but it still hasn't opened. Big mess. Corruption, construction delays, and safety errors. Now it sits there growing weeds and housing rats. Many Berliners are angry or embarrassed by this, but the longer I can use ugly old Tegel, the better."

Well, thought Brodie, maybe the famed German efficiency was a bit of a national myth. They were mere mortals, with corrupt government officials and idiot contractors just like everywhere else. That was comforting.

"Also," said Ulrich, "they should never have

121

closed Tempelhof Airport. It was historic. The Berlin Airlift. You know?"

"Yes," said Brodie. Not to mention it was the airport of the Third Reich, and probably had an Adolf Hitler VIP lounge.

Ulrich continued, "Now it is a public park. So maybe that is good."

Brodie changed the subject. "We saw anti-immigrant protests on the news."

Ulrich nodded. "Yes. I assume you know about your compatriot who was killed?"

"We do," said Taylor.

"It is a tragic thing."

Brodie asked, "Who organized the protest?"

"Af D. You know this group?"

"No," said Brodie, though he was sure Taylor could have supplied a twenty-minute briefing.

"Alternative für Deutschland," said Ulrich. "They are a right-wing, populist political party. Very nationalist. Very . . . Well, some say too much admiration for . . . another time."

"Right." Brodie often relied on local cabbies and hired drivers to cut through the bullshit while on overseas assignments, and he figured he'd give Ulrich a try. "How do you feel about this group?"

Ulrich shrugged. "I think some of these people are maybe crazy. But they also have an argument. I have no hate in my heart, sir.

But also I value tradition. Does this make sense?"

"Perfect sense," said Brodie, who thought Ulrich had spent too much time around diplomats. "The news is saying this murder was an act of Islamic terrorism. I guess there are a lot of Muslims that live around where it happened?"

Ulrich nodded. "Yes, sir. Neukölln. These days we call it Little Damascus for all the Syrian refugees. The ones that the Chancellor let in." He added, "As an act of compassion."

Taylor asked, "Do you know this neighborhood?"

"I have no reason to go there, miss. But the young people like it. They are more adventurous. My granddaughter, for instance, she spends time there with her friends. Clubs and art galleries and things such as that."

Brodie asked, "Is it dangerous?"

"Well . . . yes, maybe a little. But not because of terrorism or anything like this. It is a problem of drugs and gangs." He hesitated and said, "This American was a detective, correct? I think it was a criminal gang who did it."

Brodie nodded. The drug trade and terrorism were not mutually exclusive problems, with the former often funding the latter, so maybe that was what Vance was on the trail of. In which case his murder was not so much an act of terrorism as a gang hit to snuff out an investigation and preserve a lucrative criminal enterprise. But that didn't explain why Vance was conducting his work in secret. Although it might explain his missing eye.

On a related subject, Brodie wasn't so sure that Taylor booking them in a hotel in Neukölln was that good an idea after all. If a drug gang had killed one nosy American, two more would make three.

Ulrich turned onto a main road and they drove through a commercial area of car dealerships, gas stations, and light industry.

Ulrich asked, "Have you been to Berlin before?"

"I haven't," said Taylor.

"Once," said Brodie. "In 2000. Did you live here then?"

"Yes. All my life. Friedrichshain. In the East. I was six years old when the Wall went up."

"That must have been . . . traumatic," said Taylor.

Ulrich nodded. "August thirteenth, 1961. We call it Stacheldrahtsonntag. Barbed Wire Sunday. My mother and I went out for a walk that morning, and we noticed many people out on the street, talking excitedly and moving toward a line of barbed wire, and soldiers and police along the main street. They had done this at night, while we slept, along the whole border. I asked my mother, 'What is

124

this?' She didn't know. She was frightened, I remember. All of our neighbors were as well. By the afternoon she must have heard the Party propaganda and told me the barbed wire was to keep the fascists out. Well, fascists meant Nazis, and those people destroyed Germany and the world. So I thought, this is good. But then . . . I saw that the barbed wire kept us in." He was quiet for a moment, then said in a faraway tone, "We had family on the other side. Some we never saw again. The rest, not for twenty-eight years."

"That's very sad," said Taylor. "Cruel."

Brodie asked, "Did you witness the Wall coming down?"

Ulrich perked up as he said with pride, "I helped tear it down, sir. November 1989. You have seen those pictures of the people with sledgehammers? I was one of them." He laughed and added, "The best labor of my life."

Brodie said, "When I was here, a teenager sold me a piece of the Wall for twenty deutsche marks."

"In 2000? I'm sorry to say that was a piece of sidewalk, Mr. Brodie."

"It came with a certificate."

Ulrich laughed again. "You know, the best part was seeing the Grenztruppen — the East German border guards — just watching me with my sledgehammer. They could do nothing. Those . . . bastards. Excuse me."

125

Well, apparently Ulrich's diplomatic reserve didn't extend to the old regime that had oppressed him and stolen his childhood and his manhood.

He continued without prompting, "I learned something important in these moments. You see, the guards still had their guns as they watched us break their ugly Wall, climb over it, cross the border. But they could do nothing. The man holding the gun is not the problem. The problem is the people above this man who is carrying the gun, the puppet masters, pulling the strings." Ulrich added, "But we cut all the strings. Not on the day the Wall fell, but in the months before, bit by bit. This is the real work of resistance. The part not on the television. And so, when the end came, it seemed to come quickly. Like a rotten tree that falls in a wind. It was already dead."

This reminded Brodie of other conversations he'd had with people who lived in the former Soviet Bloc. The events of 1989 that had toppled Communist governments from Berlin to Bucharest seemed to happen all at once, at least from the point of view of an outsider. But the stage had been set in the months and years before. Not only by dissidents such as Ulrich, but by the totalitarian governments themselves, who built their regimes on a weak foundation of lies, repression, and stupidity. Many of the people who lived here knew it was coming. The CIA and other Western Intel agencies totally missed the signs.

Brodie said, "Still, they had the guns. You were all very brave."

Ulrich shrugged. "We were tired of being afraid. Tired of being abused. It was as simple as that. Once you cross this line, it is almost . . . easy. We didn't want to die, but we were prepared to. We knew we had a chance to take those bastards down, and we could not afford to let the moment pass." Ulrich glanced at Taylor in the rearview. "Excuse my language, miss."

"No fucking problem," Taylor assured him.

They all got a laugh at that.

They entered a residential neighborhood of handsome prewar apartment buildings and storefronts, and then the buildings quickly transitioned to a hodgepodge of more recent construction.

Berlin was not a beautiful city in any traditional sense. It didn't have much in the way of architectural uniformity or charm, which was a result of it being bombed and then blown to hell in street-to-street fighting, then divided into four occupation zones — American, British, French, and Russian — then split in two by the Wall. But what it lacked in traditional beauty it more than made up for with its sheer intrigue. During his last visit, Brodie remembered feeling that every corner of the city had a story to tell. And most of those stories didn't have happy endings.

They crossed the Spree River and entered onto a wide six-lane boulevard with thick growths of bare trees on either side.

Ulrich gestured out the window. "This is the Tiergarten, which Mr. Brodie might remember. Beautiful park, even in winter. The eastern end of the park is across the street from your embassy. Good for a nice walk."

They approached a traffic circle surrounding a tall decorative stone column that Brodie recalled from his last visit. The column was ringed with sculptures of gilded cannons, and on top was a bronze statue of a winged woman holding aloft a wreath of laurels and a lance.

Ulrich, who had probably heard "What is that?" a few hundred times, anticipated the question and said, "That is the Victory Column. Built in 1873 by Prussia to commemorate military conquests that expanded the German Empire. On top is Victoria, Roman goddess of victory."

Brodie looked up at Victoria, her feathered wings and raised lance shining in the bright morning sun. He imagined that contemporary Germans were a little more comfortable with displays of martial pride like this one, which predated the Third Reich.

128

They rounded the traffic circle and then continued east along the boulevard that cut through the Tiergarten. In a few minutes they passed another monument on their left, a modernist stone colonnade behind a large plaza. A brass statue of a helmeted soldier stood on a high pedestal, flanked on either side by artillery guns and tanks. The pedestal featured Cyrillic writing etched in gold.

Taylor looked at it out the window as they drove past. "What is that?"

"It is one of the Soviet War Memorials," said Ulrich. "For the Red Army soldiers who died in the battle for the city. Much of the marble used to build it was taken from the ruins of Hitler's Reich Chancellery."

Brodie remembered this from his last visit. The Soviets had built this memorial on the spot where they had buried thousands of their own dead within the Tiergarten, which had been reduced to a charred wilderness from incendiary bombings and from the Red Army's advance into the heart of the city.

Brodie eyed the colossal Soviet soldier towering over the now regrown trees of the Tiergarten. He wondered if it was disturbing for Berliners out for a stroll in the park to have to see a prominent memorial to the sacrifices of the conquering army, while no memorials existed to their own soldiers who had fought and died for the most hated regime in history. This was a complicated place.

Ulrich eyed the memorial as they drove past it and said, "The Soviets are gone, but it was part of the German reunification treaty to keep these memorials. In order to . . . honor the men who defeated the fascists."

Ulrich said that last part as if he didn't exactly agree with the reasoning. Indeed, the Red Army did deserve much of the credit for defeating Hitler. But they also flattened Berlin and other German cities in their path, and raped millions of German women before and after the fall of the Reich. To the victor go the spoils. History hung over this city like a shroud.

Ulrich said, "Up ahead is the Brandenburg Gate. Built by King Friedrich Wilhelm the Second in 1791. This serves as a passageway to Unter den Linden, the main boulevard in the city center and also where your embassy is. The boulevard used to lead straight to the Royal Palace, which was badly damaged in the war and then demolished by the Communists, but has now been rebuilt."

Brodie looked at the iconic Brandenburg Gate ahead of them. A row of neoclassical columns formed five passageways, through which Berliners on bike and on foot were passing in both directions, which was not possible when the Brandenburg Gate divided East and West Berlin. Atop the structure was a sculpture of a horse-drawn chariot carrying Victoria, who must have been the Germans' favorite Roman goddess.

As they got closer to the gate, Brodie noticed mottled patches of lighter-colored stone along the lengths of the Doric columns, where the sandstone had been replaced to cover bullet holes and pockmarks from grenade and bomb shrapnel.

Ulrich made a right turn at the T-intersection in front of the gate, and they passed along the eastern edge of the Tiergarten. Ulrich pointed to their left. "This is the embassy here." He added, "We will go around to the back."

Brodie and Taylor looked out the driver's-side window. From here they could see the western side of the embassy, which was a modern, fairly nondescript four-story sandstone building. Brodie noticed a Berlin Police officer standing near a small side entrance. Knee-high security bollards lined the curb between the road and the tree-lined cobblestone sidewalk, and a metal fence stood in front of the embassy walls. A few pedestrians passed by.

Ulrich drove a block past the embassy and then made a left. He again pointed out his window. "This is the Holocaust Memorial. The architect is an American Jew."

Brodie and Taylor looked out at a field of thousands of rectangular stone slabs arrayed

131

in long rows. The slabs were suggestive of a cemetery — or perhaps a mass grave. They all appeared to be the same shape but varied in height from a few inches high to over fifteen feet tall, and followed the curves of the ground beneath them, creating ripples across the field. Two teenagers sat on top of one of the slabs. A tourist family took a selfie.

This place, like the memorial of the Soviet soldier flanked by howitzers and tanks in the Tiergarten, seemed to be not only a monument to a dark past, but — due to its central location — a piece of public art. A place not only prominent but unavoidable. Maybe that was the point.

They passed the memorial, and Ulrich made a series of turns to bring them around to the back of the embassy. As they approached the rear of the building he pulled onto a narrow shoulder and stopped in front of a row of security bollards.

Ahead of them stood a short, stocky man in his mid-forties with a full head of dirty-blond hair. He was dressed in a black topcoat and holding a walkie. He and Ulrich exchanged waves, and the man said something into the walkie. After a moment the security bollards lowered into the ground, and Ulrich pulled the Mercedes forward onto the embassy property.

Ulrich parked the car near the rear entrance, a glass entryway with a security booth next to it. A Berlin Police officer was inside the booth, watching them without much interest.

Ulrich said, "I am to take you to your hotel when you are ready."

"Good," said Brodie.

Ulrich asked, "May I ask where you are staying?"

"What were you told?"

Ulrich looked at Brodie, then Taylor. "They told me the Art Hotel in Neukölln. But that must be a mistake."

Brodie replied, "We heard the cocktail lounge was terrific."

Ulrich informed them, "I believe it is a Muslim-owned establishment. No alcohol."

"Holy . . . Are you kidding?"

"No, sir."

Taylor interjected, "That's where we're staying."

"Yes, madam."

Brodie and Taylor climbed out and the stocky man approached them, extending his hand. "Mr. Brodie, Ms. Taylor. Welcome to the embassy. My name is Jason Butler, assistant legal attaché."

Brodie shook his hand. "Call me Scott."

Taylor also shook his hand and said, "Maggie."

Butler smiled at them both. "All right, Scott and Maggie. We're happy to have you on the team."

Whenever Brodie heard that he'd be part of a "team," he wanted to reach for his service weapon, but unfortunately he was unarmed. He said to FBI Agent Butler, "Look forward to meeting the rest of the team."

Butler flashed another grin and then said something in German to Ulrich, who spoke perfect English, but Butler wanted to show off his German.

Ulrich responded in English, "Very good, Mr. Butler. I will be here."

Butler nodded, then said to his guests, "Ulrich will hold your luggage and then take you to your hotel after the meeting. Sound good?"

"Sounds fine," said Taylor.

"Excellent. This way, please." Butler led them toward the entryway.

Brodie thought that Jason Butler had something of a Boy Scout vibe, which he'd found to be a common trait among FBI agents. He'd also found that was no reason to underestimate them. Or to trust them.

Butler pulled open the glass double doors and they entered a wide marble hallway. A Marine guard in full dress uniform stood at attention next to an American flag.

The Marine saluted them, so apparently the Marine Embassy Guard had been alerted to their military officer ranks despite their civilian dress. Nice touch. Brodie and Taylor, who rarely took or gave a salute on the job, remembered to return the salute.

Butler led them down the hallway, passing a few closed doors. "I'll take you to the front lobby where you can relax while we're getting things set up for the briefing. How was your flight in?"

"Fine," said Brodie. "Except for the Lufthansa pilots detouring over London for a practice bombing run."

Butler ignored the bad joke and said, "I've been doing some reading on Mr. Vance, and it sounds like he had a remarkable career."

"Yes," said Brodie. "We lost a good one."

Taylor asked, "Who will be running the briefing?"

"Sharon Whitmore, the senior legal attaché."

"Will the BKA and the Berlin Police be present?"

"Both will be represented," replied Butler. He added, "It will be a very comprehensive briefing."

"Good," said Brodie. "And after it's over we will need access to the crime scene."

"I'm sure that can be arranged."

"By who?"

"By the BKA. The Federal Police, who are running this investigation. They have control of the crime scene and custody of all evidence."

Taylor said to Brodie, "We'll put in a request with the BKA officer at the briefing."

"Actually," said Butler, "we can handle that

135

for you." He added, "Though we have no investigative authority, we have a lot of experience coordinating with German law enforcement."

Brodie said, "And we have a lot of experience investigating homicides."

"I'm sure you do. But this homicide is politically sensitive. We all need to keep open lines of communication here and be clear on our needs and requirements. To that end, I want you to relay any requests you have pertaining to this investigation to me directly."

Brodie took that to mean, *Don't do anything without clearing it with the FBI.*

He replied, "We will keep all lines of communication open. I will let you know about all of my and Maggie's needs."

Butler flashed another smile, this one not so convincing. "Good."

They entered the front lobby, a modestly sized room with mostly glass walls. The eastern-facing wall offered a view of a large interior courtyard dotted with trees and benches, and the western wall faced the street and the edge of the Tiergarten. There was another hallway entrance at the far end of the lobby that, based on Brodie's experience in American embassies, led to the front entrance and the security desk.

Butler led them to a cluster of leather club chairs near a polished flagstone wall. "Make yourselves comfortable and I'll let you know when we're ready for you."

Taylor said, "Thank you, Jason."

Butler looked at Taylor and smiled as he said, "You're most welcome." He walked off quickly.

Brodie and Taylor sat in facing chairs. Brodie watched Butler as he trotted across the lobby, then disappeared from view. He pictured the guy taking a secret elevator up to the NSA listening station where he could spy on everyone in the lobby. Brodie eyed a potted fern next to his chair and pushed aside one of the leaves.

"What are you doing?"

"Sweeping for bugs."

"Maybe I shouldn't have told you about that. You're paranoid enough."

"What did you think of Agent Butler? Please communicate in hand signals only."

"He was fine. As for you, I think you still have some things to learn about making friends and influencing people."

"I don't need more friends."

"How about allies?"

"Jason Butler is not our ally. He is an FBI agent and a bureaucratic roadblock between us and the German Federal Police, the BKA, who are actually running this investigation. And the BKA, in turn, is another roadblock. You understand this intuitively, which is why you got us hotel rooms away from this place with views overlooking the crime scene."

"That's not exactly what I was thinking —"

"Listen, Maggie. Humans are clannish by nature. We divide ourselves by nation, race, religion, sports teams, and beer brands. You and I are part of a large and powerful clan called the U.S. military, and that little twerp is not."

"Don't be the kind of soldier who has contempt for civilians. It's unbecoming."

"My point is that the FBI is its own clan too, and they are looking at this thing the way Feds do — hung up on jurisdiction and procedure. And that's fine, they're basically diplomats here and that's part of their job. They have to live and work in this country every day, and they can't burn bridges that they'll need again when the next case comes along. We are outsiders. And we have a different job and different motivations. Harry Vance was one of us."

Taylor looked Brodie in the eyes. "You're hungry for a fight. But you ought to wait until someone actually fucks with you before starting one."

"I won't have long to wait."

Taylor had no response.

Brodie spotted a tall man in a blue Army service uniform entering the lobby from the front entrance. The man saw them and headed in their direction. As he got closer Brodie saw he was in his early fifties with short military-cut gray hair, a ruddy face, and angular features. He wore the silver star of a brigadier general on his shoulders and had a chest full of ribbons.

Brodie and Taylor stood, ready to salute as the man approached, but he extended his hand.

"Ms. Taylor, Mr. Brodie. I'm General Frank Kiernan, defense attaché."

They all shook hands.

Brodie said, "Pleasure to meet you, sir. Colonel Dombroski speaks highly of you."

Kiernan smiled. "Haven't seen Stan in eight years. He has no idea what this place has done to me." He gestured to the club chairs. "Let's sit."

They all sat. Kiernan looked between the two of them and said, "Hell of a thing."

Brodie nodded. "Yes, sir."

"I've got my theories. I'm sure you have yours. You ought to know I've spoken with Mark Jenkins, Harry Vance's former partner. He's out for blood. Everyone in the Fifth MP is. Understandable. But General Hackett made the right decision in not letting them handle it and sending you two."

Taylor said, "Thank you, sir. Is there anything you can share with us about your conversation with Mark Jenkins?"

"Plenty. But you might be better off speaking to him directly." He took a business card from his pocket and handed it to Taylor. "My card. His cell is written on the back. He's staying at the Radisson, not too far from here. He's already spoken to the FBI and the BKA, but he sounded eager to confer with his own people."

"We'll get in touch ASAP," said Taylor.

"Good. So where did they put you up?"

Brodie said, "Ms. Taylor has put us in the Art Hotel."

"Where is that?"

"It's in Neukölln," said Taylor. "We wanted to get a sense of the area."

"Okay . . . Well, I guess that makes sense. But if it's a dump I'm sure the embassy can help relocate you."

Brodie asked, "How long have you been in-country, General?"

"Six years," said Kiernan. "It's an interesting posting. Modern Germany is a nation somewhat unique in world history — a rich, successful country that is in many ways afraid of its own power."

Taylor said, "They seem to be exerting a lot of power over the rest of Europe."

"*Economic* power," said Kiernan. "And maybe that's part of the key to their success, fully committing to that tool because the rest of their toolbox has been shut. But their military has gradually been spreading its wings, so to speak, in the last twenty years. It's been an interesting process to see from the inside."

Brodie nodded. German resentment over their forced disarmament after the First World War was one of the contributing factors to Hitler's rise to power, and during the Cold War, West Germany's military had a purely defensive posture and never saw combat. After reunification, the unified German military — the Bundeswehr — slowly stepped onto the world stage, first in Kosovo and then Afghanistan. It was now deployed all over the world, which made some people nervous.

Kiernan continued, "It's the ongoing guns and butter debate with the Germans," referring to the competing priorities of military and social welfare spending. "And it's easy enough for the pacifist politicians here and the rest of Europe to scare the crap out of the public and the world about the bogeyman of a large and powerful German military. But it's happening."

"You believe that's a good thing?" asked Brodie.

"Sure," said Kiernan. "So long as you stay on their good side." He chuckled and said, "A German tourist drives to the French border and hands his passport to the guard. Border guard asks, 'Occupation?' and the German says, 'No no no, just visiting.' "

Kiernan laughed at his own bad joke. Brodie and Taylor smiled. This guy had definitely been here too long.

141

Kiernan's smile faded and he appeared lost in thought. After a moment he said, "You two did a hell of a job on the Mercer case."

Officially, there was no such case, and if there was, Brodie and Taylor had nothing to do with it. So neither of them responded.

Kiernan stared at Brodie, unblinking. "The official story is bullshit, of course."

Again, Brodie didn't respond, and neither did Taylor.

The general looked between the two of them. "You did what you had to do. But your reputation from the Mercer case precedes you, and there are people here who don't like you."

Meaning the CIA. And maybe military Intel guys who were somehow involved in the Mercer business.

Since they were on the subject of people who might want to kill them — and since Taylor had not yet brought it up as she'd said she would — Brodie said, "General, Ms. Taylor and I would like to be issued sidearms."

Kiernan raised an eyebrow. "This is Germany, Mr. Brodie, not Venezuela. You don't need a gun here."

"With all due respect, sir, we are working a homicide case in which the victim is an Army CID agent, and until we have a better understanding of the motive, it's reasonable to believe that Ms. Taylor and I could be targets." He wasn't sure he believed that, but it sounded good.

Kiernan thought for a moment, and nodded. "You make a point. The Germans are very strict about allowing foreign agents to carry firearms, but I will look into it."

"Thank you, sir."

Just then Jason Butler walked back into the lobby and headed toward them.

Kiernan watched Butler approaching and said, "I've had to deal with this guy more in the last twenty-four hours than in the whole two years he's been stationed here."

As they stood and walked toward Butler, Kiernan said to Brodie and Taylor, "I doubt you are in any mortal danger in this country, but you're about to enter a snake pit of bureaucracy and bullshit that has its own way of taking years off your life. So, as any commander would tell his troops before battle — watch your ass."

CHAPTER 8

Jason Butler led them to a second-floor conference room with a long table. Five people were already seated, speaking quietly. At the head of the table stood a woman in her late fifties with shoulder-length brown hair, wearing a navy-blue suit. She approached Brodie and Taylor and extended her hand.

"Mr. Brodie, Ms. Taylor. I'm Sharon Whitmore, legal attaché. Welcome to Berlin."

They all shook. Brodie regarded FBI Agent Whitmore, who had alert brown eyes but something of a world-weary demeanor.

Taylor said, "We're glad to be on the team."

Brodie, who was not glad to be on the team, said, "Nice meeting you."

Whitmore gestured to the conference table. "Please have a seat. There are name cards."

Brodie and Taylor made perfunctory greetings as they found their adjacent seats that corresponded to printed placards propped up on the table. General Kiernan and Jason

Butler took their seats near Whitmore's.

Set behind each placard was a bottle of German mineral water, a small stack of briefing materials, and a notepad and pen. A pile of apple strudel sat on a plate in the dead center of the table where no one could reach it. In a CID Quantico conference room, a box of donuts lasted about ninety seconds, but this strudel had probably been sitting there since Christmas.

Across from Brodie and Taylor were two uniformed men, talking quietly in German. The guy on the left was a dark-skinned man around Brodie's age in a navy-blue Berlin Police uniform. His placard IDed him as Police Captain Omar Soliman, obviously an Arabic name. Brodie wondered if Captain Soliman was in the Berlin PD's counterterrorism division. Or maybe he was homicide, and Neukölln was his beat.

The other uniformed man was Chief Inspector Erlich Schröder. He was in his mid-fifties, a rail-thin, severe-looking guy with deep-set blue eyes and thinning strawberry-blond hair. He was dressed in an olive-drab collared shirt with epaulettes, which Brodie assumed was the uniform of the federal police force — the Bundeskriminalamt, or BKA.

Also at the table was FBI Special Agent David Kim, who looked to be of Korean descent, mid-forties, dressed in a tailored black suit and white dress shirt with no tie. Mr. Kim

145

was in polite conversation with the person seated next to him, Sarah Hopkins of the U.S. State Department, an attractive woman of about thirty in a tan suit with oversized glasses and brunette hair pulled back in a tight bun. And next to her was another State Department rep, Howard Fensterman, a bald man in his mid-fifties who wore a rumpled blue suit and was sipping mineral water while reviewing the stack of papers in front of him. So, there were a total of ten people in this room, all with the same stated goal and different unstated agendas.

Brodie noted that this was an interior room with no windows, and was most likely a SCIF, a Sensitive Compartmented Information Facility, that was secure against electronic eavesdropping — a safe room that was safe from everything except grandstanding and bullshit. A lot of these types of rooms required you to turn in your phone and other electronic devices before entering, but an embassy SCIF might have different protocols. Brodie checked his phone and noted that he had no cell signal.

Brodie took a pen from the table and scribbled a note to Taylor on his pad: THE STRUDEL IS POISONED.

Taylor read the note, then wrote beneath it: HAVE A PIECE.

Sharon Whitmore took her seat at the head of the table and everyone turned their attention toward her.

"Welcome, and thank you all for being here." She paused and scanned the faces around the table. "We are here because of the tragic death of U.S. Army CID Special Agent Harry Vance early Sunday morning. I am confident that the joint efforts of the individuals in this room, and the organizations you represent, will deliver justice for Mr. Vance. We are grateful to have the full cooperation and considerable expertise of the Bundeskriminalamt as well as the Berlin Police, represented here by Chief Inspector Schröder and Captain Soliman, respectively."

The two uniformed men nodded in acknowledgment.

"I would also like to extend a special welcome — as well as condolences — to our two visiting special agents from the Army Criminal Investigation Division, Chief Warrant Officers Scott Brodie and Maggie Taylor." She looked at them. "We will find justice for your fallen colleague."

Taylor said, "Thank you."

Brodie nodded.

Whitmore continued, "Everyone in this room has the proper security clearance to hear the information that will be presented. Feel free to take written notes, but please no recording devices. Now" — she gestured around the room — "I'd like to have everyone introduce themselves, so we all know

147

who's who. I am Agent Sharon Whitmore of the Federal Bureau of Investigation and the senior legal attaché for the Berlin embassy." She looked to her left, where Jason Butler was sitting.

"Agent Jason Butler, FBI. Assistant legal attaché."

The general was next. "General Frank Kiernan. U.S. Army. Defense attaché." He added, "I am in constant communication with senior officials in all branches of the German military, who are keeping a close watch on this case due to the obvious national security implications. But I will leave it to German civilian law enforcement" — he gestured to Schröder and Soliman — "to determine what, if any, intelligence is to be shared with their military counterparts."

In other words, the general's German military contacts were going to want to know what was said in this room, and Kiernan was assuring the BKA and Berlin PD that he was tight-lipped. The web of competing agendas, loyalties, and bureaucracies represented around this table was migraine-inducing.

The man next to Kiernan said, "David Kim, FBI. Here from the New York field office."

That was interesting, thought Brodie. Outside talent. The only reason Brodie could think of for bringing David Kim all the way from New York was that he was a counter-

asshole. It's always best to set the bar low before clearing it.

And last but not least, Maggie Taylor. "Warrant Officer Maggie Taylor, U.S. Army CID Special Agent. I did not know Mr. Vance personally, but he was a respected and valued colleague within CID. We all feel this loss, and we are determined to assist in delivering justice."

So, thought Brodie, there it was. Ten blind mice, which was eight more than they needed.

Whitmore spoke. "Thank you, Ms. Taylor, and thank you, everyone, for your introductions. Before we get into the specifics of the case, I would like to briefly address the political climate in which this investigation is being conducted. Yesterday, just outside this embassy, a large far-right demonstration was held. The protest was quickly organized without permission from the city and included a number of individuals looking to foment violence."

Whitmore looked at Captain Soliman. "We rely on the Berlin Police to provide embassy security. One of your officers was assaulted, as you know. About a dozen people were arrested for various other incidents."

Soliman nodded. "There were fourteen arrests."

Whitmore asked, "And how is the injured officer?"

"A broken rib. But he'll be okay."

151

Whitmore nodded. "I'm happy to hear that. All right, we will first turn to Mr. Fensterman for a little more context."

Howard Fensterman glanced at a sheet of paper in front of him. "Yes. Thank you, Agent Whitmore. One of the aspects of my job is to monitor and analyze the day-to-day political environment within Germany, as well as broader political trends within the country, and the significance of any of these developments as they relate to American interests." He paused and looked around the table. "There is a rising white nationalist movement here in Germany. Its center of influence is in Dresden and other parts of the former East, where lagging economic growth and other factors provide fertile ground for right-wing populist influence driven in large part by a demonization of immigrants. Increasingly, these movements are finding traction within Berlin itself. These extremists have been legitimized by one of Germany's political parties, Af D — Alternative for Germany — which has a right-wing nationalist platform. They organized yesterday's rally. Af D currently has eighty-nine seats in the Bundestag, making it the largest party in the opposition. Mr. Vance's murder provides a perfect opportunity for them to amplify their anti-immigrant — and specifically anti-Muslim — rhetoric. They have officially condemned the assault of the police officer yesterday, which is in keeping with their pattern of using inciteful and inflammatory rhetoric and then distancing themselves when that rhetoric leads to unlawful and violent actions of their own making."

Brodie eyed Captain Soliman and Chief Inspector Schröder, both of whom looked uncomfortable with Fensterman's analysis.

Fensterman continued, "There are other groups in Germany with more extreme views and less political power than Af D, but they use Af D as a legitimizing front for their extremism. We believe that — regardless of the outcome of this investigation — Mr. Vance's murder will be exploited as a galvanizing moment for an emboldened far-right movement. I'm not an investigator. I leave that job to others in this room. But I wish everyone to be mindful of the political environment in which this investigation is being conducted." He added, "Thank you."

Brodie wasn't entirely sure what the point of this presentation was — except to signal that if it turned out that a Muslim immigrant had killed Vance, all hell might break loose. And if they discovered the killer was not an immigrant or a Muslim . . . all hell might break loose anyway if the right-wing crazies decided to try to delegitimize the investigation's findings that didn't fit their agenda. Mr. Fensterman was just doing his job, of course, but the last thing a good criminal

153

investigator should be thinking about is the political implications of his findings.

Ms. Whitmore said, "Thank you, Mr. Fensterman. I have heard from embassy security that another unauthorized protest is massing out front as we speak, and the police presence has been increased to avoid a repeat of yesterday's disturbances. Now we will turn to the details of the investigation, and we'll begin with Captain Soliman, who will run us through the homicide division's findings."

Captain Soliman nodded. "Thank you, Ms. Whitmore." He picked up a remote control and pointed it toward a flat-screen TV hanging on the wall at the far end of the room. He pushed a button and a photo of a park appeared, and he said in near-perfect English, "This is Körnerpark, in Neukölln, where Mr. Vance's body was discovered early Sunday morning." He pressed the button, and the next picture came up, a photo of a grassy clearing within the park. In the center of the clearing, a gray-haired man lay on his back. He was wearing a camel-hair topcoat, dark slacks, and brown oxford shoes. His left arm was splayed to the side and slightly above his head, and his right arm rested partially on his chest. A cap of some kind lay in the grass near his head. Soliman continued, "The body was found in an open area in the park's northeast corner at approximately six-thirty

154

Sunday morning, by a woman walking her dog."

Brodie looked at Harry's face, which he could only see from a distance in the wide image. His single right eye stared open to the sky. Where his left eye had been, Brodie could barely make out a small patch of dark blood.

Soliman went to the next slide, which was a close-up photo of the very small entry wound near Vance's ear. Soliman said, "Mr. Vance was shot in the right temple with a single standard-velocity twenty-two-caliber long rifle round. The bullet lodged in the brain and was removed during the autopsy. Ballistics is currently analyzing it."

Brodie processed that. Twenty-two-caliber long rifle bullets were one of the most common and widely used rounds for civilian bolt-action and semi-automatic rifles, and were often employed for target practice and for hunting small or medium-sized game. This caliber round was much more widely used in the U.S., while European rifles tended to use 5.56-millimeter NATO rounds, which were about the same caliber but in a larger cartridge and with a higher velocity. The .22-caliber long rifle fired a slower, more lightweight round, which would explain why there was no exit wound.

Soliman switched to an overhead diagram of Körnerpark. The location of Vance's body was illustrated, as well as the locations of trees and paths. There was a hashed line leading from the body to the street running along the east side of the park. Soliman continued, "This line here represents the likely trajectory of the bullet. I should note that Körnerpark is sunken approximately six meters below street level. Based on the angle of entry, it is believed that the gunman was on the sidewalk above the park and shot Mr. Vance from a distance of approximately sixty meters. This distance would be consistent with the cranial wound and the bullet's depth of travel."

Brodie looked at the hashed line illustrating the hypothesized bullet trajectory. The killer knew he wouldn't need anything more powerful than a .22 LR round for shooting someone at close range. Sixty meters — about two hundred feet — was well within the range for a fatal head shot, and the gunman made sure of it by striking the temple, the softest part of the skull. One of the greatest advantages of .22 LR ammo — both for hunters and for murderers in the middle of a dense urban area — is that due to its low velocity and small cartridge it doesn't make much of a sound when fired. It's also quiet enough to not require a silencer, which slows down the bullet and, in this case, could have dropped the velocity of a .22 LR round to such a degree that a fatal head shot from sixty meters was unlikely. In any case, this was obviously not a random murder. It was planned and premeditated.

Soliman continued, "Berlin saw heavy rain throughout the day Saturday, and we have analyzed impressions in the grass and mud inside the park to determine precisely where Mr. Vance was standing when he was struck, and we have also determined the body was not moved after the fatal shot. This analysis has allowed us to approximate the location of the shooter, and we will be able to confirm it once further analysis of the cranial wound is completed." Soliman continued talking, describing what Vance was wearing at the time of his death — slacks, dress shirt, plus a camel-hair topcoat, scarf, and a flat cap — and then listed the items found on Mr. Vance's person, remarking on the absence of a cell phone and the likelihood that it was taken by the perpetrator or an accomplice. Soliman also mentioned the Beretta M9 that Vance was holding in his coat pocket and said that the mag was fully loaded and that, according to an initial analysis, the weapon had not been fired recently.

Then Soliman said, "There was also what we believe to be a postmortem injury to the body." He clicked to the next photo, which was a close-up image of Vance's hollowed-out left eye socket. "Someone — we can assume the killer or an accomplice — removed Mr. Vance's left eye from its socket using a sharp object. We mentioned this in our initial report, but the information has subsequently been withheld, in the event a group or individual were to come forward with this detail when claiming responsibility. Thus, you will not find this information in the briefing materials you have been provided." He added, "Nor should this detail be shared with anyone outside of this room."

Brodie nodded. His theory on that was correct. The more interesting question was why the perp had done this in the first place. As proof of responsibility? Souvenir collection by a psychotic serial killer? Or, to send a message.

David Kim said aloud, "An eye for an eye."

The room was silent for a moment. Then Captain Soliman said, "This type of mutilation could fit into a number of criminal profiles. My people are looking back through a decade of homicide records to see if a similar mutilation was performed on any prior victims."

Taylor said, "Sounds like you're looking for a serial killer."

"It is one of many theories," said Soliman. "Another would be, as Mr. Kim alluded to, an attempt by an individual or group to send a message, perhaps related to a case Mr. Vance had been investigating. But I'd prefer not to enter into this kind of speculation until we have more information."

158

Brodie stared at Harry Vance's empty eye socket. The eyelid was intact, and it appeared as if whoever had performed the incision had done so with care, to preserve the eyeball. The killer, or the killer's accomplice, was not rushed, or nervous. They were dealing with pros.

Soliman pressed the remote and went to another slide, this one a photograph of a stone stairway. He continued, "These stairs are at the southern entrance to the park. Based on the location of Mr. Vance's footprints in the mud, we believe he descended into the park from this staircase, off Schierker Straße, and then walked north through the park to his final location."

Captain Soliman moved on to the next slide, a black-and-white image from a closed-circuit security camera. It showed the corner of a city block, and a metro station in front of elevated train tracks. A figure in a long, light-colored coat and cap was walking on the street away from the station. Soliman said, "This image is taken from footage recorded by a security camera and shows a figure who we believe to be Mr. Vance exiting the Berlin-Neukölln metro station. As you can see, it is time-stamped two-fifty-two in the morning. It is an approximately five-minute walk from this location to Körnerpark."

Brodie asked, "Have you shown this footage to anyone who knew Vance?"

Captain Soliman looked a little annoyed by another interruption to his presentation. He set down the remote and looked at Brodie. "No, Mr. Brodie. We have not."

"Well, I'm sure his partner, Mark Jenkins, would like to see the security tape and could easily confirm or refute your ID. I'd like to see the tape too."

Chief Inspector Schröder interjected, "We are in contact with Mr. Jenkins and I'm certain he will be helpful in this investigation."

Brodie asked, "What about the train line for that stop? Where was Harry Vance coming from? Have you reviewed footage near other stations?"

Schröder offered a tight smile and said in slightly accented English, "Thank you for your thorough questions, Mr. Brodie," which was actually German for "fuck you." He continued, "The Neukölln station is serviced by both the U-Bahn and S-Bahn railway systems. These systems combined contain over two hundred stations. Our officers, with the assistance of the Berlin Police" — he nodded toward Captain Soliman — "are collecting and reviewing security camera footage near these stations where it is available. The late hour of Mr. Vance's travels makes this process slightly less daunting. As you can imagine, we are very interested in where he was coming from and who he was associating with in the hours and days before his murder."

David Kim piped in, "And still no one's come forward? We don't know who he had been in contact with while in Berlin?"

Captain Soliman nodded. "That is correct."

Brodie asked, "Do we know when Vance arrived in Berlin?"

Chief Inspector Schröder looked at him with his severe blue eyes and said, "This is a complex case with many details to work through, Mr. Brodie, and Captain Soliman and I have structured our briefing for both efficiency and clarity," which was German for "shut the fuck up." A few days here and Brodie would be fluent.

Captain Soliman, who seemed a bit more accommodating than the tight-ass BKA chief inspector, added, "We have spoken to Mr. Vance's commanding officer in Kaiserslautern, Colonel William Trask, and also to Mr. Vance's partner, Mark Jenkins. Mr. Vance informed both of these men nine days ago — that would be last Sunday — that he was leaving for Berlin on Tuesday and would be back by early the following week. According to Mr. Jenkins, his partner usually took the train between Kaiserslautern and Berlin, and we have confirmed that a ticket was issued in his name by Deutsche Bahn. We are currently reviewing security camera footage from the

Kaiserslautern station, as well as the stations in Mannheim and Hanover — one of which he would have needed to use as a transfer point — and footage from the Berlin central station where he would have arrived. We hope to reconstruct Mr. Vance's journey and to determine if he had contact with anyone during that journey, as well as to determine where he went once he arrived in Berlin. He did not tell either his commanding officer or his partner the purpose of his trip, beyond saying that it was personal."

Taylor asked, "Did either of them speculate as to why he was coming here?"

Soliman nodded. "He was in the process of a divorce. Both his colleagues believed that he was traveling for romantic purposes."

Brodie estimated that Kaiserslautern to Berlin was about a five-hour train ride, not including the transfer. *There are easier ways to get laid, Harry.*

And while Vance might have been following his dick or his heart, that probably wasn't why he was shot by a sniper lying in wait for him in a park in Neukölln. Brodie looked at Chief Inspector Schröder and asked, "Can I assume you have information on what terrorism cases Vance was working in the past few months?"

Schröder replied, "Colonel Trask shared information that may prove useful."

"Such as?"

Schröder looked at Brodie. "These cases involved classified U.S. military intelligence. I am authorized to receive, but not authorized to share, such intelligence. I am sure you will have no problem obtaining that information yourself." He added, "From your own people."

"Thank you." Brodie asked Captain Soliman, "Has the Berlin Police checked hotel registrations to see if a Mr. Harry Vance was or had ever been a guest?"

Soliman nodded. "We are in the process of doing that. But it is a big task in a big city. And there are thousands of Airbnbs, and rooms for rent where few questions are asked."

"Right. Let me know if you get a hit."

Soliman nodded.

Well, if Harry was here for a woman, he was probably staying with her, assuming she was a local. But if he was with a woman, why hadn't she come forward?

David Kim said, "Can we cut to the chase? We're all wondering if this murder is in some way linked to Islamic terrorism. Right? I'd like to hear some theories, and then I'll share my own."

Brodie looked at Kim. This guy didn't act like a Fed. Too much spark.

Schröder cleared his throat and said, "I was getting to that, Mr. Kim." He turned to Soliman. "Before I do, is there any other information you wish to share, Captain?"

Soliman shook his head. "We will update everyone when we receive further results from our forensics analysis, as well as if we find anything in the security camera footage or discover where Mr. Vance stayed in Berlin."

Sharon Whitmore said, "Thank you, Captain."

Schröder said, "Now I will address the potential counterterrorism aspects of this case. Neukölln is a large borough with a very diverse population. Among this population are former refugees from Lebanon, the Palestinian territories, Iraq, and most recently Syria and Libya. It should go without saying that the majority of this population are law-abiding and contributing members of German society who have come here to make a better life for themselves and their families."

Brodie knew through experience that that PC preamble meant the chief inspector was about to say something less than flattering about the fine people of Neukölln.

"However," continued Schröder, "Neukölln has also become one of the focal points of extremist Islamic ideology in Germany. Mosques and other gathering spaces are used for recruitment, as well as for leveraging large networks of religious adherents to raise funds for overseas extremist groups, which is illegal in Germany. Our agents are closely monitoring all of this, though I am not at liberty to share details of ongoing investigations. If we determine that Mr. Vance's murder is linked to Islamic extremists, we will be as forthcoming as possible."

Brodie noted the "as possible" and hoped there would be other sources of Intel on potential links between Harry's murder and Islamic terrorism. Like, for instance, Captain Soliman, who in addition to being familiar with the community was a fellow cop and therefore less slippery than Schröder, a federal intelligence agent.

"Captain Soliman," said Brodie, "can you share any details about the presence of terrorist groups in Neukölln?"

Soliman shifted in his seat. "I am a homicide investigator, Mr. Brodie. Terrorism and national security are not my areas of expertise or my duties."

"But Neukölln is your beat. And I believe homicide is one of the terrorists' favorite hobbies."

Captain Soliman nodded and thought for a moment, then said, "As you have certainly noticed, I myself am Arab — Moroccan — and I am personally invested in rooting out violent extremism from my community. I cannot discuss particular groups and where they may or may not be operating. That is Chief Inspector Schröder's purview. But I can tell you that these groups are a very real problem, and a threat not only to the country, but to the community of recent immigrants who are particularly vulnerable to their propaganda and false promises."

Brodie thought about that. On some level he understood why, if you're living in a hellhole like Syria and fighting for your life in the middle of a brutal civil war, you might join up with the most ruthless jihadi head-choppers you could find. Like an inmate in prison, you want the strongest and meanest motherf-ers on your side.

But if you're lucky enough to get your ass to a nice place like Germany, what's the draw? These terrorist cells probably operated something like a cult, offering a sense of community, purpose, and maybe even power to people who had lost all three, or had never had anything to begin with.

Brodie regarded Captain Soliman, who reminded him of Arab Americans he had known and worked with over the course of his career — men and women in the FBI, the Defense Intelligence Agency, and other organizations that were fighting the War on Terror. They were often the most gung-ho about the cause. This was partly because, as Captain Soliman had said, they had a personal investment in catching the sickos who were giving their religion and culture a bad name. But Brodie sensed that they were also motivated by a need to prove themselves and reflect well on their own people by example.

This was an unfair but maybe unavoidable burden.

Schröder said, "Thank you, Captain Soliman. I could not agree more. As I said, if we find that any of our on-the-ground intelligence is relevant to the murder of Mr. Vance, we will share it to the extent that we can. Now, Mr. Butler has informed me that our out-of-town guests wish to visit the crime scene. We can —"

David Kim interrupted, "You have a Hezbollah problem, Chief Inspector."

Schröder pursed his lips. "Excuse me?"

Kim looked around the room. "For any of you who are not aware, Hezbollah is a legally recognized entity in Germany and in most of the European Union."

Schröder said, "That is not true, Mr. Kim. The militant arm of Hezbollah is banned. And I assure you that the political arm is closely monitored."

"Yeah," said Kim. He raised his right hand and clenched his fist. "When I get into a fight, I throw the first punch with this." Then he raised his left hand. "And I call this my political arm."

General Kiernan laughed.

Whitmore said, "Agent Kim, please get to the point."

"Right," said Kim. "So, as I'm sure everyone in this room knows, Hezbollah is a Shia organization, and Shi'ism is the minority sect.

They're not dreaming of a world caliphate like the Sunni crazies in ISIS and al Qaeda. Their goals are material, political, rooted in a degree of pragmatism and power politics. Iran is the largest and most powerful Shia country. Iran funds and supports Hezbollah, as well as Shia militias in Iraq and the Shia regime in Syria. Why? Geopolitics. Iran and her allies are a check on the power of Saudi Arabia and the Gulf states, as well as Israel and the United States. Iran also participates in political assassinations for the same reasons. Hezbollah and other militant Shia groups generally don't go out of their way to kill civilians or otherwise mount big, flashy attacks. They prefer hard targets. Players in the game, so to speak. So when I first heard about the murder of Mr. Vance, and learned that he was a counterterrorism investigator, I immediately thought of Hezbollah. He may have been investigating them, or maybe he had already put some of their people away. So, they killed him for it."

Well, thought Brodie, David Kim was either a counterterrorism specialist or pretending to be one. Either way, that info about the political wing of Hezbollah still being legal was interesting. Why would Germany tolerate that? More than other liberal European countries, Germany was open and demonstrative about its support for Israel — for obvious historical reasons — and Hezbollah

168

was Israel's mortal enemy.

Chief Inspector Schröder said, "Interesting, Mr. Kim. But that is pure conjecture."

Brodie said, "This is a briefing, not a trial. Nothing wrong with conjecture." He looked at Captain Soliman. "What is Hezbollah's presence in Neukölln?"

Captain Soliman appeared conflicted. He clearly wanted to be helpful, but the chief inspector outranked him and was probably burying his heel into the guy's foot. He said, "You can trust that Inspector Schröder will share all relevant information when — and if — the need arises."

Brodie looked at Schröder. "I look forward to that."

Agent Whitmore said, "There is much we need to ponder. By this time tomorrow, we ought to have a better reconstruction of Mr. Vance's travels as well as, hopefully, some additional forensics data." She looked at Omar Soliman. "Have arrangements been made for our visiting agents to see the crime scene?"

Captain Soliman replied, "Yes. I will be going there now to personally walk them through." He looked at Brodie and Taylor, then Agent Kim. "Please meet me at the southern entrance of Körnerpark."

Taylor said, "Thank you, Captain."

Whitmore announced, "This meeting is adjourned. I would like to reconvene at the same time tomorrow morning if that is amenable." She looked at Soliman and Schröder. "Gentlemen, would that fit with your schedules?"

Both men nodded. Whitmore looked around the room to get assent from the group, and everyone indicated that they could be back in this room at 9 A.M. tomorrow for a second helping of briefing, bullshit, and strudel.

Whitmore said, "Good. If there are any questions, concerns, requests in the meantime, please direct them to me or Jason. Good day, everyone."

Whitmore stood and everyone followed. The Germans left quickly without a word to anyone. Sarah Hopkins and Howard Fensterman, the two State Department reps who were probably only there to say they were there — as well as to listen and take notes — departed as well. Brodie watched General Kiernan flip through the briefing materials in front of him before rolling them up in his hand, rising from his chair, and declaring to his compatriots, "This is my day of Germans." He explained, "I've got meetings all day at the Defense Ministry." On the way out he said to Brodie and Taylor, "Call Mark Jenkins."

Taylor said, "We will, sir. Thank you."

"And call me if you need anything." He walked out of the room.

Brodie and Taylor threw on their coats, and

Taylor put her and Brodie's briefing materials in her satchel.

Jason Butler handed his business card to Taylor and said, "Call me for anything else you need."

Brodie replied, "I will."

Butler gave Brodie a look and left the room.

Sharon Whitmore said, "I trust that was informative."

"It was a start," said Brodie.

"I see you're staying in Neukölln."

Taylor nodded.

"Why?"

Brodie replied, "We're on a tight budget."

Agent Whitmore did not smile.

Taylor said, "We're cops. We want to know our beat."

Whitmore nodded, then looked at them and said, "I'm not going to insult you with a description of the limits of our jurisdiction and authority because you are both accomplished professionals who already understand that. But I will ask, are you willing to accept these limitations?"

Brodie made eye contact with Ms. Whitmore. She could obviously smell trouble from these two out-of-town CID agents and she wanted to nip any problems in the bud, which was admirable but also futile. Brodie usually dealt with these kinds of people by saying annoying and stupid things until they left him alone, and he was about to tell her that

171

limitations only inspire creativity, but before he could say anything Taylor chimed in: "We do understand. And we will follow your lead. We don't want to step on anyone's toes. But we are eager to help and are highly motivated to find our colleague's killer."

Ms. Whitmore nodded. "Of course."

Taylor was better at the bullshit than Brodie. Sometimes he worried that she actually believed her own bullshit.

David Kim approached and extended his hand to Brodie and Taylor. "Scott, Maggie. Good to be working with you both."

They all shook. Taylor said, "Nice to meet you."

Brodie and David Kim made eye contact. Kim had short black hair and a steady, confident stare. He was a few inches shorter than Brodie, and solidly built. His suit, dress shirt, and topcoat looked tailored and a little high-end, definitely a cut above standard-issue Fed wear. And unlike every male FBI agent Brodie had ever encountered, he didn't wear a tie. He was a man with his own style, probably in more ways than one.

Kim said, "I'm told an embassy driver is waiting on you guys so I hope I can bum a ride."

Brodie said, "Sure."

Kim looked at Sharon Whitmore, his FBI colleague. "Captain Soliman seemed up-front and all right. Herr Schröder could have walked off the set of Stalag 17."

Whitmore gave him a deadpan look, then turned to Brodie and Taylor and said, "Agent Kim only alluded to his background, but he is one of the New York field office's premiere counterterrorism experts, and has been a valuable asset to us on past cases." As if to say, *And that's the only reason we put up with him.*

Brodie asked Kim, "How confident are you that your particular expertise will be required?"

Kim shrugged. "I'm not sure at all. Maybe we'll find out tomorrow that Mr. Vance was mistaken for a rival gang member or something. Wrong place, wrong time. But in my experience, if they bother to send me, then that means I have a job to do."

Should Brodie tell him that when all you have is a hammer, every problem looks like a nail? He'd probably heard that line a few times. David Kim seemed like a sharp and motivated agent and — for now, at least — was probably a good ally to have.

Brodie, Taylor, and Kim wished Ms. Whitmore a good day, left the briefing room, and headed for the elevator.

Brodie asked Taylor, "Thoughts? Impressions?"

"The Germans cooperated as much as they needed to and no more," said Taylor. "They don't want to come to us with anything half-baked because they don't trust us to keep that information to ourselves, or to avoid the temptation to act."

"Agreed."

Kim nodded. "That's their playbook. They're control freaks. Then again, so are we, so can't really fault them for it. The problem arises when their caginess starts to affect their work product."

Taylor said to Kim, "It sounds like you've worked with Agent Whitmore in the past."

"Indirectly."

"In Berlin?"

"Yes. And that's about all I can say about that." He asked, "You folks been here before?"

Brodie said, "I was here twenty years ago. During college. Researching a paper on monkey business."

Kim laughed. "Where was college?"

"NYU."

"My adopted city. Great town."

"Where were you before New York?"

"All over. My folks moved from Seoul to LA in the late seventies when I was three, ran a grocery in K-town until it got burned to the ground in the '92 riots, then we moved to a suburb of Phoenix. I did my undergrad at Yale, and my law degree at Stanford, then joined the FBI soon after. Been in New York my entire career."

Brodie said to Taylor, "A Yalie. I think we

found our CIA plant."

Kim laughed. "Those geniuses tried to recruit me in college, actually. They showed up at our senior year job fair. Thought I was Chinese."

They took the elevator to the ground floor and walked to the rear entrance, where the Marine guard again saluted them. Brodie and Taylor returned the salute as they exited and headed toward the parked Mercedes, where Ulrich was standing and smoking a cigarette.

Brodie introduced Ulrich to Kim, then climbed in the front passenger seat as Taylor and Kim got in the back. Ulrich swung the car around and radioed someone, and the security bollards lowered. He pulled onto the road. "We go to your hotel?"

"The park across the street from the hotel," said Brodie.

Ulrich nodded and headed toward Körnerpark, where Harry Vance had gone alone, in the dead of night, for reasons unknown to Brodie, but known to Harry Vance. If Vance was there to meet someone, that someone was Fate.

The embassy briefing had been, as expected, a little substance and a lot of nothing. There were no answers to be found in a conference room full of competing egos and turf war pissing matches. Scott Brodie had no idea where this investigation would ultimately lead, but in a homicide case the road to justice always begins where the victim's life ended.

CHAPTER 9

Ulrich drove his American passengers to Körnerpark and Brodie told Ulrich to drop their bags off at the Art Hotel, and he was free to go.

Brodie, Taylor, and FBI Agent David Kim joined Berlin Police Captain Omar Soliman on an open expanse of frosty lawn in the northeast section of Körnerpark. At the perimeter of the block-square, sunken park, tall, bare trees towered above the twenty-foot-high retaining wall that marked its boundary. Nearby was a circular pool with a fountain that had been turned off and was filled with rainwater and dead leaves.

Brodie imagined this was a popular spot for locals on warm days — and when it was not the secured scene of a homicide. Now they were the only ones here.

Detective Soliman pointed to five white flags stuck in the frigid grass — one for Harry Vance's head and one for each of his extremities. "The right leg," said Soliman, "was bent to the side. And his left arm was above his head. This is consistent with a gunshot striking him in the right temple while he was facing north. He fell back and to the left." He added, unnecessarily, "Due to the deceleration forces of the bullet strike."

Taylor pointed to a line of yellow flags leading north from the site of the body. "What do those indicate?"

Soliman replied, "Footprints leading toward the body, then away from the body. Our forensic people created plaster casts on Sunday when the impressions were fresh. We also found muddy shoe or boot prints going up the stairs of the park's northern entrance over there. They end at the curb. We believe that after the killer shot Mr. Vance, he may have given the murder weapon — the rifle — to an accomplice so that he would be clean when he descended into the park to check that the victim was dead, take his cell phone, and perform the mutilation."

Perform the mutilation. That made it sound somehow both clinical and barbaric.

Soliman added, "Then the killer left using the same stairway and, we believe, got into a waiting vehicle."

Kim pointed to a line of blue flags leading in the opposite direction. "And those are the victim's footprints?"

"Yes," said Soliman.

Brodie spotted a few red flags at various

distances from where the body had been, which he knew without asking were markers for blood splatter.

Brodie looked around the park. It was a relatively straightforward crime scene and a relatively simple kill. Victim approached from the south, was sniped from somewhere to the east, and then the killer entered and exited the park from the north. The heavy rain and cold weather on the day before the murder would have kept visitors out of the park and also created something of a clean slate for the footprints of the victim and of the killer to be formed, then documented. Not much different from how a crime scene was processed back home.

Brodie looked to the eastern edge of the park, which sloped up toward street level and was the only side without a retaining wall. An iron fence separated the park from the sidewalk. "Let's take a look at where you believe the shooter fired from."

Captain Soliman nodded. "Follow me."

Brodie, Taylor, and Kim trailed Soliman along a paved path that sloped upward to an opening in the iron fence on the east side of the park, where a strip of yellow crime scene tape stretched across the entrance. The tape was printed with German words beginning with <u>ACHTUNG!</u>, which always gets everyone's attention. A Berlin Police officer stood nearby.

It had been over forty-eight hours since the discovery of the body, and this was an unusually long time to maintain a closed crime scene in a public place, so Brodie assumed they were still running crime scene analysis and forensics. Or maybe they had kept the park closed for the benefit of their American guests, to show how cooperative they were being. The Berlin Police probably cared more about maintaining good optics with the Americans than they did about inconveniencing the residents of Neukölln.

They ducked under the tape and stepped onto a small cobblestone side street. Soliman turned right and they followed him for about thirty feet. "Based upon analysis of the bullet's trajectory," he said, "we believe the killer stood approximately here, and fired the bullet from a height of one point six meters. That would mean the killer stands at a height of approximately one point eight five meters."

Brodie nodded. A little over six feet tall. Statistically above average height for an Arabic male. Or for anyone. He turned around and looked at the rows of five-story apartment buildings across the street. The cobblestone road was narrow, and the buildings were only about twenty-five feet from the edge of the park.

Brodie looked down into the park where Harry Vance had been standing when the small bullet entered his skull and ended his life. Did Harry have a split second of understanding of what had just happened to him? Probably. The bullet-pierced brain took a few long seconds before it stopped processing information. Maybe longer.

Brodie said to Captain Soliman, "I assume you scoured this area for a shell casing?"

"Of course." He added, as though giving a classroom lesson, "No professional assassin would leave an ejected shell casing behind."

Brodie nodded. But sometimes they did. Because they dashed off as soon as they pulled the trigger. This killer, however, walked into the park to finish his business. But first he retrieved the shell casing, which wouldn't be easy in the dark. Then he ditched the rifle and the casing — probably with an accomplice — then walked into the park to examine his kill. Like he had all the time in the world. This was a cool customer. A pro.

Brodie asked Soliman, "And there were no eyewitnesses? No one heard anything?"

Soliman replied, "We are still questioning residents." He added, "It was about three o'clock in the morning."

Brodie nodded, though not satisfied with the answer.

Soliman checked his watch and said, "I am due back at headquarters. I expect we will have more concrete information for you at tomorrow's briefing."

David Kim said, "All we ask for, Captain

181

Soliman, is collegial cooperation and total candor."

Soliman looked at him. "And all I ask of you in return is an understanding of the sensitive nature of this investigation." He gestured around them. "This whole neighborhood is holding its breath."

Taylor asked, "For what?"

He looked at her. "For whatever happens in a neighborhood full of Arabs when a white man is murdered. I will see you tomorrow morning." He walked off toward his parked police car, leaving the three Americans to speak freely and speculate wildly.

Brodie said, "Total candor notwithstanding, I think they have someone who saw or heard something. Maybe more than one."

Kim said, "Maybe. Soliman is protective of this neighborhood and the people in it, and I get that." He added, "Also, he's protective of his turf."

"Right," said Brodie. "It can't be easy being an Arab Muslim Berlin cop."

Kim replied, "Divided loyalties are never easy."

Taylor said, "I'm sure he's a cop first."

No one responded.

Brodie looked into the park. The iron fence was about eight feet tall, with wide openings between the bars. This location offered a clear and unobstructed view of the spot where Vance had been standing. In fact, Harry

Vance would have made a good target standing almost anywhere in this park. What was he thinking?

Brodie peered through a gap between the bars and tried to put himself in the shoes of the killer.

This was, obviously, not a crime of opportunity. The killer had chosen a .22-caliber rifle because he knew he would be firing in a densely populated neighborhood and needed a weapon that could kill from a distance without making too much noise. But the low-velocity bullets were also not a sure bet for a lethal shot. Sixty meters was fairly close, especially for a rifle, but still no guarantee that the bullet would penetrate the cranium, especially if the shooter did not hit his target precisely in the temple. Brodie looked around and noticed there was no streetlight on the corner, nor any lights within the park near Vance's position. So maybe the killer had used a night scope.

Taylor said, "This was a skilled marksman. Maybe a hired gun."

"Or a trained terrorist," said Kim. "Hezbollah has plenty of decent snipers."

David Kim was really leaning into the Hezbollah thing. And he might be right, but Brodie was biased against the first explanation offered. Why should things be so easy? Or simple?

Taylor was looking into the park. "The

shooter took a very unnecessary risk. The murder was committed late at night, but this is a late-night town, and he could have been spotted. But he got away with the shot, and then instead of leaving the scene he went down into the park. It was worth the risk to nab the cell phone, which would take all of two seconds and might contain incriminating information, but extracting the eye would take longer."

Brodie said, "It was just as important to the killer as the cell phone. As a message. Or proof of responsibility. Or both." He added, "We also don't know if the sniper was the same person who took the phone and eye. Could have been an accomplice in the park."

Kim said, "We need to know what cases Vance was working. Who was looking to send a message? And who is the message for?"

Brodie nodded. "Aside from the political and international intrigue aspects of this case, we need to work it as a standard homicide."

Taylor agreed, but FBI Agent David Kim looked like he wanted to roll his eyes at the two cops.

Brodie turned and scanned the row of apartment buildings across the road from the park. "We need to look for possible witnesses."

"Good luck in this neighborhood," said Kim.

But as if on cue, an old woman in a long

coat and red hijab appeared, pushing a shopping cart full of groceries toward the front door of an apartment building. She stopped at the base of the stoop.

Brodie crossed the street and smiled at her. "Guten Morgen."

The woman stared at Brodie as he approached. Taylor and Kim followed.

Brodie took hold of her cart and carried it up the stoop. She smiled, nodded, and said in halting German, "Danke, junger Mann."

Brodie smiled back at the woman as he came down the steps and said to Taylor, "In your best Army Language School Arabic, ask her if she heard anything unusual in the early morning hours of Sunday."

"Scott, we are not authorized to question civilians."

"She just told me to ask her any question about the murder. Didn't you hear her?"

"Scott —"

Kim said something to the woman in Arabic. She seemed surprised that this Asian man spoke her native tongue. They engaged in a brief conversation, and she seemed to loosen up.

Kim said to Brodie and Taylor, "This woman, Amina, says she was shocked to hear about the murder. This is generally a quiet neighborhood. She slept all through the night, as she already told the German police, but they also questioned a young woman who lives above her, and she believes this woman did hear something."

Brodie asked, "Is this woman home?"

Kim said something to Amina, who responded as she gestured toward the stoop. She climbed the stairs, then pressed the buzzer. After a moment a fuzzy voice came through the speaker. The two spoke over the intercom in Arabic; then Amina said something to Kim, unlocked the front door, and pulled her shopping cart inside. She shut the door behind her.

Kim said, "She asked us to wait here. Fatima is coming down."

Taylor said something to Kim in Arabic, and he replied.

Brodie said, "Excuse me."

"I was complimenting David on his Arabic," said Taylor.

"Why don't you compliment me on my initiative?"

"I did. In Arabic."

The door of the apartment building opened and a nice-looking woman of about twenty-five stuck her head out and said in English, "What's up?"

Brodie looked at the young woman. She had long dark hair, no hijab, and wore jeans and a thick sweater. She had a stud nose piercing and a small tattoo of some kind on the side of her neck. He asked, "Fatima?"

She nodded.

Taylor said, "We were told you may have heard something unusual on the night of the murder."

She scanned the three people who were obviously not Germans and asked, in good English, "Who are you? I already talked to the police."

Taylor held up her creds. "I am Maggie Taylor and this is Scott Brodie and David Kim. We are American federal investigators assisting your government."

"Then shouldn't you already know what I told them?"

Fatima seemed distrustful of authority, which Brodie generally appreciated, though it was inconvenient when he was the authority. He said, "We'd like to hear it from you directly."

Fatima thought about that, hesitated, then stepped out of the doorway and sat on the stoop. She took a pack of cigarettes from her pocket, shook one out, and lit up. "Okay, I was coming back from the club. The street was quiet. I went upstairs to my apartment." She gestured with her cigarette at the building behind her. "I'm on the third floor here. I open my window to have a cigarette — the window faces the park — and then I hear this sound, a weird sound, like a kind of pop. It didn't sound like a gunshot, but then I remembered always hearing about people not thinking guns sound in real life like they do in the movies, so . . ." She trailed off for a moment. "I thought maybe I was being paranoid, but I looked at my phone to see what time it was, thinking in my head maybe someone will ask me what time I heard this sound. It was three-twenty-five."

Brodie asked, "Did you see anyone?"

"No. Yesterday I saw where the body had been found. But I can't see that part of the park from my window. Blocked by trees."

Kim asked, "Did you see anyone on the street or sidewalk?"

"I didn't see anyone on the sidewalk, but I did a see a car driving down Jonasstraße. That's the street on the north side of the park."

Brodie asked, "What kind of car was it?"

She shook her head. "Don't know."

Taylor asked, "Sedan? Van? Truck?"

Fatima replied, "I really don't know. It wasn't a giant truck. I guess I would have noticed that. Like, a regular car probably."

Brodie asked, "What color? Dark? Light?"

Fatima thought for a moment. "Dark, I think. I could only really see the taillights. It was just driving, not, like, screeching away. I thought it was probably nothing. But then I heard on the news that a guy got shot, so . . ."

Brodie thought about that. Vance was seen on security tape leaving the metro station at 2:52 A.M., and it was only a five- or six-minute walk between the station and the park. If Vance had gone directly to Körner-park, he would have been waiting almost thirty minutes before the fatal shot. What was he doing in that thirty minutes? The foot-prints told two different stories. It was possible that Vance did meet with someone in the park before being sniped. That person spoke with Vance about something, then gave a signal to the gunman up on the street, who had plenty of time to line up his shot. The sniper pulled the trigger, and then the person who had been speaking to Vance took his cell phone, carved out his left eye, and left the park quickly, and both men left in the car.

Or maybe Vance went somewhere else to have the meet, and he was cutting through the park afterward on the way back to the train station. Or he stopped to get a drink or a coffee or to buy a pack of cigarettes before the Körnerpark rendezvous. There were two, three, or more scenarios that fit the bare facts. Well, at least they had an exact time of death, if Fatima had heard the shot.

Fatima was looking up at them, probably wondering when they were going to go bother someone else. Brodie asked, "Anything else you can think to tell us about this?"

"No," said Fatima. She took a drag. "Every-one around here is scared. Whenever this neighborhood gets attention, it's not for anything good and it's not good for anyone here."

Taylor said, "We hope with the cooperation of the people here, we can find the perpetrator and conclude this investigation. Quickly."

Fatima laughed, took another drag. "You don't get it. It doesn't matter who did it, or why. When something bad happens near a bunch of Muslims, there's things that happen. Mosques will be raided by the police. People will be harassed. I have a friend who's Syrian, teaches art to children at a local school, but his cousin who he barely knows fought with the rebels in Aleppo, which of course means my friend must be in al Qaeda or ISIS. He's followed all the time. I'm sure the police will find a reason to bring him in for questioning about this murder."

Kim said something to her in Arabic, and whatever it was seemed to piss her off. She spat something back at him, and then Kim said to Brodie and Taylor, "Let's go."

Taylor thanked Fatima and they walked away, toward the southern edge of the park.

Brodie asked, "What was that about?"

Kim replied, "I told her that extremism is a community problem. The community suffers by it, but the community is also central to combatting terrorism, and the community is complicit when they don't cooperate."

"Sounds like an FBI brochure you've memorized," said Brodie.

"More like an FBI brochure I wrote. And I believe it. Mosques wouldn't be raided if they weren't used for recruitment. And if a family member is a member of a terrorist group, the odds that other members of that family are also involved are statistically much higher. Will innocent people be hassled? Of course. But I'll happily inconvenience and intimidate a hundred innocent people to save one innocent life."

Brodie could easily agree with this point of view. Then again, Mr. Kim might be underestimating the psychological impact of the endless inconveniences and intimidations — not to mention humiliations — of being part of a religious, ethnic, or nationality group that is always suspected of violence and subversion. Brodie had seen that in Iraq. The real horrors of war got the headlines, like the massacre of civilians by Blackwater contractors, or the prisoner abuse at Abu Ghraib. But it was the everyday grind — the military convoys barreling through neighborhoods, smashing cars and snarling traffic; the endless nighttime raids on houses and apartments that terrorized civilians and almost never netted any bad guys or weapons; the checkpoints, the blast walls, the Green Zone fortress in the middle of the capital — these were the things that pissed off and alienated the average Iraqi and made them feel like second-class people in their own country.

The dynamic here was different, of course. This was an immigrant community in an advanced Western country. But in a place like Neukölln, police and Intel people needed local support, and heavy-handed police tactics had a way of turning potential friends into potential foes.

Taylor, getting back to the case, said, "Fatima heard the shot at three-twenty-five. That's an interesting timeline."

Brodie nodded. "Vance may have stopped somewhere. Check what businesses between the metro station and this park would have been open after three A.M. Sunday morning."

Taylor took out her phone and ran a search while Brodie and Kim checked their phones for messages. After a minute she said, "I see three places either on or immediately off of Karl-Marx Straße, which was the road Vance probably walked down, that were open after three. A noodle shop called Wunderschön Saigon, a hookah bar called Ember Berlin, and what looks like a dance club called Proletariat."

Did Harry Vance go clubbing for twenty minutes before a dangerous rendezvous? Probably not. But he could have stopped for some pho or a coffee and a smoke. Brodie said, "We should check out all three of those spots late tonight. If we're lucky, we'll find staff who are working the same shifts they did on Sunday and can maybe ID a photo of Harry Vance."

"Sounds like a plan," said Taylor. She

added, "It's Turkish psychedelic rock tonight at Proletariat."

"My favorite genre," said Brodie. "Meanwhile, I want to take a look at the metro station where Vance got out. Let's do his walk in reverse." He looked at Kim, who was still checking his phone. "Are you joining us?"

"Yeah," said Kim. "And I've got something to show you on the way."

They turned at the corner onto Schierker Straße, and walked another block to Karl-Marx Straße, a larger four-lane road. As they walked south along Karl-Marx, they passed a number of handsome old five-story buildings with pitched roofs interspersed with nondescript prefab concrete apartment blocks. The street was lined with pharmacies, cell phone stores, delis, a couple of kebab takeout joints, and a Turkish café. The pedestrians appeared pretty diverse, and in general the place gave the impression of a bustling and vibrant working-class neighborhood.

The name of the street — Karl Marx — was obviously a leftover from when this was Communist East Berlin. Maybe, thought Brodie, in a year or two it would get its old name back — whatever that was. Or a new name: Diversity Straße.

As for the buildings, the nice ones were prewar, and the new ones marked the places where a thousand-pound British or American bomb had reduced the previous building to rubble.

Brodie considered his encounter with Amina and Fatima. Officially and publicly, the German government welcomed immigrants and refugees from the Mideast. And the government was probably sincere — and also wanted to show the world how much nicer they were than the Nazis. The German people on the other hand . . . well, they were divided on the issue of immigrants, especially Muslim immigrants. And this division between liberal and traditional Germans was the fuel that fed the fire of what the Germans called the far-right political parties, but what other people called the neo-Nazis.

And all of that, Brodie knew, had to be factored into the investigation of Harry Vance's murder. And if — when — the murder was solved, this political and social tension would have consequences far beyond the murder itself.

After a block Kim led them to another side street, then down a curving road, mostly residential, then turned a corner at a café and stopped.

"There," said Kim, pointing across the street at a five-story yellow concrete building, which was about twice the width of the adjacent apartment buildings.

"The Al Mahdi Islamic Center," said Kim. "It's not a mosque, per se, though they do have a prayer hall. It's a hub for the Shi'ite Muslim community here. They have cultural events, charity drives, educational programs. That sort of thing."

Brodie asked, "Do they have Bingo?"

"No. But it's also suspected of being a center of recruitment and fundraising for Hezbollah military operations. See that?" He nodded at a parked gray van farther down the street. "That's probably police surveillance. The police also have a mobile unit that circles about every half hour. This place is being watched, and they know they're being watched. I would be surprised if they didn't get raided soon." He added, "This is privileged information, and not to be shared."

Brodie asked, "Is there a particular reason you're telling us about this place?"

Kim said, "You're going to talk to Vance's CID partner, Mark Jenkins, and if you're lucky you'll get a piece of the puzzle from him." He looked at the building. "And this might be another piece. Keep it in mind." He added, "It's good to share."

Brodie understood that Kim wanted whatever info they might get from Mark Jenkins, so he was giving something of value as prepayment. Kim, like many FBI Special Agents, had probably worked on a number of Joint Terrorism Task Forces — JTTFs — which in New York usually involved joint operations between the FBI and the NYPD.

Kim was used to the give-and-take of working with other agencies, as well as the currency of favors that often existed in local law enforcement. That attitude generally sat well with Scott Brodie. But David Kim also seemed arrogant and thought he knew everything, which did not sit so well with Brodie, because Chief Warrant Officer Scott Brodie was the one who in fact knew everything.

Kim eyed the building as he continued, "Sometimes the way your target reacts after they know they are being surveilled is as valuable and interesting as what you might find behind the closed doors. And sometimes it's not so much about who is coming and going, but who *stops* coming and going once they know they're being watched. But that only gets you so much. Like I said, expect a raid on this place in the next day or two."

Well, thought Brodie, David Kim was sounding very confident in his conclusions. The fact that Harry Vance, a counterterrorism investigator, was murdered a few blocks away from what was possibly a nexus of recruitment and financing for Hezbollah definitely added some weight to Kim's interpretation of the case. Then again, the German and the American counterterrorism people could be wrong about this place. They could actually be wrong about everything. Wouldn't be the first time.

Brodie eyed the suspected surveillance van,

196

which made him think about the suspected spy nest on the roof of the American embassy. He asked Kim, "Have you heard anything from our Comrades in Arms?" Meaning CIA.

Kim replied, "Not me. And I never will. Schröder might have a CIA contact, but maybe not. The BKA is roughly equivalent to the FBI, whereas the German equivalent to our CIA is the BND. Don't ask me to pronounce what that stands for because I can't. The CIA and the BND are undoubtedly in touch on this case, and you'll notice neither outfit had a rep in the briefing room."

Right. Civilian Intel officers believed they were deities among mortals and wouldn't suffer the indignity of sitting through a tedious briefing. That was everyone else's job.

They doubled back to Karl-Marx Straße and walked another block to the metro station, a boxy brick building that sat below elevated train tracks. Yellow lettering above the entrance said: BAHNHOF NEUKÖLLN. Another sign on the building showed the "S" logo for the S-Bahn system, and the name of the stop, BERLIN-NEUKÖLLN. An entrance for the underground U-Bahn station stood in front of the building.

Brodie spotted a tall metal pole topped with two security cameras pointed in opposite directions. These cameras must have been the source of the footage of Vance leaving the metro station.

Brodie looked again at the metro stop. Anyone seeing the surveillance footage in its entirety could easily determine which metro system Harry Vance had used. If he had exited the station doors, it meant he'd come here from the S-Bahn elevated train. If he was coming up the underground stairs, he had used the U-Bahn. In either case, that would be a clue as to where Vance had come from. Yet Captain Soliman and Chief Inspector Schröder had only shown them a still shot from after Vance exited, and neither man had mentioned this detail. Were they withholding information and clues? Did they regard their American guests as simply along for the ride, and not requiring or deserving of this level of detailed information? Brodie was looking forward to disabusing them of that notion.

Taylor, who must have been thinking the same thing, said, "Our German colleagues pretended they didn't know which system Vance used, but it should be obvious from the security cameras."

"What's also obvious," said Kim, "is that they are willfully withholding details. First the time of the gunshot, now this. Turf-protecting. And arrogance."

Brodie said, "Which gives us good grounds to demand to see all of their surveillance footage and any witness testimony." He said to Kim, "You say you've worked with Sharon

Whitmore before. Will she be our ally on this?"

Kim nodded. "She's a cautious person, but she won't back down from a fight if she thinks she's getting cut out of important Intel."

"Good."

"So, would you suggest we lodge a formal complaint today? Or catch them with their pants down at tomorrow's meeting?"

Brodie replied, "The second option sounds more fun. And possibly more effective. My instincts tell me that the Germans are especially susceptible to embarrassment."

Kim smiled. "As Churchill said, the Germans are either at your feet or at your throat."

"Or asking to see your papers."

Kim laughed.

Making fun of the Germans was easy sport, and great bonding. Brodie glanced at his partner, who wasn't enjoying a laugh.

Taylor said, "You are both making a lot of assumptions about our hosts. A formal complaint is an overreaction. *I* will bring up these issues tomorrow. Tactfully."

Brodie nodded. "Good idea."

Kim checked his watch. "All right. I need to head back to Mitte. I hear that you folks got a hotel in the neighborhood?"

Brodie nodded. "The Art Hotel. I think they charge by the hour."

Taylor added, perhaps defensively, "It

overlooks Körnerpark."

Kim smiled. "Good move." He said, "If you're going my way, we can share a cab."

Check-in at the nearby Art Hotel wasn't until 2 P.M., so this was a good time to go to Mitte — Berlin's central district — for a meetup with Mark Jenkins. But Brodie wanted some time with his partner minus David Kim so they could speak freely. He said to Kim, "Maggie and I will grab a bite here before we check in."

Kim nodded. "Okay. Well, we're off to a good start." He flagged a cab sitting at a red light across the street, then turned back to his compatriots. "Listen, since you're staying around here, do me a favor and circle back to the Al Mahdi Center later, see if that police van is still there."

Brodie replied, "We can do that."

"And, obviously, if you get the feeling a raid is about to happen, try to witness it. They tend to do these things in the early morning."

Brodie had the distinct and very bad feeling that he was being given orders by the FBI. He didn't respond.

"We'll keep it in mind," said Taylor. "And we'll see you tomorrow at the embassy."

Kim took his business card out of his jacket and handed it to her. "Call me before then if you see or hear anything you think I should know." He jogged across the street and hopped in the taxi, and it drove off.

"I should dislike him," said Brodie. "But I don't."

"He reminds me of someone else who I should dislike, but don't." She added, "Also, he's Hezbollah-obsessed. He makes a good case, but it might be the wrong one."

Brodie nodded. It occurred to him that in all this speculation, there was one big question no one had even tried to answer: If Harry Vance was really here for a romantic rendezvous with a woman — or perhaps, to keep an open mind, a man — then why hadn't that person contacted the police after learning or hearing about his death? One explanation was that this person was married, as Vance was, so had to keep quiet. Or this person was somehow connected to the murder. Either responsible for it, or fearful of becoming the next corpse. Or maybe Harry's romantic interest was already dead. In any case, as every amateur sleuth knows, "Cherchez la femme."

Brodie saw that Taylor was dialing the handwritten number on the back of General Kiernan's business card. She put the phone to her ear and said, "Hello? Mark Jenkins? It's Maggie Taylor, CID . . . Yes, I'm in Berlin . . . Yes, this is awful." She looked at Brodie as she listened for a moment. "Oh . . . All right. I understand. Good. See you soon."

She hung up and said, "The Alexanderplatz

201

Radisson. He wants to meet in his room."
She added, "He thinks he's being followed."

"By who?"

Taylor shrugged. "Didn't say."

Brodie had dealt with paranoid associates of murder victims before. When someone's family member or colleague gets clipped, it tends to rattle people, even if they had nothing to do with the reason for the homicide. But Mark Jenkins wasn't some paranoid civilian. He was a highly trained CID Special Agent. If he thought he had something to fear, then he probably did. And if he thought he was being followed, then he probably was.

Brodie said to Taylor, "I think we are entering the world of smoke and mirrors."

Taylor nodded. "Again."

CHAPTER 10

Brodie and Taylor grabbed some shawarma from a hole-in-the-wall place in the neighborhood. They ate it as they walked to the metro, where they boarded the elevated S-Bahn toward Alexanderplatz for their meetup with Mark Jenkins.

The train was half-empty at this hour and they found an isolated spot toward the end of one of the cars and sat across from each other. The train pulled out of the station and they watched the city slide by out the windows.

Brodie asked, "What do you think of Berlin so far?"

"Nice embassy conference room. Picturesque crime scene. Better shawarma than I can get in Kentucky."

"Neukölln seems . . . not sinister by day, maybe a little edgy by night. Maybe Vance was just bar crawling, then realized he caught a tail."

"Does not compute, Mr. Brodie. He was

there to meet someone."

"Right. That was one reason he was in Berlin. The other is a woman."

Taylor nodded, thought for a moment. "If he really was coming to Berlin on a regular basis for a romantic fling, why hasn't his lady come forward?"

"Maybe it was a honeytrap. A seductress hired to get info from CID Agent Vance. The fastest way to a man's secrets is through his schwantz."

"I bet I know what that is."

"Right. It's Yiddish, not German. I dated a Jewish girl at NYU who taught me Yiddish. Mostly the dirty words."

She ignored that and said, "A honeytrap also does not compute. Unless Harry Vance is not the same man you described."

"Right. Harry was a pro." He added, "Let's hear what Mark Jenkins has to say."

Taylor nodded.

Brodie watched out the window as the elevated train rumbled over the city. He looked north toward Alexanderplatz and the adjacent Berlin TV Tower, an imposing concrete shaft topped with a steel sphere and a broadcast antenna. It was built by the East Germans as a display of Communist power and ingenuity, and had since morphed from a symbol of Cold War division into an icon of a united Germany — just like the Brandenburg Gate and the remnants of the Wall, and probably a dozen other sights and symbols in this city of multiple personality disorders. The tower was still used for broadcasting, and Brodie recalled that it contained a rotating restaurant where you could enjoy some of the best views and worst food in all of Berlin. Beware of restaurants that rotate.

"The Pope's revenge," said Taylor.

"What?"

She pointed out the window toward the tower. "The sunlight makes a cross on the sphere. I read that during the Cold War it was called the Pope's revenge."

Brodie looked at the cross of sunlight on the paneled sphere. He didn't put a whole lot of stock in spiritual symbolism, and he'd never seen the Virgin Mary in his morning pancakes. But he hoped this accidental refraction of sunlight had brought a little solace — or at least bitter amusement — to the Christians forced by circumstance to live on the wrong side of the Wall, where the state religion was no religion.

They changed trains, and after a few more stops they got out at Alexanderplatz Station, a large structure with a vaulted roof and a bustling platform.

Brodie walked toward a newsstand where there was a rack of German and international newspapers, each featuring a photo of Harry Vance on its front page. A few German dailies named the neighborhood of Neukölln in their screaming headlines.

Brodie spotted the London *Times* and grabbed a copy, then brought it to the register.

The clerk, a thick balding man in his early fifties, said, "Drei fünfzig."

Brodie handed the man a ten-euro note, and as the clerk was counting out change he asked Brodie, "British? American?"

"Canadian," he replied as he always did to that question. Everyone liked Canadians.

The man nodded and gestured to the folded-up paper on the counter. "The Russians."

Brodie did not respond.

"Fucking Putin. He wants no trust between people. And so" — he jabbed the paper — "make it look like Muslim terrorist. Yes?"

Jackpot. A new theory, straight from the Berlin street. "Clever," said Brodie.

The man seemed happy to have an audience and leaned across the counter. "The Russen have their testicles everywhere."

"Excuse me?"

"Like octopus. Reaching all over. The white nationalists. The German military, the Bundestag, big corporations. They want to rip Germany in two parts again. Do you see this?"

"Yes," said Brodie. "They won't get away with it."

"Of course they will!"

206

"Okay. Well, that's too bad —"

"We have become weak and stupid. We have it coming."

"Don't be so hard on yourself. Auf Wiedersehen."

Brodie took the paper and scooped up the change, and he and Taylor headed toward a stairway that led down to the street.

She said, "Your new friend sounds like he's in a Cold War time warp."

"That, or history is repeating itself." He added, "Keep an open mind."

They walked downstairs and exited onto the northern section of Alexanderplatz, a large square surrounded by modern buildings containing shops, cafés, and a department store. The massive TV tower loomed behind the train station they'd just left. A chill wind blew across the open Platz and pedestrians bundled in winter coats hurriedly crisscrossed the square.

Taylor pointed to a wide blue-glass tower at the far end. "There's the Radisson."

As they walked toward the hotel Brodie observed the blank modern buildings around them. Like a lot of places in Berlin, this spot was steeped in a vanished history. Brodie recalled from his long-ago guided tour of the city that Alexanderplatz was named after one of the Russian czars to commemorate a state visit, back when this square must have been ringed with ornate imperial buildings. Most of the current buildings looked like they'd been constructed in the last thirty years, meaning that a lot of the junk the Commies had built after clearing away the rubble of the destroyed city had itself been swept away by developers after the fall of the Wall. Berlin, it seemed, was as defined by its absences as by what you could see.

They reached the hotel and entered the lobby, which was modern and clean but not high-end, the kind of place you could submit to the Army travel office for reimbursement without raising an eyebrow.

Jenkins had given Taylor his room number over the phone, so they headed directly to the elevator and took it up to the fifth floor, then walked down a long carpeted corridor until they found his room and knocked.

A voice asked through the door, "Who's there?"

Brodie replied, "Scott Brodie and Maggie Taylor."

The door opened and a man quickly stepped aside and gestured them in without a word. They walked into the small room and he shut the door behind them and bolted it.

Brodie looked at Mark Jenkins. He was in his late forties, of average height, with an olive complexion and black wavy hair. He had large dark eyes that darted between the two of them.

He shook hands with Taylor and then

Brodie, who said, "We're sorry about Harry."

"Yeah. Me too. Everyone at Fifth MP is sorry." Jenkins gestured at a few chairs around a small circular table in the corner of the room. "Hungry? They've got room service. It's okay."

"No thank you," said Brodie. He noticed Jenkins' Beretta in a holster on the nightstand, which triggered trigger-envy.

Jenkins ran his hand through his hair as he looked around the room searching for something. He grabbed a bottle of clear liquid from the top of the dresser along with three plastic cups and set the cups on the table. He held up the bottle. "Some schnapps that Harry brought me from one of his trips here. High-quality but a little abrasive. Like the man himself."

He sat down and poured a triple shot in each cup, which was a little more alcohol than Brodie was used to drinking before noon. But he wasn't about to deny the man a toast to his fallen colleague.

Jenkins lifted his cup. "To Harry Vance. A real pro, a true friend, and a damned good man."

They tapped their cups together and downed the schnapps.

It was harsh stuff, and for Brodie it brought back a few bad college memories. For Taylor, it was probably a step down from Kentucky moonshine.

Jenkins set his empty cup down on the table and said, "I checked out both of you. I wanted to know who they put in charge of finding Harry's killer."

"The Germans are in charge," said Brodie.

"Officially," said Jenkins.

Brodie nodded.

Jenkins continued, "But you're not going to leave the murder of an American soldier in the hands of a foreign country."

Taylor replied, "We'll do what has to be done."

Jenkins nodded. "I know you will." He looked at both of them. "You two were in Venezuela. Kyle Mercer."

Brodie replied, "We can neither confirm nor deny."

Jenkins smiled. "Well, everyone knows." He added, "You two are more famous in the Fifth MP Battalion than you might know."

Neither Brodie nor Taylor responded.

Jenkins continued, "For the record, I do not agree with CID's decision to have the Fifth MP stand down in this investigation."

"I understand," said Brodie. "But we have our orders."

Jenkins nodded. "Me too. Mine are to get out of Berlin."

"Will you?" asked Taylor.

"Yes." He looked at her. "But only because I believe this investigation is in good hands."

"We appreciate your confidence," said Taylor. She added, "Tell us about being followed."

Jenkins poured himself another. "Yesterday evening, after being interviewed at BKA headquarters by Chief Inspector Schröder. When I left the interview I was a little worked up and decided to walk back to the hotel. A good hour walk. There were two guys. One of them came down from the nearby S-Bahn platform, like he was expecting me to take the train and then saw I was walking. The other guy was on a park bench."

Taylor asked, "Did you get a good look at them?"

He shook his head. "Long black coats, winter caps — I set out at six and it was already dark. One guy stayed on the other side of the street, the other maybe thirty feet behind me. It was either the worst tail job I've ever seen, or they were trying to intimidate me. I tried to shake them a few times just for fun, but they stuck like glue until I got back here. And then this morning, I went out for a walk after breakfast, and there's this guy standing outside the hotel using his phone, and I'm watching him. I swear the asshole is taking pictures of me. Just the way he's holding the phone, the angle of it. Too far away to make him out, but same long black coat and cap. And after I start walking across the square in his direction, the guy walks away. Quickly. And then he stops at the fountain in the middle of Alexanderplatz and makes a phone call, and while he's on the phone I see him glancing my way. This guy was not subtle. So I keep walking toward him, and he scoots off and disappears into the underground U-Bahn station. I followed but I lost him."

Brodie asked, "White guy? Arab?"

Jenkins shrugged. "Between the hat, the sunglasses, and the distance I couldn't tell. Same with the guys last night."

Brodie nodded. If these guys really were amateurs, Jenkins could have shaken them, and probably wouldn't have lost the guy in the underground. They sounded like pros, and this sounded like intimidation. "Did you report this to the police or the BKA?"

"I left a message for Chief Inspector Schröder this morning."

Taylor said, "The obvious conclusion is you were being harassed because of your relationship to the victim. Maybe the perpetrators assumed you were working the homicide." She added, "But how did they know you were in Berlin? Or who you were? Or where you were?"

Jenkins replied, "I don't know. That's the troubling part." He looked at his guests. "When the bad guys have good Intel, that's not good."

Brodie nodded. Assuming Mark Jenkins saw what he said he saw, then whoever killed

212

Harry Vance was just the tip of a much larger and smarter group who had access to inside information.

Taylor, thinking along the same lines, said, "This all suggests organized crime of some sort. Or maybe a terror network. Do you have any information about what Harry was doing here in Berlin?"

Jenkins looked at her. "I don't have information. What I do have is informed speculation." He thought for a moment, then added, "I assumed Harry was having an affair with someone here. His trips to Berlin started a few months before he and Julie separated."

Taylor asked, "He never spoke to you about these trips?"

"No. Harry was a very private person. I didn't even know his marriage was on the rocks until he moved out. And I used to go to their house for dinner at least once a week." He smiled as he added, "I'm a confirmed bachelor, and I think Julie thought I needed a home-cooked meal every once in a while."

Taylor asked, "Have you spoken with Julie since she was notified of her husband's death?"

He nodded. "She's devastated. She spoke with the police, but as far as I know she doesn't have any more of a clue than I do about what Harry was up to in Berlin. She just assumed it was work-related."

Brodie said, "Harry must have understood that other assumptions would be made by his colleagues about his trips here."

"I got the impression that he understood that I thought something was going on, and he was happy to leave it there." Jenkins looked at his empty schnapps cup like he was thinking about another refill. "He has — had — two kids. Great kids. Fifteen and seventeen." He made eye contact with Brodie. "He was a good father. A good man."

Brodie nodded.

"But . . . these trips. They started getting more frequent."

Brodie asked, "How often?"

"I don't know. Maybe every few weeks for a few days at a time. Unless we were working a big case. He didn't let it get in the way of his work. But the thing is, once he and Julie separated and he moved out, he was supposed to get the kids a couple nights a week, work permitting. And he started missing his nights so he could come to Berlin. And yeah, from the outside it's easy to imagine a guy in an unhappy marriage getting caught up with a new fling, letting that get in the way of being around for his kids. That's a common story. But Harry wasn't a common guy."

Brodie said, "I had the pleasure of knowing him many years ago. He was one of my instructors in Special Agent training. Oh-five."

Jenkins smiled. "Can't imagine Harry as a teacher."

"He was impressive," said Brodie. "Wasn't overly enamored with the sound of his own voice like a lot of them, and he got to the point. Also, unlike a lot of the male instructors, Harry didn't hit on his female students." Brodie glanced at Taylor, who'd had her fling with her instructor, CIA Officer Trent Chilcott. But Taylor wasn't taking the bait. He continued, "Hard to believe that a straight arrow like Harry Vance was following his dick to Berlin to see a woman."

Jenkins shrugged. "That's what it looked like."

Brodie asked, "How many CID agents in the Fifth MP?"

"In Kaiserslautern, about sixty."

"That's not a big group."

"No," said Jenkins. "And they're all gossips. The men worse than the women. Harry's trips here were the subject of a lot of conversation and speculation. And the problem was, the less he talked, the more everyone else talked."

"And you're suggesting that there may have been a woman, but that you don't believe that would have been enough to take him away from his children in the middle of a divorce."

Jenkins nodded. "But I could believe him being absent because of a case."

"A case that his commanding officer and his own partner knew nothing about."

Jenkins looked at him. "We're counterterror. We have a narrowly defined mandate. So, he could have gotten involved in something outside of that mandate and that's why he kept it to himself."

"Was that in his nature?" asked Taylor. "To go rogue like that?"

Jenkins shook his head. "Harry was obsessive about his work . . . but keeping me in the dark and doing an end-run around Colonel Trask, that's something else. So, whatever reason I come up with for Harry's trips here, I'm seeing a pattern of behavior that doesn't really fit the man."

Brodie asked, "Could any of your recent cases have made Harry or you a target?"

"You never know. But with most of our cases, we're not dealing with pros. We're dealing with a lot of young, self-radicalized idiots looking for a fast track to fame and their allotted seventy-two virgins in Paradise. So, we prevent fantasies from becoming reality, bad plans from becoming operational, and we try to keep stupid people from getting lucky. Every once in a while you find a radicalized a-hole who has actual high-level contacts in hot spots like Afghanistan, Syria. Mostly al Qaeda and ISIS. Those are the ones you really need to worry about. But CID agents are just not high-priority targets. And all of

Harry's knowledge of ongoing terrorist cases is redundant to mine, and to our commanding officer and in some cases other colleagues. So it doesn't make sense from a tactical standpoint for a smart or even stupid terrorist to target a CID guy."

That might be true, but Special Agent Jenkins might also have acquired an exaggerated sense of his own ability to get inside the heads of the crazies he'd spent his career hunting. Brodie said, "Sometimes the driving force is simple revenge. Anything like that?"

Jenkins nodded. "Yeah. We did have one case that was a little different. Two months back, Harry and I got approached by a couple of our CID colleagues who work narcotics. They were investigating a heroin ring being run by a few Arabic translators — Iraqi and Syrian nationals — who worked at the American base in Mannheim. Narcotics looped us in because they'd figured out these guys were wiring money to certain individuals in Baghdad who were members of Asaib Ahl al-Haq, which in case you don't know is a powerful Shi'ite militia group with close ties to the Iranian regime. We usually refer to the group simply as the Khazali network after the founder, Qais Khazali."

Brodie had never heard of the Khazali network. They might have come along after his time in Iraq. But he did know about other Iraqi Shi'ite militias that received funding,

217

training, and weapons from Iran, and also sometimes acted as muscle for the Shi'ite-dominated government in Baghdad. These militias had also — with Iran's help — become experts at constructing and deploying the roadside IEDs that had sent hundreds of American soldiers to Landstuhl for re-assembly and rehab — or home in body bags. Brodie had seen a few of those blasts up close and personal, and he'd lost a few friends to them. He asked, "Where were these translators selling the heroin?"

"Some on base. But they also had a couple of American accomplices, Army transpo guys who were helping them smuggle the stuff in U.S. military convoys. All over Germany and into France." He looked at Brodie and Taylor. "This was a big operation. When we made our arrests, we really screwed the terrorist groups relying on that money."

Taylor asked, "Does this militia have any connection with Hezbollah?"

Jenkins nodded. "One of the Khazali network's first operations was fighting alongside Hezbollah in the 2006 Lebanon-Israeli War. And more recently they both fought together in Syria against ISIS." He thought for a moment and asked, rhetorically, "So, is Hezbollah or the Khazali network under orders to ice the CID agents who put a dent in their funding network? Well, maybe it wouldn't be the craziest thing I've heard lately. But . . ."

He trailed off for a moment. "Doesn't explain what Harry was doing in Berlin in the first place, in some Muslim quarter of the city, at a park in the middle of the night with his hand wrapped around his M9 like he's expecting trouble."

Brodie told Jenkins about the Shi'ite Al Mahdi Islamic Center that FBI Agent Kim had shown them, and the place's suspected ties to Hezbollah. "Kim expects it's under surveillance and will be raided soon."

Jenkins processed that. "An FBI agent volunteering information? That's a new one."

"He's expecting something in return."

Jenkins looked at him. "The heroin smuggling case is an ongoing investigation. The arrests were reported, but the press hasn't connected the dots to terrorism and we're not going to help them do that until it's wrapped up tight. But the FBI is always trying to stick their noses into our counterterror investigations, so your guy Kim might already know about this. Use your judgment."

Taylor asked, "Do you know anything about the Al Mahdi Center?"

Jenkins shook his head. "Almost all our cases involve Sunni extremists, people loyal to al Qaeda or ISIS. But I mention the Khazali network because a case like that is pretty rare. The Shi'ites don't come on our radar so often these days, and it's harder for me to predict their motivations and behavior.

But if Harry was investigating this Shi'ite center in Neukölln, he would have involved me. Even if his jurisdiction was a little . . . tenuous."

Scott Brodie knew all about tenuous jurisdiction. The CID mandate was to investigate crimes that involved the U.S. Army, and CID agents occasionally landed in trouble for interpreting that a little too broadly. Mark Jenkins and Harry Vance had been investigating a narcotics case that involved using Army personnel and Army equipment to distribute drugs in order to fund a militia that was tied to Iran, a state sponsor of terrorism. That was pretty clear-cut. But if Vance had somehow gotten himself involved in an investigation of Hezbollah's fundraising and recruitment network in Berlin, that was maybe a bridge too far. But even if that *was* what he was up to, would it get him whacked?

Killing a cop investigating you was generally a bad tactic, since the ones still standing were that much more motivated to take your ass down. The Italian Mafia understood that and had a rule that law enforcement officers were never to be targeted — unless they were crooked cops in on the game. Brodie doubted that Hezbollah practiced that discretion, but it did raise the possibility that Harry Vance was a crooked cop. Which might explain his trips to Berlin.

Jenkins said, "Just to set the record straight

220

about why we're meeting in this hotel room, it's because I'm being followed and I'm linked to Harry, and there's no reason for you two to be linked to me and get on the radar of the guys who've been tailing me."

Brodie nodded. Mark Jenkins didn't want his colleagues to think he was hiding in his hotel room to avoid the fate of his partner. In some ways, Berlin could be more dangerous than a lawless place like Venezuela. Why? Because here, in civilization, you could easily let your guard down. And then you were dead. And surprised that you were.

Brodie asked, "Does Chief Inspector Schröder know about this heroin-smuggling case?"

"I mentioned it to him yesterday. German Feds were involved in the investigation so he already knew about it, but didn't know that Harry was one of the CID detectives on the case." He looked at Brodie. "Schröder said he'd be at your briefing this morning."

"He was," said Brodie.

"What was your impression?"

"A bit of a tight-ass."

"How was the briefing?"

"They put on a decent show. But no back-stage access."

"Yeah. Sounds right."

Brodie asked, "Did Schröder give you information about the postmortem mutilation?"

Jenkins looked at him and nodded. "Sick bastards."

Taylor asked, "Do you have anything to add to the prevailing theories?"

He shook his head. "If it's a message, I'm not getting it. I'm more of the mind that a group will use this unreported detail to verify responsibility. Or, we're dealing with a serial killer with an eye collection in his freezer, and Harry was a random target. But I wouldn't bet on that."

Taylor changed subjects. "In the briefing, no one mentioned Harry's personal computer."

Jenkins said, "He had a work laptop. Apparently he didn't take it with him this trip. BKA officials in Kaiserslautern gained entry to his off-base apartment and located it. But I doubt they'll find anything interesting."

"Why?"

"Harry conducted a lot of his business on his phone, using encrypted communication. He told me he didn't trust DOD's in-house network security."

"What kind of phone did he have?"

"A Samsung maybe? Android-based. Schröder asked me the same question. They've contacted Deutsche Telekom to get tracking data, but I guarantee you Harry turned off any kind of location sharing, and I know he used a mobile VPN. He was pretty diligent about digital privacy and security."

Probably because he saw firsthand in his investigations just how much information the average schmuck was sharing with the telecom companies — and thus with the cops — without even knowing it.

Jenkins took the schnapps bottle and popped it open. He poured himself another shot and offered the bottle to Brodie, who took it and examined it. It looked like a homemade small-batch concoction, a glass bottle with a rubber and metal swing top and a simple white label that said <u>KRÄUTER-SCHNAPS</u>.

"Where did you say Harry got this?"

"Not sure. Some specialty place, I think."

"Did he ever bring you a bottle of this before?"

Jenkins nodded. "Once before. We drank most of it together, and he brought another bottle to me after his last Berlin trip."

"Exact same stuff?"

"Yeah."

Brodie looked at Taylor, who was already tapping away on her phone. He said to her, "There's no commercial markings, so look for a distillery specializing in schnapps."

Taylor nodded as she looked at her phone.

Jenkins, who wasn't firing on all cylinders thanks to the schnapps and the grief, said, "I should have thought of that."

Taylor was quiet for a moment, then said, "Found it. Identical bottle design. It's made by Preussische Schnapsmanufaktur. I guess, Prussian Schnapps Manufacturer. In Prenzlauer Berg."

Brodie recognized the name of the Berlin neighborhood but couldn't recall anything about it.

Jenkins offered, "Prenzlauer Berg is kind of artsy, upscale, gentrified. Picturesque. One of the few parts of the city that didn't get totally flattened in the war."

Brodie looked at Jenkins. "Thank you for your help."

Jenkins nodded, and they all rose from their chairs.

Taylor said, "This is the part where I would tell the person I've interviewed to call me if they think of anything else, but I know you've already run every angle and detail in your mind before we even walked in the door."

Jenkins looked at her. "I appreciate you saying that. But the truth is I'm gutted by Harry's death and not at the top of my game. If I do think of anything else — or if I get tailed again — I will let you know. I'm driving back to Kaiserslautern tomorrow." He added, "I'd leave today, but Schröder asked me to stick around in case something comes up."

Brodie wanted to suggest that Warrant Officer Jenkins cut back on the day drinking, but he said, "We will get justice for Harry."

Jenkins looked him in the eyes. "I know you will."

Jenkins walked them to the door and opened it. As they stepped into the hallway he hung in the doorway, something still on his mind. He said, "Harry wasn't just my partner. He was a close friend. If he was investigating something and he was keeping it from me, it was big, and it was dangerous. So big and dangerous that he couldn't take a single risk, of a single person knowing. Even a person who he trusted with his life." He asked, not rhetorically, "What the hell could that be?"

Taylor said, "We're going to find out."

Brodie suggested, "Keep an eye on your ass."

They turned and walked down the hall as Jenkins shut the door.

After a minute Taylor said, "He's really hurting."

Ms. Taylor had an excess of empathy, which Brodie thought made up for his deficit. He said, "He's a walking example of being too close to a case to work it right."

"I hope you'd be as torn up if something happened to me."

"I'd be devastated," he assured her.

"You'd drink yourself to death."

"I'd at least start smoking again."

They took the elevator down to the lobby and walked out into the bright winter day.

The wind had died down but the day had grown colder, and a frozen stillness hung in the air.

Brodie looked around. Through the windows of a nearby café he could see that the tables were packed with a lunch crowd. Shoppers walked hurriedly in and out of the large department store on the western side of Alexanderplatz, and people flowed out of the train station that bisected the expansive plaza. Beyond the station, Brodie could see a line of tourists at the base of the TV tower, waiting their turn to ride an elevator to the top for a panoramic view of the city.

Something about this city felt so mundane, so banal, so at odds with its tragic and disastrous history. But the past never dies, even when it's been bombed and bulldozed and replaced with a shopping mall. It's still in the air, and in the earth beneath your feet, and in the hearts and minds of those old enough to remember.

Brodie spotted an old man sitting on a concrete bench ringing a graffiti-covered fountain in the center of the square. The man shakily brought a cigarette to his lips and took a drag. *What has this man seen in his life?*

A memory came back to Brodie of his last time here in 2000. He had been drinking with his old roommate Adam Kogan in a biergarten next to the Berlin Zoo. It was a perfect spring day — sun shining, birds chirping, two friends getting tipsy and scoping the pretty girls in their short dresses.

But Kogan had taken a dark turn, as he sometimes did after too many drinks. He was staring at an elderly German man — maybe early eighties — sitting alone at a nearby table having lunch.

"What's he seen, Scott?" asked Kogan. "What's he done?"

Brodie had looked at the man, who probably would have been in his early twenties at the start of World War II. "Maybe nothing," said Brodie. "Maybe he was just a soldier doing his duty and following orders."

Kogan had slammed his beer down. "No such thing as just a soldier doing his fucking duty and following fucking orders. He was a fucking Nazi!"

He'd said it loud enough for other patrons to hear, and maybe the old guy himself, though he didn't react. Brodie and Kogan left soon after.

Brodie watched the old man by the Alexanderplatz fountain, who squinted against the harsh winter sun as he smoked his cigarette. He was probably born around the beginning of the war, and had spent his childhood in a country reduced to rubble and ash. A country of women and children, whose men were missing, dead, or maimed and broken . . . hard to comprehend all that.

Had this man lived in East Germany? Had

227

he found a job with the state? The Stasi — the East German secret police — had deployed a spy or informer for every six citizens. It was the most heavily surveilled police state in history. And in the blink of an eye — when the Wall fell — the police state became a liberal democracy. But it doesn't work that way.

What's he seen? What's he done?

Harry Vance wasn't just here for a fling. Brodie was sure of that. Harry was searching for something, bringing light to the dark corners of this place. And someone killed him for it.

CHAPTER 11

Brodie and Taylor stopped at a café on Alexanderplatz and picked up black coffees to go, antidotes for the schnapps.

As they left the café Taylor consulted her phone and said, "The distillery is a thirty-minute walk."

"That means it's a five-minute taxi ride."

"We need to walk off the alcohol and jet lag."

No use arguing with someone who liked to make easy things difficult.

They walked north from Alexanderplatz on Karl-Liebknecht Straße, a wide road lined with broad, nondescript buildings. After a block they cut into a small neighborhood and found themselves on a quiet tree-lined cobblestone street.

Taylor said, "The charm sort of sneaks up on you here, doesn't it?"

Brodie tried not to link everything in Berlin back to the war, but he couldn't help wondering how much of the modern cityscape was determined by where some British or American bomber pilot happened to release his payload. Or where the apocalyptic battles between Russian soldiers and die-hard German defenders had been fought.

They walked and sipped their steaming coffees and Brodie looked at Taylor. Her cheeks were flushed from the cold and her blond hair rustled in the light wind. A few piggish thoughts invaded his mind and Taylor asked, "What are you thinking?"

"I'm thinking it's a good time to call Colonel Dombroski."

"You never think that."

She was onto him. Although calling the boss now wasn't a bad idea. The first report was the easy one — before they needed to ask permission to do something crazy, or ask forgiveness because they'd already done it. He said, "I'm working on my communication skills."

Brodie took out his phone and checked the time. It was half past noon, so 6:30 A.M. in Virginia. Would he catch the colonel out on a predawn run? Probably not. But by now Dombroski would at least be up and caffeinated.

He opened Signal — an app that offered end-to-end encrypted communication — and dialed the boss.

Dombroski picked up after a couple of rings. "Guten Tag, Herr Brodie."

"Good morning, sir. I am calling you with Ms. Taylor. We had our embassy briefing this morning, toured the crime scene with Berlin Police Captain Omar Soliman and FBI Agent David Kim, and have just concluded an interview with Harry Vance's partner, Mark Jenkins."

"Good. Are the local authorities being helpful?"

"We are experiencing the famed German warmth and hospitality."

"You're no treat either, Scott, but I'm sure you can all work together."

"Yes, sir. Though we've already discovered some relevant details that were not mentioned in the briefing."

"Don't waste your time with pissing matches. But if it's serious you can talk to Agent Whitmore about getting the Germans to show all their cards. As you know, that's part of the legat's job."

"Yes, sir."

Dombroski asked, "Anything new or interesting at the crime scene?"

"Not really." He briefed his boss on the crime scene visit, omitting his unauthorized questioning of Fatima.

"Sounds like you've been busy."

"We hit the ground running, Colonel."

Dombroski had no response to that, but said, "They took his eye."

"Right."

"Why?"

"Don't know. Don't want to speculate."

"It's a message."

"Yes, sir."

"You need to find the sons of bitches who did this."

It sounded to Brodie like his mandate had just been broadened. Unofficially. "Yes, sir."

"Does anyone there have any suspects?"

"If they do, they're not sharing. But Mark Jenkins has some theories he shared with me and Ms. Taylor."

"Let's hear it."

Brodie filled the colonel in on the terrorism and narcotics case in Mannheim that Jenkins and Vance had been working involving the Khazali network. "Jenkins made it clear that this Iranian-backed Shi'ite militia is different than the lone wolves or small cells of Sunni extremists that CID usually investigates, and that it's possible the Khazali network or an allied group was ordered to assassinate law enforcement involved in the case."

"That's interesting," said Dombroski. "I already put in a general records request with Colonel Trask, but I can flag that narcotics case in particular. Might give us some names and details that Mr. Jenkins was unwilling or unable to share."

"Good idea." Brodie also reported Agent David Kim's Intel about the allegedly Hezbollah-linked Islamic center that was a few blocks from the park where Vance was murdered. "We believe it is reasonable to assume there is some sort of operational connection between Hezbollah and the Khazali network."

Dombroski thought about that for a moment. "A picture is forming, but don't stare at it too much. Question your assumptions."

"I always do. Along with everyone else's."

"I know. Meanwhile, it's a minor miracle that you made a friend in the FBI. See what other details you can get from Agent Kim, and if we get our hands on the CID case records, we might be able to make some concrete connections."

"Yes, sir."

"And of course you will share your theories with the German authorities."

"Of course." The BKA already knew about the CID narcotics case, and of course they knew about the Al Mahdi Center in Neukölln, but it was possible they had yet to consider a connection between the two. Brodie made a mental note to forget to tell them.

Brodie added, "I should also tell you that Mr. Jenkins believes he is being followed. Two separate incidents." He briefly recounted what Mark Jenkins had told them. "This would seem to bolster the theory that a terrorist or other criminal organization is responsible for the murder."

Dombroski thought about that for a moment. "I don't know Mark Jenkins. Would you consider him a reliable narrator?"

"He and Harry were close, and he's angry and grieving, but I believe this happened. Though I am having a hard time understanding why. It makes no sense to try to intimidate a CID agent like this. It's pointless, high-risk, and counterproductive."

"Terrorists specialize in pointless and high-risk." He asked, "How is Ms. Taylor?"

Brodie turned to Taylor, who was sight-seeing as they walked but obviously listening to Brodie's side of the conversation. "She's grateful to be working with a real pro again."

Taylor rolled her eyes, then smiled.

Dombroski said, "You might be projecting, but I'm glad it's working out so far. Anything else to report?"

Should he tell the colonel that they were going beyond their authority and trying to locate Harry Vance's possible mystery love interest? Probably not. The colonel was expecting them to show initiative, but that didn't mean he always wanted to know about it. "Nothing else to report, sir."

"How's the weather?"

"Sucks."

"How's your hotel?"

"We haven't checked in yet."

"What are you doing now?"

More unauthorized detective work, but you

should never outright lie to your commanding officer, so Brodie spun it. "The hotel we're staying at is Muslim-owned, so no bar, so we're looking for a liquor store." He glanced at Taylor, who was smiling appreciatively at his cleverly worded bullshit.

Dombroski said, "All right. I will let you know once I hear back from Colonel Trask, and you will report again around this time tomorrow, if not sooner."

"Yes, sir. And I'll be mindful of the time difference."

"If it's important, it doesn't matter what time it is. I sleep like crap these days anyway. Something you have to look forward to when you're on the wrong side of fifty."

"Yes, sir. Anything further?"

"Negative further."

Dombroski hung up and Brodie put his phone back in his pocket.

Taylor asked, "Has he requested records from Kaiserslautern?"

"He has. Waiting to hear."

They reached a wide four-lane road with cable car tracks running down the middle. They crossed, then Taylor consulted the map on her phone. "We are now in Prenzlauer Berg. The distillery is a few blocks north."

They walked down another narrow cobblestone street, then made a couple of turns within the neighborhood. They passed cafés that looked like they offered al fresco dining in warmer weather, a biergarten that appeared closed down for the season, a number of bars, a couple of trendy-looking coffee shops full of trendy-looking people, a few high-end boutiques and baby stores, and a park with a playground. Unlike the other parts of Berlin they'd seen so far, Prenzlauer Berg had some of the feel of an old European city center, and probably had the rents and property values to match.

Taylor said, "Just up there."

They approached a wide storefront at the base of a cream-colored turn-of-the-century building. There was a large display window showcasing bottles, wooden casks, and clay growlers of various spirits. Painted gold lettering on the window said: <u>PREUSSISCHE SCHNAPSMANUFAKTUR</u>.

They entered the shop and were greeted by a man of about thirty in a fitted collared shirt and skinny jeans. He had slicked-back blond hair, a bushy beard and mustache, and a sleeve of tattoos on his right arm. He smiled to his customers in the otherwise empty store. "Guten Tag."

"Guten Tag," said Taylor.

They walked over to a row of shelves featuring dozens of clear and amber-colored glass bottles similar to the one that Jenkins had. Along the wall next to the shelves were two six-foot-tall old copper stills along with a small plaque in German, probably describing their history.

Brodie looked to the back of the store, where a glass-paneled wall with a door led to a large room full of distillery equipment.

"Wir machen jeden Mittwoch und Freitag Führungen."

"Sorry," said Brodie, "we don't speak German."

"Ah!" said the man. "Welcome. My name is Johannes. I was saying that we do tours of the facility every Wednesday and Friday." He asked, "Is there something in particular you were looking for? We do offer tastings."

"No thank you. I already had my schnapps this morning."

Taylor asked, "Do you have other retail outlets in Berlin?"

"No," said Johannes. "Everything is made and sold here. We even create custom blends for customers who request them. If you find an old or rare bottle of schnapps and bring it here, we can re-create it."

"Incredible," said Brodie, suddenly realizing there was such a thing as a schnapps snob. "What if I bring you a bottle of scotch?"

Johannes smiled. "Then I say thank you and we drink it." He asked, "Where are you visiting from?"

"Toronto," said Brodie.

"Ah. I hear it is a wonderful city."

Brodie approached the counter. "Your store was recommended to us by an American friend of ours."

"Yes? I might know him."

Taylor opened her satchel and pulled out the copy of the *Times* with Vance's face on the front page and set it on the counter in front of Johannes.

Brodie said, "We were supposed to meet him here in Berlin. News broke while we were mid-flight."

Johannes' face dropped as he looked at the picture. "I am so sorry. Yes, I've seen him in here a few times. Nice gentleman. I was shocked when I saw his picture on the news."

Taylor said, "We were looking forward to meeting his lady friend and were hoping we could still find her."

Johannes nodded. "Yes. She must be devastated. Nice woman. They seemed happy."

"Harry never gave us her contact," said Brodie. "Do you know a way we might find her?"

Johannes thought a moment. "I'm not sure. I don't even know her full name . . . just Anna. She paid in cash. No credit card." He added, "She used to come here alone over the years, and then started to bring your friend with her."

Taylor said, "We were supposed to meet them at Café König on Stargarder Straße, so we assumed she lived in the area."

Johannes shook his head. "I am sorry. I just don't know."

Brodie looked at the man. At the risk of sounding like a cop, he asked, "When did you see them last?"

"Last week, I think. Yes. Maybe Thursday evening."

Taylor said, "We really lost touch and I guess we're desperate for information about him. He was excited to introduce us to Anna but really didn't tell us much about her. But maybe you can." She added, "I'm sorry if this is inappropriate."

"No, no," said Johannes with some sympathy. "It's all right. She was younger than your friend, maybe mid-thirties. Good-looking woman, brunette, kind of petite." He thought for a moment. "You know, I recall that one time a few months ago she came in and forgot her wallet. She said she was going home to get it and that didn't take very long, so I suppose she does live nearby."

In his mind Brodie ran through all the questions that an investigator would ask but a friend wouldn't: *How often did Anna come here with Harry? How would you describe their behavior toward each other? Was there a noticeable change in either of their demeanors on their last visit?*

They could tin the guy and go into full detective mode, but Brodie felt he was going to have plenty of reasons in the coming days to cross some jurisdictional lines and piss off the Germans, and it was best to choose his transgressions. He did ask, however, "Was she German?" He added, "I mean, ethnic German?"

If Johannes wondered why they didn't know this, he didn't comment, but said, "Yes. A Berliner by her accent."

Brodie bought an expensive bottle of schnapps to thank the man, and to make up for the Art Hotel's lack of amenities. Then he said to Johannes, "If Anna comes here again, please tell her that Mr. Vance's American friends came by. Jack and Lisa." He took a pen from his jacket pocket, then wrote his phone number on the back of the store's business card and slid it to Johannes. "And please give me a call if you see Anna."

Johannes nodded. "I will. I'm sorry I couldn't be more helpful. And my condolences on your loss."

They thanked him again, left the store, and continued walking along the street.

Taylor said, "An attractive brunette woman named Anna, petite, German, in her mid-thirties, who lives in a few-block radius of this store. It's not great, but it's something."

"And she likes schnapps. I'll just strike up a conversation with every good-looking petite brunette we come across."

"I'm sure you would enjoy that. But for the moment, let's work with what we have."

"Right. Let's assume Harry Vance was staying with her."

"That's fair."

"And let's assume he took the metro to Neukölln after leaving her apartment."

"A little less fair. He could have been coming from anywhere."

"He could have been," said Brodie. "But let's assume he wasn't out and about all night carrying his M9. He left Anna's place sometime after two A.M. What are the nearby stations?"

Taylor pulled up the GPS on her phone and analyzed it for a minute. "The closest station from here is the U-Bahn on Eberswalder Straße. Next closest is the Prenzlauer Allee S-Bahn, and then to the northwest is the Schönhauser Allee station which serves both systems."

"Good." He pulled out his cell phone along with FBI Agent Jason Butler's business card and dialed the number.

Butler picked up after a couple rings. "Guten Tag."

"Guten Tag. It's Scott Brodie."

"Mr. Brodie. How can I help you?"

"Ms. Taylor and I have uncovered some information that will be helpful to the investigation which should not wait until tomorrow's briefing. In the days before his death Harry Vance was with a German woman named Anna, last name unknown, brunette in her mid-thirties, who lives in the neighborhood of Prenzlauer Berg."

Butler processed that and asked, "How did you come across this information?"

Brodie explained about the schnapps store, making it clear that they did not present themselves as CID agents. He added, "What we'd like to do is hit every bar, restaurant, and shop in this area with Harry Vance's picture and see who else might be able to provide a description or full name of this Anna."

"This is a job for the Berlin Police, Mr. Brodie."

"Right. Giving us information that we ask for is another part of their job. So Ms. Taylor and I would like to see all the CCTV footage in Prenzlauer Berg that the German authorities have access to, beginning from six A.M. Saturday morning, up until the early morning hours of Sunday when Vance likely boarded a train from here in Prenzlauer to Neukölln, and including the three metro stops of Eberswalder Straße, Schönhauser Allee, and Prenzlauer Allee."

"I can put in that request for you. Though I wonder what you believe you'll find that the Germans could not."

"Well, we already found something that the Germans could not, and we've only been in town a few hours."

Jason Butler did not respond for a moment. Then he said, "I'm sure the German investigators will find your information useful. Thank you for sharing."

"I want the CCTV footage."

Butler replied, "Even if they honor the request, you'll be disappointed with what you get. Public security cameras other than those in metro stations have been legal in Germany for less than two years and are still not widespread. Given their history, the Germans have a lot of . . . sensitivities about surveillance."

Well, that sounded like a good instinct in the birthplace of the Gestapo and the Stasi.

Butler continued, "This lack of surveillance cameras has caused a lot of problems for the authorities, particularly in investigating terrorist attacks that have occurred in public places that you might assume have surveillance cameras but actually don't. But that is beginning to change because of terrorism and crime. The police are starting to experiment with facial recognition software."

"Maybe they had the right idea the first time."

"I'm surprised to hear a CID agent say that."

"I surprise myself sometimes."

Scott Brodie probably had more of a libertarian streak than a government employee and military criminal investigator should, and he sympathized with where the German public was coming from. Thank God neither the Nazis nor the East German Communists had lasted long enough to get their hands on facial recognition software, not to mention surveillance drones and satellites. The problem was, there's always another evil around the corner. Technological innovation might be a line trending ever upward, but history is a circle.

Butler continued, "All this is to say, if the Germans agree to your request and then don't give you much, please don't misinterpret that as a lack of candor or cooperation."

Apparently Jason Butler had internalized Scott Brodie's distrust of authority and he was already doing damage control.

Brodie said, "Understood. Thank you for your assistance, Jason."

"Of course. Is there anything else?"

He thought about filling Butler in on the narcotics case that Vance had worked, but he decided to wait and see if Schröder brought it up in the briefing. "Nothing else."

"I will let you know what the police say about the CCTV footage."

"You need to be less diplomatic. Push them."

Brodie hung up and turned to Taylor. "Butler is putting in a request. Though apparently the Germans had their fill of Big Brother and don't like being watched, so there might not be much security camera footage outside the metro stops."

"I haven't noticed any on our walk." She added, "It's check-in time at the Art Hotel."

"If our bags got stolen, can we stay some-place nicer?"

"If we only have the clothes on our backs, the Art Hotel is where we'll fit in best." She added, "If we are following Harry Vance's late-night journey through Neukölln later, I need a nap. I suggest you do the same."

"Good idea."

Or maybe he'd recon the neighborhood while Taylor got her beauty sleep. Whenever he was alone and unarmed, interesting things seemed to happen to him.

CHAPTER 12

Brodie and Taylor took a cab to the Art Hotel, a gray stucco building on a tree-lined street along the south side of Körnerpark. As they got out of the cab Brodie noticed that a Berlin Police officer was still stationed at the southern entrance to the park, though the yellow crime scene tape had been removed.

They made their way through the glass doors of the hotel into a small reception area. The hardwood floors looked clean and there were no signs of peeling paint, or flickering bulbs, or skittering rats. So far, so good.

They approached the reception desk, a big beechwood counter with the words <u>ART HOTEL</u> bolted to the front. A few canvases of abstract art hung on the white walls. There was no one behind the desk.

Brodie rang a bell on the counter, and in a moment a door in the back opened and a slender man in his seventies shuffled out. He had a dusky complexion and bushy gray eyebrows, and wore a white button-down linen shirt and khakis.

The man smiled. "Willkommen. Deutsch? Englisch?"

"English," said Taylor.

"Very good. My name is Mustafa. Welcome to the Art Hotel."

"Thank you," said Taylor. "We have two single rooms booked under Magnolia Taylor." She put her passport on the counter, as did Brodie.

Mustafa glanced at both passports, then clacked away at a desktop computer in front of him. "Yes, I see. Six nights."

Taylor said, "With an option to extend."

Mustafa smiled. "There is always an option to extend a visit. Alas, not so with life."

Great, Brodie thought, a philosopher check-in clerk. He said to Mustafa, "In life, there is no charge for an early checkout. How about here?"

Mustafa assured him, "No charge." He added with a smile, "A small fee."

Taylor interrupted the path toward enlightenment and said, "We requested adjacent rooms."

"Yes, miss. And I use the card on file for additional charges?"

"Yes. And I believe you are holding our bags."

He nodded, turned around, and shouted something in another language. It didn't sound like Arabic to Brodie's ears. Probably

Turkish.

In a moment the door swung open and a skinny, sullen teenager — possibly Mustafa's grandson who'd been roped into the family business — walked out pulling Brodie's and Taylor's roller bags and brought them around the counter.

The boy looked between Brodie and Taylor and mumbled something in German.

"English!" barked Mustafa.

The kid flinched, then said, "I hope you enjoy your stay."

Taylor smiled. "Danke schön."

The kid returned to the back room as Mustafa took two keycards out of a drawer and input something on the computer.

Brodie gestured to the abstract canvas hanging behind him. "Nice art."

Mustafa turned to see what he was pointing to. "Yes? You like?" He didn't seem so sure about it himself.

"Bold color choices."

"A hundred fifty euros if you want."

"It looks perfect where it is."

Mustafa shrugged and went back to his computer. "All local artists. Every room, different painting on the wall. The price is also on the wall."

"Modern art should be priceless."

"Yes. I agree." Mustafa slotted a keycard into a programmer. He punched a button and then handed the card to Taylor with her passport. "Room three-oh-three. Third floor, park view."

"Danke."

He programmed another card and handed it with his passport to Brodie. "Room three-oh-five. Next door. The boy, Ayaz, will bring your bags up." He added, "A small tip."

"We can manage," said Brodie.

"As you wish." Mustafa gestured to an open doorway in the lobby. "Stairs over there."

Brodie asked, "Where's the elevator?"

"No elevator. On the second floor is the kitchen for everyone. There is free coffee and tea. You use the fridge, you put name on your food."

Brodie asked, "*My* name? Or the name of the food?"

Taylor said, "Scott. Stop."

"Yes, ma'am."

Mustafa handed them a slip of paper. "Web address for Wi-Fi login. Seven euros per day."

Taylor asked, "Any recommendations for dinner spots around here?"

Mustafa reached under the counter and produced a sheet of paper listing local places to eat and drink, as well as a few sightseeing spots. Brodie scanned the list for the three places that they intended to check out tonight and noticed only the club — Proletariat — made the list.

Taylor slipped the paper in her satchel and asked, "Is it safe around here? I'm noticing a lot of police everywhere."

Mustafa hesitated, then said, "In the park across the street . . . there was an incident."

Taylor asked, "What kind of incident?"

"I am not sure, miss. Maybe gang stuff." It must have occurred to Mustafa that he was frightening his paying guests and he added, "This is nothing for you to worry about. The area is very safe."

"Well," said Brodie, "it is now with all these cops around."

Mustafa's look darkened. He lowered his voice. "All these new Arabs cause problems. My people" — he pounded his chest — "Turkish. We have been here a long time. My family came from Ankara, 1962. No problems."

Brodie was sure that the neo-Nazis didn't make such fine distinctions. MUSLIME RAUS.

They thanked Mustafa and went to the small adjoining room that contained vending machines and the stairway.

Brodie gestured to Taylor's suitcase, which was about twice the size of his own. "May I?"

"No, but thanks for asking." Taylor humped up the steps with her large roller bag, and Brodie followed. They should have tipped the kid.

The second-floor kitchen looked barebones but clean, just like the lobby and hopefully the rooms. There were multiple signs in

German, English, Spanish, and French taped all over the place, instructing the young and clueless backpackers who were probably the Art Hotel's main customer base that they needed to label their items in the fridge, wash their dirty dishes, and not leave their food out.

They climbed to the third floor, walked down a short hallway, and located their adjacent rooms. The end of the hallway featured a small window with a view of the street and Körnerpark.

Brodie looked out the window. The Art Hotel aligned approximately with the mid-point of the park, and the northeast corner where Vance was killed was visible through the bare trees. The crime scene marker flags had been removed, and a few teenagers in winter parkas were skateboarding around the fountain. Apparently Körnerpark was back open to the public.

Brodie said, "Probably more than any other building on the park perimeter, people here could have been awake past three A.M. If we run into other guests, let's find out if anyone heard or saw anything."

Taylor replied, "I'm sure the Germans have already thought of that and have checked here for witnesses." She walked to her door. "I'm going to get some sleep. We have a late night ahead of us."

Their eyes met and Brodie thought back to

their last assignment, and a similar moment. Two people, far from home, standing in a hotel hallway in front of their respective rooms. Last time, he'd wondered if at some point one of them would end up in the other's room and the other's bed.

But now it felt different. There was still tension here, but they'd experienced a different kind of intimacy in Venezuela — the intimacy of battle, of almost losing their lives and relying on each other for survival. All in all, they both probably would have had a better time sleeping together.

"Scott."

He refocused.

"You did that thing where you look either lost in thought or in the middle of a stroke."

"I'm fine. Just need a hot shower and a cold beer from the minibar."

Taylor did her best Mustafa impression: "Beer warm. Shower cold. Ten euros."

Brodie smiled. "Meet at seven?"

"Make it eight."

"See you later."

She inserted her keycard, opened the door, then paused and looked back at him. "I'm glad we're working this together, Mr. Brodie."

"Likewise, Ms. Taylor."

She went into her room and closed the door behind her.

Brodie entered his room and bolted the door. It was a small, minimalist box with white walls, a double bed, and a desk and dresser that looked like they were from IKEA. A small flat-screen TV was bolted to the dresser and reinforced with a security cable, and the hotel's titular art hung over the bed. The piece in Brodie's room looked like someone had accidentally spilled red and blue paint across the canvas. It was titled <u>SYNCHRONICITY</u> and could be his for eighty euros.

There was a window across the room that looked over the park where Chief Warrant Officer Harry Vance had exited this life. And he had done so, apparently, while on some sort of official or unofficial mission, gun in hand. That was the way to go. Better than a nursing home. Brodie should be so lucky.

He took off his coat and tossed it over the desk chair, then kicked off his shoes. He grabbed the TV remote and sat on the bed, then turned on CNN International, where he saw, of all things, footage of downtown Caracas, Venezuela. Thousands of people had taken to the streets to protest President Nicolás Maduro and support some guy that the legislature had recognized as the real president. The chyron read: "LEGITIMACY CRISIS IN VENEZUELA."

Apparently the country had only continued its downward spiral since he and Taylor left, which was as predictable as it was depressing. Just like when he saw a news story about

253

some awful shit happening in Iraq, he had no desire to revisit a place where he'd almost died. Been there, done that, bought the T-shirt. He stripped down and walked into the small bathroom.

There was a handheld open shower, a sink, and a toilet. The shower wasn't hot, but it was warm, and as he showered, he thought about the case. They'd absorbed a lot of information today, and at some point you need to stop and try to separate the facts from the clutter, and the clues from the bullshit.

First, the search for the mysterious Anna might be a pointless exercise. Her failure to go to the police was suspicious, but people make bad choices all the time for no reason other than being scared or stupid. She might just be a person with poor judgment, who'd had a fling with a married man who had met a bad end and now wanted to wash her hands of it.

Then there was the Hezbollah-linked Al Mahdi Center, which might not actually be Hezbollah-linked and might also have nothing to do with Vance's murder. Same went for the narcotics case with the Khazali network. Harry Vance and Mark Jenkins had spent their careers pursuing dangerous and violent people, and then Harry Vance met a violent end. Those two things were not ipso facto related, but the killing seemed premeditated.

The most concrete thing, in fact — outside of whatever forensics evidence the Germans were discovering — was the fact that Mark Jenkins had been followed in what sounded like a blatant act of intimidation.

But why bother trying to scare Jenkins? You intimidate civilian witnesses to shut them up. But not a U.S. Army Warrant Officer who was a senior CID Special Agent in counterterrorism and a close associate of the victim. It didn't track. And when things don't track, you need to pay attention to them.

Of course, all of this was assuming that Mark Jenkins wasn't suffering from paranoid delusions. Alcohol could do that. So could twenty-five years on this job.

Brodie got out of the shower, dried off, shaved, and got dressed in a fresh button-down shirt and black denim jeans, then put on his shoes and socks and winter coat. Time for a stroll.

CHAPTER 13

Brodie stepped through the glass doors of the Art Hotel into the cold winter afternoon. The sun set a little earlier in this part of the world, and the shadows were already long at a quarter past four. Brodie crossed the street and walked along the southern edge of Körnerpark. He approached the Berlin Police officer at the park entrance. "Guten Tag."

The officer nodded to him. "Guten Tag."

Brodie descended the stone steps and walked around the central fountain, where the teens were still at it on their skateboards, a few feet from where Harry Vance had lain dead. They ignored him as he walked toward the steps up to the northern entrance.

He climbed the steps to Jonasstraße, which was where Captain Soliman surmised Vance's killer got into a getaway car, and where Fatima had seen a car drive away shortly after hearing the gunshot. Directly across the street was a decrepit-looking concrete apartment building, and Brodie wondered if anyone in this building got a better look at the car or the gunman. He looked around for surveillance cameras, but there were none.

He walked east along Jonasstraße, a quiet residential street, and reached Karl-Marx Straße. Directly across the street was a handsome old brick church, and on either side were rows of apartment buildings with street-level commerce.

Brodie crossed Karl-Marx, then turned onto a side street and retraced the route to the Al Mahdi Islamic Center. As he approached it, he spotted a blue-and-white van marked POLIZEI parked at the curb nearby. Behind the wheel was a police officer in black combat fatigues. Flanking the front entrance of the Al Mahdi Center were two more officers, also head-to-toe in black fatigues, each holding an assault rifle. The word POLIZEI was emblazoned across their body armor.

A little farther down the road on Brodie's side of the street was the same gray van that David Kim had suggested was a surveillance vehicle.

Brodie pulled out his phone and called Kim, who picked up after one ring.

"Scott. Hi. Crack the case?"

"Tomorrow. For now, I'm at the Al Mahdi Islamic Center and the gray van is where we left it, and there's now a police van and a couple of heavily armed cops that are guarding the center."

Kim let him know, "I heard through channels that there has been a threat against mosques in the area because of the murder. Probably nothing, but the authorities have to take these things seriously even if it's just one idiot making a phone call."

Brodie watched as three Arab men in coats and skullcaps walked between the police officers and into the center. Neither the Arabs nor the cops acknowledged each other. "So you think they're standing guard, but also conducting surveillance and planning a raid?"

"That is what's happening. You've got a place that is suspected of Islamic terrorist links and now also a possible target of white-supremacist terrorist activity. So the police have to protect the people that they're going to bust later." Kim thought that was funny and laughed.

Brodie changed the subject and told Kim about the narcotics and terrorism case in Mannheim that Vance and Jenkins had worked together. "Were you aware of this case?"

"I was aware of it generally, and I just got briefed an hour ago by my superior in New York that Mr. Vance was one of the investigating agents. CID ought to make every agent involved in the Mannheim investigation aware that they may be a target."

Well, that might be overreacting. But maybe not. He said, "Mr. Jenkins thinks he already

258

is a target." He described his and Taylor's meeting with Mark Jenkins, and the man's account of being followed.

Kim processed that. "He needs to get out of Berlin."

"He is. Tomorrow. At the moment, he's lying low in his hotel room. Chief Inspector Schröder is aware of all this."

"Good. Maybe they need to provide a protective detail."

"I think Mr. Jenkins is more than capable of taking care of himself and asking for help if he needs it."

"Right."

Brodie asked, "Have you heard of the Khazali network?"

"I have."

"Tell me."

Kim replied, "I've read the bio they sent me on you. You served in Iraq. Oh-three and oh-four, mostly Baghdad. So I assume you're aware of the Mahdi Army."

Brodie was well aware of the Mahdi Army, a Shi'ite militia run by a radical cleric named Muqtada al-Sadr that had set up de facto rule in one of the most violent quarters of Baghdad during the war. "We exchanged gunfire with the Mahdi Army on a few occasions."

"I'm glad they couldn't shoot straight."

"They killed two of my men."

"Sorry."

Brodie didn't respond.

Kim continued, "Qais Khazali used to be one of al-Sadr's lieutenants but was expelled from the group for going rogue. He started his own militia to direct attacks on U.S. troops. Khazali also ran death squads to kill Iraqi Sunnis. These guys are financed and trained by the Iranian Quds Force and have fought side by side with Hezbollah." He added, "This is all starting to come together."

"Not in my mind."

"You're a criminal investigator, Scott. I'm a counterterrorism expert, specifically Islamic terrorism." He added, "We think differently."

"You want me to think like an FBI guy? I'd need a brain injury for that."

Kim laughed. "No. We can complement each other's area of expertise. We don't need to butt heads."

"Right. Meanwhile, I think you're reaching for the closest answer instead of the right one."

"All I'm doing is sniffing around and following the scent. And I'm telling you there's a stench coming from that Al Mahdi Center."

Brodie looked across the street at the building. A couple of male Arab teens with their heads in their phones were walking toward the entrance and almost bumped into the heavily armed cops, who reprimanded them in German. The kids apologized and went quickly inside. He asked, "Has the BKA questioned anyone associated with the Islamic center?"

"That sounds like a question for the BKA."

"I'm asking you."

"I don't have an inside track. Maybe Whit-more does. But I doubt she'll tell you any-thing outside of the regularly scheduled programming. You and I aren't here to solve the case. We're here to plant our asses around that briefing table." He added, "Optics."

"I get it. But I have other plans."

"Yeah, I like to earn my paycheck too. All I'm saying is, look where the signs point. Khazali network. Heroin. Hezbollah. When it comes to these Shia militias, don't think ji-hadis blowing themselves up and chopping off heads. Think gangsters. Think Mafia. There's a Lebanese or an Iranian Pablo Es-cobar somewhere in all this. Army CID cut off their funding source and they wanted to send a message, which is: Fuck with us and we fuck with you." He added, "An eye for an eye."

Brodie suddenly missed all the deathly dull FBI agents he'd dealt with throughout his career. David Kim was something else; a man preaching a gospel that he insisted others hear and believe. Brodie said, "I am here representing the United States Army in an investigation that to my knowledge has yet to uncover any evidence, even circumstantial. And we have no named suspects — only the usual collection of Islamic militants. But I'll keep an open mind."

"Please do." Probably sensing he'd come on too strong, Kim added, "I appreciate you calling me to report, Scott. I know you didn't have to do that."

"I expect you to do the same." Brodie hung up.

Maybe Kim was right, and the obvious explanation was the right one. Maybe it had been so long since Brodie had had a real case that he didn't want it to be solved too quickly. Or by someone else.

A mournful prayer emanated from the Islamic center. A man's voice, deep and solemn, was amplified from a speaker somewhere on the rooftop and reverberated down the narrow street.

Brodie remembered the call to prayer from his time in Iraq. One call always came around this time of day, when the sun was slipping below the horizon.

Another group of Arabs — a handful of men in skullcaps and two women in hijabs — hurried through the doors. Brodie watched as the doors slowly swung shut. As the sky darkened the streetlamps blinked on up and down the street.

What were you doing here, Harry?

Vance's lady friend Anna lived on the other side of the city. So why had Vance come to Neukölln? Well, if David Kim was right that Vance was conducting a secret investigation, and that investigation was related to the case involving the Khazali network and perhaps Hezbollah, then that very well could have led Harry Vance to this place.

Before he realized what he was doing, Brodie had crossed the street and was approaching the Al Mahdi Islamic Center. As he walked toward the door one of the cops stepped in front of him.

"Was wollen Sie hier?"

Brodie realized he was being racially profiled by these cops charged with protecting the Islamic center from violent white nationalists. He said, "I'm going to prayers."

The cops exchanged a look, then the one in front of him asked in English, "You Muslim?"

"Of course. How about you?"

The cop didn't reply, but said, "We need to see ID."

Brodie produced his passport and handed it to the cop, who flipped through it and matched the photo with the man, then handed it back. "We must check you."

"Fine."

The cop slung his assault rifle, then gave Brodie a pat-down. Satisfied that he wasn't armed, the cop stepped aside and said, "You go."

"Allahu Akbar," said Brodie. He opened the door and stepped inside.

CHAPTER 14

Brodie stood in a small foyer with brown linoleum flooring and yellow walls. A narrow staircase led to the second floor. Near the stairs was a folding table covered in religious pamphlets, and an easel with a whiteboard written in Arabic that looked like a list of scheduled events.

A few posters hung on the walls featuring religious leaders. Brodie spotted Ayatollah Khamenei, the Supreme Leader of Iran, who was dressed in a black robe and turban, superimposed next to a long Arabic quote. Another poster featured a man he recognized as Ayatollah Ali al-Sistani, the top Shi'ite religious figure in Iraq. Brodie had seen both men's images plastered all over Shia areas of Baghdad, usually accompanied by a photo of Hassan Nasrallah, the leader of Hezbollah, whose photo was nowhere to be seen here in the lobby. Probably a wise choice in the event the police switched from guarding the doors to kicking them in.

On a less political note were posters and photos that highlighted the center's community activities — hosting talks, preparing communal dinners, providing religious instruction to teens. One photo showed a group of children working on a farm somewhere in the countryside. There was also a colorful mural of children holding hands that was made out of construction paper and dried macaroni.

An elderly Arab man entered the lobby and asked Brodie something in German. Brodie nodded, which had a decent chance of being the right answer. The man stared at him a moment, then climbed the stairs.

Brodie started to wonder what he was doing here. Had Harry Vance come to this place? And if he had, wouldn't the police surveillance detail have picked him up, and subsequently shared that sighting with the BKA officials investigating Vance's murder? Unless, of course, one arm of the German national security apparatus did not always talk to the other, which happened all the time in America. It was also possible that Chief Inspector Schröder and Captain Soliman did have information that Vance had paid a visit to the Al Mahdi Islamic Center and forgot to include it in that morning's briefing. That was actually easy to believe, given their track record so far. Either way, this was a long shot, but you never knew where pay dirt was until you dug. Time to push on.

Brodie waited a moment, then climbed the narrow staircase to the second floor, which featured a large landing covered in plush maroon carpeting. A window directly ahead looked out to the street, and a window on the opposite side of the landing faced an interior courtyard with a few trees and picnic furniture. On the walls were several flags featuring gilded Arabic script next to three closed doors.

He could hear voices coming from the third floor — quiet conversation, a little laughter.

He climbed the stairs to the next landing, where about ten Arab men of various ages were chatting near a closed door while taking off their shoes. A few women in hijabs clustered at the far end of the landing near another door, and Brodie guessed these were the two gender-segregated prayer spaces.

The conversation died down as everyone looked at Brodie. A portly man in his mid-forties wearing a knit sweater and glasses smiled at Brodie and said something in German.

"I am sorry to disturb you," said Brodie. "Is there someone here who speaks English?"

The man nodded. "Englisch, ja. Einen Moment." He opened the door, stuck his head in, and called out for someone.

In a moment another man came through the door. He was in his late twenties and wore

266

a collared shirt, khakis, and a skullcap over curly black hair. He said to Brodie, "Greetings, my friend. My name is Caleb. How may we help you?"

"I'm searching for truth and justice."

"As are we all." He asked, "Are you of our faith?"

"Thinkin' about it."

"Yes? We have people here who can guide you."

"Great." He stuck out his hand. "My name is Jack Davis."

They shook.

Brodie lowered his voice and said, "I'm also here because my friend Harry Vance was killed in the nearby park, which I'm sure you've seen on the news."

Caleb looked at him with genuine concern. "I am so sorry, Mr. Davis. Yes, we all know of this. A terrible crime."

"Right. Look, I know the police are working on it, but I came here as his friend to try to understand this. To find out where he'd been and who'd seen him in the time before his death." He looked at Caleb and asked, "Do you know of anyone in your congregation or in your community who may have seen him, interacted with him? I'm going door to door around here just trying to get some answers."

Caleb stared at him and didn't respond right away. Then he said, "I believe you should speak with Imam Hassan." He gestured to the door. "You may join us for the maghrib first if you wish. People of all faiths are welcome."

"Thank you, but I'll wait here."

"Of course. It is maybe fifteen minutes."

Caleb went back into the prayer hall and the other men finished removing their shoes and followed. The women at the far end of the room looked at Brodie with some apprehension before disappearing into the women's prayer hall.

Brodie sat down on a bench near the window. After a minute he could faintly hear the prayer getting under way.

Well, he hadn't been met with a blanket denial, and no one had thrown him out. He imagined everyone in this congregation and the larger Muslim community in Berlin must be on edge, despite Caleb's earnest friendliness.

He knew he should not have gone off on his own without his partner for backup, or at least should have told her where he was going. That was the rule. Maybe one of the few good rules. Harry had broken the rule, and look what happened to him.

So before he wound up missing — or held hostage and forced to work on the macaroni board — maybe he should call Taylor and tell her what he was up to so that she had enough time to get pissed off at him and then cool down again before dinner. But he had nothing to report yet beyond the fact that he'd done something impulsive and maybe stupid, which wasn't really news.

He got up and walked to the window looking down into the courtyard. He now noticed a small fenced-off area that contained a children's jungle gym and some toys. This place didn't feel like a nexus for terrorism. Then again, it wouldn't be a very effective front if it did.

He stood near the two doorways, listening to the sunset prayer. The imam was chanting in Arabic, occasionally pausing for a response from the congregation. It sounded like both doorways led to the same room, and the men and women were probably divided by a partition.

As the prayers continued, he walked to the street-facing window and looked out. The sun had set, and an orange afterglow sat above the rooftops, fading into a darkening sky. Down on the street, the surveillance van remained at its post, possibly taking photographs and conducting electronic eavesdropping to uncover links between this place and a terrorist militia a continent away. Meanwhile the kitted-out cops stood sentry at the door in case some neo-Nazis decided to show up with homemade bombs or assault rifles. What a world.

It sounded like the prayers had wrapped up

and the imam was speaking informally, maybe reminding everyone of the upcoming bake sale while passing around the collection plate, or whatever their version of that was.

Once the imam finished, people began to emerge from both doorways, chatting as they put on their shoes. Caleb approached Brodie along with an elderly man with a short gray beard who wore a flowing black robe and a white turban. The man stared at Brodie with his deep-set eyes, then said something in Arabic and walked away.

Caleb seemed a little uncomfortable. "Imam Hassan says we will talk in the hallway. Come."

Caleb and Brodie followed the imam into a hallway near the stairs lit by dim fluorescents. The imam stopped walking once they seemed out of earshot of the congregants. He asked Brodie, "Who is you?"

"Jack Davis. As I told Caleb, I'm a friend of the American who was killed in the nearby park. I'm going around the neighborhood seeing if anyone saw him or interacted with him in his final days."

The imam, who seemed to know a little English, nodded. "Sorry for you friend."

"Thank you."

"You friend police."

"Yes. Military police. United States Army."

"And you?"

"I'm a used car salesman."

"Yes? And where you sleep in Berlin?"

"Look, I'm here to —"

The imam raised his hand to interrupt. "Police come. Talk to me." He looked at Brodie. "You see police? Outside?"

"Yes."

"They here" — he jabbed his finger toward the floor — "because person say come kill us. My daughter here. Caleb mother here. Little children here. This my home. They come kill us in home." He pointed at Brodie. "Because of you friend. Muslim people kill him, yes? This they think. Always think Muslims bad people."

"No one is accusing you of anything." Except maybe supporting and financing Hezbollah, but he probably shouldn't bring that up.

Caleb said, "Someone defaced the center with spray paint early this morning."

"I'm sorry to hear that," said Brodie.

Caleb continued, "We talked to the police because we must, and because it was our duty as members of the community. But we need to think of our own safety, and not speak to . . . outsiders."

The imam said something, and Caleb translated: "The imam wishes me to escort you out."

Brodie looked at the imam, who stared back at him with his intense dark eyes. Brodie said, "Thank you for your hospitality."

Caleb said to Brodie, "We usually open our hearts to strangers. But this is now, sadly, a time of distrust. A time of danger for us all."

Well, he could understand how these people felt under siege, but it was also possible that the imam — and perhaps Caleb — knew something they weren't telling him. Unfortunately, he had zero leverage to find out what that was.

Brodie said, "I don't need an escort."

"I insist," said Caleb, who gestured back toward the landing. "You understand."

Brodie walked down the stairs to the first floor, with Caleb following. When Brodie reached the lobby, he walked to the front door and turned to Caleb, who was standing near the foot of the stairs. "I hope your people told the truth to the police."

"We do not tolerate lies in the house of God, Mr. Davis."

"Right."

Brodie stepped outside and passed between the two armed cops. He walked along the front of the Islamic center, then stopped to look at the wall next to one of the ground-floor windows. It appeared to have been freshly painted and was illuminated in the white glow of a nearby streetlamp.

He looked closer. Bleeding through the single coat of fresh paint he could make out the unmistakable image of a spray-painted swastika.

CHAPTER 15

Maggie Taylor sipped her white wine and looked at Brodie across the small, candlelit cocktail table. They were at an intimate bar on a side street off Karl-Marx Straße, a place with dim lighting, a quiet clientele, and a ten-page cocktail menu. Old German cabaret music played softly in the background. Brodie had just told his partner about his excursion to the Al Mahdi Center, and she seemed to still be processing it.

"Taylor."

She refocused.

"Any positive thoughts on what I told you?"

She was quiet again for a moment. The flickering flame of the tea light danced over her features. Then she said, "When I was at Fort Campbell, I saw the on-base therapist."

Brodie didn't respond.

"She told me that I get myself involved with dangerous, untrustworthy, and oftentimes unstable men, and the reasons for this date back to the trauma I experienced in my child-hood."

He assumed the trauma she was referring to was her mother blowing away her father with a shotgun, which would screw anyone up. As for the men, she must be thinking about Trent. Not Scott Brodie. He said, "Makes sense."

"I alternate between the roles of child and mother, either allowing myself to be dominated and controlled by these men or burdened with the responsibility of providing discipline and comfort to them. Both roles are attempts to fill voids in my life, and both hold me back from being a strong and independent woman."

This sounded like a three-drink conversation, but they were only on their first round. Brodie said, "I think you are a strong and independent woman."

"I don't need your validation."

"Of course." He took a swig of his doppelbock beer, which had a high alcohol content, but maybe not high enough.

Taylor continued, "So my first impulse now is to chastise you for being so impulsive and reckless, for possibly endangering yourself and compromising both of our roles in this investigation. But a reprimand from me is what you expect, and on some level it's what you want and what you need." Taylor looked him in the eyes. "I refuse to waste my time with someone who does not respect me, Scott. Pull this shit again and I walk."

Maggie Taylor had changed. Psychobabble aside, she was more self-assured, self-possessed, and maybe even self-centered in a way that was probably good for her. And where did that leave him? In need of his own shrink, maybe. Though he didn't need to pay someone by the hour to tell him that there was an adolescent boy inside of him who made half of his decisions.

He said, "You're right. I should have called you before doing that so we could confer, and I apologize. But you need to know that I do respect you."

"Not enough, Scott."

"I'll work on it."

She finished her wine and stood. "I'm getting us another round." She walked to the bar.

Brodie watched her approach the bar and start chatting up the young male bartender, who seemed to enjoy the attention from the pretty American woman.

Brodie drank his beer as he scanned the place, noticing that most of the patrons were in their thirties or older, probably thanks to the high-priced cocktails. This bar was obviously a product of Neukölln's gentrification. On the exposed brick wall at the far end of the room he spotted a Gay Pride flag, as well as a sign that said in English REFUGEES

WELCOME, which was a nice sentiment, though he wasn't sure if the refugees could afford the fourteen-euro martinis.

He also noticed a large black-and-white placard that said FCK AFD. He thought he could fill in the missing vowel in the first word, and he remembered that AfD, Alternative for Germany, was the right-wing political party that had organized the anti-Muslim protest outside the American Embassy in reaction to Vance's murder.

This place certainly had its liberal credentials in order, which reminded him that despite the right-wing populism roiling Europe and parts of Germany itself, Berlin was still a very progressive city. Then again, it had been a liberal, cosmopolitan place during the Weimar Republic too, right up until the day Adolf Hitler became chancellor.

Brodie's phone rang. He didn't recognize the number, but when on assignment you always pick up. "Brodie."

"Mr. Brodie, it's Jason Butler. I heard back from the Berlin Police. An officer will meet you at the embassy after our briefing and remain with you while you review the security footage that you requested. He will provide a laptop for viewing, and you can use one of our empty offices."

"Great. I'm sure the police were happy to oblige."

"Not exactly. But they like to cooperate on

the small asks so that they can say no to the big ones."

"Anything else?"

"I was told to let you know that the only available footage within Prenzlauer Berg is from the three metro stops you requested, and that the authorities have already reviewed every minute of that footage as part of the investigation."

"Well, I'm happy to waste my time and theirs."

"I'm sure. See you at the briefing."

Brodie hung up as Taylor returned with their drinks and sat down. "Who was that?"

"Butler. We can check out the security camera footage after the briefing."

"Great." She slid his beer to him. "The bartender gave me some dinner recommends. A few really good Turkish spots and a few fusion places."

"What about German food?"

"We might be in the wrong neighborhood for that. In fact, we might be in the wrong city. This is a very international town."

"I'm sure we can hunt down a schnitzel."

She was quiet for a moment, then leaned forward and lowered her voice. "Did you get the sense that these men at the Islamic center knew you were there under false pretenses?"

"I turned in a pretty good performance, as I always do, but . . . maybe. With all the death threats they're getting, they're suspicious of strangers."

"Or," said Taylor, "they were already primed to distrust an American coming to them for information because one already had, possibly also misrepresenting himself."

Brodie nodded. "Possibly. Whether or not Harry showed up there, they know something."

"If he did go there, I'd want to know if he also went to other mosques or Islamic religious centers around here. Was he investigating something concrete and specific to the Al Mahdi Center, or just going on a fishing expedition around the neighborhood?"

"Maybe we should go mosque-to-mosque to see if Harry paid a visit."

"I think you've already stepped beyond our mandate. We need to tread carefully."

"Then I guess we also need to cancel tonight's rounds."

Taylor shook her head, then smiled. "We're just having a night on the town. It's not our fault if we stumble onto some clues along the way."

Brodie got started on his second stein of doppelbock. If they kept up at this rate, they were bound to stumble onto something.

As for Maggie Taylor, when it was she who broke the rules, it was okay. Not so for Scott Brodie. Interesting.

More importantly, Maggie Taylor was willing to push the envelope on this case for the same reason he was: to resurrect a career that had been damaged by the Mercer case. And this made things easier for him. They both understood that this case was a make-or-break. They had nothing to lose if they screwed up. And when you have nothing to lose, you do things your way. Meaning the right way.

Harry Vance, who was apparently doing things his way, would agree. If he were alive. But he was dead. Because he was doing things his way.

CHAPTER 16

Brodie and Taylor had dinner at one of the bartender's recommends, a trendy spot located in a converted old laundromat named, appropriately, the Laundromat. The washing machines had been swapped for tables, but the place otherwise looked like a laundromat — harsh overhead fluorescents, a polished concrete floor, and exposed brick walls slapped with white paint. The fare was upscale continental, and the prices would raise some eyebrows when they turned in their expenses. "Laundromat, two hundred euros, Mr. Brodie?"

Taylor said to her partner, "My instincts tell me that Harry's lady friend, Anna, will know why Harry was in Berlin."

"He was here for her."

"That's not what got him killed. And she'll know what he was working on here."

Brodie had had the same thought, and nodded. He himself did not share his cases with his girlfriends, but lots of men did. Pillow talk. Usually the woman was uninterested, or pretended she was. Sometimes the woman was *too* interested. And she wasn't in bed with the guy because of love. Or maybe he'd read too many spy novels. Well, they wouldn't have any answers about Anna until they found her. He glanced at the menu. "I might try the stuffed pig anus."

"That would be appropriate."

They navigated the French language menu with German subtitles with the help of the waiter, avoiding internal organs.

The chatted as they ate, catching up on a few things, sort of reconnecting, each trying to figure out how the other one had changed, and whether it was for the better.

After dinner they both had some cognac to brace themselves against the cold night ahead.

They left the restaurant and found their way back to Karl-Marx Straße, then headed south toward Wunderschön Saigon, the Vietnamese noodle shop that was the first stop in their quest to reconstruct what they thought could be Harry Vance's late-night journey through Neukölln.

The air had grown colder, and a freezing gust barreled down the wide road. Taylor zipped up her long black winter coat and pulled down her knit wool cap.

It was half past ten and the streets were light on pedestrians, but the indoor cafés and bars were packed.

They reached Wunderschön Saigon, a narrow storefront with a lit-up sign and a front window covered with laminated pictures of big bowls of pho.

They entered and looked around. There were a few small tables, and a counter with stools that ran along the left wall. The place was full of multicultural patrons chatting and slurping. In the back was an ordering counter in front of an open kitchen.

They approached the counter, where a petite fifty-something Vietnamese woman in an apron had her back turned to them and was shouting something to the kitchen staff. She turned around and faced them. "Ja?"

"Guten Abend," said Taylor. "Sprechen Sie Englisch?"

"Englisch? Nein." The woman pushed a laminated menu across the counter and jabbed her index finger over the various pictures of pho. "Hühnchen. Schweinefleisch. Gemüse. Okay?"

"Danke schön," said Taylor. The woman moved on to another customer.

A voice from behind them said, "Hey, my friends."

Brodie and Taylor turned as a teenager of African descent with close-cropped bleached-blond hair got up from his table and approached them. "I help you order, yeah?"

"Thank you," said Brodie.

"You got it, my man. Best pho in the fucking city right here. Americans?"

"Yes," said Taylor.

The kid nodded. "All right. Love America."

"You don't hear that every day," said Brodie. "Listen, do you know about the murder in that park down the street?"

"Oh yeah," said the kid. "Everybody knows about that, my man. Got sniped or something."

"He was a friend of ours," said Taylor. "We are helping his family try to figure out where he went on the night he was killed." She nodded toward the Vietnamese woman behind the counter.

The kid looked like he regretted his offer to help. "Oh. So sorry. Yeah . . . I can try." He approached the counter and said something loudly in German. The Vietnamese woman finished up an order, then walked toward them and listened as the kid spoke quietly. She glared at Brodie and Taylor and said something to them in harsh-sounding German.

The kid said to them, "Yo . . . She said she already talked to the police. She thinks you're reporters or something and she don't want to talk to you."

"Tell her we're friends of the victim," said Brodie. "Can she tell us what she told the police?" He added, "We'll pay her for her time."

The teen said something to the woman, who shook her head and barked at him in German. "She says she knows nothing. That's what she told the police. She says you need to order or leave."

Taylor looked at the woman. "Danke." She said to the teen, "Thanks for your help."

"You got it, my friends. Sorry about your mate. It's brutal out there."

"It is," said Brodie. "Take care of yourself."

Brodie and Taylor stepped back out into the cold night and Taylor said, "I have a feeling that wherever we go, Chief Inspector Schröder will have already been."

"We might be retracing Schröder's steps, but we are looking with different eyes. Redundancy in an investigation is a good thing, a fail-safe against incompetence, bias, and — in this case — German arrogance."

"What about American arrogance?"

"That's what makes the world go round."

They continued south along Karl-Marx Straße and approached the hookah lounge, Ember Berlin, which was at the base of a five-story apartment building. The ground-floor frontage was all glass and the place looked busy. A red neon sign that said EMBER BERLIN HOOKAH LOUNGE spanned the length of the building.

They entered. The place was kind of gaudy, with white vinyl seating, mirrored walls, and blue and purple club lights splashed across large Turkish tapestries hanging from the ceiling. Middle Eastern pop music was playing low in the background.

The clientele was mixed — a couple of clusters of old Middle Eastern men puffing away at hookahs and drinking tea, and a few groups of diverse twenty- and thirty-somethings smoking and sharing pitchers of beer.

A Turkish man in his forties wearing an electric-blue dress shirt and sporting greased-back hair approached them, smiling as he gestured to the tables. "Setz dich hin wo du willst."

"Danke," said Brodie.

They found a two-person round table toward the back and sat down, and the man brought over a couple of menus and said something to them in German.

Brodie said, "We'd like a hookah. Do you have apple?"

The man nodded. "Apfel, ja. Uh . . . drink? Beer?"

"Ja," said Brodie. "Zwei Pils."

"Warsteiner?"

"My favorite."

The man nodded, took the menus, and walked off.

Taylor said, "I haven't smoked a hookah since college."

"The synthetic flavors will take you back."

"And I haven't had a man order for me

without asking what I wanted since before that, in Tennessee."

"This is a real nostalgia trip for you."

Taylor looked around the place. "Do we think our friend came here?"

"Well, if he came to Neukölln to meet someone in relation to an Islamic terrorism investigation, this seems more like the place for that than a Vietnamese noodle shop or a loud, trendy nightclub."

"Assuming he came to this neighborhood for a meeting. But why then go through the park, which is north of here? After the meeting, he could have doubled back to the train station he'd arrived from."

Brodie shrugged.

Taylor shook her head. "Doesn't feel right. The meet — if there was a meet — was in the park. Or was supposed to be in the park."

Well, this was all useless speculation unless and until they got some real Intel. Brodie looked over at their host, who was now sitting near the door. The man yawned and looked at his watch.

Brodie checked his own watch. Ten fifty-five. "Let's see if there's a changing of the guard at eleven."

Another Turkish man, a lanky guy in his mid-twenties wearing a red button-down shirt and jeans, entered from a back room carrying two pints of beer. He placed them on their table and smiled. "Enjoy."

"Danke," said Taylor.

They watched as the young man returned to the back room, then emerged a moment later with a small pot full of coals and a pair of tongs. He went around the room replacing the coals atop the guests' hookahs, then said something to the older man at the front. The older guy got up, threw on a thick coat, and left.

Brodie watched as the young man returned to the back room.

Taylor said, "I guess there's our night shift."

In a minute the young man re-emerged with their hookah and placed it on the table. He put a few hot coals on top of the tobacco bowl, then used a plastic mouthpiece from his pocket to take a few deep drags to get the coals going. He exhaled a long puff into the ceiling, then removed his mouthpiece, placed the hose on the table, and gave them each their own mouthpieces. "Can I bring you anything else?"

Brodie gestured at an empty chair. "Do you have a minute?"

The man appeared a little confused, then looked around the place to see that no one was flagging him. He hesitantly sat down.

Brodie fitted his mouthpiece on the hose and took a long drag. The rush of tobacco gave him a nice buzz and a little jolt of energy to counteract the beer and cognac.

Brodie offered the hose to Taylor, who

shook her head; then he held it out to the young man, who smiled and said, "No, please. But thank you, sir."

Brodie extended his hand. "Name's Jack."

The man shook his hand. "Faruk."

Taylor extended her hand and they shook. "Lisa."

Brodie gave Faruk the same spiel about them being concerned friends of the murdered American, whose movements they were attempting to retrace for his family. Faruk seemed to react to this line of bullshit a little differently than the guys at the Islamic center, or the teen and the Vietnamese woman at the noodle shop. He looked nervous. Tense.

"I am sorry about your friend. But I think you should maybe talk to my uncle. He just left. You should come back tomorrow."

Taylor asked, "Does your uncle usually leave around this time?"

Faruk nodded.

"How late are you here?"

"Closing. Usually around four on weekends. Two on weeknights."

Brodie asked, "Were you here Saturday night?"

Faruk nodded again.

"Have you seen news coverage about the murder and are you aware of what the victim looked like?"

"Yes."

"Did you see Harry Vance at this establishment the night he was murdered?"

Faruk didn't answer. His eyes darted between Brodie and Taylor. After a moment he said, "The police . . . interviewed my uncle. He told them he did not see this man."

Taylor pointed out, "Your uncle wasn't here at three A.M., when the victim would have been. You were."

"Yeah," said Faruk. "I didn't see him."

Brodie asked, "Did the police speak with you?"

"No."

"Why not?"

"I don't know."

"Maybe your uncle didn't mention you were working that night."

Faruk didn't respond.

"Was it a busy night?" asked Brodie.

Faruk looked at him. "Yes."

"Anyone else here helping you with the tables?"

"No."

Brodie nodded and shared a look with Taylor. After a moment Brodie took another puff from the hookah and breathed out a long trail of smoke. Then he took out his smartphone, Googled Harry Vance, and pulled up the now ubiquitous military portrait photo. He slid the phone to Faruk. "Look again. Think back to that night. Did you see this man?"

Faruk swallowed hard as he stared at Vance's picture. Just then one of the old guys in the corner called for him and he shot up from his chair. "I'm sorry. Excuse me."

He picked up his pot of coals and walked quickly away.

Taylor said, "You're acting like a cop."

"I am a cop."

"So what's the move?"

Brodie took a drink of his beer and eyed Faruk as the man refreshed the coals on his guests' hookah, then hurried across the room toward the back door. Brodie said, "Time for a direct approach."

He got up, headed for the back door, and intercepted Faruk before he was able to reach it.

"Sir, I'm sorry, but I must —"

Brodie grabbed Faruk's forearm and pulled him into a small vestibule that led to the restrooms. Brodie produced his CID creds and held them up. "I am Scott Brodie of the United States Army Criminal Investigation Division, investigating the murder of Special Agent Harry Vance. We have strong reason to believe he visited this establishment on the night of his murder. If you or your uncle withheld information from investigators, you could go to prison. Be truthful with me now, and that won't happen. Do you understand?"

Faruk stared at Brodie's badge case and nodded slowly.

"Did you see the victim here on Saturday night?"

Faruk nodded again.

"When?"

Faruk thought for a moment. "It was . . . between two and three, I'm not sure when."

"Closer to two or closer to three?"

"Closer to three."

"Was he with anyone?"

Faruk shook his head. "He was alone, only here for maybe ten minutes. Ordered a coffee."

"How did he seem to you? Nervous? Calm? Tense?"

"I am not sure. I wasn't paying such close attention."

"Was he using his phone?"

"Yes."

"Did he leave in a hurry?"

Faruk thought for a moment. "I guess you could say this. He didn't ask for a check. Just left cash on the table and walked out."

Brodie nodded. Was Harry expecting to meet someone here who never showed? Or setting up the meeting on his phone? Or killing time and keeping warm and caffeinated before the meeting in the park? This maybe wasn't the lead he was hoping for. "Do you have security cameras in here?"

"No, sir."

"I want you to think carefully, was there anything out of the ordinary here? Did anyone else act strangely, or change their behavior, once he came in?"

Faruk thought about that. "Not really. No, I would say not."

"And did your uncle tell the police he was working that night, to protect you and spare you a police interview?"

Faruk did not respond.

"Guy comes in and has a coffee and leaves. Maybe ten minutes later someone shoots him dead. That doesn't make you or anyone in this place guilty."

Faruk looked him in the eyes. "It's not about him. It's about the other people here. There were two . . . powerful men here, sir. If I tell the police that this American came here, they want to know who else was here at that time, then I have to give them names, and then some people who don't like the police attention so much, they get attention, and this is not so good for me. Not so good for my uncle."

Brodie nodded. *Powerful men.* In other words, members of a local crime syndicate. "Tell me about these men."

Faruk shook his head. "I can't."

"You can and you will."

"I have done nothing wrong."

"I disagree. You are in the process of obstructing justice."

Faruk looked back into the lounge.

"Look at *me,* Faruk."

The young man looked at him. Sweat was beading on his brow. If Taylor were doing this, she probably would have gone for a softer approach. Maybe he should ease up. He said, "Forget names. Tell me about these powerful men in Neukölln. Who are they? What kind of business are they in?"

Faruk nodded, grateful to be asked a question he could answer. "They are Arabs. From Lebanon, mostly. They have been here awhile. There are ten families here in Neukölln. They run gambling, prostitution, drugs . . . sometimes robbery. Bad things. They keep to themselves. They take care of . . . problems without involving the police."

"And the guys who were here, did they take notice of Harry Vance?"

"They take notice of everyone."

"Did they arrive before or after him?"

"Before. Maybe an hour before."

"How long did they stay after he left?"

"A while. Until about four-thirty."

"I thought you closed at four."

"We do. But men like that, you don't kick them out."

Brodie thought a moment. Did Harry Vance fall down an investigative rabbit hole that brought him to the attention of the Arab crime families? Was that why he got clipped? The whole thing could have been a setup to get him into a park alone, late at night.

He looked at Faruk. He could keep pressing, but since he had no jurisdictional leg to stand on here, it might be better to kick this up to Schröder and let him make whatever threats were more specific to German law.

Brodie said, "Thank you, Faruk. You've been helpful. You'll be hearing from the police, who will be looking forward to your cooperation."

Faruk looked at the floor. "I did nothing wrong."

"I'll need your contact information."

Faruk gave Brodie his cell phone number, which Brodie typed into his phone. He said to Faruk, "Look at me."

The man looked at him.

"You are doing the right thing. And I promise you that the police will be discreet."

The young man nodded, then shuffled off into the back room.

Brodie returned to the table, where Taylor was sipping her beer. She looked up at him. "Anything?"

Brodie nodded. "Leave a big tip and let's get out of here."

Taylor put a fifty-euro note on the table and they left the hookah lounge. As they walked north along Karl-Marx Straße, Brodie gave Taylor the rundown of his conversation with Faruk.

She said, "So we've moved on from terrorism to organized crime."

"I'm not so sure there's a bright line between them."

Taylor nodded. "In my preparation for this

case I did some reading on the Arab clans. That's what they call them. Most of the families came here as refugees of the civil war in Lebanon during the seventies and eighties. Some trace their lineage back to parts of Turkey, and they are almost exclusively Sunni."

"So, they might not be involved in financing Shia militia that are friendly to Iran."

"I'm not sure how religious they are. If money is to be made, maybe they don't care. You and I don't really understand this world and we should be careful about our assumptions."

"There's a lot of moving parts here," said Brodie. "And we don't even know the names of the parts."

They continued along Karl-Marx Straße. Taylor said, "Well, we've discovered something new. But I don't feel we're any closer to finding the killer."

"We're not," Brodie assured her. "But we've reconstructed Harry's movements and times from the U-Bahn, to Ember Berlin, to Körnerpark, where his journey ended."

"Why did he stop at Ember Berlin?"

"If we had his cell phone we might know."

"Why was he here? In Berlin. In this neighborhood?"

"Anna knows why."

"We need to find her."

"We are hot on her trail. Consider her found."

"I can see why some people mistake your self-assuredness for monumental arrogance."

"They don't know me like you do, Maggie."

She had no response to that and asked, "You still want to go to Proletariat?"

"Why not?"

"Based on Vance's timeline, he couldn't have stopped there before or after Ember Berlin."

"But he may have been there on another night. Also, we need a drink. And the Art Hotel has no bar."

"I have that bottle of schnapps in my room."

Brodie hesitated. Was she offering just schnapps? Or schnapps with a chaser?

"Scott?"

"Let's stick to the plan."

"Okay . . ."

They continued on in silence.

CHAPTER 17

Brodie and Taylor found themselves in a quiet residential neighborhood, somewhere east of Karl-Marx Straße. Taylor glanced at her cell phone, then up at a nondescript gray stucco building, covered with graffiti, and saw the street number stenciled above the steel door. There seemed to be no proprietary name on the building, but Brodie spotted a piece of spray-painted graffiti that said, <u>PROLE-TARIAT</u>, which he brought to Taylor's attention. "Here it is. Right above 'Peace, love, and kill the capitalists.' "

She glanced at the graffiti, and asked, "Do you want to go in?"

"We have nothing to lose but our euros." He opened the door and they walked in.

The place felt warm compared to the frigid street, and Brodie scoped out the dimly lit lounge.

A long bar ran along the left wall of the large room, but only two people sat there. Neon beer lights hung on black walls plastered with flyers, and electronic dance music played from wall-mounted speakers. Café tables were scattered around the concrete floor, all empty except for one where a couple sat, obviously having a tiff.

A red curtain hanging on the far wall must have led to the music venue in the back room, and Brodie could occasionally hear electric guitars and drums.

Taylor walked to the bar and Brodie followed. She sat and unzipped her coat. Brodie sat beside her.

Behind the bar stood a full-bodied woman in her mid-twenties with dyed, henna-red hair and arms covered in tattoos. "Was kann ich dir bringen?"

Either Brodie was starting to understand German, or the barmaid was speaking English with half a load on. He asked Taylor, "Vas is du drinkin', comrade?"

She ignored him and said to the barmaid, "Ein Whiskey, bitte."

"Make it zwei," said Brodie.

The barmaid grabbed two glasses and a bottle of something and doled out two generous pours. She slid the glasses to them and said, "Zwanzig euros."

Taylor put a fifty on the bar and asked the woman, "Do you speak English?"

She hesitated, then replied, "Yes. A bit."

Taylor said, "We are looking for an American friend." She put her cell phone on the bar. "This man." She added, "An American soldier, stationed here."

The barmaid looked at the Army photograph of Harry Vance, then at Taylor, but said nothing.

Taylor took a chance and said, "We know he comes here. When was the last time you saw him?"

"This morning."

Taylor looked at her. Unless she worked in the morgue, she hadn't seen Harry Vance this morning. "Are you sure?"

"He . . . I saw this photograph. On the television." She looked at Taylor again, then at Brodie. "On the news . . ."

Brodie asked, "Had you seen him before that? In here?"

"No. I never seen him."

Taylor pushed the fifty-euro note toward her. "Keep the change."

The barmaid hesitated, then took the money. She moved off to take another order.

Brodie picked up his glass of whiskey and Taylor did the same. They clinked glasses and Brodie said, "Well, Ember Berlin was a piece of the puzzle."

Taylor sipped her whiskey thoughtfully. "A small piece. In a big puzzle." She asked, "Will we share that?"

"We don't share. We trade."

"Don't get yourself in trouble."

"I live there."

"I guess I better keep my distance."

Brodie smiled, then said, "We did our due diligence here. Do you want to finish this shit whiskey or head back to the hotel?"

"Let's get our money's worth." Taylor took another sip, then set her glass down and slowly spun it with her fingers. She looked like she had something on her mind. After a moment she said, "You know, I was miserable at Fort Campbell."

Brodie didn't respond.

"Steve was a good partner, and we were clearing cases. That should have been enough. But it wasn't." She looked at Brodie. "And I realized . . . everything that happened on our last mission together, it made me feel something I hadn't felt since my time in Afghanistan. The way everything was . . . heightened."

Brodie looked her in the eyes. "I understand."

At first glance, Maggie Taylor was disciplined, rational, and career-driven. That's how most people in CID would have described her. But on a closer look, she was a person who rushed headlong into danger in a way that was more than just brave, and she made a lot of risky decisions — not the least of which was agreeing to be Scott Brodie's partner.

He asked, "When you told your people at Fort Campbell that you were leaving to take another case with me, what did they say?"

She hesitated. "I was told that it was a career-making case with a career-killing partner." She added, "And that Colonel Dombroski was a fool for giving this case to you, and it was only because of his blind loyalty to you that you have not been relieved of duty."

Brodie didn't respond.

"I'm sorry, Scott. I didn't want to tell you that."

"Maggie, I wouldn't have lasted this long if I gave a shit what people say." He picked up his drink and said, "Here's to dragging you down with me."

They clinked glasses and drank.

Taylor said, "This morning, sitting through that briefing, I was thinking that this was going to turn out just how we feared, we'd be spectators in our own investigation. And the only thing that made me feel better was the thought that at least I'm with you." She looked at him. "Someone who understands what's missing."

Brodie looked at her. They were two vets screwed up by two different wars. And even though they'd traded their combat fatigues for civilian suits, they hadn't left the military — and hadn't really left the war either. Brodie knew this about himself, and now Taylor was figuring it out.

Taylor stared off, a bit glassy-eyed now.

Then she turned back to him and said, "I want to dance."

"I can't imagine that feeling."

Taylor smiled at him. "C'mon, Scott. Live a little."

"I live at the bar."

She got up and put her hand on his arm. He grudgingly got off the stool and they walked through the red curtain and down a dark hallway that opened to a large room with a dance floor and a stage at the back. Onstage, a twenty-something Turkish hipster guy was on electric guitar, cranking out a vaguely Middle Eastern groove. A young woman in a tight T-shirt, miniskirt, and fishnets was cooing some breathy lyrics in Turkish into the microphone. Behind them, a floppy-haired drummer tapped out a down-tempo beat. Multicolored spotlights pulsed above the stage and on the dance floor.

"This is great," said Taylor.

"It's something."

They walked onto the dance floor where a few dozen people were dancing or shuffling to the beat as they drank. It was a diverse, all-ages crowd. A gray-haired Turkish man who was high on life or maybe something else was really getting into it with a young German girl.

Taylor closed her eyes and started moving her body to the music, then looked up at Brodie and said, "C'mon, partner."

He started dancing. Taylor looked up at him, the kaleidoscope of colors flashing over her face as she inched closer to him, swaying her hips to the music. She was a good dancer. She smiled at him.

Brodie's head was swimming from the whiskey and the hypnotic light show. The hooky guitar line and driving drumbeat kept repeating over and over as he and Taylor drew closer to each other. He put his hand on her waist. She had her eyes closed and was feeling the music. The singer let out a high note. Taylor pressed into him.

Over Taylor's shoulder Brodie noticed a man staring at them across the dance floor. He lost sight of the guy in the crowd for a moment, then spotted him again, skirting the edge of the crowd and watching them. He was Middle Eastern–looking, mid-thirties, short in stature, and wearing a black bomber jacket and dark pants.

The music changed to something more up-tempo, and Taylor kept pace. Brodie maintained a visual on the guy, who was momentarily lit up by the club lights as he texted something on his phone and then brought his gaze back to them.

Well, things were getting interesting on this dance floor in more ways than one. Brodie pulled Taylor close and whispered in her ear, "We might have a tail." He led Taylor toward the edge of the dance floor and said, "Back to the front."

They walked quickly up the hallway to the front room and sat at the bar. Brodie eyed the red curtain partition. The barmaid asked if they wanted another drink and Brodie declined.

Suddenly the door to the street swung open and Brodie noticed three men entering. They wore black topcoats and black pants and looked Middle Eastern. They glanced around the dimly lit lounge. One of the men fixed his eyes on Brodie and Taylor and said something to the other two, who followed his gaze.

Brodie said to Taylor, "I don't think they're here for the music."

She nodded.

Brodie said, "Put your right hand in your coat pocket."

She nodded again and put her hand in her pocket, signaling to the men that she was armed and ready to pull. Brodie did the same, finding a toothpick in his pocket, which would not pass as a 9mm Beretta if he pulled it. Brodie recalled General Kiernan's words of wisdom: *This is Germany, Mr. Brodie, not Venezuela. You don't need a gun here.*

The man in the bomber jacket emerged through the red curtain and nodded his head toward Brodie as he passed them. Two of the men in topcoats moved toward the bar, and the tallest guy stood by the exit, which confirmed to Brodie what he already knew: These guys were not here to dance.

One of the men took a seat at the bar, leaving an empty stool between him and Brodie. The other man stood behind them.

The barmaid said something in German to the seated guy, who replied, "Coke, bitte."

Brodie looked openly at the guy at the bar and they made eye contact. The guy smiled and nodded, as though acknowledging Brodie's presence. He also noted Brodie's hand in his pocket.

Brodie continued to look at the man seated next to him. He was a thick, barrel-chested guy of about fifty-five with short salt-and-pepper hair that was plastered with pomade. His deep-set eyes were cloaked in shadow above a prominent nose. He wore a black T-shirt and an expensive-looking gray suit beneath his topcoat, and a thin gold chain around his neck. Several jeweled rings adorned the fingers of his hand resting on the bar.

The Coke arrived and the man held it up toward Brodie and said, "Cheers," as though he knew what language to use.

If Brodie had his gun, he would have pulled it, said, "Cheers," and put a round through the glass. Well, maybe not. But a nice thought.

The man turned in his seat toward Brodie and put out his hand. "My name is Rafeeq Nasir. What is your name?"

"Mr. Beretta."

Nasir withdrew his hand.

Brodie gestured to Taylor. "And this is Mrs. Beretta. Nice to meet you."

It occurred to Brodie that he might have totally misread this, which would be funny. Not to mention racially insensitive. But the guy in the bomber jacket had definitely followed them to the bar, and these guys had all positioned themselves like pros. When it looks like trouble, it is.

Nasir again glanced at where Brodie's hand was deep in his pocket, probably thinking the same thing. Nasir said, "You are, I believe, Mr. Jack Davis."

Well, the visit to the Islamic center had shaken something out of the tree. In this business, whatever you're looking for will usually find you before you find it.

"How do you know my name?"

Nasir gestured to the man in the bomber jacket. "Hasan told me. He was told by Caleb at the Al Mahdi Islamic Center."

Brodie looked at Hasan, who stood with his back against the wall. Unlike the three pros who had just entered, Hasan actually looked somewhat uncomfortable with this situation.

Brodie turned back to Nasir. "I told Caleb my name, not my evening itinerary."

Nasir smiled. "Well, then, I must admit that my friend Hasan has been following you since you left the center."

Neither Brodie nor Taylor had picked up the tail until the dance floor. Maybe because they weren't looking for one. But they should have been.

Taylor asked, "Why were you following us?"

Nasir glanced at Taylor as though Brodie's camel had just started talking. He didn't reply.

So Brodie asked the same question.

Nasir replied, "I have some information for you."

"Okay. Let's hear it."

He looked around the lounge. "Someplace more private. I have a car outside. We can speak there."

"I don't get into cars with strangers. Look, pal, if you got something to say, say it. There's nobody in this fucking joint."

Nasir summoned the barmaid and said something to her in German, and they chatted. The barmaid seemed to sense — or knew from experience — that Mr. Nasir felt very comfortable here and was used to getting what he wanted.

Nasir said to Brodie, "The bar lady says there is a manager's office in the back which we can use."

Brodie looked at Taylor. "What's the stupidest thing I can do?"

"Hard to top what you've already done."

Nasir interrupted, "This lady stays here. My two companions stay there. We go to this office with Hasan."

Taylor replied before Brodie could, "You don't make the rules. We make the rules."

Nasir didn't like that, but he said nothing and looked at both of them. By now he knew that these two Americans were more than the bereaved friends of their deceased compatriot. Which was why he'd had them followed all night.

Nasir said to Brodie, "You asked for information. I am here to give it to you."

Taylor interjected, "You could have done that about six hours ago."

Nasir was getting annoyed at the American woman and said, bluntly, "If we wanted to kidnap you — or kill you — that would already be done."

Brodie said to Taylor, "He makes a good point."

She ignored Brodie and said to Nasir, "Are you selling this information? Or giving it away?"

Nasir replied, "It is free." He added, "I don't need your money."

"What do you need?"

"I need peace. I don't need trouble for my people, or my community. This is all I want."

Taylor and Brodie exchanged glances, and Taylor gave him a slight nod.

Brodie was the boss, but Taylor had more experience in dealing with Middle Eastern types. Brodie had been in Iraq to kill the bad guys; Taylor had been in Afghanistan to talk to them. "Okay," he said to Nasir. "Thank you for giving up your evening to follow us around. We'd like to hear what you have to say. And here's the deal — you and I and this lady go in the back room. All your friends stay here." Brodie and Taylor stood.

Nasir hesitated, then said, "Hasan comes too. He has information that you should hear from him directly." He added, "Unlike me and my friends here, he is harmless. A civilian."

Brodie eyed Hasan, who actually looked scared shitless. He said, "Fine."

Nasir got off his barstool. He threw a hundred on the bar, and the barmaid gave him a key and said something to him in German.

Nasir turned to his man standing close by and spoke to him in Arabic. The man replied.

Brodie glanced at Taylor, who spoke passable Arabic, and she nodded, indicating that what she'd heard wasn't something like, "Let's kill these bastards in the back room."

Nasir led the way back through the red curtain and into the hallway, with Hasan close behind him and Brodie and Taylor following. Beyond the hall Brodie could see the dancing and music were still going.

On the left wall of the hallway were two doors labeled W.C. To the right was a door marked <u>PRIVAT</u>, which Nasir opened with the key.

He led them all into a small, windowless office furnished with a simple gray steel desk, steel shelves, and four olive-drab, wood-and-canvas camp chairs.

Brodie turned a chair to face the door and Taylor did the same, then Brodie slid two chairs against the closed door and motioned Nasir and Hasan to sit, which they did.

Brodie and Taylor sat facing the two men and the door, their hands still in their empty pockets.

Nasir asked the obvious question. "Who are you?"

Brodie replied, "We're not here to answer questions."

Taylor added, "You came to us."

Nasir reminded her, "Your friend here came to the Islamic center. Under false pretenses."

Taylor did not reply, but Brodie could hear her thinking, *That wasn't my fucking idea.*

Brodie said to Nasir, "You're on."

He nodded and looked at them. "As I said, my name is Rafeeq Nasir. If you were from around here, that name would mean a great deal to you. I have prominence in this community, and my people rely on me." He added, "The murder of Mr. Vance has made a lot of people nervous and is bad for business. Well, maybe not your business. What are you? FBI? American Army?"

Brodie regarded the man. Mr. Nasir seemed eager to tell them what he knew, and when a guy is eager to sell, he'll settle for scraps in return. Unless he was about to feed them bullshit, in which case you get what you pay for. Brodie said, "Army CID."

"May I see your identification?"

"I'm not asking to see yours. Don't ask to see mine."

Nasir smiled and said something in Arabic to Hasan, who did not appear to find any of this funny. They exchanged a few words, and once again Brodie relied on his partner to discern whether the men were discussing how best to kill the Americans and chop up their bodies.

Nasir turned back to them and said, "It will be easy for me to find your names on my own, but to be honest it is not so important." He gestured to Hasan. "My friend here, he is a good man. A pious man. And like any good Muslim he is ready to help a stranger in need." He looked at Brodie. "Even those who come to a place of worship with words of deceit." He then patted Hasan's arm to signal for the man to talk.

Hasan cleared his throat and looked at Brodie and Taylor. He spoke in slow, halting English: "I saw this man, Harry Vance. He come to our center on Thursday. He speak to the imam. He give a different name. Say he is a writer . . . a reporter. He is looking for

311

Iraqis who come to live in Berlin after the war in Iraq."

Well, that confirmed Brodie's suspicion that Harry had been to the Al Mahdi Center. But . . . Iraqi refugees? What was that about?

Hasan continued, "I hear of this. I am from Iraq, I come here to live in 2006. I call Mr. Vance, he asks me questions about myself. Where I am from. What I do in Iraq before Germany. He tells me he look for Ba'ath people . . . Saddam's people . . . who come to Berlin after the war."

Brodie considered that. Saddam Hussein was dead, his Ba'ath Party had been dissolved, and most Iraqis who had held any prominence within the regime had been killed in battle, thrown in jail, or sent straight to Hell through a hangman's noose.

Nasir stepped in. "Hasan does not know these kinds of men. But he knows Rafeeq Nasir, and I know everyone. Wishing to be helpful to the American, Hasan comes to me. But I am not so trusting. I want to know what this American wants. I had also heard that he had gone to other mosques in the neighborhood — Sunni mosques — with the same request. So I call Mr. Vance to find out what he really wants. He tells me something about writing a story on the legacy of the war, or something. Whatever. All bullshit anyway, yes? This I could tell. He was a detective, like you, trying to get information."

"How could you be so sure?" asked Taylor.

Nasir looked at her. "I have talked to police and I have talked to reporters, and I can tell the difference."

Well, thought Brodie, being undercover wasn't really Harry Vance's area of expertise. His routine was good enough to work on the civilians at the Al Mahdi Center, but not on a shrewd denizen of the criminal underworld.

Nasir continued, "I told Mr. Vance I knew a few people who fit this description — former Iraqi Ba'ath Party men who had re-settled in Germany — but I needed to understand more about what he was working on before I would be willing to share their identities. He eventually got to the point of what he was really looking for — not political people, but former military or intelligence officers from Saddam's regime. And then I understood that Mr. Vance was looking for a *particular* man, a former Ba'ath Party military intelligence officer who he knew lived in Berlin and perhaps in Neukölln."

"How did you come to that conclusion?" asked Brodie.

"Because I knew of a man who fit this description, living in Neukölln, who had taken a new identity since immigrating. I think Mr. Vance had learned that this man lived in Berlin, and that he had changed his name, and Mr. Vance was trying to locate this Iraqi under his new identity." He added, "So

313

I gave Mr. Vance the name. And three days later, Mr. Vance is dead."

Taylor asked, "Who is this man?"

"His real name was Tariq Qasim. The rumors were that he worked in military intelligence for Saddam's special warfare program." He looked at Brodie. "You understand?"

Brodie gave a slight nod. *Special warfare.* Which meant biological, chemical, and nuclear weapons. He didn't know why Harry was looking for Tariq Qasim, but this case had suddenly taken on a new and more frightening dimension.

Nasir added, "After Saddam was overthrown, Qasim came here and changed his name to Abbas al-Hamdani. He started a new life. He had a shoe store a few blocks from here. So I gave Mr. Vance his cell phone number."

Brodie wondered if this was all an elaborate lie to gum up the investigation. But if Rafeeq Nasir was involved with Vance's murder, he was taking an enormous risk in having this encounter just to drop some bullshit in the pipeline.

Brodie asked, "Why are you helping us?"

"I don't like dead Americans in my neighborhood. There are police everywhere now. Also the right-wing Germans who threaten my people with violence. I want you to solve this case, and quickly." He smiled and added,

314

"You can tell the German investigators how helpful Rafeeq Nasir was to you."

Actually, the Germans might decide that Rafeeq Nasir was suspect number one. But the man seemed confident in his story — even if it was part bullshit — and confident he was not going to get pegged for this murder.

Taylor asked, "If you knew Harry Vance was law enforcement, why did you help him and reveal al-Hamdani's identity?"

Nasir shrugged. "Hamdani owed me money. So I owed him nothing."

She asked, "How do we find this man?"

Nasir replied, "You can't. No one has seen Abbas al-Hamdani since Friday evening, when he was spotted by a few people having tea at a café. He was supposed to open his shoe store at noon on Saturday, but he never arrived. And no one can reach him by phone. Then early the following morning, Mr. Vance's body was found in the park." He added, "I doubt al-Hamdani's body will ever be found."

Taylor asked, "Did he live alone?"

Nasir nodded. "His wife died a few years ago."

Brodie said, "If Hamdani was Vance's killer, he could have skipped town."

Nasir laughed. "Abbas was a sad, old, fat little man. Not capable of killing."

Taylor pointed out, "He worked with weapons of mass destruction, but he wasn't capable of killing someone?"

Nasir shook his head. "Making choices that kill thousands, that's easy. Pulling the trigger and killing one man . . ." He trailed off, as if he were recalling some personal experiences with that activity. It occurred to Brodie that if Mr. Nasir was as important as he claimed to be, he was also a dangerous man, and Brodie would have liked something in his pocket other than a toothpick.

Nasir continued, "As for Hamdani going into hiding because his identity was discovered, this is not so easy either. This requires resources and powerful allies, things he no longer had. No, I am certain that whoever killed Harry Vance also killed Abbas al-Hamdani."

Taylor said, "And the killer got rid of Hamdani's body, but left Vance to be discovered in a city park."

Nasir looked at her. "I'm sure you can figure that one out. If Mr. Vance's murder was not an act of Islamic terrorism, what better place for his body to show up than Neukölln? This is a useful distraction, yes? It makes people like you waste your time investigating the wrong things. And the press gets to blame their favorite villain, the Arabs." He continued, "The German authorities already know about Mr. Vance's trip to the Al Mahdi Center and his request for information about

Iraqi immigrants. The police interviewed people at the Islamic center, including Hasan here. Everyone was truthful that they either did not speak to Mr. Vance or spoke to him briefly but gave him no information. Everyone, that is, except Hasan, who lied and claimed he never spoke with Mr. Vance." He threw a critical look at Hasan, who was staring at the floor. "He was trying to protect me, you see. He meant well, but it was the wrong choice. Never tell a lie that gets you in more trouble than the truth. Hasan will contact the police tomorrow and correct his statement, and deal with the consequences."

Nasir said something to Hasan in Arabic. Hasan nodded, fished a scrap of paper out of his back pocket, and gave it to Brodie. On the paper was a handwritten phone number.

Nasir explained, "Should you need to contact Hasan directly for any follow-up."

Brodie put the paper in his jacket pocket and regarded Hasan. The man had escaped the hell of his own war-torn country for a better life in Europe, only to find himself under the thumb of a warlord by another name.

Nasir said, "I am sure you will agree I have been very helpful."

Brodie replied, "You're helping yourself."

Nasir said, "Our interests align. If they didn't, we would have a problem."

"Is that a threat?"

Nasir looked him in the eyes. "I do not threaten. I just say how it is." He eyed their hands in their pockets. "And when I deceive, I do a better job of it than you, and the late Mr. Vance." He stood, and they all rose from their chairs. "I hope that your stay in our neighborhood is productive, and brief." He added, with a smile, "But you should find better lodgings. That place is a shithole."

Brodie wondered if Mustafa was late on his protection payments. More importantly, Rafeeq Nasir was letting them know that he knew where they slept, which made sense if Hasan had been following Brodie since his visit to the Islamic center.

Taylor said, "You made your point. Now drop the surveillance. Or *you* will be the one with the problem."

Rafeeq Nasir looked like he was not used to being talked to like that, especially by a woman, but he tried to hide his annoyance and said calmly, "I grew up during the civil war in Lebanon. Every street of my neighborhood in Beirut was a death trap of snipers and mines and ambushes. If you let your guard down, you were dead. I learned many lessons in this and formed some useful habits. I keep my eyes on my neighborhood."

Well, if Nasir truly had eyes everywhere around here, he'd know who had killed Harry Vance.

Brodie thought back to Mark Jenkins' account of being followed. Could that have been Nasir's people? It might make sense that they'd want to keep an eye on him, but how would they even know who he was in relation to Vance, and that he was in town and staying in Alexanderplatz? Rafeeq Nasir might be lord of his fiefdom here in Neukölln, but that didn't mean he was capable of IDing and locating Mark Jenkins. There were also Faruk's "powerful men" present at Ember Berlin at the same time as Harry. Neukölln was an interesting and complex place.

Brodie asked Nasir, "Did you have someone watching Vance the night of his murder?"

"Why would I do that?"

"Well, two guys in your line of work were at the Ember Berlin hookah lounge at the same time as Vance, about thirty minutes before he was killed."

Nasir thought about that a moment. "My men do not go to this place. But I know who does."

"Who?"

"A different family. I will look into it." He added, "But this was likely a coincidence. People like us don't kill policemen. It is bad for business."

"Unless it *was* business," said Taylor.

Nasir shot her a look. "Wild speculation can be dangerous for everyone."

Brodie suddenly saw Rafeeq Nasir in a different light — not as a street thug, or a mobster, but as a merchant of information in a competitive market whose organization had failed him.

Long before the Gestapo or the Stasi, crime families had always had their own primitive but effective versions of intelligence outfits. Eyes on the street. Ears to the ground. A network of informants, like Hasan, who had gone out of his way to follow Brodie for hours, probably without even being ordered to do so. Hasan just knew what was expected of him. There had been a murder in Rafeeq Nasir's hood, and the boss had no clue who had done it, or why. That had to be fixed.

Brodie said, "You will be hearing from the German authorities."

"I will look forward to it, as always." Nasir pulled the two chairs away from the office door and opened it, then gestured for Brodie and Taylor to exit.

Brodie said, "We're not leaving yet. But you and your men are."

Nasir nodded and said, "As you wish." He led Hasan out of the office, then turned back to them and said, "May you deliver justice for your colleague. Swiftly." He walked out and shut the door behind him.

CHAPTER 18

Brodie and Taylor sat at the bar in Proletariat. They both needed a shot of caffeine, and Brodie asked the barmaid, "Do you have coffee?"

"Nein."

Brodie held up two fingers. "Good. We'll take two of the nine."

"Bitte?"

Taylor said to the barmaid, "Two Cokes, bitte."

She nodded and moved off.

Brodie said to Taylor, "She probably thinks we converted to Islam in the manager's office." He suggested, "Order a brandy."

"Are you done?"

"I think so."

The barmaid put the Cokes in front of them. "No charge."

"Thank you," said Taylor. She took out her phone and said to Brodie, "I'll get us an Uber."

He reminded her, "I make the tactical decisions, Ms. Taylor. We'll walk. I want to find a kebab joint."

"You can walk. I'm riding back to the hotel."

"You're insubordinate."

"I learned from the best." She added, "I can't believe you missed the opportunity to make a joke about using 'Uber' in Germany."

"Low-hanging fruit."

"When has that stopped you?"

The only military women who spoke to him like this were the ones he'd slept with. Maybe this was foreplay.

They sipped their Cokes for a minute, then Taylor's phone dinged. She stood and zipped her coat. "Car's here." She said to the barmaid, "Gute Nacht."

The barmaid looked at them and said, "Those men . . . you need to be careful."

"Thank you," said Taylor.

They walked to the door and Brodie said, "Tactical exit." Taylor told him the license plate number of their car, and he opened the door while she stayed behind.

Out in the frigid air, Brodie checked out the dimly lit street, his hand in his pocket. The Uber idled at the curb, and a few other vehicles were parked, but looked empty. No sign of their Arab Tony Soprano or his friends.

He gave the bar door two raps, signaling all-clear, then went to the taxi and opened the rear passenger door as Taylor came out and headed for the open door.

As she slid in and over, Brodie slid in beside her, pulling the door closed.

The driver, who appeared Middle Eastern, looked at his smartphone to confirm the destination. "Körnerpark?"

"Ja," said Taylor.

The taxi moved off.

Taylor said to Brodie, "I compliment you on your good security and good judgment."

Brodie replied, "But when the bad guys make you change how you live, they win."

"They also win when they kill you."

They rode in silence, and the dark streets of Berlin glided by out the window. As they approached Körnerpark and the Art Hotel, Brodie asked the driver, "English?"

The man replied, "Little."

"East side of Körnerpark, bitte. Wittmannsdorfer Straße."

The driver nodded.

Taylor said to Brodie, "I'd pinned the south side. Closest to our hotel, which is where we're going."

"I want to walk through the park. We haven't surveyed it at night."

"You can sleep in the park for all I care. I'm going to the hotel."

The driver said, "Man killed in park. American." He added, "But park safe."

"Sounds safe," said Brodie. "Where are you from?"

"Syria. Not safe."

"It's all relative."

"Yes? Where you go?"

Brodie looked at Taylor, who stayed silent. She was tired, and probably also tired of her partner's bullshit. But after a moment she said to the driver, "East side of the park. Wittmannsdorfer Straße."

They pulled up on the side street at the east end of the park, Brodie paid, and they got out.

They walked to the wrought-iron fence and looked down into Körnerpark. They were standing in roughly the same spot that Captain Soliman believed the killer had stood for his kill shot. As Brodie had noted earlier, there was no streetlamp nearby. And now, looking down into the park at night, Brodie appreciated how dark the area was where Vance had been standing when he was shot. Perhaps he'd chosen that spot deliberately, as it was a distance from any of the streetlamps that lined the park's paved pathways. If so, it was a gesture toward operational security, but not nearly good enough. Especially against a trained marksman with a night vision scope.

Taylor stood next to Brodie and looked down into the dark greenery. She said, "Harry Vance was working a secret investigation in the days before his murder, an investigation that somehow involved Iraqi immigrants and maybe Saddam Hussein's military intelligence apparatus and WMD programs. Maybe someone was selling secrets. Or, God forbid, a few dozen vials of anthrax. But Vance told no one. Why?"

"So you're choosing to believe Nasir?"

Taylor handed him her phone, which featured what appeared to be a surveillance photo of Rafeeq Nasir getting out of a black Mercedes.

Taylor said, "He is who he said he is. Heads the third-largest Arab crime family in Berlin. He's indirectly implicated in five unsolved homicides." She added, "Tonight could have gone differently."

"Right. I could have not gone to the Al Mahdi Center, and not shaken something out of the tree, and then we would not have received vital Intel that completely reframes this case."

"Good luck is a poor substitute for good judgment. And eventually, good luck runs out."

"Good judgment is no substitute for calculated risk and aggressive action."

"You're not in the infantry anymore, Scott."

"It's all the same. I survived Baghdad, and I will survive Berlin."

"You had a gun in Baghdad."

Good point. Brodie said, "Let's walk through the park."

They went to the eastern entrance and

stepped over a chain, then headed down into the park.

As they walked, Taylor said, "Back to the ill-fated Harry Vance. What is his *motive* for his secrecy? I don't see motive."

"Let's for a moment assume the worst of the departed. He was selling Intel or maybe something worse."

"Do you really believe he was capable of that?"

"People surprise you. Especially when they're under financial strain or thinking with the wrong head."

Taylor thought about that. "Anna knows what this is about."

"The clues you haven't found yet always look the juiciest."

Taylor looked at him. "Harry went to a lot of trouble to see this woman. I think they were close. And if he was keeping a secret from everyone, that didn't include her."

Well, Ms. Taylor did know a few things about sleeping with a guy weighed down by secrets. As if anticipating what Brodie was thinking, she added, "I wish I could forget most of the things Trent told me. It was like . . . he'd confide in me, to gauge my re-action. Not to shock me, but . . . to get some reassurance from me that he hadn't lost his soul."

"He was also compromising you."

She had no reply.

Well, apparently CIA Officer Trent Chilcott's idea of pillow talk involved Black Ops and extrajudicial assassinations. Creepy. Was he at least good in the sack? Brodie hoped not. He said, "We will find Anna tomorrow."

"She might be the key. But I guess she could also lead nowhere. Just an innocent and ignorant woman who happened to be shtupping the murder victim."

"Good Yiddish."

"Thanks. I Googled it."

They walked off the path into the grass near the central fountain and Brodie looked around. A fine mist filled the air, and a glowing half-moon bled through the thick clouds above.

Taylor said, "This is where Harry was standing."

"More or less."

Taylor looked around the dim park and asked, "Would you have met someone here who you didn't know at three in the morning?"

"Not without backup." Maybe.

"Me neither. And Harry was smart. Experienced. So, *what* was he thinking?"

Brodie thought about that. "Harry brought his piece, and he was holding it when he died, so it's not that he wasn't apprehensive. I think this park wasn't part of the plan. He wanted to meet . . . let's say this guy Abbas al-Hamdani, if we choose to believe Nasir.

Harry wanted to meet Hamdani in public. At the hookah lounge. Then he gets a message: 'Hey, Harry, let's meet in this creepy park instead.' And Harry says sure."

"Why would he agree to that? Just insist on the original plan. Or threaten to walk."

"He had no leverage," said Brodie. "He needed something from Hamdani, not the other way around. Also, maybe he felt he had nothing to fear from this guy. He wasn't meeting with an al Qaeda informant or another bad actor. Sounds like Hamdani was middle management in a defunct regime. Far from power, far from influence. But he had *something.* Something Harry perceived as valuable — but not dangerous."

"The guy worked with the most deadly weapons on the planet."

"A long time ago." He added, without thinking, "Unexploded ordnance."

"What?"

He looked at the surrounding buildings. "Over a million tons of bombs were dropped on Germany during the war, and a lot of them didn't explode. And every few months somewhere in this country they're digging a rail tunnel or a foundation pit for a new building, and they find one of these things, an old 'fuck you' from the past, and people need to evacuate so a special team can dispose of the bomb before it blows everyone up."

"Is this a metaphor?"

"Yeah . . . Harry was digging for something. Something buried from the past. But what he didn't know was that down there in the sands of time was an old bomb that had been waiting to explode."

Taylor didn't respond. They both stood in silence for a minute. On the street above, they heard a glass bottle shatter, followed by a drunken cackle.

Taylor yawned. "All right, Mr. Brodie, a lot to think about. Let no one say you don't show a girl an interesting time."

They walked up the stairs on the south side of the park, then crossed the street and entered the Art Hotel.

The Turkish kid, Ayaz, was behind the desk playing with his cell phone and he barely looked up. Brodie asked him, "What time do you lock the front door?"

"Soon."

"Lock it now." He added, "We are not expecting any visitors. But Ms. Taylor's husband is looking for us. Do not let anyone in who you don't know. And call our rooms if anyone comes looking for us. Understand?"

Ayaz nodded.

Brodie put a fifty-euro note on the counter. "Fifty more if you call us."

The tip seemed to get Ayaz's attention. He looked at Brodie and said, "Yes, sir."

Brodie and Taylor headed toward the staircase. She asked him, "Is that something you learned in class, or learned in life?"

"Both."

They ascended the staircase and passed the second-floor kitchen, where a group of backpackers, male and female, were sitting around a table, speaking French and sharing a few pizzas and a bottle of wine. They looked up, and a few of them smiled and motioned for Brodie and Taylor to join them. Taylor said something to them in French, and they all laughed.

"What did you tell them?"

"I said, 'Sorry, I have to get this old man to bed.' "

"That's not funny."

"It is in French."

They walked up to the third floor and stopped at their rooms. Taylor turned to Brodie. "We did okay tonight."

"We did."

"You're a good detective, Mr. Brodie." She smiled. "And a decent dancer."

"Don't tell anyone."

She smiled again, then swiped her keycard and turned the doorknob. Then she looked at him and said, "We need to be careful. Risks need to be worth taking. Or else . . . we're just being self-indulgent. And self-destructive."

Was she still talking about the case? After a moment she asked, "What time are we out the door?"

"Eight-thirty for the nine A.M. briefing."

"That doesn't leave time for breakfast."

"That strudel will still be on the conference table."

She smiled. "Good night." She entered her room and Brodie watched the door slowly shut behind her, which also closed the door on any more reckless choices and excitement for the night. But there was always tomorrow.

Brodie walked into his room and switched on the lights, tossed off his coat, and chugged a couple of glasses of water from the tap. He realized that he needed to update Dombroski, which was the last thing he felt like doing. He'd had maybe three hours of sleep in the last thirty-six and was ready to crash. He'd make it short.

He sat on the edge of the bed and called the colonel, who picked up after one ring. "Good evening, Mr. Brodie."

"Good evening, sir."

"It's late there."

"Yes, sir. It has been a long and productive night."

"I want to hear about it. But first, I spoke with Colonel Trask a few hours ago, he's giving us Vance and Jenkins' CID reports from the past eighteen months. He's securely transmitting them to the Defense Attaché Office in the embassy, where you can retrieve them tomorrow when you go for your briefing. Minimal redactions. Hopefully some good reading."

"I'm glad the Fifth MP is being co-operative."

"They want this done right. And I assured Colonel Trask that I had my two best agents on the case."

"Thank you for your confidence and your compliment."

"I want Scott Brodie's ego working *for* me, not against me." He added, "Update me on your progress."

"I think we found out what Vance was doing here in Neukölln. He was looking for a military Intel officer in Saddam Hussein's special warfare program who immigrated to Germany after the war. Guy named Tariq Qasim."

"Who told you this?"

"A Lebanese mobster, name of Rafeeq Nasir."

"And how did you get in contact with this gentleman?"

"He found us. Long story. Nasir claims he's helping us because he wants this case wrapped up quickly so that the cops-to-robbers ratio in his neighborhood goes down."

"How did you come to this man's attention? Just being your discreet self?"

He told Dombroski about his visit to the Al Mahdi Islamic Center, and being subsequently followed by Hasan, as well as Vance's original visit there. He also told Dombroski about the man Faruk whom they'd questioned at the hookah lounge. "So, Vance goes to this mosque looking for former Iraqi Ba'athists — and, according to my underworld source, he went to a handful of other mosques in the area as well — then he gets a name and number from Rafeeq Nasir, then gets in touch with this Iraqi guy Tariq Qasim, apparently arranges a meeting at the hookah lounge, and . . . Qasim doesn't show, and Harry goes for a walk through the park, or the guy changes the meeting place to the park instead of the lounge. Either way, sounds like a setup."

"It also sounds like we have a suspect. Tariq Qasim."

"Right. The problem is Qasim has disappeared."

"He's fled."

"Or he's dead. Nasir believes that whoever killed Harry also killed Qasim."

"Is that a theory of his? Or did he personally wrap piano wire around the guy's neck?"

"I don't think he's involved beyond what he told us. Otherwise he took too big of a risk revealing himself to us."

"Maybe he's an idiot who thought he was being clever. There's a lot of that going around."

"I don't think so, sir."

Dombroski thought about that. "You were

face-to-face with Mr. Nasir, so I trust your instincts. But I'm sure the German authorities will be labeling him a person of interest."

"I'm sure. But I don't want to get off track. This Iraqi guy is the key. Tariq Qasim. After he came to Germany, he changed his name to Abbas al-Hamdani. We need to find out more about him." Brodie reminded Dombroski, "Tariq Qasim was involved with Iraqi weapons of mass destruction."

"All right. I'll run both those names by a couple Intel guys I trust with experience in Iraq, see if anything comes back."

"Thank you, sir."

"Anything else?"

He told the colonel about their excursion in Prenzlauer Berg, and the woman named Anna whom they were going to try to find tomorrow with the help of the metro surveillance footage.

"You've been busy, Scott. Almost a Teutonic work ethic."

"Must be something in the water." He added, "I get the sense that we are sometimes walking in the German investigator's footsteps." He mentioned Fatima, the eyewitness they'd located earlier in the day, who had already spoken with the police, and also the cops who had already paid visits to the Vietnamese noodle shop and the hookah lounge. "None of this was mentioned in the briefing. Nor was the fact that the authorities were already aware of Harry's visit to the Al Mahdi Islamic Center."

Dombroski processed that. "This is a complex investigation, and the Germans have multiple agencies on this. Multiple streams of Intel. I'm not surprised there's a bottleneck in disseminating information."

"That's a very generous interpretation, sir."

"Listen, Scott. I know you, and I know you like to keep your cards close to the chest until you have a winning hand. But that's not the game you're playing. You have gone well beyond your mandate, but you've also got a lot to show for it, which should mitigate some of the fallout with the FBI and the Germans. You share what you know, as you learn it, and without conditions. This is about justice for Harry Vance. Not about you."

"I don't need to be reminded of that, Colonel."

"But you do need to be reminded not to get hung up on process with these people, because they are bound to disappoint you and piss you off. That's baked into the cake."

"I understand."

Dombroski asked, "And how is Ms. Taylor?"

"Doing a good job."

"And you're working well together?"

"We are."

"Anything further?"

"Nothing further."

Dombroski was silent a moment. "It sounds like you're back in the shit, Scott. Right where you want to be."

"Trouble has a way of finding me, sir."

"I think it's because you paint a target on your ass."

"Yes, sir."

"Get some rest, Mr. Brodie." Dombroski hung up.

Brodie set an alarm on his phone, then plugged it in on the end table, threw off his clothes, and hit the lights. He collapsed onto the cheap mattress and stared up at the abstract art above the bed, which looked a little better in the dark. Outside, the mist had turned into rain that pattered against the window.

His closed his eyes and imagined the man he remembered, Chief Warrant Officer Harry Vance. He was in front of the class at the Army MP School in Fort Leonard Wood, discussing the organizational structure of terrorist cells. His lecturing style was always a bit dry, almost aloof. But he didn't need to try hard to make his students care about what he was saying. There were killers out there who could strike anywhere at any time, and the guy at the front of the room was giving the eager agents-in-training the tools for stopping them.

Brodie took this vision of the man and put him on a five-hour train across Germany to see a woman named Anna, who was maybe the love of his life, or maybe just a diversion from a failed marriage. He imagined them walking around picturesque Prenzlauer Berg, shopping for small-batch schnapps.

Brodie then pictured Vance knocking on doors of mosques throughout Neukölln pretending to be a journalist. Sitting in a hookah lounge waiting to meet a man with intimate knowledge of the deadliest weapons ever made. Descending into a dark city park in the last moments of his life. The shot. The fall. A figure descending the steps, a sharp object in hand, coming to collect a gruesome trophy . . . *An eye for an eye.*

The relationship with Anna wasn't a cover for the investigation, and the investigation wasn't a cover for the relationship. Both were well-kept secrets. So maybe both were part of the same thing.

You're not solving a puzzle. You're defusing a bomb.

Vance had said that about his own work in counterterror in the post-9/11 era, where the crimes and atrocities existed on a continuum, one following the next. While Harry Vance gathered evidence and testimony and looked for suspects on a case, the next attack was in the nascent stages of being executed. Vance's caseload wasn't a ledger of unrelated crimes — it was a timeline of attacks and attempted attacks in a generational war.

And now, maybe that war had come here, to Berlin. And as Brodie and Taylor sought justice for their colleague, they also had to pick up his fallen sword and carry on. Brodie wished his old teacher could give him some clues.

Brodie lay in silence, listening to the rain and the wind and the sporadic sounds of cars and motorbikes, and the occasional revelers on the street below as the night wound down in the short hours before dawn. And as he drifted off, he reminded himself of something he had learned long ago: The dead can speak. You just have to know how to listen.

CHAPTER 19

Brodie and Taylor left the Art Hotel at 8:30 A.M. and headed toward Karl-Marx Straße, where they could get a taxi to the embassy.

A cold wind blew the damp, misty air under a slate-gray sky. Another perfect day in Berlin. Brodie asked, "Did you remember your sunscreen?"

She smiled. "I applied motor oil so I don't rust."

They stopped at a café on Karl-Marx to get two black coffees to go, then they left the café and walked along the wide avenue, burning off some alcohol and replacing it with caffeine.

Brodie said, "Vance and Jenkins' CID case files have been transmitted from the Fift MP Battalion to the Defense Attaché Office, where we can retrieve a printout."

"How do you know that?"

"I called Dombroski last night."

She looked annoyed. "I expect to be present when you speak to him."

"I realized I needed to call him after we got to our rooms." He added, "I would have knocked on your door, but you looked tired."

She was silent for a moment, then started to reply just as a booming sound thundered from somewhere, and Brodie felt the sidewalk shake.

He looked at Taylor, who stared back at him.

A few cars slowed down, and pedestrians stopped walking and looked around apprehensively before continuing on their way — likely coming up with a mundane explanation for whatever that loud noise was. No one expects to hear an explosion during morning rush hour, but Brodie and Taylor knew this sound, which was the same all over the world.

They dropped their coffees and ran across the four-lane road and down a side street toward where the blast had come from. The sounds of chaos grew louder: Tires screeching. Honking cars. A man shouting something in Arabic. A woman screaming.

They rounded a corner onto a narrow street lined with tightly packed residential buildings and storefronts.

A block ahead of them, a five-story apartment building was billowing smoke and fire from its top floor. Most of the top story was gone, and the pitched tile roof sagged. Rubble and shards of glass were scattered across the sidewalk and the street, which was choked with stopped cars. Ash drifted onto pedestrians staring up at the huge column of fire and smoke that rose into the gray sky.

As Brodie and Taylor continued and got closer to the site of the blast, they spotted a middle-aged Arab woman sitting on the curb, her hand over her bloodstained hijab, and a scattering of debris around her. A young German man was crouching next to her while speaking urgently into his cell phone.

Taylor approached the woman and spoke to her in Arabic. The woman seemed dazed but responded. Taylor laid the woman down on the sidewalk, took her pulse, and listened to her breathing, then turned to Brodie. "Sounds okay." She moved the woman's hand away from her head, and pulled back the hijab to reveal a bloody gash across her forehead. Taylor replaced the hijab over the wound.

The young man said in English, "Ambulance. Five minutes."

"Can you stay with her until it arrives?"

"Yes."

Taylor took the man's hand and placed it over the bleeding wound. "Pressure. Okay?"

He nodded. "Okay."

They continued toward the building. Two Berlin Police officers were now on the scene, as frightened residents ran out of the flaming building. Emergency service sirens were wailing in the distance.

341

When they were about twenty yards from the blast site, a black police van screeched up and five cops wearing helmets and body armor piled out, carrying assault rifles. Two policemen flanked the door to the apartment building while the others went to get drivers back in their cars so they could clear the street and close it off. The two cops at the door entered the building.

Brodie looked at the smoking building. Almost the entire fifth-floor façade had blown off, and the roof, sitting on unanchored rafters, looked like it could collapse any minute and slide into the street.

Through the missing façade Brodie could see part of the destroyed apartment, blackened from the blast. An overturned metal desk sat near the edge of the hole, its legs twisted and deformed. He thought he saw a charred arm sticking out from the opening.

A uniformed Berlin Police officer stepped in front of them and raised a gloved hand. "Halt. Wir schließen den Bereich."

They stopped walking as another cop wrapped police tape between street signs to cordon off the area.

Brodie looked around. Across the street, a mass of curious onlookers had gathered on the sidewalk, and his eyes landed on a middle-aged Arab man in a ratty winter coat sitting on the curb, staring up at the smoldering building. He seemed to be crying. Brodie wondered if the guy was a refugee from Syria or Iraq who thought he was done with this shit.

As for the older German residents of Neukölln, they thought they were done with this shit in 1945. But the shit goes on.

Brodie's cell phone rang and he pulled it out of his pocket. He didn't recognize the number, but answered, "Brodie."

"Good morning, Scott. It's Sharon Whitmore." Brodie put the phone on speaker so Taylor could hear. "I just received word that Chief Inspector Schröder and Captain Soliman are no longer available for the briefing, so we're postponing it."

"I think I've got a clue what they're doing instead." He informed her, "There's been an explosion here in Neukölln."

"Oh God . . . What happened? Are you both okay?"

"We're fine. But the top floor of an apartment building is not."

"Okay . . . accident? Gas leak?"

"I don't think so."

She processed that. "All right. I will let you know when I hear from the BKA. Meanwhile . . ." She paused a moment. "Stay safe."

Brodie had a feeling what she really wanted to say was, "Stay out of it." He informed her, "We have business at the Defense Attaché Office. We'll be at the embassy shortly."

She didn't ask what business, but said,

"Okay. Security has your names, and you can contact me directly if you need anything. FYI, the right-wing crazies are at it again here in Pariser Platz. Even bigger crowd than the last two days."

"Thanks for the heads-up." He added, "Hell of a morning."

"Hell of a world, Mr. Brodie. Talk to you later." She hung up.

Brodie slipped his phone in his pocket and said to Taylor, "It's a beautiful world. But the people suck."

She nodded, then looked back at the blast site as a fire engine pulled up. "Assuming it was a bomb, it was a targeted assassination."

"It would seem so." He added, "But we don't know if it was terrorism, criminal, or personal." He looked back at the building as firemen jumped out of their truck and charged inside. He'd seen this scene too many times in Baghdad. The fire, the debris, the fear. But that was another place, and another life. "Traffic will be a mess for a while. Let's take the U-Bahn."

They headed down the road away from the scene. They passed a parked ambulance where two EMTs were loading the woman they'd helped onto a stretcher.

They kept walking and Taylor said, "I can smell the burning fuel oil."

"Me too. But maybe it's only in our heads."

"It's in our souls, Scott."

"Right." What the brain buries, is buried in the soul.

CHAPTER 20

Brodie and Taylor emerged from the Brandenburger Tor U-Bahn station onto the tree-lined median between the east- and west-bound lanes of bustling Unter den Linden, the wide boulevard that ran through the heart of central Berlin. This venerable old street had become touristy with souvenir shops and a Madame Tussauds Museum. Brodie wondered if they had Hitler in wax. In any case, no one seemed to have any idea what was happening across town.

They crossed the road and headed west toward the Brandenburg Gate, passing a large, stately building that Brodie recognized as the historic Hotel Adlon, which, according to his college classmate Adam Kogan, had been Der Führer's favorite place to have afternoon tea, and which had been connected by a secret tunnel to Hitler's Reich Chancellery. Kogan, after a long night of drinking with Brodie and two German ladies, had insisted on going to the Adlon's opulent and expensive lobby bar, and after a few rounds of overpriced cocktails, Kogan had pissed in the lobby's ornate fountain, yelling, "Fuck Hitler!" which was either a creative way of skipping out on the bar tab or a heartfelt political statement. Maybe both. If Kogan had just pissed in the fountain, without the "Fuck Hitler," he'd be committing a crime. The "Fuck Hitler" had elevated the public urination to an expression of anti-Nazi activism, which caused some conflict with the hotel security guys, who decided to kick them out rather than call the police. In exchange, Kogan and his friends had to promise never to return to the Adlon, and Kogan had to put his dick back in his pants. *Schnell!*

"Scott?"

"Yeah . . . ?"

"Where'd you go?"

"I . . . was just remembering a night at the Adlon Hotel when I was here for my spring break."

"Good memories, I hope."

"Yeah. We got comped."

"Lucky you."

And later got laid. "Very lucky night." He said, "I'll take you there one night if we're here long enough. Great bar." He added, "Beautiful lobby with a fountain."

"Sounds good." She asked, "Why did you get comped?"

"I'll tell you when we're there." But not

show her.

Up ahead was Pariser Platz, a large cobblestone square that stood in front of the Brandenburg Gate. In the center of the square were about a hundred demonstrators waving flags and chanting.

As they got closer, Brodie spotted German and American flags, and a large banner being held by two men that featured the logo of the AfD party along with the words ISLAMISIERUNG STOPPEN!, which didn't really require a translation.

Amidst the flags was a sign bearing an unflattering photo of the German Chancellor with a big X over it, as well as signs that featured the portrait of Harry Vance. Brodie also spotted a fat bearded guy waving a flag he didn't recognize — white with a black Nordic cross and a Prussian eagle in the center, and the red, black, and white tricolor of the old German Empire in the upper corner beneath an iron cross.

Taylor followed his look. "That's the imperial war flag. A favorite of white nationalists here, since it's illegal to use Nazi imagery."

Brodie watched the old battle flag rippling in the wind. He understood why Germans would want to ban the swastika, but killing symbols doesn't kill the thing behind the symbol. And now the old banner of the Kaiser's armies was dusted off for a new century, and with terrible new meaning.

The crowd switched from German to English and began chanting in unison: "We are the people! We are the people!" That didn't sound malicious, but Brodie was sure he was missing some context.

In between the protestors and the embassy was a strip of landscaped lawn surrounded by a low railing. Brodie and Taylor entered the square and rounded the south side of the greenspace to avoid cutting through the protest. Brodie now spotted a line of kitted-out Berlin Police officers near the embassy, and another group of officers across the square near what appeared to be the French Embassy. After Monday's violence, the police weren't taking any chances.

Brodie and Taylor approached the American Embassy's glass-and-steel entrance, where a stone-faced U.S. Marine stood at attention. But before they could enter, a voice called out from behind them: "Hey! You! Americans!"

They turned toward the voice. A thirty-something German man with a shaved head was holding an America flag on a pole over his shoulder. He raised his right hand in a fist. "We. Are. The people!" He added, "Muslims out!"

"Fuck you," suggested Brodie.

The man looked surprised. "What?"

Taylor said, "C'mon, Scott."

Brodie stepped toward the guy. "You dishonor my flag."

The man's lips curled into a sneer. "You dishonor your race."

"Asshole." Brodie advanced on the guy.

Taylor grabbed his arm. "Not worth it, Scott. Not even a little."

Brodie noticed two of the police officers coming closer to them. He said to the skinhead, "Your grandpa already tried this shit. Didn't work out so well."

He turned and walked to the embassy entrance, with Taylor close behind. The German guy continued shouting at him in a mix of German and English, but Brodie blocked it out as he and Taylor showed their passports to the Marine guard, then pushed open the doors to the embassy.

They entered a glass-ceilinged rotunda, where the marble walls were etched with the preamble to the U.S. Constitution — WE THE PEOPLE . . . — along with a large American flag. They showed their passports and IDs to the security man behind the front desk who, as promised by Ms. Whitmore, had instructions to let them through without an appointment. The man also had a note from Jason Butler with the room number where they were to meet the Berlin Police officer to review the security footage at ten o'clock.

The security man gave them directions to the Defense Attaché Office, and they went through a metal detector and rounded a corner into the lobby where they had waited yesterday before the briefing.

Standing near the floor-to-ceiling windows facing the inner courtyard was David Kim, dressed in his tailored black suit — sans tie — and a long topcoat. He was tapping something out on his phone, then looked up and spotted them. "Hey! Guys!" He marched across the lobby. "You hear what happened in Neukölln?"

"We saw it," said Brodie.

"Wow." He looked them over as if inspecting for damage. "You guys all right?"

"We're fine," said Taylor. "But it was awful to see."

"News isn't saying much, and the BKA won't tell us anything. What did it look like to you?"

"Like a bomb went off inside a top-floor apartment," said Taylor.

Kim nodded as he thought about that.

Brodie said, "Maybe it was Hezbollah."

Kim looked at him. "I know you're being facetious, Scott, but it did cross my mind. They like to use remote bombs to carry out assassinations."

Brodie pointed out, "But if you've already gained access to your victim's apartment, why bother with a bomb?"

"Terrorists like to make grand statements. You know that."

"Right."

Kim thought, then said, "The Weather Underground. Remember them?"

Taylor replied, "Way before I was born."

"Greenwich Village bombing — 1970."

Brodie nodded. As the son of hippies who had lived in the Village in the sixties and seventies, Brodie knew all about the Weather Underground, a left-wing terrorist group who accidentally blew up a townhouse in the Village while making a bomb that killed three of their own. "So, you think Jihadi Johnny wasn't paying attention in bomb-making class and accidentally connected the yellow wire instead of the red one?"

"Maybe. It depends on IDing the blood and guts that the forensic squad is collecting in mortal remains bags."

"Thank you for that image," said Brodie. "We're due at the Defense Attaché Office, so let's walk and talk."

As they walked across the lobby toward the elevators, Kim said, "I guess you saw the psychos out front."

"Scott almost started a fight with one of them," said Taylor, in a tone that was neither accusatory nor affirmative.

"I would have liked to see that. The Germans are in major denial about their white nationalist problem. It makes a lot of them uncomfortable, for obvious reasons."

They reached the elevator and Taylor punched the call button. She said, "Maybe it's best to deprive them of attention. Keep them marginalized."

Kim shook his head. "Too late for that. They're in the Bundestag, for God's sake. They're also in the military. And the BKA. And the police. And that's just the public-facing institutions. Every year they get a little bolder. A little more willing to say out loud what they used to say in private."

Brodie observed, "There's a lot of that going around."

Kim nodded and continued, "Their trend toward radicalization isn't that different from the jihadists, really. We've got over a decade of social media now that's foisting garbage into people's brains, increasing social alienation and atomization, and inciting incidents that draw new people into the movement. In this case, the murder of Harry Vance, U.S. Army officer."

The elevator arrived and Brodie hit the button for the third floor. As the doors slid shut Brodie asked Kim, "Does the name Tariq Qasim mean anything to you?"

Kim thought for a moment. "Doesn't ring a bell."

"What about Abbas al-Hamdani?"

"No. Who are they?"

"Same guy. Tariq Qasim took the name Abbas al-Hamdani when he moved from Iraq to Germany sometime after the fall of Saddam. He was in Saddam's special warfare program, a.k.a. weapons of mass destruction."

"Now you're making me nervous."

"Maybe we should all be," said Taylor. "Harry Vance was looking to meet Tariq Qasim in the days before his death. And now Qasim is missing."

The doors opened and they stepped into a wide hallway as a young man and woman in suits walked by and stepped into a nearby office. Brodie and Taylor gave Kim a rundown of their encounter with Rafeeq Nasir and the information he'd provided. Kim listened, but said nothing.

Brodie asked, "What do you know about the Arab clans?"

"Nothing," said Kim. "Which means they don't have anything to do with me or terrorism."

"Maybe they do," said Taylor.

Kim replied, "If there was anything to know, I would at least have some sense of it. But I'll look for this Iraqi guy under both names in our data bank."

"Let us know what you find," said Brodie. "We'll catch up after the briefing, whenever that is."

Kim nodded. He pushed the call button and the elevator doors opened. He paused, then turned back to them. "An American CID terrorism investigator is shot dead, and a few days later and a few blocks away, a bomb goes off. Two remarkable events separated by a few days and a few blocks. Co-incidence? Or correlation?"

"Chaos," said Brodie. "That's what most of the world is, most of the time."

Kim smiled. "Yes. Most of the time. Ciao." He stepped in and the elevator doors closed behind him.

Brodie and Taylor stood in silence for a moment. Taylor said, "He makes a point. About a connection."

"It's a point that I'm sure already occurred to you, as it did to me. But it's not useful or productive to throw around conspiracy theories until we have more facts. Maybe we'll find some in Harry's CID case reports."

They walked down the hallway to a door labeled DEFENSE ATTACHÉ OFFICE. There was no buzzer or call box, so Brodie knocked on the door and opened it.

They entered a windowless, modern office with four desks spaced evenly around the room, each occupied by a young person in a military service uniform in front of a computer. A hallway at the far end led to a few closed doors, probably the offices for General Frank Kiernan and the subordinate attachés who represented the individual service branches.

A twenty-something woman, wearing the dark-blue uniform of an Air Force enlisted person, looked up at them and smiled. Her nametag read "Hodges" and her rank was

Sergeant. "How may I help you?"

Taylor said, "Sergeant, I am Chief Warrant Officer Taylor and this is Chief Warrant Officer Brodie. We are retrieving documents from the Fifth MP Battalion."

Sergeant Hodges stood and saluted, and the other three enlisteds — two Army PFCs and a Marine Corporal — did the same.

Brodie and Taylor returned their salutes, and Brodie said, "As you were," and they returned to their seats, except Sergeant Hodges. Military protocol could be stressful. As warrant officers, they were to be saluted by any enlisted personnel in any branch of the military. But because Brodie and Taylor spent most of their time in civilian dress, service members did not know their rank upon sight and would awkwardly scramble to salute once they did. If Brodie had his way, fist bumps would do.

Brodie and Taylor showed Sergeant Hodges their IDs, and she retrieved a thick paper folio from one of her desk drawers and handed it to Taylor. "Here you are, ma'am. May I ask one of you to sign this release?"

She slid a paper across her desk, which Brodie quickly scanned. It was to acknowledge receipt of documents containing classified intelligence, and it was full of threatening legalese about how much shit they'd be in if they duplicated, transferred, or otherwise disseminated any of it.

356

He signed, then said to Sergeant Hodges, "General Kiernan told us he'd leave two sidearms here for us."

She went directly into panic mode. "Uh . . . I don't . . ." She looked around, as though searching for two guns that might have escaped her attention.

Brodie said, "We'll sign for them."

"Sir . . . I —"

"Scott."

"That's okay," Brodie assured Sergeant Hodges. "But when you see General Kiernan, please remind him that Warrant Officers Brodie and Taylor would like to have their guns."

"Yes, sir."

"With nice holsters and ten fully loaded clips. That's five each."

"Yes, sir."

"Thank you, Sergeant."

Brodie and Taylor exchanged salutes with Sergeant Hodges and left the office.

In the hallway, Taylor said, "You frightened her."

"Not as frightened as I was last night when I put my hand in my pocket and grabbed a toothpick." He asked, "How about you?"

"Point made. But let's go through official channels and not frighten the troops."

"General Kiernan will get the message."

She had no reply.

Brodie checked his watch: 9:34 A.M. "We've

got almost half an hour to kill. Let's see if we can get in early to the room Butler set aside for us."

Taylor nodded as they headed back to the elevator.

Neither Brodie nor Taylor was looking forward to watching hours of security footage that might or might not answer some of the many questions surrounding this case. The Berlin Police had already reviewed all the footage, as Jason Butler was eager to let them know, and maybe they were wasting their time. But in Scott Brodie's experience, how hard you look at the evidence sometimes depends on how badly you want the answers.

Chapter 21

Jason Butler had provided them with a small office on the embassy's fourth floor. The room held only a desk and a few chairs, and was also being used to store cartons of paper; the lifeblood of a bureaucracy. Brodie and Taylor flipped through Harry Vance's CID case reports they'd just gotten from Sergeant Hodges while waiting for someone from the Berlin police force to arrive with the video surveillance footage.

The door opened and a gaunt young man entered carrying a satchel and introduced himself as Berlin Police Officer Franz Lindoff.

As Lindoff set up his laptop, he informed them, "You must not touch the hard drive."

"Why not?" asked Brodie.

Lindoff, in the long German tradition of not asking or answering questions that began with "why," replied, "They tell me, so I tell you. If you touch it, I will tell them."

"Right. You're just following orders."

Lindoff plugged in the drive, then took a seat on a chair against the wall and began fiddling with a tablet. Taylor pulled her chair up to the laptop and started scrolling through the files as Brodie sat beside her. They had footage for all three requested metro stops, and each file appeared to contain two-hour blocks of footage.

"Let's begin at the beginning," said Taylor. "Schönhauser Allee, Saturday, six A.M., the day before the murder."

She opened the video file, which showed a wide-angle, black-and-white shot of a city street corner in the early morning hours. The angle afforded a view of the intersection, where a few delivery trucks and cars rolled through, with very light pedestrian traffic.

Taylor ran the footage at high speed, and whenever they saw a figure enter the frame she slowed it down. They went through the files, looking for Harry Vance, and the images became color after sunrise, when the road and foot traffic picked up. By 8:30 A.M. the rain had started, and people were carrying umbrellas, which made IDing them even harder. Officer Lindoff checked his watch. "How long?"

"As long as it takes," said Brodie.

Lindoff sighed loudly and went back to his tablet.

Taylor asked Brodie, "Would you even recognize him if you saw him? And I'm sure

360

there are multiple entrances to this station that the camera doesn't cover."

Brodie nodded. "Okay. New strategy. Harry entered the hookah lounge at about three A.M., give or take. It's a five-minute walk to there from the Neukölln metro. Coming from Prenzlauer Berg, let's say that's a twenty-minute trip from stop to stop. So he could have entered one of these metro stops around two-thirty A.M."

Taylor took out her phone and pulled up a map of the metro system. "Forget Eberswalder Straße. There's no way to go from there to Neukölln without a transfer, so he probably didn't use that station. The other two stops are direct and are on the same line. Schönhauser is one stop before Prenzlauer if you're headed in the direction of Neukölln. Pick one."

"Prenzlauer," said Brodie, on a hunch and also because he couldn't pronounce Schönhauser.

Taylor pulled up a new file. "Prenzlauer Allee. Two A.M."

The footage showed another black-and-white night vision shot. This security camera appeared to be situated over a street-level staircase that went down to the recessed tracks. In the foreground was the top of the stairs, and beyond that was the sidewalk and a wide road. On the other side of the road was the entrance to a small side street.

They began watching. Brodie said, "Remember, light-colored camel-hair coat and a flat cap."

"Also remember, if it was obvious, Berlin PD would have spotted him already."

They watched as people went up or down the metro steps. It was a cold winter night in Berlin, and the foot traffic was minimal. They sped through the footage. No sign of Harry.

"Wait," said Brodie. "Back up."

Taylor rewound the footage.

"There."

It was time-stamped 2:24 A.M. She said, "I don't see anything."

"Across the street." He pointed at the screen where a tiny figure in the distance was walking along the sidewalk on the far side of the road, illuminated by a streetlamp.

"That's, like, five pixels."

"Light-colored coat and a hat," said Brodie. "Back it up a little more."

She rewound the footage. The figure had come from the side street, barely visible in the corner of the frame.

"Harry had a kind of funny gait," said Brodie. "You remember that about people. A big stride even though he wasn't that tall. See how that guy is walking?"

They watched the figure walk along the road. Taylor said, "I think you're desperate."

"Maybe. But that's still him."

"He's not even going into the metro stop."

Brodie pulled up a map of Berlin on his phone and zeroed in on the area around the Prenzlauer Allee station. He switched the view to a satellite image. "Look. There's another metro entrance farther east. Probably to access the other side of the tracks. He just crossed the street at a different spot and used a different staircase that didn't have a camera."

Taylor looked at the satellite image. "Maybe."

"And look at this." He pointed on the map to the side street that the figure had emerged from. "It's a dead-end street."

Taylor nodded but didn't seem convinced.

"Pull up the previous file and let's watch that street."

She pulled up the midnight to 2 A.M. file and ran a high-speed playback as they kept their eyes on the distant side street. A few people came and went, but not the same figure in the light-colored coat.

Brodie said, "He was staying at her place that night. And her place is on that side street."

"This is a stretch."

Brodie pulled up a street-view image and showed it to Taylor. "It's a short street with fewer than twenty buildings, and some of them look like single-occupancy homes. We could spend another eight hours here, or we could go check out this single city block where Harry Vance's lady friend might be living."

Taylor still didn't seem convinced, but she nodded.

Brodie said to Officer Lindoff, "We're done here."

Lindoff looked up, pleasantly surprised. "Yes?"

"I didn't touch the hard drive."

"This is good."

Brodie and Taylor stood and put on their coats. Taylor said, "It's a thin lead, Scott."

"A lead is a lead. Especially when you don't have any others. Let's go find Anna."

CHAPTER 22

Brodie and Taylor worked their way along the east side of a narrow cobblestone street that dead-ended at a tall brick apartment building. It was a residential street except for a trendy-looking Japanese ramen restaurant that didn't open until evening.

Brodie inspected the call box in front of a narrow, cream-colored apartment building, looking for an Anna. He said to Taylor, "Last names only."

"Let's check the next one."

The next building was a five-story nineteenth-century apartment building that was painted orange with white trim. Brodie looked at the call box. "Okay, this one has first initials, and two A names. 'A. Schiller' and 'A. Albrecht.' "

Taylor typed on her phone, then said, "I see a few Anna Schillers in Berlin . . . One appears to be an older woman who owns a bookstore. Got some address hits too . . ." She looked up at Brodie. "No addresses for this street. But Anna Schiller could be unlisted. Or recently moved."

"Try Anna Albrecht."

Taylor worked at her phone again. "Oh. Okay, this might be something. Anna Albrecht is a curator at an art gallery in Kreuzberg. The gallery has a website . . . She has a bio . . . Let me run this page through a translator." After a minute Taylor handed him her phone, and he read a short bio describing Anna Albrecht as "a longtime resident of Prenzlauer Berg with extensive experience in the Berlin avant-garde art scene." The bio included a photo of Ms. Albrecht, a very attractive woman in her mid-thirties with a short pixie haircut, high cheekbones, and big brown eyes, which sort of matched the description given to them by Johannes at the schnapps store. Brodie handed the phone back to Taylor. "I'd take a ten-hour round-trip train ride for her."

"I'm sure you would." Taylor looked up at the building. "Maybe not a bad lead after all. Let's see." She pressed the buzzer for Apartment 3B. They waited a moment. No response.

"Entschuldigen Sie."

A fifty-something woman in a fur hat and peacoat approached the door, along with a yappy miniature black schnauzer on a leash.

Brodie and Taylor stepped aside as the woman unlocked the heavy wooden door and pushed it open. She held it for them and smiled.

"Danke schön," said Taylor.

They entered a high-ceilinged foyer with a ceramic-tile floor leading to a wide staircase. They lingered in the foyer as the woman climbed the stairs, talking to her schnauzer, who barked replies.

When the conversation stopped, Brodie and Taylor climbed the stairs to the third floor, where there were two wooden doors on a small landing, 3A and 3B. They approached 3B and Brodie knocked.

They waited. Brodie knocked again and said loudly, "Anna Albrecht. My name is Scott Brodie. I was a friend of Harry's and I would like to speak with you."

Nothing. Brodie twisted the old doorknob, which was locked. But from the sound of the knocks the door wasn't too thick. He'd breached his share of doors in training and in combat, and this one wouldn't put up much of a fight.

Taylor knew what her partner was thinking. She whispered, "This might not even be the right Anna. Plus, we have no jurisdiction and no warrant. This is breaking and entering."

"We have the right apartment. This woman had an ongoing romantic relationship with the murder victim and has not come forward. Maybe she killed him. Or maybe she's dead." He reminded her, "You know the rules of forced entry."

"Maybe she *did* go to the police. Another detail they conveniently forgot to put in their briefing."

That was possible, but not probable. "Even our German colleagues wouldn't withhold information that would explain the murder victim's presence in Berlin."

Taylor said, "We can call Agent Whitmore or Chief Inspector Schröder and have a team of BKA officers sent here."

Brodie stared at the closed door. Taylor's suggestion was the right way to make an entry. Then again, Scott Brodie had been sent here to get answers, and the answers were behind that door. More importantly, he'd already announced himself. If Anna Albrecht was home and had something to hide, she could be destroying evidence — or slipping out the window and down a fire escape — while they waited for the police to show up. Or she really could be dead or dying.

Brodie said, "I'm going in. You can leave."

Taylor looked offended. "We're partners. We both live and die by your bad choices."

"Right."

She eyed the door. "Aim just left of the doorknob."

"I've done this a few times."

He stepped back, then brought his foot up and slammed it next to the doorknob, feeling it crack. He shouldered the door and it flew open. This is where they'd pull their guns if they had guns, but Brodie settled for, "Police! Hands up!"

They rushed into a small foyer with a table and coatrack. To their left was a hallway leading to a kitchen.

"Scott . . ."

He turned to his right. Another hallway led to an open door about fifteen feet away, and standing in the doorway was a petite woman in her thirties with pixie-cut black hair dressed in a gray tank top and jeans.

She was pointing a rifle at them.

CHAPTER 23

The woman with the rifle spoke in almost unaccented English, "Who are you?"

Taylor replied in a calm voice, "My name is Maggie Taylor, and this is my partner, Scott Brodie. We are U.S. Army CID Agents investigating the murder of our colleague CID Agent Harry Vance. Are you Anna Albrecht?"

"You know I am."

"We have received information that you were acquainted with the deceased."

As the woman stared at Taylor, Brodie glanced at her rifle. It was a bolt-action with a wooden stock, though he couldn't tell more without getting closer. The woman had the rifle butt braced against her shoulder, with the barrel aimed at Brodie's midsection. Her finger was wrapped around the trigger, which meant either she was about to shoot him or, more likely, had not internalized the basic rules of trigger discipline.

"We are unarmed," said Brodie. "Please lower your weapon."

Anna tightened her grip on the rifle. "I don't believe you."

Taylor said, "We are sorry for breaching your door. There was a concern that something had happened to you."

Anna kept her eyes locked on Brodie. "Something did happen to me," she said in a quiet, intense voice. "Harry was murdered."

"We're very sorry," said Taylor.

Brodie said, "He was a good man."

"You knew him?"

Brodie nodded. "He was my instructor many years ago."

"When?"

"Two thousand five."

"Where?"

"The Army MP School in Fort Leonard Wood, Missouri."

"All right . . . Show me your CID identification."

Apparently, thought Brodie, she'd learned something from her lover.

He said, "Mine is in my inside jacket pocket. I'm going to reach for it now." He slowly reached for his badge case and pulled it out, and Taylor did the same.

Anna glanced at their badges, nodded, then slowly lowered the rifle. "You had no right to break in here."

"You had a responsibility to go to the police," said Brodie. "If you had, we wouldn't be here." He also informed her, "The fact

371

that you didn't go to the police makes you a suspect."

Anna stared at him. Ms. Albrecht was even more of a looker in person, and she had a kind of crackling energy to her. She asked, "How did you find me?"

"Dumb luck," Brodie replied.

Taylor asked, "Why didn't you go to the police?"

"I don't have to answer any of your questions."

"That is true," said Taylor. "But we all want the same thing, Ms. Albrecht. Justice for Harry."

"Justice. Right." Anna clicked the rifle on safety and leaned it against the wall, then walked toward them and stopped in front of Taylor. "You're very pretty."

"Thank you."

"Too pretty for a cop. I bet that causes you some problems."

"No problems."

Anna looked at Brodie. "I could have blown your head off."

"Have you ever shot a person before?" Like Harry Vance?

"No. But there's always a first time."

Brodie asked, "Where'd you get the rifle?"

"I inherited it from my father. He inherited it from his father, who was a veteran of the First World War."

"Right." Brodie glanced at the rifle, which

looked military. Probably a Mauser, so the caliber would be larger than the .22 that had killed Harry. Did that eliminate Ms. Albrecht as a suspect? Maybe. Unless she had an arsenal somewhere. He advised her, "Always keep your finger outside of the trigger guard unless you're about to shoot."

"I *was* about to shoot." She explained, "You could have been here to kill me. Like they killed Harry."

"*Who* killed Harry?"

She shrugged, then thought a moment. "Perhaps . . . not who you think."

Brodie and Taylor exchanged glances, and Taylor said, "We need to speak to you."

She nodded, went to the splintered door, shut it, and slid a chain lock in place, then led them to the kitchen, a compact room with dark tile flooring, aging cabinets, and a small breakfast table shoved in the corner. A slender window next to the fridge looked out on a small interior courtyard.

Anna put water and grounds into a metal coffeepot, lit her gas range with a match, then set the pot over the flame and grabbed a pack of cigarettes from her jeans pocket. She held the pack out to Brodie and Taylor, who both declined.

She shoved a cigarette in her mouth and lit up using the flame from the gas range, which seemed to Brodie like a bad idea. She gestured with the cigarette. "They shoot you for this in the States, yes?"

"Only on a second offense," Brodie assured her.

Anna blew out a stream of smoke as she leaned against the counter and eyed him. "What did he teach you?"

"Harry was a counterterrorism instructor," said Brodie. "A very good one."

"And now you use his training."

"In a way. We are not counterterrorism specialists."

"Do you think a terrorist killed him?"

"We're not at liberty to discuss that."

"How did you find me?"

"We're not at liberty to discuss that either."

"If I call the Bundeskriminalamt headquarters and give them your names, will they know who you are?"

"They will," said Taylor. "But it's probably better for all of us if you don't do that."

Anna made a look of exaggerated concern. "Why is that? You don't get on well with the German police?"

Brodie said, "We're happy to be on the team."

She laughed. "Yes? I don't like the police."

"Harry was a policeman."

Anna looked away. "Harry was different."

Taylor asked, "Is that why you haven't come forward? You don't trust the police?"

Anna eyed Taylor for a moment but didn't respond.

Brodie asked, "What was Harry doing here in Berlin?"

"He was doing me."

"Right. Beyond recreational activities."

"Why do you think I'm not enough reason for a man to come to Berlin?"

Brodie smiled. She made a good point. But he knew there was more to Harry's visits. That was why Harry was dead. "Help us."

Anna thought for a moment, crossed her arms. A trail of cigarette smoke coiled up past her face. "He was helping *me* with something."

"With what?"

Anna didn't respond.

Taylor said, "If you don't speak to us, we'll make a few phone calls, and you can instead have this conversation in German. Maybe from a jail cell."

Anna stared at Taylor. A half-smile crept over her face. "People don't see you coming, do they?"

The coffeemaker hissed and spurted steam. Anna turned off the range, then took down three espresso cups from her cupboard and filled them. "It's strong. Do you need sugar?"

They both declined. Anna handed each of them a cup and saucer. "We'll talk in the living room."

She led them through the hallway into a large living room with tall windows that faced the interior courtyard. The walls were adorned with original plaster moldings and a few large pieces of modern art that looked a little better than the stuff at the Art Hotel.

Anna directed them to a sagging orange couch against the far wall as she sat on a battered leather Chesterfield across from them.

Brodie set his cup on the large coffee table, which was covered with art magazines and a glass marijuana pipe that could use a good cleaning. A crystal ashtray was piled with cigarette butts. Brodie and Taylor took off their coats and tossed them on the arms of the couch and sat.

Anna set her cup down and looked between them with her intense brown eyes. "No weapons. No warrant. And probably no one else has any idea that you're here."

"We're part of a team," said Brodie.

"The Americans don't play well with others."

"We try."

"No. You are arrogant."

"Correct."

"All right. Who are you working with here?"

"The BKA and the Berlin Police. Plus our FBI."

"What about intelligence agencies?"

"I'm not at liberty to say."

Taylor said, "I'm not sure how this is relevant."

Anna looked at her. "I'm interested in spies, Ms. Taylor. You might say I'm preoccupied with them. My father was a spy. A double agent for your government."

That was a surprise. Brodie said, "We thank him for his service."

"Well, you can't. He's dead. Executed by the Stasi after his cover was blown. They killed him two weeks before the Wall fell. How is that for bad timing?"

"I'm sorry," said Taylor.

"So am I." Anna took a long drag on her cigarette. "He was a Stasi man himself. Manfred Albrecht. Records analyst." She looked between her two guests. "Do you know how many records the Stasi kept on its citizens? Well, I'll tell you. One hundred and eleven kilometers, when placed end-to-end."

That was about seventy miles of paperwork, thought Brodie, a true image of Hell. Considering the small size of East Germany and the brief time it existed — just about forty years — the average East German could probably have expected at least some detail of their personal life or the lives of their immediate family to be in that vast secret police archive.

Anna continued, "You could commit the smallest infraction and end up getting spied on for years. And every piece of this surveillance generates a report. My father's job was to find connections and patterns between all the suspected enemies of the state, which was virtually everyone who lived in that giant prison."

Brodie and Taylor exchanged glances. Anna was talking, so they stayed silent.

Anna continued, "I was young when it all ended, but . . . I do remember a general *feeling*. Like, everything was heavy. Everyone was on edge. A lot of drinking. There were constant shortages of everything except alcohol. I'm sure the whole thing would have collapsed a lot sooner if they'd ever run out of alcohol."

Well, this was depressing. But what did it have to do with Harry Vance getting killed in Neukölln while looking for an Iraqi WMD specialist? This didn't feel like a practiced monologue, or something building to an alibi; more like some dark thing that had been weighing on her and that she was trying to unload. And when a potential witness — or suspect — was feeling chatty, it was always best to stay silent, or now and then encourage them, and eventually lead them back to what you were really there to talk about.

Brodie asked, "What kind of intelligence did your father provide the American government?"

"Many things," said Anna. "He began working for the Stasi in 1978 and was providing information to the West by at least 1985. And unlike a lot of his colleagues, he wasn't restricted to a certain department. He had access to all the archives." She added, "He was ideally placed to be a mole. Until someone blew his cover."

"Who?" asked Taylor.

Anna looked at her. "This is the question my family has been trying to answer for thirty years."

Taylor and Brodie again exchanged glances. This seemed to be going somewhere, though Brodie still couldn't tell why Ms. Albrecht was spilling her guts to them, or what any of this had to do with the murder of Harry Vance.

Anna stared at the table for a moment, then looked at them. "One Sunday morning in September 1989, men in dark suits came to our door. I was six years old. They arrested all of us and put each of us in a separate car to be taken for interrogation. Can you imagine? Interrogating a six-year-old? I remember being terrified, sitting in this horrible green room . . ." She trailed off, her mind going back to that room, but she didn't seem to want to share the details. "They let me and my mother out after a few days. My mother knew nothing about my father's activities — he knew that if either of them was ever arrested, her ignorance might save her. I guess they believed her." She paused. "I never saw my father again."

Anna looked toward the window. The dull gray light illuminated her somber eyes. "They phoned my mother sometime at the end of October, told her where and when to expect the burial. You got full service in the German Democratic Republic. Cradle to grave. They tried you, they executed you, and they planned the goddamn funeral." She laughed bitterly and looked at Brodie and Taylor. "One of your politicians, I can't remember his name, he said something about the Vietnam War that has always stayed with me: 'How do you ask a man to be the last to die for a mistake?' Well, that was my father. The last to die before the Wall came down . . . That whole country was a goddamn mistake. A travesty."

They all sat in silence for a moment. Taylor said, "I am so sorry."

Anna shrugged and stubbed out her cigarette in the ashtray piled with butts. "After the Wall fell a couple of weeks later, my mother began going through all the official channels to try to learn about what had happened to her husband, how he'd been caught. The reunified government set up the Stasi Records Agency so any East German could find their own reports, see if they were spied on, find out if your friends and neighbors were informing on you or your family. But there were restrictions. Any report that involved a foreign government — including West Germany — was still locked away. State secrets. So, no luck. But my mother was a stubborn old bitch." Anna smiled to herself. "She wouldn't quit. She petitioned every

380

government agency that might have some loose connection to state intelligence. She hounded politicians. She contacted journalists. For years and years. But, nothing. Until one day."

Anna got up and walked to an old wooden desk across the room. She opened the bottom drawer and pulled out a thick manila envelope, then tossed it on the coffee table and sat back down.

Taylor picked up the envelope and pulled out a thick stack of typewritten documents. They were all slightly misshapen, jagged on the edges, their surfaces shiny from the heavy application of clear tape. Brodie watched as Taylor flipped through the pages, and he realized that every page had been shredded and meticulously reassembled.

Anna said, "When it was clear that East Germany was finished, the bastards in every Stasi office in the country started shredding everything. And when their shredders broke down, they began ripping up all the records by hand. When the Stasi headquarters was stormed by the people, the Stasi men fled and left behind thousands of bags of paper scraps. The most difficult jigsaw puzzle in the world. But also, one of the most important. To this day, thirty years later, a group of people sit in an office in a little town outside Nuremberg, trying to piece together the past. We call them the puzzle women."

"This is incredible," said Taylor as she flipped through the stack of reassembled pages, all in German. "Is this record about your father?"

"Not exactly," said Anna. "That record is unique. Not a surveillance report, but a comprehensive record of the activities of an American double agent, a military man, who was betraying your country and giving information to the Stasi. His identity was so secret that his name is not even used in this top secret document. He is referred to only by his code name, Odin."

Anna looked at her American guests to see if they recognized this name. She explained, "Odin is the chief god in Germanic mythology and folklore. God of war, death, wisdom, and many other things."

Brodie said, "That's a pretty wide mandate. Even for a god." He added, "And a pretty grandiose code name for a traitor."

Anna nodded. "Fitting too. The god Odin would seek greater knowledge by disguising himself and wandering among mortals." She gestured to the papers with her cigarette. "Sometime in 1999, someone who was working in the Records Agency received this report from the puzzle women, along with official instructions to turn it over to state intelligence. Well, whoever read it realized what they had in their hands, and instead of turning it in to be put in some secret vault forever, this person brought the report to my mother. People working in the Records Agency knew how many years she had been looking for information on her husband. You see, this report implicates Odin in blowing the cover of four different Stasi agents who were working for the West. Each man was caught, each man was executed. The last of these four men was my father."

Brodie asked, "Was Odin ever caught?"

Anna shook her head. "His identity remains unknown."

Brodie processed that. Throughout the Cold War, there had been a number of Americans who had betrayed their country and sold secrets to the Communists, but only three known moles within the American Intel community had ever betrayed foreign double agents in a matter that led to those agents' deaths — Edward Lee Howard and Aldrich Ames of the CIA, and Robert Hanssen of the FBI. Howard had managed to escape to Moscow. Ames and Hanssen were both currently serving life sentences without parole.

It was almost inconceivable that there was a fourth American traitor out there with such a high body count who had never been discovered or caught, and whose ability to escape justice was not itself a matter of public knowledge. And this traitor was someone in the U.S. military, no less. *Odin.*

Brodie eyed the stack of yellowing typewritten pages that Taylor was still holding, their thousands of shredded pieces carefully reconstructed like a museum artifact. It looked real. And in his gut, it felt real too.

Anna continued, "My mother died nine years ago, never getting the answers she sought. I'd seen what this obsession had done to her, and I promised myself that I would let the past lie. Then I fell in love with a stubborn American CID agent who heard this story — from me — and vowed to discover Odin's identity. To find this American traitor and bring him to justice. But also to get justice for my father. And my mother. And me. And for Harry's efforts," she said, her eyes now shining with tears, "someone killed him."

CHAPTER 24

Brodie looked at Anna, who was staring back at them. He noticed a large painting on the wall behind her featuring thick black strokes on white canvas. On a closer look it appeared to be an abstract rendering of the Berlin Wall.

This city was full of ghosts — and ghost stories, like the one they'd just heard. The duplicitous American spy, Odin, who had been on the wrong side of history yet had somehow escaped its judgment. And the brave Stasi man, Anna's father, secretly defying a dictatorship, betrayed and killed just before he could relish his own taste of freedom.

It was an interesting story. Maybe even a true one. But did it have anything to do with Harry's murder? This Odin, whoever he was, would probably be at least seventy years old by now. More likely, he was dead. The past mattered. But thirty years later, did it matter enough to kill for?

Brodie asked Anna, "What was Harry actually doing to discover Odin's identity?"

Anna shook her head. "He was keeping me in the dark. He said it was to protect me, which I thought was a bit melodramatic. To me this was like a curiosity, uncovering a sad piece of family history. Not something that was still . . . alive." She looked at Brodie. "Something that could still hurt people."

Taylor said in a soft voice, "Anna, we have information about why Harry was in Neukölln, and what he was investigating. We don't have all the answers yet, but . . . he was a counterterrorism investigator. And what he was involved in, we believe is related to Islamic terrorism in one way or another." She put the Stasi documents on the coffee table and asked, "Do the names Tariq Qasim or Abbas al-Hamdani mean anything to you?"

"No." She looked between the two of them. "You don't get it. *This*" — she pointed to the documents on the coffee table — "is what he was doing. He took it seriously. And so should you."

"We do," said Taylor. "But you need to consider the possibility that this . . . Odin case is not related to Harry's death. Also, nothing you have told us justifies why you have not spoken to the authorities. We can arrange —"

Anna interrupted, "The *authorities* shot my father for treason and dumped him in a cold grave. Do you know that there were more people conducting surveillance at his funeral than actual mourners? Little men with their little cameras. Seeing who was there, who came to honor the memory of an enemy of the state. And if you had the audacity to weep, maybe you'd end up on one of their dreaded lists for the rest of your life." She shook her head, lit up another cigarette. "The *authorities*. Fuck them."

Taylor leaned forward. "I do not mean to minimize your grief, Ms. Albrecht, and I'm sorry if that's how it came off. But that grotesque system is over, that country is done, those people are powerless. And now you have an obligation to help find Harry's killer. The police are no longer your enemies."

Anna smiled tightly. "So says the police-woman." She looked down at the paperwork on the table. "I used to think, who cares who Odin is? Or was? East Germany killed my father. The system killed my father. This American traitor, Odin . . . I wasn't going to pour all my anger and grief into him like my mother did. I wasn't going to give him that power. Then Harry came into my life. I think it offended him on a personal and professional level, the idea of someone in the American military having done this, having betrayed his country and gotten away with it. Harry was doing what he thought was right. Stubborn, like my mother. And now dead like her too." She took a long drag, then thought for a moment. "I'll talk to your police friends. And if I mysteriously vanish, maybe then you'll take this seriously."

Taylor said, "That will not happen."

Anna ignored that as she rose and walked back to the desk and pulled out another manila envelope. She handed it to Taylor. "Take this. Harry translated the Stasi report into English."

Taylor slipped the envelope into her satchel. "Thank you. We'll read it."

Brodie asked, "When your mother first got this report, did she alert any government authorities?"

"Of course," said Anna. "She wanted their help. She wanted to keep the original, so she gave them a photocopy and claimed it was the only version she was given. She made up some story of how she got the documents in order to protect her contact in the Records Agency. She knew that if the government doubted its authenticity, they'd try to procure the original. But her contact informed her that they never did. Which made her think that they already knew about Odin, as did your government."

Brodie thought about that. If the U.S. and West Germany lost four undercover agents over the course of a decade, they obviously knew they had a mole. And when the Cold War abruptly ended one November evening in 1989, there were plenty of reasons why both countries might want the whole thing to be memory-holed. He asked, "What about the other three people? Their families? Do they know about this report?"

Anna nodded. "My mother contacted them, but . . . you will find that not many citizens of the former East Germany want to revisit the past."

Taylor seemed incredulous. "Even those whose family members were executed?"

"What makes you so sure that those people didn't believe that their husbands and fathers got what they deserved? Or that they weren't at least ashamed of their actions? East Germany was full of true believers, and that faith in the virtues of the state didn't just lift like a spell when Germany unified. After the Nazis, there was Nuremberg. They hanged the bastards. But after East Germany, there was no equivalent. Erich Mielke, the head of the Stasi, you know what happened to him? He died of old age. And the General Secretary, Erich Honecker? He was supposed to stand trial for his many crimes against the people, but they took pity on the bastard because he had terminal cancer. He was allowed to live in exile in Chile, where he died an old man. There was no justice and so there was no reckoning. No consequences. And therefore no redemption." She took a long drag. "The world will never let us forget the Nazis, and why should they? But the Communists . . .

that is something different. There is a permission to forget, and all too many Germans take permission."

Brodie considered that. East Germany had lost the Cold War, and the price of defeat was full integration into a vibrant democracy that had become the economic powerhouse of Europe. And unlike other vanquished nations at the end of a war, the worst crimes committed by East Germany were against her own people. And even distinguishing the perpetrators from the victims was difficult in a system that had managed to turn half the country into collaborators and snitches. No wonder everyone wanted to forget. To move on.

Well, they'd really gotten into the weeds on this Cold War stuff, but Brodie still had some meat-and-potatoes investigating to do. He switched gears and asked, "How did you and Harry first meet?"

Anna took a deep breath. "I met Harry last July. I'm a curator at a gallery in Kreuzberg, and we'd just opened a new show. We'd been trying to highlight new voices, you know, marginalized voices. And especially with all the refugees coming in, I decided I wanted to find the artists among them, support them in creating new work. So I did. Artists from Syria, Afghanistan, Iraq. Challenging subject matter. Some of it quite grim. I knew it might be too much for our regular clientele, and I was right. Visits dropped off. But this square-jawed American walks in one day. He's drawn to the work, and we start talking. Harry tells me he is a military investigator, and he even tells me a little of what he does, and I have this terrible feeling that he's come to my gallery looking for terrorists. But he said he was just in town for a meeting or something. But he was a naturally curious man. An empathetic man. And he . . ." She trailed off for a moment. Then she tapped her chest over her heart. "He held a lot of darkness in here. I could feel that. There was something about him I needed to understand, to figure out. Most of the men I date, they are shallow little boys pretending to be deep. But Harry was the opposite. A deep well, but trying to hide it. I was immediately drawn to him."

Vance could be considered the strong silent type, and there was definitely a kind of woman attracted to a man with inner demons. Of course, Anna Albrecht had a few demons of her own. Maybe she'd recognized a fellow traveler.

Brodie wondered if Vance was really pulled in by the artwork he saw through the gallery window, or by the very attractive gallery curator. But maybe that was too cynical. All men are pigs, but some are more dedicated to the role than others.

Anna continued, "We had a nice couple of days. He left, but we stayed in touch. And then he would start visiting every few weeks."

Brodie asked, "Did you know he was married?"

"Of course," replied Anna, as if offended. "We shared everything. We did not lie to each other. He still loved his wife. He told me that. Who says that to the woman they are cheating with? Harry had a kind of stupid honesty about him."

Taylor said, "His wife might disagree."

Anna shot her a look. "That's not my business."

Brodie asked, "When did Harry arrive in Berlin for this last visit?"

"Tuesday. Late afternoon. I was busy and couldn't meet him at the train station, so we met in the neighborhood around six-thirty."

"Did he have a key to your apartment?"

"No. He didn't want one. Except when he was staying here. So, we met at the Japanese place across the street."

"Were you together from Tuesday until early Sunday morning?"

She shook her head. "I'd go to work in the morning, and he'd go do . . . whatever it was he was doing. We saw each other in the evenings, and the weekend." That seemed to bring up something painful, and she added, "Sunday morning I rolled over toward him, but his side of the bed was empty. I saw he'd texted my phone, said he couldn't sleep and was going for a walk, would be back by dawn.

I called him and he didn't answer. I tried again. And again. And then . . ." She paused. "I was a wreck all of Sunday. I wanted to contact the police, but I told myself that would be overreacting . . . and the police might contact his wife . . . And then the news comes, Monday morning. I learn along with everyone else. His wife is the one who gets the phone call, yes? I was just . . ." She trailed off.

That was the price of being the other woman. Harry might have given his heart to Anna, but it didn't come with next-of-kin status and a legally binding contract.

Brodie asked, "Was Harry's wife aware of your relationship?"

"He was getting divorced."

"Please answer the question."

She hesitated. "No."

"She must have suspected something."

"We didn't talk about it," said Anna brusquely. "By our third time together, he told me he was getting a divorce. It was that simple. He was unhappy. I made him happy. And if you find happiness in this shit world, you grab it and don't let go."

It seemed that Ms. Albrecht was more defensive about this topic than about with-holding key information from the police who were investigating her boyfriend's murder. Also, something about this wasn't making sense. Why wouldn't Harry have told his wife,

Julie, about the affair when filing for divorce? Once the deed was done, why not come clean? Shame? A desire for a more amicable and speedy settlement?

Then Brodie thought about Mark Jenkins, whom Harry had also kept in the dark about this relationship, and who seemed perplexed about what Harry could have been up to in Berlin that was so secretive that he wouldn't share it with his CID partner and close friend.

This secrecy could all be explained by the Uniform Code of Military Justice: Adultery was a punishable offense. So were actions unbecoming an officer. Not to mention actions that brought discredit to the Army. Having an affair was not a career builder. And that might be the answer to Harry's silence on the subject.

But maybe now they had another answer. *Odin.* Harry's relationship with Anna and his hunt for the American traitor were part of the same thing in Harry's mind. To tell his wife or his partner about Anna Albrecht was to risk revealing what he was really doing in Berlin beyond a romantic dalliance.

Was Harry using this woman? Did he just happen upon her art gallery? Or was he seeking her out because he already knew about her father and her family's search for justice? In other words, was Harry Vance on a case? Not according to Mark Jenkins, or Colonel Trask, or anyone else at 5th MP. Well, something was propelling Warrant Officer Vance forward on this search for Odin, and Brodie needed to figure out if there was more to it than a keen romantic interest in Ms. Albrecht, and moral outrage over the American military traitor who had betrayed his country, and betrayed Anna's father. Something more in the present.

Brodie asked, "Is there anything Harry mentioned — or something you might have overheard — that could shed some light on who he was in contact with while he was in Berlin?"

Anna shook her head.

"Maybe you saw something on his phone."

Anna shot him a look. "I saw nothing on his phone. I respected his privacy. We trusted each other."

Taylor said, "Harry must have left some of his belongings here."

Anna nodded. "Clothes, mostly. Plus his passport, which he told me he always traveled with, even within Germany, in case he got unexpected orders to travel abroad. His bag sat there on the floor in my bedroom, I didn't know what to do with it. I didn't even want to touch it. I eventually got up the nerve to throw it in my wardrobe."

Brodie asked, "May we see it?"

"Why?"

"I won't know until I see it."

Anna stood and led them back into the

hallway, into a bright, airy bedroom with tall windows facing the street.

The room was a mess. Unmade bed, pillows tossed on the floor, books and loose papers on every surface. Anna opened a tall wooden wardrobe across from the bed and retrieved a black nylon overnight bag, which she handed to Brodie. "Some of his shirts and slacks are still hanging in here, everything else is in the bag."

Brodie set the bag on the bed and opened it. Socks, boxer shorts, a few T-shirts and undershirts. He pulled out a worn paperback copy of Joseph Conrad's *The Secret Agent* and handed it to Taylor. "Appropriate reading."

Taylor flipped through the book to see if anything had been slipped between the pages. "I read this in college. Terrorists, espionage, betrayal. Good stuff." She set it on the bed.

The only other thing of note in the bag was Harry's passport, which Brodie flipped through. As expected, it was full of entry stamps for various European countries as well as a few places that were no one's idea of tourist hot spots — Iraq, Yemen, Pakistan, Libya. The oldest stamp was from Algeria in 2013. The most recent was from Poland in 2018.

Brodie closed the passport and said to Anna, "This is State Department property, and I am handing it over to the American

Embassy."

Anna nodded.

Brodie slipped the passport in his jacket pocket and gestured to the wardrobe. "May I?"

Anna stepped aside, and Brodie observed three button-down dress shirts, two pairs of dark slacks, and a navy-blue sports jacket hanging in the wardrobe next to Anna's clothing. He checked the pockets of the dress shirts and slacks, which were empty. Then he reached into the inside pocket of the jacket and felt something. He pulled it out.

It was a small manila envelope a little larger than a credit card. He opened it and withdrew what appeared to be a glass microscope slide, about three inches long. In the center of the glass was a nickel-sized drop of liquid with a slightly purple hue.

He held it up to Taylor. "What do you think this is?"

Taylor looked at it closely. "Judging by the color, it might be some kind of pathogen with a contrast stain applied to it. They're supposed to be labeled."

A small white sticker was affixed to one end of the slide, featuring a string of six handwritten numbers. There was no other labeling.

Brodie turned to Anna and showed it to her. "Any idea what this is?"

She looked at the slide and shook her head. This needed to be marked as evidence and turned over to the German police. Or maybe not. Brodie returned the slide to the envelope and put it in his jacket pocket with the passport. He asked Anna, "Any of his other belongings here?"

"Toiletries. In the bathroom."

"Was he taking any prescription medication?"

"Not that I'm aware of." She gestured to the overnight bag. "Are you done with it?"

"Yes. Hold on to all this for now. You will be turning it over to the German authorities."

She didn't respond to that, but said, "It's all I have left of him."

Taylor said, "We understand. But it's not yours."

Anna nodded and left the bedroom. Brodie and Taylor followed her back to the hallway. She informed them, "I have nothing more to say."

Taylor glanced at Brodie, who nodded. She said to Anna, "Thank you for your assistance, and we are sorry again for your loss."

Brodie added, "Someone from the BKA will be in touch about taking a statement from you, and they will also be collecting your rifle for ballistics, and Harry's belongings as evidence." He added, "You need to be honest with them about why you have not come forward."

"Yes, I will tell them I honestly don't trust

the police."

"Right. But here's some free advice: Don't antagonize people who have the power to charge you with obstruction of justice."

"Who's paying to fix my front door?"

"Give us the bill when we see you next."

"Oh, are we doing this again?"

"I'm sure we'll have more questions for you once we read the Stasi documents."

She looked at Brodie. "The only question is why this American traitor was never caught, and who is protecting him now."

Brodie replied, "By now, he may have faced justice in a much higher court."

"I don't believe in any of that," said Anna. "There is justice in this world or none at all."

Taylor took Anna's phone number and gave her both of their cell numbers; then they left the apartment and walked down the stairs and out to the street. A light flurry had begun, and the flakes were collecting on the cobblestones.

Taylor said, "Well, that was . . . something . . ."

Brodie nodded. "Good info. Wrong case."

Taylor asked, "What did you think of her?"

"Before or after she threatened to blow my head off?"

"She showed restraint, actually. And a fair amount of trust in people who had just broken into her apartment."

"Maybe that's her fatal flaw. Overly trusting. Maybe Harry was snowing her about trying to find her father's killer. Stringing her along."

"Do you think he would do that?"

"I didn't know him well enough to say. But he seemed like an honest guy."

"Except for the extramarital affair."

"If nothing else, he was earnest. And diligent. Maybe he'd managed to dig into old Stasi archives or even U.S. counterintelligence reports to try to discover Odin's identity. But is that why he was in a park in the middle of the night in an Arab neighborhood holding his Beretta? I doubt it. But we'll look at the Stasi report."

His phone rang. He pulled it out of his pocket and saw it was Sharon Whitmore. He answered, "Brodie."

"Scott, when can you be at the embassy?"

"Fifteen minutes. Why?"

"There's been a major development."

"Can I get a tease?"

She hesitated a moment. "The bombing in Neukölln has provided some new evidence."

"See you soon."

"Good." She hung up.

Brodie slipped the phone back in his pocket. He watched as the snow drifted past the old buildings and the bare trees lining the sidewalk. *Two remarkable events separated by a few days and a few blocks.* Maybe it wasn't chaos after all. Maybe there was some awful unifying logic to all this.

"Who was that?"

"Whitmore. She needs us at the embassy ASAP. The bombing in Neukölln has led to new evidence in our case."

"Well, at least they're calling it a bombing, and not a cooking accident." She looked off, thinking. After a moment she said, "Last night I felt like this case was almost making sense."

"Whiskey will do that."

"And then there's this." She gestured to Anna's building. "What does an American spying for the Stasi have to do with Iraqi military intelligence, or weapons of mass destruction, or now this bombing?"

"Don't forget Hezbollah and the Lebanese Mafia." He added, "Anna is paranoid. Grief-stricken. Harry's death stirred up a lot of things that she thought she'd buried."

"The hysterical woman."

"That's not what I said."

"It's implied."

"What do you want me to say, Taylor? A CID counterterrorism investigator is clipped in the middle of an Arab neighborhood while trying to locate an Iraqi ex-Ba'athist with knowledge of the most terrible weapons known to man, and now a bomb blows up in that same neighborhood and apparently has something to do with Harry's murder. That paints a kind of picture. A scary picture, actu-

401

ally. But also a coherent one. As for Anna . . . I think she's stuck in the past. You and I can only begin to imagine what she's gone through. Growing up in a place like that. Those bastards taking her father from her at such a young age. But the world moves on, and the problem is that the pain doesn't move on with it."

Taylor thought about that. "She's traumatized."

He nodded. "And with the murder of Harry, twice over."

"We at least owe it to her to take her claims seriously. To see what's there."

"We always see what's there."

"We do. But we don't always understand what we see."

"I do."

"Then tell me what that thing is that you took from Harry's jacket."

"His passport."

"The *other* thing, Scott."

"I have no frickin' idea."

CHAPTER 25

The far-right protestors who had clogged Pariser Platz that morning appeared to have gone home for the day, or to another location. A few cyclists and pedestrians weaved between the columns of the Brandenburg Gate.

Brodie and Taylor navigated the embassy security check, then took the elevator to the second floor and walked to the conference room.

Sharon Whitmore and Jason Butler sat together at the far end of the conference table. No one else was there.

Brodie asked, "Are we early?"

"It's just us," said Whitmore. She gestured to the chairs across from them. "Please sit."

They took the two seats that were set up with water bottles and blank pads. Brodie noticed that the plate of strudel was still there. Must have been a plastic replica sourced from an IKEA showroom. Probably bugged.

Taylor asked, "Where is everyone?"

"The Germans have got their hands full," said Whitmore. "Chief Inspector Schröder called me about an hour ago to brief me about the bomb blast. I briefed Agent Kim immediately thereafter. As for the others" — she gestured to the empty chairs — "this has become a need-to-know matter."

Interesting. It made sense to exclude the State Department reps, but Brodie thought General Kiernan had a need to know.

Whitmore continued, "The blast that you both witnessed this morning was caused by an improvised explosive device consisting of ammonium nitrate and fuel oil. Three bodies were recovered from the apartment." She consulted some handwritten notes in front of her. "Two of the bodies have been identified as Abdul Aziz and Yosef Rahman, Syrian refugees who had immigrated to Germany approximately six months ago. They were both renters of the apartment. The third body was sitting closest to the detonation and will take longer to identify, but is possibly Zahid Bishara, their third roommate, who emigrated from Syria at the same time. Based on an initial analysis of the remnants of the device, which included a receiver and a detonator, the German authorities believe that the explosion was accidental, and that the victims were in the final stages of building a bomb that would be placed elsewhere and remotely detonated."

Well, that gave some credence to David Kim's theory. Bomb-making didn't leave a lot of room for error.

Whitmore continued, "Two cell phones were recovered at the scene, and technicians are currently at work gaining access to them. A laptop computer was sitting on a desk near the explosion, and any data on it is likely unsalvageable. However, the authorities located a USB thumb drive in one of the desk drawers which contained several images. The first few were of a dark-green Mercedes sedan parked in an underground lot. Different angles, including the underside of the car. These were time-stamped around seven A.M. yesterday morning, and geo-tagged to the Radisson Hotel in Alexanderplatz."

Brodie and Taylor exchanged glances, knowing what Whitmore was going to say next.

She looked at them. "The BKA has confirmed that the vehicle in the photos belongs to Mark Jenkins, Mr. Vance's former partner. The remainder of the photos on the flash drive are surveillance photos of Mr. Jenkins in Alexanderplatz. This is consistent with Mr. Jenkins' own account of being followed and surveilled by several individuals. The authorities believe that the bomb was intended for Mr. Jenkins' car."

Brodie asked, "Is Jenkins still in town?"

"He was preparing to depart this afternoon, but after I called him and briefed him on this, he has chosen to remain in Berlin until Mr. Vance's memorial service in Kaiserslautern this weekend."

Brodie wasn't surprised that Jenkins was sticking around. The guy didn't want to give the appearance of turning tail. As with any proud and occasionally stupid military man, cheating death was just an invitation to play the odds again.

More interestingly, Ms. Whitmore had just revealed that after receiving this information from the chief inspector, she had decided to conduct three separate briefings. Mark Jenkins, David Kim, and now Brodie and Taylor, with Jason Butler present. Why?

Whitmore looked again at her notes. "Several weapons were recovered from the apartment. Among them was a Heckler and Koch MP5 semi-automatic submachine gun with a night vision scope. This particular weapon had been converted for use with twenty-two long rifle rounds. Captain Soliman's team is running ballistics to determine if it was the rifle used to kill Mr. Vance, though he seemed confident they will discover that it was. And I share his confidence."

Taylor asked, "How can you be so sure?"

Whitmore looked at her. "Because of the other piece of evidence that they recovered. In the apartment freezer was a glass jar that contained a human eyeball."

The briefing room was silent as they absorbed what Whitmore had just said. There was physical evidence — the photos — linking the three dead men to the murder victim's partner, Mark Jenkins, and there was a potential murder weapon, and potential forensic evidence of the murder victim himself. The eyeball. Assuming the ballistics and genetic testing didn't offer up any surprises, this was case closed. Except, of course, for discovering motive and possible co-conspirators.

Taylor asked, "Do you have anything on these three Syrians?"

Whitmore replied, "They all emigrated from the city of Idlib in northwestern Syria. For most of the Syrian civil war and up to today, Idlib has been under the control of various Sunni extremist rebel groups, many of which have ties to al Qaeda. Inspector Schröder informed me that refugees from this particular part of Syria receive increased scrutiny and screening by the German government during the asylum application process. The authorities are currently looking further into these men's recent activities as well as their backgrounds, including — with the aid of our Defense Department — any connection that these individuals may have had to past or ongoing criminal investigations within Army CID or other American military law enforcement entities. Meanwhile, Berlin PD is canvassing Neukölln and questioning residents about the movements of these men in the last few days and weeks, as well as any known associations they may have had with radical groups."

She paused for a moment and looked between Brodie and Taylor. "The working theory is that a Sunni extremist group has chosen to assassinate American counterterrorism agents in Germany — and possibly Mr. Vance and Mr. Jenkins in particular — as revenge for some particular law enforcement action."

Brodie thought about that. Sunni extremists such as al Qaeda were the mortal enemies of Shi'ite terror groups like Hezbollah, which meant Agent Kim's favorite theory had just gone up in smoke along with the suspects. Hopefully he'd taken it okay.

On that subject, Brodie asked, "Why are we being briefed separately from Agent Kim?"

Whitmore pursed her lips. "Agent Kim is a CT expert with a top secret security clearance, and I wanted him to be able to speak freely to me about any intelligence that might inform this case without concern for what was being shared outside of the Bureau."

The FBI liked to keep it in the family. So did the Army. But on a case like this you were at least supposed to pretend that civilian and military law enforcement were one big happy family. Or at least related by marriage. Agent Whitmore appeared to be dropping the pretense.

"Speaking of Agent Kim," said Jason Butler, who seemed to have been waiting for his cue, "he asked us to give this to you." He slid a manila envelope across the conference table. "The FBI file on Tariq Qasim, a.k.a. Abbas al-Hamdani."

Taylor took the envelope. "Agent Kim has set a good example for interagency cooperation."

Whitmore, who was not setting a good example, did not reply.

Butler said, "Makes for interesting reading. Qasim was a colonel in the Iraqi Army, a military Intel guy who helped coordinate and execute Saddam's nerve gas attacks against the Iranians during the Iran-Iraq War in the eighties. Not much other info on him until after the 2003 American invasion, when he was the leader of an insurgent cell focused on killing his own people — Iraqi civilians who worked with the U.S.-led Coalition Provisional Authority. These terrorist activities are the reason Qasim was in our database in the first place. He switched sides a couple years later and joined the Sunni Awakening, which, as you may know, worked for us." He added, "I assume this is the only reason a guy with such a murderous background was granted asylum here in Germany."

Brodie knew of the Sunni Awakening — otherwise known as the Sons of Iraq — who were a coalition of Sunni tribes paid by the U.S. military to fight and kill the al Qaeda jihadists within their communities. They were mostly led by tribal elders as well as guys like Tariq Qasim — former officers in Saddam's military who saw an opportunity to switch to the winning team and get paid in the process.

Members of the Awakening were, unsurprisingly, marked for death by al Qaeda and their cohorts, who saw them as traitors to their sect and collaborators with the American infidels. It wasn't difficult for Brodie to imagine how a man like Qasim could secure asylum in the West as a political refugee. War criminals are bad until they're on your payroll, doing your bidding. And now Brodie wondered if Qasim had switched sides yet again and gotten himself involved with a Sunni extremist cell here in Germany that was assassinating American military counterterrorism agents.

Butler looked at Brodie and Taylor. "Do you have any idea why Mr. Vance would have been seeking this man out?"

"No," said Taylor. "We were hoping the FBI file would shed some light."

"It didn't to us, nor to Agent Kim. We shared a copy of Qasim's file with the BKA as well as with Mark Jenkins, who was not familiar with the names Tariq Qasim or his alias, Abbas al-Hamdani."

Whitmore added, "It is possible that Colonel Qasim had an operational connection to these Syrian bomb-makers, and that all of them were somehow related to an investigation that Mr. Vance was conducting without the knowledge or authorization of his commanding officer. It is also possible that Qasim has nothing to do with our investigation, and that you were given inaccurate information by your source, perhaps intentionally." She added, unnecessarily, "That's done all the time."

Jason Butler said to Brodie and Taylor, "Agent Kim explained to us the circumstances through which you obtained this name. At first I thought maybe Kim was making a joke, or you were BSing him."

"You might not like our methods," said Brodie, "but we don't trade in bullshit."

Butler ignored that. "I looked into this Rafeeq Nasir. You're both lucky to be alive."

"Luck had nothing to do with it."

Jason Butler leaned forward and clasped his hands together on the table, which he'd probably seen an FBI interrogator do on television. "What we want to know is, why would this Mr. Nasir help you? Why call attention to himself in the first place? And why should we trust anything he has to say?"

"We got on his radar," said Brodie. "And he wanted to know who was poking around his neighborhood. And he wants it to stop. Bad for business. If we hadn't been CID agents then maybe, as you suggested, we'd be dead. Who knows? And, frankly, at this point who cares? We got Intel, and we have now shared it with our good friends at the Bureau."

"It is difficult," said Whitmore, "to isolate this information from the source." She added, "And the extraordinarily reckless fashion in which it was acquired. I'm surprised that you believed any of what Rafeeq Nasir told you."

Brodie looked at Sharon Whitmore, who was staring back at him. This woman was hard to read. After a moment, she dropped the bomb: "We are concerned that your conduct is negatively impacting this investigation."

And now Brodie understood why General Kiernan wasn't here, and why David Kim had been briefed separately. When you're getting ready to shiv someone, it's best not to have any of their potential allies in the room.

Taylor asked, "Are we being relieved of our duties?"

Whitmore replied, "I have no authority to do that. But it is my role to advise your superiors of any actions I believe might improve the cooperation between American and German law enforcement. And even setting aside your blatant disregard for jurisdictional boundaries and your cavalier behavior which endangered your lives as well as the success of this investigation, the nature of this case has fundamentally changed since this morning. I will be recommending to the Provost Marshal General that he dispatch a team from the Fifth MP to take over the CID's role in this investigation, specifically a team from the Terrorism and Criminal Investigation Unit in which Mr. Vance served. They will have a more comprehensive understanding of the national security context behind the assassination of Mr. Vance and the planned assassination of Mr. Jenkins."

Brodie was sure that General Hackett would jump at an excuse to summon them back to the States. Would Colonel Dombroski have their backs? Hard to say. Did they even *want* this case if the legal attaché was treating them like this? Well, yes. Wounded pride is no excuse to abandon your duty.

As for Ms. Whitmore, she was a diplomat, and she wouldn't risk alienating the two CID agents on her team unless she was fairly confident that her recommendation was enough to send them home. Of course, she could have done this all behind their backs, without this face-to-face meeting. But that wasn't the Bureau's way. She was required to brief them until the moment they were no longer assigned to this case. In the FBI, even betrayal was by-the-book.

Whitmore assured them, "This is not personal. I am doing my job, which is to shepherd this case to a successful conclusion."

Brodie said, "A good shepherd can spot the wolves in sheep's clothing."

She stared at him with her unblinking brown eyes. "And who is that, in your estimation?"

"I don't know yet," replied Brodie. "But it's not us." He dug a scrap of paper out of his jacket pocket and tossed it on the table.

Whitmore picked up the paper and looked at it. "A phone number."

"For a man named Hasan. He is a congregant at the Al Mahdi Islamic Center in Neukölln, and he put Harry Vance in touch with Rafeeq Nasir. He lied to German investigators about this, out of fear of reprisal from Nasir, but he is now prepared to amend his statement."

Butler asked, "Last name?"

"We'll leave the detective work to you." Brodie looked at a note on his phone, then jotted another name and number on the pad in front of him and slid it across the table. "And this is Faruk. Works at the Ember Berlin hookah lounge on Karl-Marx Straße in Neukölln. He saw Mr. Vance the night of his murder. He also lied to German investigators, and for a similar reason to why Hasan lied. The Lebanese mobs in Neukölln have a lot of power, and people are easily intimidated by them. Faruk is also ready to amend his official statement."

If Jason Butler was impressed, he didn't say so, but he did say, "I don't know how you found these people — or how they found you — but it appears that they told you what you wanted to hear, or what they wanted you to hear. In any case, it seems that you have stepped into off-limits territory."

"That's where all the answers are, Jason."

Butler had no reply.

Taylor, following her partner's lead, transcribed a note from her phone to her pad and slid it over. "And this is the address and phone number for Anna Albrecht, Harry's lover here in Berlin. We interviewed her in person, at her apartment, and she had some interesting stories to tell that she is ready to repeat to the German authorities." She added, "Mr. Vance's personal effects are in her apartment."

Except, thought Brodie, for the microscope slide that he had in his pocket, and which he decided not to hand over.

Whitmore remained poker-faced as she stared at the pad containing Anna Albrecht's contact info, but Jason Butler looked like he'd lost another hand of five-card stud. He asked, "How did you find her?"

Brodie replied, "We were looking for her. We find people we're looking for."

Butler had no response to Brodie's arrogance, but informed Brodie and Taylor,

"This woman had an intimate relationship with the murder victim and did not identify herself to the police. She could be a flight risk. And if she skips town —"

Brodie interrupted, "It was obvious to us within three minutes of meeting her that she was a witness, not a suspect." He added, because he and Taylor were going to be sacked anyway, "I'm sure it would be obvious even to an FBI agent, Jason."

Butler did not reply directly to the insult, but said, "You know, I began my FBI career in the Boston field office. I often had to work with local law enforcement. Staties were mostly professional. But the Boston detectives . . . the cops . . . they were always about their instincts, their *guts*. A lot of posturing and BS from little cowboys with big chips on their shoulders. And when it hit the fan, you couldn't count on them. You'd see the fraud you always knew was there."

Brodie said, "I'm sure the feeling was mutual."

Whitmore said, "Gentlemen, please."

Brodie enjoyed a good pissing match, but it was time to return to business. He took Harry Vance's passport from his pocket and put it on the table in front of Whitmore. "We took this from Mr. Vance's personal possessions that were in Ms. Albrecht's apartment. It is the property of the United States government, and I return it to you."

Whitmore opened the passport and flipped through it, but said nothing.

Taylor said to FBI Agents Whitmore and Butler, "My instincts tell me you're not going to congratulate us on a job well done."

Neither Whitmore nor Butler responded, but Butler said, "You'll write a report on all this . . . all you've done since you've been here. And if Ms. Albrecht skips town, you're in a world of trouble."

Brodie assured him, "We can find her again."

Whitmore was looking increasingly uncomfortable with this conversation and placed her hand on Butler's arm, which was enough to shut him up.

Brodie said to Whitmore, "I'm glad to see you've got him on a short leash. Might also need a muzzle."

She stared at him. "You have gone *way* beyond your authority."

"That's easy to do when we had no authority to begin with."

"You understood the parameters of this assignment when you accepted it. I see now that you had no intention of respecting those parameters." She looked at Taylor. "I have to say, I expected much more professionalism from the CID."

Taylor looked pissed off, and said, "The motto of the CID is 'Do What Has to Be Done.' And we did."

Whitmore ignored that as she produced a dark-blue folder from the pile of paperwork in front of her and slid it across the table. "As long as you are the agents on this case and have not yet been relieved of your duty, I am obligated to share any pertinent information provided by German law enforcement. There's a preliminary report on the Neukölln bombing prepared by the BKA and translated by my office, as well as a list from Berlin PD of any sightings of Mr. Vance on public surveillance cameras from when he arrived at the Berlin central train station on Tuesday to when he disembarked the metro in Neukölln in the early hours of Sunday — the night of his death."

Taylor took the folder and slipped it into her satchel.

Whitmore added, "I regret that our working relationship is ending this way. But as the embassy legal attaché, I will do what I believe I must in order to find justice for Mr. Vance."

"Right," said Brodie as he stood and grabbed his coat. "And I promise you, so will we."

CHAPTER 26

Scott Brodie and Maggie Taylor strode in silence across Pariser Platz. Finally Taylor said, "Well, they turned out to be assholes."

"Comes with the territory." He added, "Not excusing them, but working in a foreign country is a balancing act."

"I'm sure they were assholes back in the States."

"Maybe we bring out the worst in people."

"Speak for yourself." She added, "Actually, you're an asshole."

"Only when I work with you."

They both got a smile out of that.

Taylor said, "More importantly, we're about to be relieved of our duties."

"That's what happens when you show personal initiative in government work."

She glanced at him as they walked. "Dombroski will go to bat for us."

"He used all his goodwill with General Hackett to get us on this case, and I don't think he's got much left to go against the recommendation of the legal attaché."

"Call him."

"He'll call us when he's ready to pull the plug on us. No reason to hasten the inevitable."

She looked at him. "You're just accepting this?"

"I'm acknowledging the situation. It's up to us how we respond, but I guarantee you that whining to the boss will do nothing." He added, "Dombroski is worried about his own ass by now."

Taylor said, "He stuck his neck out to get us this assignment."

"He should have known better."

They exited the square and walked east along tree-lined Unter den Linden. A light dusting of snow was settling over the city beneath a rolling gray sky.

Taylor looked deep in thought. "The bombing seems to have answered the question of who killed Harry Vance, but the proposed motive sounds vague and I'm not sure I buy it." She looked at him. "What do you think?"

"I think that Mark Jenkins and David Kim both gave us some compelling reasons as to why Iranian-backed Shi'ite militias might have had a hand in killing Harry. And now suddenly we're dealing with Syrian bombmakers who might have a connection to al Qaeda. Plus there's Qasim, a former Saddam loyalist and WMD officer whose last-known affiliation was helping us hunt down and kill al Qaeda terrorists in Iraq. Never mind the whole Stasi business with Anna. It's like we keep finding puzzle pieces, but they're all for different puzzles."

Taylor considered that. "We need to stay focused on motive. Not just of the killers, but of the victim. Harry was looking for Odin, and he was also looking for Tariq Qasim. We don't know if those two things are linked, but one of them has got to be connected to his murder."

"Right. And if locating Tariq Qasim — or other Iraqi military Intel people — was part of an official counterterrorism investigation, Mark Jenkins would have been looped in. There's something else going on."

Taylor gestured at her satchel. "Maybe the Stasi report from Ms. Albrecht or the law enforcement reports we received from Whitmore will give us some answers."

"Save the reading for the flight home. I think we've got a few hours at most before Hackett tells Dombroski to yank us. Meanwhile, we have time for maybe one more play."

She looked at him. "You, Mr. Brodie, are a bloodhound without a scent. Or, to put it in military terms, a homing missile without a heat signature. We need more information before we can make another move."

She had a point. He pulled out his phone

and ran a Google search for Abbas al-Hamdani, Tariq Qasim's alias. He got a few hits for listings in the German white pages, but only one with an address in Berlin, an apartment on Stuttgarter Straße. Was this their guy? Possibly. Colonel Tariq Qasim wanted to live an anonymous life, and he probably assumed that taking an alias would offer enough protection from his past, and had not thought to make sure that alias was delisted from the online phone directory.

Taylor asked, "What are you doing?"

"Picking up a scent." He entered the address in his GPS and saw that Mr. Hamdani lived on a small street on the eastern edge of Neukölln. He checked his watch. "It's eleven thirty-five. Based on Whitmore's timeline, she couldn't have spoken to Kim more than an hour ago, which is when she would have received the FBI file on Qasim and then passed it on to the BKA. We might be able to check Qasim's apartment before Schröder's people get the same idea."

Taylor thought for a moment. "You seem determined to make this a race between getting sent home or being arrested by the Germans."

"There's a third option. Cracking this case before anyone else."

"You're delusional."

"I'm motivated."

"Yes, but by what?"

"Same as always. Duty and justice."

"I was thinking spite, arrogance, and a nose-diving career."

"Whatever gets the job done."

CHAPTER 27

They took a taxi to Neukölln, and as they rode, Taylor pulled out the FBI file on Tariq Qasim and looked it over. She read aloud in a low voice, "Qasim was an ambitious young officer and fierce Saddam Hussein loyalist throughout the 1970s. When Iraq invaded Iran in September 1980, Colonel Qasim was ideally positioned to take on a prominent role in the war effort. He was instrumental in devising the most effective methods of deploying sarin gas, mustard gas, and other deadly chemical agents against Iranian military units and Iranian civilians in villages near the Iraqi border. Qasim's efforts were bolstered in the final years of the war in part by the exploitation of dual-use materials supplied by the United States and other allied nations."

Brodie absorbed that. "Dual-use" was political doublespeak for military tech that could have peaceful, civilian applications, but could also be weaponized. If the U.S. was sending "dual-use materials" to a guy like Colonel Qasim in the middle of a brutal war with the Iranians, it probably wasn't Kevlar vests.

Brodie said, "It's no secret that we gave Iraq assistance during that war. But I assumed it was things like military intelligence, maybe conventional munitions. This sounds like something else."

Taylor added, "The Soviets also supported Iraq in the war. In fact, the Iran-Iraq War is one of the only Cold War–era conflicts I can think of where the U.S. and the Russians were on the same side."

Brodie nodded. "Everyone was freaked out by the crazies in Iran. So, Colonel Qasim was getting clandestine WMD assistance from our government. And possibly from the Soviets as well."

"Right."

Brodie couldn't quite get past the fact that the United States had assisted Saddam Hussein with his WMD program — the same WMD program that Scott Brodie and over a hundred thousand other American soldiers were sent to Iraq decades later to destroy. Of course, it turned out that Saddam had done the job of destroying the weapons himself throughout the nineties, while simultaneously encouraging the impression that he'd secretly held on to some of them, in what he thought was a clever ploy to deter the Americans and their allies from launching an invasion — but was actually a green light for the gang of warmongers in Washington thirsty for blood. Wrong move, Saddam.

Brodie tried to refocus on the case. The truth was, he'd never imagined this murder in Berlin would bring up so much Iraqi history, which in turn brought up a lot of Scott Brodie history. He said to Taylor, "The takeaway is that our person of interest in this case, Colonel Tariq Qasim, was using some nasty stuff, and some of it was supplied by our own government. Is this relevant to our homicide investigation?"

Taylor thought for a moment, then said, "We don't know yet. But maybe."

Brodie looked out the window as the taxi wound through the streets of Neukölln. Traffic was light but the cars were slowed by the snow, which was becoming heavier. Only a few pedestrians were out and about.

They passed a mosque, with a Berlin PD van parked out front and two officers with assault rifles flanking the entrance. By now reports on the nearby explosion would be all over the news, though undoubtedly with some key details missing. Brodie had a feeling that Neukölln and other Muslim neighborhoods were going to be under the eye for a while.

The cabbie turned onto Stuttgarter Straße, a tree-lined cobblestone street, and stopped in front of a dilapidated postwar apartment block covered with peeling mustard-yellow stucco and graffiti. "Wir sind da."

Brodie paid the driver, and they exited the taxi and approached the building where Tariq Qasim, a.k.a. Abbas al-Hamdani, lived — if he was still alive.

They walked into the foyer and Brodie looked at the call box. A few of the buttons had handwritten names on strips of tape, but Hamdani's apartment, 2D, had no name listed. Brodie pushed the button and waited. As expected, no response. He checked the glass-paneled door to the lobby. It was locked. "We'll wait for someone to come in or out."

"You're going soft, Scott. Let's just kick down the door."

He couldn't tell if she was serious or if she was mocking him. Actually, he could tell.

Taylor looked at her watch. "Let's give it five minutes."

"Three."

"It's about the time for midday prayers. Someone will be coming out."

"You couldn't get me out to pray on a day like this." He added, "Good thinking."

"Somebody has to."

Brodie didn't reply. He and Taylor waited in the outer foyer. After a few minutes, they could see through the glass-paneled door two middle-aged men in winter coats coming down the stairs and walking across the lobby toward them.

The two men opened the door and looked at Brodie and Taylor, probably thinking, *There goes the neighborhood,* as they exited the building.

Taylor pushed the door open before it shut and locked, then held it for Brodie, who entered the lobby with Taylor behind him.

They crossed the small lobby to the staircase and climbed to the second-floor landing, where there were four doors that led to the apartments. They approached apartment 2D, and Brodie noticed it had no peephole and no deadlock. But maybe there was a bolt or chain on the inside. He said to Taylor, "Say we're the police."

There was no doorbell, so Taylor knocked hard on the door and shouted something in Arabic.

They waited. No answer. Brodie put his ear to the door and said, "He's either not home, he's sleeping, he's frightened, or he's dead."

"Or injured," said Taylor, quoting from the manual of forced entry.

"Or maybe having sex in the shower. Okay . . ." Brodie looked at the door, which was more substantial than Anna's. "We can do this."

"Not without alerting half the building."

"We're cops. You just shouted that. We have ID."

"Try the doorknob. That's what burglars do first."

He tried the knob, and to his surprise it turned and he heard and felt the bolt slide. He looked at Taylor and nodded.

This was where they'd draw their guns and again ID themselves as police. But they had no guns, and their status was at best ambiguous. Brodie waved Taylor back, then pushed the door open a few inches and peered inside.

You never knew what you were going to find on the other side of an unlocked door. Usually nothing, but sometimes a dead body. Brodie sniffed the air, but couldn't detect that distinctive smell of a decomposing corpse.

Sometimes danger lurked in a quiet apartment; someone waiting in ambush, like in Baghdad, or in Anna's apartment, for that matter.

He motioned for Taylor to stay put and stepped into a small foyer that led to a hallway.

As Brodie's eyes adjusted to the dim light, he noticed a small side table in the foyer. And the reason he noticed it was because it was not against the wall. It had been moved or pushed and was now toward the middle of the foyer. A ceramic bowl that had obviously been on the side table now lay on the bare wooden floor next to a set of keys.

This was a textbook sign of a struggle in

the foyer, which would explain the unlocked door. A person or persons had gained entry to 2D, either because Abbas al-Hamdani had opened the door to them, or because they had somehow secured a key or picked the lock. In either case, they'd encountered Mr. Hamdani in the foyer and apparently abducted him in some manner — either at gunpoint or by rendering him unconscious. Or they just killed him and took the body with them. But there were no signs of blood. In any case, they'd left quickly with Hamdani, and had not bothered to lock the door after them. Or Hamdani was here, dead.

Taylor had come into the foyer while Brodie was reconstructing the crime and she said in a whisper, "He got snatched."

Brodie nodded. "Okay, let's assume we're alone, but be cautious, and let's have a look around."

Taylor nodded, then closed the door and locked it.

Brodie said, "The police will be here at some point, so let's not disturb the scene too much."

"Actually, we should call the police."

"Later. From a pay phone."

"Scott —"

"The only nice thing about being fired is that you have nothing left to lose."

She didn't reply.

Up ahead were two open doorways that led

to rooms illuminated by windows. Brodie signaled for Taylor to take the left, and they quietly walked down the hall. Brodie stepped into the right-hand doorway, into a narrow, cramped kitchen. Dim gray light shone through a small window that faced an alley.

The kitchen was a mess. Dirty dishes and still water filled the sink. Some empty frozen-food boxes were strewn on the countertop, along with an ashtray full of cigarette butts. Dust, grime, and some food waste were scattered over the linoleum floor. Obviously, there was no longer a Mrs. Qasim in the picture, and Tariq Qasim had gone full bachelor.

Brodie moved back into the hallway and walked through the other doorway, which led to a modestly sized living room with two windows that also faced the alley. Taylor was checking a closet. She closed it and shook her head.

Brodie looked around. A tufted sofa sat atop a Persian rug beneath some framed landscapes of what looked like the German countryside that were at no risk of reminding Tariq Qasim of his homeland. On the coffee table were a few Arab-language newspapers and dirty coffee mugs. There was an ugly recliner facing a small flat-screen TV, and a desk tucked in the corner that was piled with papers.

Brodie signaled to Taylor, and they quietly

walked through the room to another hallway that featured two doors. One led to a small bathroom that made the kitchen look clean.

They entered the bedroom and Brodie checked under the bed while Taylor checked the closet, looking for bodies, dead or alive. The place was a pigsty; more importantly, it had obviously not been searched.

Taylor said, "I'm going to search the desk in the living room."

She left and Brodie had a closer look around. On top of an old wooden dresser stood a few framed photos. One of them appeared to be a wedding portrait of Mr. and Mrs. Qasim. They were a good-looking and happy young couple, and Brodie wondered if they'd tied the knot before or after Qasim began his successful career in deploying gases to the masses.

Another framed photo almost made Brodie do a double-take: four Iraqi men in military uniforms stood arm-in-arm in front of a tall archway made of glazed blue bricks and covered in reliefs of dragons, bulls, and lions. Brodie recognized this as the Ishtar Gate, which stood at one end of the ruins of the ancient city of Babylon about seventy miles outside of Baghdad. Brodie had an almost identical picture of himself and three of his men who had stopped at the ruins during a resupply. This photo featured Colonel Qasim and three of his fellow officers, sporting olive-drab uniforms along with the Ba'ath Party's standard-issue black berets. They all had Saddam Hussein look-alike mustaches.

Brodie looked closer at the blue Ishtar Gate, which, like much of the current-day ruins of Babylon, was actually a somewhat tacky reproduction commissioned by Saddam for his own glorification. Saddam had even — to the horror of the archeological community — stamped his own name on the bricks used for the reconstruction effort, to mimic the practice of the Babylonian king who had built the original ancient capital. In his delusions, Saddam Hussein dreamed that modern Iraq would become the new Babylon, and he the new Nebuchadnezzar. Instead, Mr. Hussein had wound up at the end of a hangman's noose. Men plan and God laughs.

Brodie remembered that the original Ishtar Gate was in fact right there in Berlin, at the Pergamon Museum only a few miles from where he was standing. Brodie had seen it with Adam Kogan, who thought they needed to add some culture to their debauchery. Brodie had never imagined, as he'd stared up at the ancient gate, that only a few years later he'd be standing in the ruins of Babylon, in desert fatigues, holding his M4 carbine. A changed man in a changed world.

Brodie moved to the closet, which was full of clothes. A rolled-up prayer rug sat on a small table at the bottom of the closet. He then checked the dresser drawers, which were also full. If Qasim had left town of his own volition, then he'd certainly packed light. Definitely a snatch job.

Brodie opened the drawer in the bedside table, which contained a leather-bound Quran. It looked like an antique, with gilt inlays on the cover and handwritten calligraphy illuminated by gold frames on every page. Likely worth at least a few thousand bucks, and not the kind of thing you'd leave behind. Brodie knew that Saddam Hussein gifted Qurans such as this to his favored politicians and military commanders.

He returned the Quran to the drawer and doubled back to the living room, where Taylor was still looking through the desk. He said, "Don't leave any fingerprints or DNA that can be traced back to you."

"A little late for that, Scott. We're up to our asses in unauthorized activities."

"We'll be okay. Nothing succeeds like success."

"Are we in the same Army?" She picked up an envelope that looked like junk mail and handed it to him. On the back of the envelope were a few handwritten words in Arabic script.

She pointed to the handwriting. "This says 'jamra,' which I've heard used to refer to coal. But I looked it up, and it can also mean 'ember.' As in, Ember Berlin. The hookah lounge where Harry was before his murder."

That sounded like a stretch, except for the fact that Vance had been looking for this man Hamdani, and based on Harry's described behavior at Ember Berlin he very well could have set up a meeting there that was then canceled, or relocated to the park.

Taylor pointed to the next word. "This says 'Storkow.' I ran a search and it's a small town southeast of here. I found this article."

Taylor handed him her phone, displaying a 1991 article from the *Boston Herald* titled, "EAST GERMANS ASSISTED IRAQIS WITH BIOLOGICAL AND CHEMICAL ARMS AT BERLIN SITE."

Taylor continued, "It says that in the 1980s, the East German Army trained Iraqis in the use of biological and chemical weapons at a facility located outside of Berlin, in the town of Storkow. Iraqi officers used Storkow as a model to build their own WMD training facility in Iraq."

"Okay. And?"

"This is it, Scott. This is the connection. Harry was looking for an American double agent working for the East Germans — Odin. And he was also looking for an Iraqi military Intel officer who specialized in biological and chemical warfare. That would be Tariq Qasim, now known as Abbas al-Hamdani. Qasim was most likely trained at this East German facility. And I'd bet you anything that Odin was there. Maybe they met. Maybe they worked together. Qasim could have IDed Odin, which is why Harry Vance was looking for him."

That was a lot of conjecture on Ms. Taylor's part. Just because Odin was spying for the Stasi didn't mean he would have any reason or desire to visit an East German military WMD facility. On the other hand, Brodie and Taylor were trying to find a connection between Harry's two extracurricular activities here in Berlin — finding Odin and finding Tariq Qasim — and this facility in Storkow could be it.

He looked at the bottom of the envelope, where he saw written 3:00 next to another Arabic word. "I'm going to guess this says Sunday."

Taylor nodded. "Vance and Hamdani were to meet at three A.M. Sunday morning at Ember Berlin to discuss something about Storkow."

"And then Hamdani didn't show. Or he told Vance to meet him in the park instead. A setup."

Taylor shook her head. "Rafeeq Nasir told us that Hamdani never opened his shoe store on Saturday. And that no one could get in touch with Hamdani all day. And you and I agree that it looks like Hamdani was snatched from here. In which case, the person Vance was in contact with in the early morning hours of Sunday was not Hamdani. Harry was set up in Körnerpark, but not by the guy he was supposed to meet. There was a third party."

"The Syrians who detonated themselves this morning."

Taylor didn't respond.

"Taylor?"

She looked at him. "Could you have asked for a more perfect crime scene? Murder weapon, physical evidence from the victim's body, a thumb drive full of photos that telegraph the killers' next victim?"

"I like crime scenes where the perps didn't splatter themselves all over the walls. Easier to question."

"That's right," said Taylor. "Dead men tell no tales."

"What are you implying? A false flag?"

"I don't know," said Taylor. "But . . . something is off here."

She took the envelope from Brodie and snapped a photo of it with her cell phone, then put it back on the desk where she'd found it. She said, "I think we've found what we can, and we don't want to have a run-in with the chief inspector."

They left the apartment and walked down the stairs and out onto the street. Brodie scanned the road. A few cars and a van waited at a red light at the nearest intersection. An old maroon Mercedes idled in front of a nearby café. After a moment a tall white-haired man in a black topcoat exited the café carrying a briefcase. He got in the car, which remained at the curb.

Taylor asked, "What are you doing?"

"Trying to be more aware than yesterday, when Rafeeq Nasir's errand boy apparently tailed us for hours."

Taylor gestured to her satchel. "We need to see if any of the material we received from the Fifth MP and the German investigators, or the report from Anna, will help us fit some more of this together."

"Maggie, I'm not sitting around reading right now. Any minute my phone is going to ring, and it's going to be the colonel telling us it's game over."

"Then turn off your phone."

"I don't think it works like that."

"We need to look over these reports, Scott."

"All right . . . so long as I can do it with a drink in my hand."

She looked around. "We need to get out of this neighborhood."

Brodie thought about the Hotel Adlon, back in Mitte near the embassy. Given their conduct so far on this case, it was kind of in keeping with the theme to go to the only spot in all of Berlin where Brodie had been banned from ever returning. He said to Taylor, "I know just the place."

438

CHAPTER 28

Scott Brodie and Maggie Taylor walked into the lobby of the Hotel Adlon on Unter den Linden and entered the bar. They were greeted by a hostess who led them to two upholstered chairs flanking a low coffee table in an isolated corner of the large lounge. It was a handsome space, with a white marble floor, exotic plants and flowers scattered around, and a soaring atrium featuring an intricate stained-glass dome. The lounge was moderately crowded with some well-dressed business types as well as a few slovenly tourists.

Taylor picked up the menu and said, "We should get some small bites."

"Order the caviar. It's on the American taxpayer."

Taylor ignored that, and when the waiter came by, she ordered a few hors d'oeuvres and a white wine.

Brodie ordered a beer, then looked over at the Elephant Fountain. It was the centerpiece of the lounge, featuring polished black stone elephants spouting water from their trunks, which might have been what had given Adam Kogan his bright idea all those years ago. Brodie had an image of his drunk friend pissing into the circular pool below the elephants, holding on to a tusk for support. He now recalled that Kogan had slipped off the edge of the fountain and back into an armchair, his own trunk still hanging out.

"What are you smiling about?"

Brodie looked at Taylor, who was laying out the paperwork from her satchel on the coffee table. "My last time here."

Taylor looked around the high-end lounge. "I can't believe you came to this place as a college student."

"We didn't stay long."

"You were supposed to tell me why you got comped."

"My roommate had a slip and fall at the fountain."

Taylor gave him a suspicious look, then tapped the papers on the coffee table. "What do you want to read?"

"You review the material from the BKA and Berlin PD while I read the Stasi report from Anna. Then we'll split the CID files."

Taylor handed him the envelope from Anna Albrecht, and Brodie opened it and removed a twenty-page document titled, "ON THE ACTIVITIES OF SECRET AGENT ODIN,

PREPARED AT THE REQUEST OF MIN-ISTER ERICH MIELKE," and which was dated October 1989.

Brodie began to read:

This report documents the aid rendered by the American agent codenamed Odin to the Ministry of State Security in its mission to uncover and liquidate traitors to the German Democratic Republic. Through his actions, Odin has helped defend the nation from the pernicious and reactionary forces in the West who would seek to dismantle the state and delay the inevitable victory of Marxism-Leninism.

A note on the contents of this report: In accordance with the new security protocols enacted by Deputy Minister Grossman of the Main Directorate for Reconnaissance, details which are irrelevant to a concise and accurate accounting of Odin's execution of his duties — yet which might reveal the identity of said asset to enemy intelligence in the event of infiltration or theft of materials — have been excised from the narrative.

Well, that would explain why this report had not yet led to the discovery of Odin's identity. Rather than rely on redactions, the Stasi had been self-censoring their own history on the assumption that traitors and spies were all around them. Probably a good bet. He continued reading:

On March 6th, 1983, Odin first made contact with an individual within the Ministry, promising valuable intelligence about pro-Western moles within the GDR state security apparatus. Odin presented himself as a high-ranking individual within the American military who was stationed in the American sector of occupied Berlin. Odin asserted that he would maintain his Berlin posting for several years to come, and thus could provide intelligence at regular and reliable intervals.

The offer was met with an appropriate level of skepticism and scrutiny. Odin's motives were evaluated, based on his own claims as well as his professional and personal circumstances. Odin's position within the American military occupation of the western sectors of Berlin granted him unique insight and access, which the Ministry deemed valuable to securing a stable and sovereign socialist state free of malicious influence by bourgeois and fascist elements.

The waiter delivered their drinks, and Brodie was grateful to have the beer to help him get through the report's tortured prose. Was something lost in translation? Or was it worse in the original German?

He continued reading. The report was written in such a vague way that even someone with a granular understanding of the American military's presence in West Berlin would not have been able to discern the covert operative's identity. A few pages in, Brodie found something interesting on the subject of Odin's motivation:

The asset, Odin, refused payment of any kind and insisted that he was driven purely by ideological conviction. This, naturally, led to a degree of doubt by his handler. The asset said he believed that while the triumph of Marxism-Leninism was desirable, it was not inevitable. On the contrary, capitalism was a powerful and malignant force that would achieve unfettered dominance in the postcolonial world unless more was done to demonstrate the successful application of an alternative economic system. It was his view that the GDR was the ideal vehicle to set a positive example for this alternative way of life. His beliefs, while clearly a product of a mind-set warped by the imperialist system within which he lived and operated, were nonetheless judged to be sincerely held, and were thus exploitable to assure the asset's continued cooperation, loyalty, and efficacy.

There were a few rambling paragraphs about why Marxism-Leninism — Communism — was of course the inevitable next phase of human society's evolution. Brodie skimmed it and then reached the section describing Odin's first success in outing a mole within the Stasi:

On November 2nd, 1983, Odin communicated to his handler that he was aware of a double agent within the Ministry. He did not know the name of the traitor, but he did potentially have access to the documents that the agent provided to American intelligence. He shared that the agent was promising information related to the National People's Army and its offensive capabilities and strategic posture. Odin's handler understood this meant that the traitor was within the Main Directorate for Reconnaissance. At Odin's direction, and with the express permission of Deputy Director Wolf, the Administration manufactured multiple erroneous intelligence reports, all identical except for a few minor alterations. These reports were distributed among many suspects within the Directorate. Once the double agent duplicated and shared his uniquely altered report with his American handler, Odin was able to acquire the intelligence documents and transfer them back to the Ministry. This strategy had the dual purpose of feeding misinformation to the Americans while also exposing an enemy of the state. It was through this technique that the Ministry was able to identify the traitor Karl Liebnick, who was arrested, tried, and executed.

The report was describing what Brodie knew to be a standard piece of counterespionage tradecraft: Flush a few turds down the pipe — the bad Intel — and see which one comes back.

It seemed to work well for Odin and his Stasi conspirators, and they used this same technique two more times, in 1984 and 1986, to blow the cover on Hans Müller and Paul Fischer. The fate of both men was summarized with the same clinical efficiency. *Arrested, tried, and executed.* Also tortured and interrogated, but that detail was left out.

As with Karl Liebnick, both Müller and Fischer had worked within the Main Directorate for Reconnaissance — German abbreviation HVA — which Brodie surmised was the foreign intelligence service within the Stasi. Their equivalent of the CIA. That made sense. While the Stasi spent much of its resources tracking and harassing its own internal dissidents and imagined dissidents, what the Americans cared about were the international players.

Brodie continued to read:

Beginning shortly after the arrest of Mr. Fischer, Deputy Director Wolf sought to explore other ways that Odin's unique access might benefit the state. At this time, Odin's handler pressed the asset for military intelligence pertaining to his branch of the American armed services. Odin refused. He maintained that since the Ministry was compromised, he would provide no intelligence that might be traceable back to him. His handler offered him a direct pipeline to Deputy Director Wolf and Director Mielke, with strict protocols that would ensure the utmost security. He still refused, and would not provide additional intelligence until all parties were confident that the Ministry had been cleansed of traitors. This was typical of the asset's intractable and stubborn nature, which could at times be detrimental to the larger mission.

So, Odin had been offered direct access to Erich Mielke, the head of the Stasi, and had turned it down. He was clearly concerned about being caught, and single-minded in his mission to rid East Germany's state security apparatus of Western spies. Which was understandable, since the Stasi — and probably the entire East German government — seemed to have a serious loyalty problem. No one at the time knew that the Cold War was coming to an end, but maybe the East German regime and the Stasi felt — even subconsciously — that they were on a sinking ship of state.

The waiter arrived with their hors d'oeuvres and set them on the coffee table. "Is there anything else I can get you?"

Taylor declined, and Brodie ordered another pilsner.

Taylor picked at the hors d'oeuvres. "I'm going through the metro system's surveillance camera sightings of Vance. Even accounting for the fact that he wasn't picked up on a camera every time he used the U-Bahn or S-Bahn, it's clear he was busy during the days. I'll need to cross-reference these stops with any relevant points of interest nearby, see if it tells us anything. How's the Stasi report reading?"

Brodie briefly described the salvaged Stasi document and added, "So far, I can deduce a few things. First, Odin was not in dire financial straits, otherwise he would have accepted payment for his services. It seemed important to him that they believed he was doing it for the cause. This was a guy with a lot of self-importance, who also valued the trust and respect of the people he was conspiring with."

Taylor nodded. "Everyone's the hero of their own story. Even traitors."

"The other thing is that Odin had access to intelligence products, perhaps from other

447

American or allied Intel agencies. So, he's an Intel guy of some sort, maybe an analyst, maybe counterintelligence. All we know is that he's military. Let's say, for the sake of argument, he's Army. He knows there's a mole in the Stasi. How? Either the mole is communicating with someone else in Army intelligence, or Odin has sufficient rank and security clearance or sufficiently developed interagency and interbranch relationships that he knows he can get access. And even if Odin gets lucky and mole number one — Karl Liebnick — was communicating with Army intelligence, what are the chances that the other three moles in the Stasi were also going through Army Intel? They could have been in contact with Air Force or Navy intelligence, or the CIA, or someone in State Department Intel. But Odin manages to identify four double agents in seven years. That's a hell of a track record. I think we are dealing with a high-ranking military intelligence officer. Colonel or above."

"That would explain the self-importance."

Brodie smiled. He continued, "We need to understand more about the Stasi foreign intelligence agency. The HVA. Set aside the docs from Berlin PD for now and research it. What role did the HVA play in state security? This report mentions the East German Army's 'offensive capabilities and strategic posture.' What is that? What were they up to around this time, or what did our Intel people think they were up to? This report is the tip of an iceberg, and a lot of what used to be below the water has probably been declassified since 1989. So you should be able to find something."

Taylor was quiet a moment. "Scott, are we investigating Harry's murder? Or are we doing the job he never finished?"

Brodie looked at her. "They might be one and the same."

CHAPTER 29

The Adlon's lounge was getting busier and rowdier, thanks to a large crowd of British corporate conference types — judging by their lanyards and nametags — who were having a good time at the bar on the company's dime. Brodie knew he could outspend them on taxpayer money if he didn't get the call from Dombroski firing him.

Meanwhile, Brodie sipped his beer and resumed reading:

In February 1988, Odin contacted his handler with a concern. He demanded a meeting with Deputy Chief Heinrich Tauchert, to be held at a specific military training facility outside of Berlin. His demand was granted. Odin entered the GDR via East Berlin using false papers and a tourist pass. He proceeded to the training facility where he met with Deputy Tauchert, who reported that the meeting went well and satisfied Odin's concerns.

During this visit, Odin had a brief interaction with visiting military officials from a client nation who were participating in a training program. Deputy Tauchert reported being surprised that Odin — who was fluent in German — spoke in English and identified himself to the foreign officials as an American defector. Deputy Tauchert considered Odin's behavior to be reckless, and believed that it raised broader concerns about Odin's commitment to strict security protocols.

Brodie stopped reading and passed Taylor the page he had just read. "I think I found what sent Harry looking for Colonel Qasim."

Taylor read the page and handed it back to Brodie. "So, Harry read this report, and researched what military facilities in East Germany had been training foreign officials. He discovered the Iraq-Storkow connection, and maybe accessed now-declassified East German files to obtain the names of Iraqi military officials who were present at the Storkow training facility in 1988."

"Right. And among those names he finds Colonel Tariq Qasim. Vance might have been able to exploit his own resources as a CID counterterrorism investigator to get information about Colonel Qasim's activities and whereabouts in the following years, and he learned that Qasim resettled in Berlin after

451

the fall of Saddam. But he couldn't locate Qasim because the man had taken a new identity. So, suspecting that, Harry did what he'd probably done before and visited mosques in Berlin, maybe starting with Neukölln, looking for men with Qasim's background."

Taylor nodded. "But if Harry had access to declassified documents about this East German military facility in Storkow, wouldn't he also have the names of East Germans who were present there? And wouldn't those individuals be easier to locate, and perhaps more likely to be able to identify Odin?"

Brodie considered that, then replied, "These declassified documents that Vance got hold of would have redactions of the names of German citizens — for legal or civil liberties reasons — but the documents would not redact the names of Iraqi military officials. One way or another, Vance believed or suspected that Tariq Qasim was present at the Storkow facility at the same time as Odin, and that Tariq was still alive, and living in Berlin under a pseudonym. Maybe Harry had some suspects in mind for Odin and was going to show Qasim some photos he'd gotten from military personnel files. It was a long shot, but for Harry it was one worth taking."

Instead, someone else took a long shot, right into Vance's head. As for the Stasi report, it put Harry's behavior in some

452

context, but so far was producing no leads of its own.

Taylor said, "The report is vague on Odin's reason for the meeting at Storkow. He had a *concern* which was *satisfied.*"

"Maybe in his official capacity as a U.S. Intel officer, Odin caught wind of something about Stasi operations that needed clarification or corroboration. Maybe something that involved this Tauchert guy."

Taylor typed on her tablet. "Heinrich Tauchert was the deputy head of the HVA. Before being promoted to deputy, he oversaw the Stasi's military intelligence division, which worked alongside the National People's Army's own Intel service." She looked up at Brodie. "He died two years ago."

Brodie nodded. "The first mole, Karl Liebnick, was sharing Intel about the National People's Army. Could be related. A joint military-Stasi operation."

"Could be."

"A joint operation that involves chemical or biological weapons."

"Maybe."

Brodie thought a moment and said, "Odin wants to help his Communist pals, but does not want to collude in a biological or chemical warfare attack on Western Europe. He demands this meeting with Tauchert at Storkow, so that he can get more information about the nature of the East German chem

453

bio program, and the Stasi's potential role in any kind of joint operation."

"I think we're getting a little ahead of ourselves."

Possibly. But the fact that East Germany even possessed a biological and chemical warfare program was news to Brodie. And the program was developed and sophisticated enough to offer training to other countries like Iraq. Did Odin learn about this facility's existence in the course of his official duties as a member of the U.S. military in West Berlin? If so, that might offer a hint as to who he was. Or had he been offered intelligence directly from someone within the Stasi that prompted his demand for the meeting at Storkow? This report was raising more questions than it was answering, and Brodie wondered how many of these questions Harry Vance had managed to answer before he was murdered.

Brodie continued reading:

In March of 1989, Odin resurfaced and reached out to his handler. While most communications over the years had been accomplished via dead drops, Odin now requested an in-person meeting at a location in West Berlin. The handler agreed to the face-to-face meeting, and afterward reported a disturbing encounter with the asset. Odin revealed that he had discovered another spy within the Ministry and was in direct communication with this person. He refused to offer up the identity of the mole, or the nature of the intelligence this traitor was sharing with him. Odin contended that if he were to give over the name of the mole it might threaten to expose his own identity, as the mole knew — or suspected — Odin's real name, or at least Odin's position within the U.S. military, which could identify him. Odin also stated that the intelligence he had received from the Stasi traitor was so sensitive, and its continued secrecy so important, that he would not give this information to his handler. Instead, he would destroy the intelligence documents he was receiving, and ensure that the traitor remained in contact with him exclusively.

This arrangement was deemed unacceptable by leadership within the Ministry, who demanded to know the identity of the traitor, and the contents of the intelligence he was passing to Odin. Odin ultimately agreed to reveal the traitor's name in exchange for a guarantee of East German residency for himself and one of his family members, along with a state pension. This guarantee was granted.

Well, thought Brodie, Odin was ready to defect to the East, while half the population of East Germany was looking to defect to the

West. And little did Odin know, in March of 1989, that East Germany would no longer exist in eight months.

The report continued, claiming that after accepting the agreement of East German residency and a pension, Odin then dropped out of contact for months without revealing the identity of the Stasi traitor. Then in July 1989 Odin reached out to change the terms of the agreement — not residency, but cash. Four million deutsche marks, which was a lot of West German money for the cash-strapped German Democratic Republic. But the Commies paid up, figuring that it was worth the risk of getting fleeced if they could bag another mole in their midst.

Their gamble paid off, to the detriment of Anna Albrecht's father. Brodie read the final page of the report:

It was in this way that the Ministry was made aware of the traitor Manfred Albrecht, who worked as a Special Analyst in the Records Department. Upon his arrest, it was discovered that Albrecht abused his unique access across multiple divisions to steal and duplicate the most highly sensitive intelligence related to joint operational plans of the Main Directorate of Reconnaissance and the National People's Army. Leadership determined that if this intelligence had fallen into the hands of the enemy, it would have brought disastrous consequences. Odin's success in establishing contact with Albrecht, and his work to protect the contents of the stolen Ministry documents from his American compatriots, will ensure the continued security and success of the German Democratic Republic and her people.

As of the writing of this report, Manfred Albrecht has been found guilty of treason and awaits sentencing.

This concludes an accounting thus far of the activities of the double agent code-named Odin, who has proven himself a resourceful ally in the battle against imperialism, and toward the cause of a more just and equal world. The German Democratic Republic owes this American a debt of gratitude and will continue to benefit from his assistance until the inevitable reunification of Germany and the global triumph of socialism over the forces of fascism.

Brodie set the report down. He looked again at the date at the top of the front page. October 1989. He imagined a Stasi bureaucrat typing these words in a dingy office not too far from where they were sitting, mere weeks before the Wall — and his entire world — would crumble. Did the bureaucrat believe in the cause, or did he just need the paycheck? Did he love his country, or fear it? Did he believe in the inevitable triumph of world Communism, or did he understand he was living inside a house of cards that was about to fold in on itself? In that land of denial, duplicity, and doublethink, the answer was maybe all of the above.

As for Odin, he seemed to have experienced a crisis of faith along the way. If he had really believed in the ultimate triumph of East Germany — and Communism — it made sense why he might want to defect — with a family member, possibly his wife — to the other side of the Iron Curtain. It sounded absurd now, but history never looks so preordained while you're living it.

And then something had happened that made Odin drop the idea of defecting and instead demand money. A lot of money. His change of heart occurred in July of 1989, when countries across Eastern Europe were roiled by protest and civil unrest that would see the collapse of every government in the Soviet Bloc before the year was done. Odin must have seen the writing on the wall. Of course, he didn't care that he was sending Manfred Albrecht to his death at the hands of a doomed regime. He just wanted to get paid.

How do you ask a man to be the last to die for a mistake?

Manfred Albrecht had almost lived in a free country. Brodie thought he was beginning to understand Anna's rage, and her and her mother's obsession with finding Odin. He thought he understood now what was driving Harry Vance too. In fact, if he'd been in Vance's shoes, he probably would have done the same thing. And possibly met the same fate.

On a related subject, considering that Stasi agents had been interrogated by Western intelligence after the dissolution of the GDR, and that surviving Stasi intelligence documents were turned over to the government of reunified Germany, it was remarkable that Odin's identity had never been discovered, and it was also a major embarrassment for the American intelligence community. No wonder they'd tried to bury it.

Brodie related the end of the report to Taylor, along with his interpretation and analysis. She nodded, thought, and asked, "But what was the information that Albrecht was passing on to Odin?"

"This report mentions intelligence about a joint operation between the HVA and the National People's Army. That's the third mention of the East German military and their relationship with the Stasi's foreign intelligence branch." He asked, "Did you find anything relevant on the HVA's activities?"

"Still looking." She paused. "The big question still is, does this Odin business have anything to do with Harry Vance's murder?

Which leads to another question: Is it possible Odin is still alive?"

Brodie considered that. "If Odin was in his thirties or forties while working for the Stasi, he'd be in his late sixties or seventies now."

"And if he *is* alive, would he be in a position to know that someone — Harry Vance — was trying to discover his identity?"

"I don't know. There would need to be some vestigial Stasi intelligence network that he was still tapped into. I don't know if such a thing exists."

"Maybe also a military or paramilitary network. Vance was killed by a skilled sniper."

"Who was likely trained in a jihadist camp somewhere in Syria or Iraq."

She looked at him. "And had a connection to Tariq Qasim."

"Maybe."

"Who subsequently had a connection to Odin."

Brodie said, "We don't know if Qasim was actually at Storkow. Maybe Vance was just hoping he was."

"But why kill Vance?"

"Maybe . . . it was a case of paranoia and misinterpreting Harry's interest in Qasim. Maybe Qasim was involved with these Syrians, and they were conspiring on a terrorist plot. When Vance, a counterterrorism agent, made contact with Qasim — a.k.a. al-Hamdani — Qasim figured the authorities

460

were onto him. So, the Syrians kill the investigator, and then plan to kill his partner, Mark Jenkins. And maybe Qasim's jihadi buddies also killed Qasim to eliminate any connection to the murder of American CID Agent Harry Vance. Harry was digging into some Cold War history and had the bad luck of reaching out to the wrong guy. Odin otherwise has nothing to do with his death."

"You're saying that Qasim, the guy who Vance was hoping might finger an American double agent from thirty years ago, just happened to be in the middle of an active terrorist plot? That's a hell of a coincidence."

"I agree. But in this screwed-up case, it's the best scenario I can think of that fits the known facts."

Taylor shook her head. "I don't buy it. There's something else going on here. We're just not seeing it."

"Better find it quick. Because right now General Hackett is sitting in his office at Quantico, trying to think of a reason not to pull his two best pain-in-the-ass agents off this high-profile case. And he's not coming up with any."

Taylor looked at him. "Sounds like you're ready to roll over and go home."

"I'm disengaging. There's a difference. There might be a connection between the Syrian bomb-makers and Qasim, and there might be a connection between Colonel

461

Qasim and Odin. But there might not be. It's a weak foundation on which to build a case, and we don't have the time or the authority to shore it up. As far as Schröder is concerned, he has his killers — the Syrians — and if ballistics comes back with a match, then he'll also have his murder weapon in the form of an HK MP5 rifle specially modified to fire the caliber of bullet that killed Harry Vance. And, of course, there's the eyeball in the freezer. And by now Schröder might also have a motive. If we want to help in the short time we have left, we should probably be focused more on what Harry Vance and Mark Jenkins were doing this past year in their counterterrorism work, and less on what the Stasi was doing thirty-odd years ago."

Taylor thought about that. "Are you playing devil's advocate? Or do you actually believe that?"

Good question. Brodie wasn't sure himself. But this case was getting more complicated by the hour, and maybe it was okay if he and Taylor were relieved of their duties here. The only thing he was sure of was the answer to the question: Career booster or career buster? If they got out now, it was a wash.

But then he thought about Harry, who by all accounts was a good man and a great agent, and apparently a good father. Anna loved him and mourned his death. Maybe his wife did too. So — petty FBI bureaucrats and

Army brass aside — what was Scott Brodie's moral duty to this man and this case?

Before he could answer Taylor's question, his phone rang. It was Dombroski. He held up the phone and said to Taylor, "Time's up."

She didn't respond.

Brodie picked up. "Guten Tag, Colonel."

"Hello, Mr. Brodie. Where are you now?"

"In a bar. With Ms. Taylor."

"Okay . . . How is everything going?"

"I think you're about to tell me."

Dombroski was silent for a moment. Then he said, "In light of the bombing this morning, and the evidence found at the scene which clearly suggests that Mr. Vance's murder was an act of terrorism, and that Mark Jenkins was the next intended victim, General Hackett has instructed Colonel Trask to dispatch a team from the Fifth MP's counterterrorism division to take over CID's role in this investigation, effective as of nine A.M. tomorrow."

"Also, I don't play well with others."

"No, you don't. And you went beyond —"

"Above and beyond. That used to count for something."

"Look . . . Scott, this is looking pretty open-and-shut. Let the Fifth MP roll it up and take the credit. We can use your and Ms. Taylor's skills better elsewhere."

"Yes, sir."

Silence, then Dombroski said, "You are be-

463

ing uncharacteristically compliant, Scott. This makes me nervous."

"Let's just say that five months in the wilderness has lowered my expectations."

Dombroski thought for a moment. "This is the Fifth MP's show. You were outside talent and General Hackett has decided he now wants insiders. Plus, you pissed off the FBI, which I knew you would." He paused a moment, then added, "By the way, I spoke to my Iraq Intel guys. Tariq Qasim ran a unit in the Sunni Awakening."

"We got ahold of his FBI record, which corroborates that."

"He killed a whole lot of al Qaeda in Ramadi."

"Good for him. Though I don't think it balances out his sins."

Dombroski asked, "You think he's still in Berlin?"

"I think he's in Hell."

Dombroski didn't reply.

"How far down the rabbit hole do you want to go, Colonel?"

Dombroski thought for a moment. "Put it all in your report, which I expect on my desk by end of day Friday."

"Yes, sir."

"The travel office will e-mail you and Ms. Taylor a flight itinerary. I told them nothing too early. Hit the town tonight. You're temporarily unemployed."

"Thank you, sir. Anything further?"

Dombroski didn't respond. Maybe he was thinking of how to end this conversation in a way that wouldn't leave his favorite agent with the impression that he'd been thrown under the bus.

After a moment Dombroski said, "It will be different when you're back here. And you can choose your partner, if that's what you want."

The colonel was clearly feeling guilty. Which was a good time for Scott Brodie to get something in return for not making this difficult. But he decided to feign compliance. "I appreciate that, sir. I look forward to discussing the details back at Quantico. Anything further?"

"Negative further. Safe travels." Dombroski hung up.

Brodie placed his phone on the coffee table and looked at Taylor, who was staring at something on her tablet and appeared to have not been listening. He said, "It's over. Flight home tomorrow. You'll be e-mailed an itinerary."

She nodded.

"For the record, I think we might be going a little far up our own asses here, Maggie. Which was also Harry's mistake. Whatever he was doing, and for whatever reason he was doing it, Vance spent most of his career hunting terrorists, and apparently the hunter became the hunted. Let's remember that the simplest explanation is usually the right one." Brodie put the Stasi report back in the envelope and placed it on the table.

Taylor was still looking down at her tablet, deep in thought.

"Taylor? Do you hear what I'm saying?"

She looked up at him. "Why didn't I think of this before?"

"What?"

She passed her tablet to him. "Take a look at the great god Odin."

Brodie took Taylor's tablet and looked at an old black-and-white sketch of the Norse god, depicted in a long cloak and holding a staff. He had only one eye — his right eye, with a gaping black hole where his left eye had been.

Taylor said, "Tell me that's a coincidence."

Brodie didn't respond. He stared at the picture of Odin, and the eye of the old god stared back. Maybe the mutilation of Harry's body *was* a message, just not the one they'd thought. Not an eye for an eye, not an act of revenge. No . . . it was a *taunt*.

I did this. I'm still here. Catch me if you can.

CHAPTER 30

Brodie stared at the picture of Odin, trying to remember the little he'd ever known about Germanic mythology.

Taylor, who must have paid more attention in class, said, "Odin took his own eye. An act of self-sacrifice to gain ultimate knowledge."

Brodie remembered Anna saying that Odin disguised himself as a wanderer to learn about the world and its people, but she'd overlooked another aspect of both the god and the man who used his name — sacrificing part of oneself to gain that knowledge. Being a double agent takes a toll. You betray your own country and people and sleep with the enemy. The prize is access to secret knowledge, and knowledge is power. But the price might be your soul.

Taylor said, "Anna insisted that the search for Odin was Harry's only focus here. If she's right, then I think that is what got him killed."

Maybe. But in a tangled case like this, you needed to make sure you were unraveling the threads in the right order. "I think Qasim is the key here. He may have been present at Storkow, and he may have met Odin there, but he is also tied to these Syrians in one way or another. When Harry made contact with Abbas al-Hamdani and presented himself as an Army CID investigator looking for a former Iraqi military intelligence officer, he sealed his own fate."

"Sounds right. Feels wrong."

"That can be the title of our report."

"What report?"

"For Dombroski. Due on his desk end of day Friday."

She shook her head. "This can't wait until Friday. We need to talk to Schröder."

"We're the walking dead now, Maggie. No one is going to work with us, and whatever we have to say is going to be seen through the lens of two desperate agents with a rapidly approaching expiration date."

Taylor thought for a moment, then pulled out her phone and dialed a number.

"Who are you calling without my permission?"

"The last man who tolerates us." After a pause, she said, "Good afternoon, Agent Kim . . . Right. We appreciate that. Listen, we have a few things we didn't get to in our debrief with Agent Whitmore, which was actually an ambush." She listened again. "I know. I understand." She made eye contact with Brodie. "We're at the Adlon, and if you have time to join us, we can talk . . . All right, meet you there in about fifteen." She hung up and looked at Brodie. "He suggested we meet outdoors — in front of the Reichstag." She added, "He sounded, as always, enthusiastic."

"He already knew about our reassignment."

Taylor nodded. "He claims he just learned that from Whitmore a few minutes ago."

"And why are we meeting him?"

"We have a duty to pass on our findings to someone we trust before we depart."

"He's an FBI counterterror guy with an agenda, Maggie. Not the best audience for our latest theories. Also, he's annoying." He said, "We should have called General Kiernan. Keep it in the family."

"My instincts say to talk to someone who isn't duty-bound to report what we say."

Brodie nodded, but said, "I'm not into protocol, but we should ask for a meeting with the legat—"

"Scott, I'd rather drink bleach than have another meeting with Sharon Whitmore and Jason Butler. Kim is our best option."

"Okay. Your call." Brodie looked for the waiter who, in his charming European way, went into hiding when he sensed someone was trying to pay the bill and leave. Brodie considered skipping out on the check as a call-back to his last time here, but no one else would get the joke.

Eventually the waiter appeared and brought them the bill. Brodie paid and was about to get up when he froze.

Across the lounge he spotted a lanky man in his seventies with close-cropped white hair. The man wore a black suit and was sitting in an armchair sipping a coffee while he read a German newspaper. A brown leather brief-case sat near his feet.

Brodie's mind flashed back to the man in Neukölln who'd climbed into the maroon Mercedes that had been idling at the curb.

"Scott? Ready?"

He gestured to the chair next to him.

Taylor came around the coffee table and took the seat next to Brodie.

He said, "White-haired guy reading the paper. Saw him near Qasim's."

Taylor glanced at the man, who kept his eyes on the paper as he lifted the coffee mug to his lips. She said, "I've seen a dozen old white men today who look like him."

Brodie studied the man. He had a round face with high cheekbones and a ruddy complexion. He seemed genuinely absorbed in his paper, or at least was doing a convincing act of it.

Taylor added, "Even if you're right, it could be a coincidence. Or even one of Schröder's men, which wouldn't surprise me."

Brodie kept his eyes on the man, who

lowered the paper to check his watch.

Taylor stood. "C'mon, Brodie. We have to meet Kim."

They left the lobby lounge and stepped out onto Unter den Linden, where the snow had turned to a light rain, and pedestrians and cars pushed through the ice and slush.

They headed west, back in the direction of Pariser Platz and the Brandenburg Gate, which was just south of the Reichstag. They passed beneath the bare linden trees, whose skeletal frames were etched in snow against the blank sky.

Brodie thought about the old man, who'd climbed in a car half a block from where Brodie and Taylor had been standing in Neukölln, and then wound up sitting in the same hotel lounge as them in a much nicer part of town. Coincidence? Possibly. But unlikely. And in this business, seeing a stranger twice in one day was one time too many.

CHAPTER 31

Brodie and Taylor stood in front of the Reichstag, a massive neo-Baroque building across the street from the Tiergarten. A cobblestone plaza stretched out before it, dotted with snow and a few tourists braving the rain.

Brodie surveyed the German parliament building as they waited for David Kim. A row of neoclassical columns stood beneath an ornate pediment with the words: <u>DEM DEUTSCHEN VOLK</u>. To the German people. Rising above the pediment was a large glass-and-steel dome, one of the few modern-looking additions to the façade. The four corners of the building featured squat towers topped with German flags waving in the cold wind.

The stone façade of the building had been repaired and restored, but it still showed the scars of bullets and shrapnel from the fierce fighting of April 1945, when the last German defenders of Berlin took a stand in the

Reichstag, and the Russians took it away from them, room by room.

Brodie could not imagine the blood that had been spilled here . . . Well, he didn't have to imagine it — he'd experienced it. Mortal combat is not as much fun as it sounds, and getting shot at gets old fast.

"What are you thinking?" asked Taylor.

"Baghdad. Fallujah."

She nodded and advised him, "As Longfellow once said, 'Let the dead past bury its dead.' "

"Right."

Brodie looked south, toward the edge of the Tiergarten and the Brandenburg Gate. He'd been keeping an eye out for a tail, but he saw no sign of their German friend from the Hotel Adlon or any other familiar-looking strangers.

After a minute he spotted FBI Agent David Kim striding across the plaza, wearing his black topcoat and carrying an umbrella.

As he approached, Taylor said, "Guten Tag. Thanks for meeting."

Kim stopped a few feet from them and smiled. "Been having an interesting day thanks to you two. Schröder brought Rafeeq Nasir and Anna Albrecht in for questioning. Invited the legats and me to observe both interviews."

Taylor asked, rhetorically, "Why weren't Scott and I invited?"

473

"Maybe Schröder thought you needed time to pack."

"He's going to miss us," said Brodie.

"Like he misses his hemorrhoids."

More importantly, Brodie and Taylor should have been there to corroborate or contradict anything that Nasir or Anna said. Clearly, the two CID cowboys from Quantico were being cut loose before they rode out of town.

Taylor asked, "Were they held?"

Kim shook his head. "Questioned and released. Nasir was told he was a person of interest." Kim chuckled. "He was very polite. I think he'd been expecting a police visit. Captain Soliman was also there, and he and Nasir seemed to have been previously acquainted, and they exchanged some words in Arabic that were not so polite. Soliman has a hard-on for this guy, which makes sense for a homicide detective working his beat, but even he probably understands that an organized crime figure wouldn't be risking this kind of exposure if he actually had any involvement in the murder of Mr. Vance or the disappearance of Tariq Qasim."

Brodie nodded in agreement. Rafeeq Nasir was an accomplished bullshit artist who probably had a major part in his high school play of A Thousand and One Arabian Nights. And Captain Soliman could easily detect his compatriot's bullshit.

"Bottom line," said Kim, "Schröder seemed

to believe that Rafeeq Nasir was being truth-ful — and helpful."

Taylor asked, "And Anna Albrecht?"

"She came in after Nasir left. Real salty. Gave Schröder a hard time, which was fun to watch. I don't think she cares much for the German police."

"Her father was murdered by the authori-ties," said Taylor. "That might explain her distrust."

"Execution by the state is not murder. Espionage is a capital crime."

Taylor pointed out, "The state in question was a murderous dictatorship."

Kim shrugged. "The GDR met the end it deserved, and the Germans are one big happy family again. Speaking of which." He gestured to the Reichstag. "Let's get out of the rain." He added, "Great view from the dome."

Brodie assured him, "I don't need a view. I need you to listen —"

"Follow me."

Brodie was getting tired of this guy's act, but he and Taylor were short on friends these days, so they followed Kim to a glass structure near the base of the Reichstag where people were waiting in line to go through a security check. After a minute they were ushered into the structure, which contained a metal detec-tor and security officers. Brodie took note that Agent Kim was unarmed. More impor-tantly, Kim had no recording device on him, and Kim now knew that Brodie and Taylor were also not wired, which was the whole point of this visit to the dome. Agent Kim was very clever. And paranoid.

They continued through the security building to an outdoor ramp that led into a small room with an elevator that took them to the top floor, where they exited into a marble lobby that opened to the expansive rooftop.

In the center of the roof was the dome, an eighty-foot-tall structure of glass plates and steel with a spiral walkway wrapping around its interior.

They entered the dome through an open doorway and Brodie looked around. An inverted cone of mirrored glass rose in the center of the space, probably to reflect sunlight on nicer days. A ring of informational placards and photos illustrating the building's tumultuous history stood in the middle of the floor. A few dozen people were ascending or descending the spiral ramp.

Brodie and Taylor followed Kim up the ramp. He stopped as they curved around to face the southwest, where they had a view of the Tiergarten. In the distance Brodie saw the low skyline of western Berlin — once known as West Berlin, an island of liberal democracy surrounded by a hostile nation.

Now, as David Kim had put it, the Germans were one big happy family again. And there was no clearer symbol of the new united

Germany than the Reichstag, which had suffered a mysterious fire during the Nazis' rise to power, been bombed by the Allies during the war, captured by the Red Army, then neglected for decades sitting alongside the Berlin Wall. Now it was restored as a symbol of the nation, the seat of the united parliament, and one of the most popular tourist attractions in the city. Like the city of Berlin as a whole, the Reichstag was a phoenix risen from the ashes, an almost impossible story of resurrection and resilience — yet pocked with scars that would never quite heal.

They looked out at the view as the light rain pattered against the glass. After a moment Kim said, "I'm sorry about how this played out."

Brodie really didn't need another obligatory apology from the FBI. Whitmore and Butler's bullshit was enough. He didn't respond. Neither did Taylor.

Kim continued, "I have an update on the case, if you want it."

"Love updates," said Brodie.

Kim nodded, then looked around to make sure no one was within earshot. He said in a low voice, "The BKA's tech specialists were able to crack one of the phones recovered at the site of the bombing. It was mostly clean — no texts, photos, or personal e-mails found. These guys sometimes use smartphones like burners, regularly wiping the memory and installing new SIM cards. But then the tech guy checks the drafts folder on the e-mail account. That's how a lot of these jihadis communicate. They share a single e-mail account, one guy writes a draft, never sends it, next guy logs in, reads the draft, and then deletes it before writing his own. No e-mail is ever sent, no recipient listed, no trace of the communication on the servers. So, the Germans found a single message in the drafts, written in Arabic. And it mentions a plan to, quote, 'execute the American agents to avenge our brothers in Tripoli.' "

Kim looked at Brodie and Taylor as if expecting a reaction. After a moment he asked, "You guys read the CID case files?"

Brodie replied, "Not yet. We've been following a different lead."

"What lead?"

"Continue."

"Okay, so about eight months ago Harry Vance and his partner, Mark Jenkins, were sent to Tripoli to arrest a prominent Syrian businessman named Jibril Saleh. Mr. Saleh had been providing intelligence to U.S. military personnel who were helping the Kurds battle ISIS in northeastern Syria. Turns out Saleh was secretly affiliated with the al Nusra Front — that's al Qaeda's Syrian franchise and a main ISIS rival — and he was using money provided to him by the U.S. Army to fund and train an al Qaeda–aligned militia in Libya. Typical double cross. So, Vance and Jenkins fly down to Libya, locate Saleh in Tripoli, and enlist the local police to assist in his arrest. Things go bad, shots fired, Saleh and his jihadi pals end up dead. And to make matters worse, the Libyan cops that CID had looped in took the bodies of Saleh and the dead jihadis and paraded them through the streets in celebration. Not good. Especially since Jibril Saleh had a lot of powerful friends back in Syria who saw pictures and video of his corpse getting dragged through the streets of Tripoli. This made the news, along with the fact that U.S. Army investigators had been involved in his death."

Brodie said, "We asked Jenkins about what recent cases might have led to him and Vance being targeted. This seems like an obvious candidate, but he only mentioned the Khazali network drug ring out of Mannheim."

Kim shrugged. "Something about Harry's murder made Jenkins suspect Shia terrorists. I made the same assumption. Looks like we were both wrong. Besides, Jenkins might be a terrorism specialist but that doesn't make him an expert on the domestic politics of Syria. Maybe he didn't understand the kind of network that Jibril Saleh still maintained in his home country, and he figured that Jibril's most dangerous allies died along with him in Libya." He added, "Or he didn't mention this because it was compartmentalized information and not to be shared without prior approval."

Taylor asked, "Any evidence that the three Syrians who blew themselves up in Neukölln had ties to Saleh or the al Nusra Front?"

Kim looked at her. "No. And no formal ties need to be established to indicate motive. Al Qaeda thrives on self-initiated attacks. That's why terrorist groups are so active on social media. Get people invested in your org from afar and they will commit violence on your behalf."

"But were any of these three Syrians previously known?" asked Brodie. "As active or aspiring militants?"

Kim shook his head. "But their years living in Idlib during al Nusra's occupation of the city could have given them all the extremist contacts, indoctrination, and military training they would have needed." Kim looked between the two of them. "You're overthinking this, guys. We've got the men who killed Harry Vance. And they're all dead. They had the motive, the murder weapon, and the deceased's eyeball in their freezer. If that don't fit, nothing does."

"What about Tariq Qasim?" asked Taylor. "How does he fit?"

"Not sure. Captain Soliman's unit interviewed people around Neukölln who knew Qasim by his alias, Abbas al-Hamdani. Apparently the man was having financial trouble, and also dealing with some mental health issues."

Maybe Colonel Qasim had been haunted by the memories of all the innocent people he'd gassed on behalf of Saddam Hussein. But that might be giving the guy too much credit. Brodie said, "Rafeeq Nasir mentioned that Qasim owed him money."

Kim nodded. "That was probably the financial trouble being referred to." He added, "Nasir will be kept under tight surveillance, and the police will continue their search for Mr. Qasim. This is an avenue we will continue to pursue with your CID colleagues."

"Our replacements," said Taylor.

Kim did not reply.

"And what about Odin?" asked Brodie.

"Hell of a story."

"More than that."

"Right. Also an embarrassment to the U.S. military and a travesty of justice."

Taylor said, "Anna thinks Harry's search for Odin is what got him killed."

"Yes, she was pretty adamant about that to Schröder and Soliman as well," said Kim. "Though she didn't do her credibility any good by failing to come forward in the first place."

"She was scared," said Taylor. "Which is understandable, given her theory of why

Harry was murdered."

"Right. Makes sense from her point of view. But we know more than she does. About this case, and also about how the world works." He looked at Taylor. "I'm starting to think maybe she did a number on you two."

Taylor stared at him. "Excuse me, David. We didn't just fall off the cabbage truck."

Kim said, "Sorry. But . . . she pulled Harry in. And he was top-shelf. She has a kind of . . . magnetism to her. I saw that. Not to mention easy to look at. Plus, the Odin case would be compelling for Vance — on a professional and personal level. But Odin has nothing to do with our case. Neither does Anna Albrecht, for that matter, other than the fact that Harry's affair with her is what placed him in Berlin, and thus in the crosshairs of a few jihadis who were looking to make a name for themselves by hitting a high-value target."

Taylor asked, "If Harry was in Berlin to see Anna, and to search for Odin, and *not* on official CID counterterrorism business, how could he have even gotten on these guys' radar in the first place?"

Kim looked at her. "I don't have all the answers. Yet. But we're getting there."

Brodie said, "Harry was shot in a park at three A.M. He was there for a reason."

"Maybe he was baited," said Kim.

"By whom?"

Kim shrugged. "To be determined."

Brodie said, "You are being handed — or fed — the case you expected to have. The perps, the motive, everything. Your biases are confirmed at every step, and that doesn't seem to bother you. They must have taught you better critical thinking skills at Quantico. Or at least at Yale."

Kim stared at him. "Now and then I've had the plug pulled on me too, Scott. Feels like shit."

"You're deflecting."

Taylor interrupted, "We have reason to believe that Colonel Qasim encountered Odin at an East German biological and chemical warfare training facility in the late eighties, and that Agent Vance had arranged a meeting with Qasim on the night of his murder to discuss this encounter."

Kim didn't reply for a moment. Then he asked, "Is this based on evidence you found at Mr. Qasim's apartment?"

Neither Brodie nor Taylor replied.

Kim seemed to enjoy catching them off-guard. "Mr. Nasir received a phone call as he was being led into BKA headquarters. One of his associates spotted you two entering Qasim's building, and Nasir shared that with Schröder."

Well, thought Brodie, Nasir had made a promise he'd keep an eye on them, and apparently he'd kept it.

483

The rainfall grew heavier and echoed in the great dome. The water splashed and streaked down the glass, reducing the panorama of Berlin to a shapeless gray wash.

Brodie suddenly felt like he was in a fishbowl, where the world looked in with clarity, but the view from the inside out was distorted and warped.

The Lebanese mob. The mystery man at the Adlon. The NSA-CIA listening station inside the embassy. The bureaucrats and brass in Berlin and Kaiserslautern and Quantico, all coordinating behind the scenes to get Brodie and Taylor off this case.

They must be close to something that needed to be left alone. Or handled by people who played the game better than CID Agents Brodie and Taylor did. Well, maybe when someone offers you a way out of a shitstorm, you should take it.

Brodie said to Kim, "Nasir already made it clear to us that he would be keeping an eye on our movements in Neukölln, which I guess is his prerogative as the local warlord. As far as our visit to Qasim's apartment, it did net some valuable Intel." He described the note about Storkow found on Qasim's desk, and the mention of Odin's visit to Storkow in the Stasi report.

Kim listened. Then he said, "You entered the apartment without a warrant and without authorization. Did you at least leave the note where you found it?"

"We did," said Brodie, "but I think you're focusing on the wrong issues here."

"On the contrary. Schröder was apoplectic when he found out you went there. Sharon had to talk him down from having you both arrested."

"She just wants us out of the country."

"You are officers of the law who seem comfortable breaking it. Anna Albrecht told us that she didn't exactly invite you in, either. And the evidence you found in Qasim's apartment is now —"

"Actionable intelligence," said Brodie.

"Actionable by whom?"

Taylor said, "Not you, apparently."

Kim was quiet a moment. A cluster of French schoolkids passed them, then he said, "I defended you to Whitmore and Butler. I tried to convince them to not make that phone call to Quantico. You both are smart, hardworking, and could not be more motivated to solve this murder. That's worth putting up with your shit, in my opinion. But I'm starting to think there is something else going on here, something almost pathological about how you both disregard and disrespect authority."

Everyone was an unlicensed psychoanalyst these days. Brodie said, "Authority is granted but respect is earned. And one without the other isn't worth much."

485

"Do they teach that at CID?"

"No. On the battlefield."

Taylor opened her satchel, removed the manila envelope, and handed it to Kim. "The Stasi report on Odin. Given to us by Anna Albrecht and translated by Harry Vance."

He looked at the envelope and asked, "Does this mention Tariq Qasim by name?"

"No."

"What about Storkow?"

"The report was deliberately vague."

"What about Iraq?"

"Read the goddamn report."

He looked between Brodie and Taylor. "I think you're reaching."

Brodie said, "That's because you think you've already solved this case."

Kim looked at him. "You want to know what I think, Scott? I think Special Agent Vance was in love, and that made him blind, and that made him stupid. So, is Colonel Qasim connected to Odin? Maybe. Was Harry really working that case and was that his sole focus here? Maybe. But is that what got him killed? No. These jihadis were gunning for him because of what happened in Libya, and he was too deep into this Cold War cold case to see it. He had stars in his eyes. Or his nose in the archives. And his dick was doing his thinking."

Taylor asked, "It's that simple?"

Kim looked at her. "You call that simple?"

486

He looked over the railing and pointed down. "You see that?"

Brodie looked down at the floor of the dome, where a circular glass panel offered a bird's-eye view of a room full of leather-upholstered chairs arranged in rows.

Kim said, "That's where the Bundestag meets. The German parliament. They put the glass there as a symbol of transparency, anyone can look in on the proceedings. The message is: Authoritarianism will never return to Germany. Nice idea. But how many tourists come here and even know that? A generation from now, what will visitors see? A kind of interesting view. A hole in the floor." He kept looking downward, then said, "We want the past to matter. To have some impact on the present. Otherwise, what's the point of anything? But the lines aren't so clear. And an old spy fighting an old war for a dead cause . . ." He shook his head. "It's lost its power, that story. It doesn't reach in. It's not *alive*. It doesn't matter anymore."

"It matters to some," said Taylor.

"Right," said Kim. "The victims." He turned toward them. "Like Anna Albrecht. They hold on to the pain, but eventually they die and the pain dies with them. And the rest of us build memorials and monuments and hope maybe someone else understands what they mean even if they will never fully feel why they matter."

Brodie thought back to the people climbing on top of the stone slabs of the Holocaust Memorial like it was a playground. This was getting bleak. He said to Taylor, "We passed on our Intel. Mission accomplished. Let's go get a drink."

Kim said, "You can't allow things to get too heavy, can you, Mr. Brodie?"

Brodie stared at him. "It's always heavy, Mr. Kim. What I carry with me. And you need to either go fuck yourself or figure out who's fucking you." He walked back down the ramp. He could hear Taylor and Kim exchange a few more words, and then Taylor followed.

She caught up with Brodie as he was exiting the dome onto the rooftop. She said, "You burned our last bridge, Scott. We might still need him."

"We don't need anyone. We are off this case. And after today there is no 'we.' "

Taylor didn't respond. The rain was falling in a steady stream now. Brodie walked toward the edge of the rooftop and looked to the east, where the sky was growing black with storm clouds.

Taylor walked up next to him. "Scott. Look at me."

He turned to her.

"We did our duty."

"Above and beyond. But no cigar." He looked up at the dome. David Kim was still standing where they'd left him, looking out over the city. "I hope Agent Whiz Kid gets his head right and realizes he's still got some work to do."

"I'll call him from the States. You should do the same."

"No. He has to call us. When it starts bothering him."

She nodded, then said, "He thinks Anna did a number on us."

Brodie hesitated, then replied, "If you mean a number on me, I won't dignify that with a response."

She didn't respond to his non-response.

They rode the elevator down to the ground floor, went back through the security building, and exited onto the plaza. A fierce wind whipped across the open expanse.

Taylor checked her phone and said, "Just got the itinerary. Ten-thirty-five flight from Tegel to Dulles. And then I've got a connection to Nashville."

Meaning Taylor wasn't even expected to be present for the Quantico report and debrief, which said something about how little their superiors valued their insights and contributions to this case.

Brodie asked, "Where do you want to ride out the storm?"

"In bed." Perhaps realizing how that sounded, she added, "I'm exhausted. We've been running on empty for a while now."

"Right." And now Brodie was thinking about what Taylor didn't mean, and how that would probably have been a fun ending to this screwed-up mission and their professional relationship. He wondered if they'd ever work a case together again. Doubtful.

They caught a cab back to the Art Hotel, where Mustafa sat at the front desk eating a sandwich that he'd probably stolen from the communal fridge. He asked between bites, "Do you enjoy Berlin?"

"No," said Brodie. "We're checking out tomorrow."

Mustafa furrowed his brow. "There is three-night minimum."

Taylor said, "Just charge the extra night."

The man smiled. "Yes, miss."

Brodie added, "Please tell the bellhop to bring our bags down at eight A.M., and have a cab waiting. For Tegel."

Mustafa said, "This is not things we do."

Brodie promised, "I'll give you a good review on Tripadvisor."

"Thank you. My cousin will take you to the airport."

They went upstairs to their respective rooms, with a tentative plan to go to dinner at nine.

Brodie went into his room and shut the door. The bed looked enticing, but the streets of Berlin were where things seemed to happen. His time was short, but it was not yet

up. He turned around and walked out of the
room.

CHAPTER 32

Scott Brodie walked through the narrow streets of Neukölln with his hood up. He checked for a tail now and then but didn't see anyone. If he had, he would have confronted them and asked — not so politely — who they were working for. German Feds? Berlin Police? FBI? CIA? Lebanese crime syndicate? Al Qaeda–affiliated terrorist group? That was an impressive list. He thought about who else he might have pissed off in his short time in Berlin. If he had a few more days, he could add a few more names.

He came across a small bar on a side street and decided to duck in to get a break from the rain.

It was a cramped, dimly lit place filled with cigarette smoke and a couple of pool tables; an old German bar in a changing neighborhood. He didn't smoke or really enjoy pool, but the vibe seemed right.

Brodie took a seat at the mostly empty bar. The bartender, a middle-aged, barrel-chested

German guy, approached. "Was kann ich dir bringen?"

Brodie eyed the taps and recalled the high-octane beer he'd enjoyed the night before. "Ein Doppelbock, bitte."

The bartender filled a half-liter glass and slid it to him. "American?"

"Is my accent that bad?"

The bartender smiled. "If it was worse, I would have guessed you were British." He added, "We don't get a lot of Americans here."

"Why's that?"

The man shrugged. "Out of the way."

"Depends where you're going."

"Holiday?"

Brodie drank his beer. "Research." He added, "I'm writing a screenplay."

"Yes? What about?"

"An American double agent who worked for the Stasi."

The bartender considered that. "This is like a historical movie?"

"It takes place now. The traitor was never caught."

"Ah."

"Sound interesting?"

The man thought a moment. "Does anyone still care about the Stasi?"

"That's the question."

A customer flagged the bartender and he excused himself.

Brodie knocked back half of his doppel-bock. "Apparently not."

"No."

Brodie looked down the bar, where an old German guy in a rumpled wool jacket was sitting a few stools away. The man had a gaunt face, dark, deep-set eyes, and a full head of brown, plastered-back hair that looked like it had been dyed with shoe polish. The old man took a long drag on a cigarette, then looked at him and said in a thick German accent, "No one gives a shit about the Stasi."

"Then I guess I'm wasting my time."

The man nodded. "Ja."

Brodie finished his beer and ordered another. He asked the old man, "What are you drinking?"

The man said something in German to the bartender, then added in English, "The American is buying."

The bartender looked at Brodie, who nodded. The bartender pulled out a bottle of clear liquid — some kind of schnapps — and poured it into a small glass, then slid it over to the man.

The man raised his glass. "Prost."

They both drank. The man moved a couple of stools closer to Brodie and extended his hand. "Friedrich."

"Scott."

They shook. Friedrich smelled like cheap

cologne and cigarettes. He hadn't brought his ashtray with him and tapped his ashes onto the bar. "You like Berlin?"

"I'm here on business."

Friedrich slapped a large hand on Brodie's arm. "Nice-looking American boy, go get some women. The German ladies are friendly. Then you will love this place."

The bartender slid the tray over to catch Friedrich's ashes, and the man ordered another schnapps. The bartender again looked at Brodie to confirm he was sponsoring the freeloader. Brodie nodded and said, "Zwei."

Friedrich finished his cigarette, stubbed out the butt, and lit another.

Brodie said, "I'm surprised you can still smoke in the bars here."

Friedrich shrugged and looked around the room. "Only small places like this. City law."

"Why small places?"

Friedrich thought about that as he enjoyed his cigarette. "It is kind of a thing such as . . . You make an agreement, a contract, in a little place like this. We all accept the smoke because we like it or because we don't give a shit. Big place, you have all kinds of persons. Different things that you expect. This little smoky place? You know what you are accepting. We all understand that death is for certain."

That sounded too existential for a municipal health statute, but this was Germany, after all. Brodie asked to bum a smoke to show his new friend that he too embraced death.

Friedrich gave him a cigarette and a matchbook. Brodie lit the unfiltered cigarette, took a drag, and coughed.

The German laughed. "Maybe you need an American menthol."

"I'm good."

The bartender set down two glasses of schnapps. Brodie finished his beer, then raised his schnapps and said, "Prost," and they both drank.

Friedrich thought a moment, then said, "This American, this double agent. Why does he do it? Help the Stasi?"

"I'm still figuring that out. That's why I'm here."

Friedrich looked at him with his dark eyes. "What is here to find?"

"People who remember what it used to be like."

Friedrich chuckled. "This is me, I think." He slapped the top of the bar. "This, here, was the West." He pointed his finger toward the door. "Three blocks that way, other side of the Wall, was my country. I worked twenty years in a lightbulb factory in Köpenick. One of the plant managers, he was a Stasi informant. Everyone knew it. What did this mean? Well, if you wanted to complain about something, about the government, about the job, you don't do it in front of him. That was it. We joked about it. Not so dramatic, like your American movies."

Brodie nodded. Interesting. But maybe not accurate. He asked, "But did you fear the Stasi?"

Friedrich waved a hand dismissively. "What was the point of this? We had enough things to worry about. Listen. For forty years people lived their lives in this place of the GDR, what you called East Germany. People loved and hated, they felt joy and pain, they fought, they fucked, they lived, they died. Just like everywhere else, okay? So, you Americans come — the reporters and the tourists — and want to talk about the Stasi. You want to talk about the Wall. But there was much more to it. Your life is not only this thing, the Stasi."

Brodie ordered another round, then took a last drag and stubbed out his cigarette.

Friedrich took a long drag and blew out a trail of smoke. He was on a schnapps-fueled roll. "You say east and west. But no. *We* were Germany. The German Democratic Republic, the place where we rejected the fascists and made a place of justice. A place of national ideas and national unity. No one starved. No one slept in the street. Every citizen was taken care of. This so-called West Berlin, it was an island of occupation inside our country. The Wall was to protect *us* from *them*. And this so-called West Germany, it was a place for pigs. A place for Nazis who escaped what they had coming. And then . . ." He trailed off and shook his head.

"And then the West won," said Brodie.

Friedrich pursed his lips. "Ja. The pigs won. And now it is a pigs' world."

The bartender brought two more glasses of schnapps, and rolled his eyes to show Brodie what he thought of Friedrich. Friedrich stared at his glass, his mind stuck in the good old days, which were actually not as good as he remembered. There was a term for this, which Brodie remembered from his trip back in 2000 — Ostalgie. Nostalgia for the Ost — the East. A coping mechanism for salvaging something from the ashes of a vanished and vanquished world.

On some level, Brodie could see where Friedrich was coming from. You lived your life in a system, and the system kind of sucked, but it was your world. Nothing was debatable and it wasn't changeable, so you focused on other things, like family, friends, working, socializing, and whether or not there would be fresh fruit at the state-run grocer on a given day. And you appreciated whatever good you could find in the system, like the fact that everyone had a roof over their head even if the roof leaked from crappy construction. And you carried on with your life. Most people don't try to change what they can't control; they don't even think about it. And the few people who did, people like Anna's father and other enemies of the state, or the hundred-plus people who tried and failed to escape over the Berlin Wall, ended up in body bags.

Friedrich kept drinking and talking, and spoke lovingly of his dead wife, then opined on the capitalist imperialists who had ruined Germany and betrayed the socialist republic, which was sounding more like utopia the more schnapps he drank. Brodie mostly listened and occasionally made up details about his own life, which was probably better than telling his new Communist friend that he was a U.S. Army criminal investigator.

After a few more shots, Friedrich began singing something that might have been the old East German national anthem. Two young German guys playing pool started making fun of him, though Friedrich didn't notice or didn't care.

Brodie was thinking about the best way to make an exit when his phone rang. It was a German number. He picked up. "Hello?"

"Scott. It's Anna Albrecht."

"One minute." He left some cash on the bar and said good-bye to Friedrich, who was pumping his fist as he sang an ode to Deutschland and barely acknowledged his drink sponsor.

Brodie stepped outside, where the rain was still falling. The sky was dark, and the streetlights had come on. He put the phone to his ear. "What can I do for you?"

"Who said you can do anything for me?" She sounded upset.

"Okay . . ."

"It was awful. The fucking police. They took Harry's things. My father's rifle. They took *me*. And the interrogation room . . . it had that kind of glass, where you know someone's on the other side but you can't see them." Something occurred to her, and she asked, "Were you there? Were you watching me?"

Ms. Albrecht was pretty fired up, and also maybe drunk, though it was hard for Brodie to tell in his own tipsy state. "I was not there."

"But you could have been."

In fact, he *should* have been, but he and Taylor were homeward bound.

Anna continued, "Chief Inspector Schröder. Such an asshole. You'd think I murdered Harry, the way he talked to me."

"Anna, you knew exactly what was going to happen. And it might have gone differently if you had been proactive about going to the police. When they come to *you,* it's definitely different. But that's the only thing you did wrong. No one thinks you had anything to do with Harry's death." He added, to be conciliatory, "Schröder is an unpleasant prick, I agree. Hopefully this will be your last interaction with him."

She was quiet for a moment. Then she

500

asked, "What's all that noise?"

"The rain."

"Why are you in the rain?"

"Because I couldn't hear you in the bar. Anything else?"

There was a long silence on the other end of the line. For a moment he thought she'd hung up; then she asked, "Who are you with at the bar?"

"I'm alone."

Another long pause. Then, "Why don't you come over here for a drink? You're . . . the only other person I know who knew Harry. We could toast his memory."

Friedrich had been an interesting drinking companion, but this was definitely a better offer. He said, "I can be there in about twenty if I can find a cab."

"You will find a cab." She hung up.

Brodie slipped his phone into his pocket and stood in the rain. Ms. Albrecht was drunk and lonely. So was Scott Brodie. Why not help each other out? He realized this might conflict with his dinner plans with Taylor. Should he invite her along? Definitely not.

He dialed Taylor, and she picked up. "Hi, Scott."

"Hi. I can't do dinner tonight."

"Why?"

"The weather sucks."

"It sounds like you're out in it."

"That's how I know it sucks. Went for a walk."

"That's not a good idea, alone at night."

"I'm fine."

"When are you coming back?"

Depends. Should he tell her that he'd made plans with a beautiful and perhaps unstable German woman who seemed to have a thing for American military men? Probably not. "Later. I just need to be alone for a while."

"All right . . . I understand. This is tough for me too." She added, "I was going to tell you at dinner, but I found some interesting things on the HVA — the Stasi's foreign Intel service. If you're interested."

He was interested, but also slightly intoxicated, and very impatient to get to Prenzlauer Berg. "Give me the CliffsNotes."

"Sure. So, the Stasi had their own paramilitary arm and they had a massive cache of weapons stored in their facilities. They had been working with the East German Army on a secret plan they called 'Day X,' which was essentially an armed invasion and takeover of West Berlin by the Stasi paramilitary, possibly coinciding with an East German Army invasion of West Germany."

"That's delusional. That would trigger a NATO military response. Not to mention a possible nuclear exchange."

Taylor said, "I'm getting the impression there were some real diehards in the Stasi leadership — and especially the HVA — who by the late eighties were getting desperate, and maybe believing too much of their own propaganda about the strength of the East German nation. Once Gorbachev took over the Soviet Union in '85, he signaled that the Soviet Union would not intervene if these Eastern Bloc countries faced an uprising, so the old guard in East Berlin started making plans independent of Moscow. And there's another aspect of this, a kind of preamble to Day X called Operation Black Harvest. East Germany's biowarfare division was working on genetically engineered bacterial, viral, and fungal agents that could infect livestock and cereal crops. The idea was to spread these agricultural bioweapons across Western Europe and disrupt their food supply. Kind of knock them on their backs before an invasion."

Maggie Taylor could always be counted on to sober him up. He asked, "Where did you find all this?"

"Day X was written about a lot in the mid-nineties as people were unearthing old Stasi archives. Operation Black Harvest is less certain. I found a single mention in a German foreign policy journal from 1992 that contained an interview with a former Stasi HVA agent. This interview generated a few news articles, but there was no corroboration. The former Stasi agent could have been making it all up. Or voicing something that was merely aspirational and never close to operational. But if it *is* true, it draws a connection between the Stasi foreign intelligence service and the East German Army's unconventional-weapons program which was run at least partly out of the facility at Storkow."

Brodie considered all that. According to the Stasi report on Odin, Manfred Albrecht had shared intelligence with Odin that was extremely sensitive and had something to do with joint operations between the East German Army and the Stasi. And Odin — a Stasi asset — had visited Storkow, an East German military facility focused on unconventional warfare, a year or so earlier over a concern about something. This could be what tied it all together. Or maybe not. Regardless, this wasn't their case anymore.

He said to Taylor, "Good research. Put all this in a memo that we will print out and deliver to the legat's office tomorrow on our way to the airport."

Taylor didn't respond for a moment. Then she said, "Odin's still out there, Scott. I feel it."

What Ms. Taylor was actually feeling was the pull of a case that she wasn't done with. And while Brodie didn't want to discourage his sometimes too literal partner from leaning on gut instinct, they had to put this investigation behind them. "Our friends in the FBI are assholes, but they are competent assholes. If there is something to all this, we have to trust they'll look into it. And we have our two CID replacements coming in who didn't get assigned to the famous Fifth MP for being idiots."

"Scott Brodie, the institutionalist."

"The realist."

"You're lying to yourself."

"What do you want from me, Maggie? You want me to run an illegal investigation with zero resources that will probably land us in prison? If you want to kick this door in, you need to do it yourself. I'm following orders for a change."

Silence for a moment. Then Taylor said in a slow, measured tone, "I don't want you to do anything except acknowledge the possibility that a traitor to the United States might still be out there, might have had a hand in the murder of our colleague, and might get away with it."

Brodie thought back to the drawing of the one-eyed god Odin. Was the mutilation of Harry's body a sadistic message from an American traitor who still walked free? Maybe. Or were Brodie and Taylor overthinking a case that was already solved? Brodie said, "Odin's probably dead."

"You don't believe that."

"Or he's an old man who will be dead soon."

"Better that he die in jail." She added, "On the plane ride here, you told me you were ready to burn it all down."

"This is not what I meant. And you know that." He added, "Don't be so egotistical that you think only you can follow up on this."

"*You* have the ego problem. I'm the conscientious one. And I'm not so sure that anyone will follow up."

"We'll follow up on that in Quantico. Also, don't forget that we're here to redeem ourselves and our careers."

"We've already missed that boat, Scott. And probably sank it."

"Right. Anything else?"

There was a long pause. Then Taylor said, "No. See you in the morning," and hung up.

Brodie shoved his phone in his pocket and walked in the rain toward a main road to find a cab.

Maggie Taylor was becoming a renegade. Maybe she was spending too much time with Scott Brodie.

Someone who understands what's missing.

That's how she had characterized him last night at the club. But what was missing in this case? And in a broader sense, what was missing in both of their lives since the Mercer case in Venezuela? A sense of purpose? Of justice?

No, that was all BS. The fact was they were both unreformed adrenaline junkies, and Maggie Taylor was currently in need of a hit.

Brodie's mind came back to Taylor's newest discoveries. Day X. Operation Black Harvest. Two more stray pieces in this chaotic jigsaw.

He thought about the puzzle women Anna had mentioned, who sifted through millions of old paper scraps, using tape and glue to reassemble the past. He wondered what their success rate was, and whether most of what they were piecing together even mattered. They'd hit the jackpot with the Odin report, but most of the archives were probably the mundanities of a petty and overbearing police state — Fritz being surveilled by Hans every day for three months because a neighbor spotted a banned book on Fritz's shelf.

Well, reconstructing that mundane report would matter to Fritz and his family. Just like finding Odin mattered to Anna Albrecht. And maybe that was enough. Maybe there was real hope in the idea that if you put back together enough of your country's shattered and shameful past, you can finally move on from it.

But that wasn't Harry Vance's battle to fight — yet he got involved anyway. And it was the last mistake he ever made.

Brodie trudged through the downpour. The darkened buildings loomed up on either side of the narrow street and seemed to tilt inward, crowding the black sky, like some canted mirage. Maybe that last schnapps was a mistake. And the two before it.

He navigated to a main road and flagged a cab. He gave the cabbie Anna's address and the car set out through the storm, its wipers at full tilt.

Brodie closed his eyes and listened to the rain.

Someone who understands what's missing.

Taylor's phrase came back to him again. It implied that Scott Brodie — as well as Maggie Taylor — approached this job in search of something beyond the law. And that could get you in trouble on a case like this, and in a city like Berlin. That could get you chasing ghosts. Or old spies.

Day X. Black Harvest. Storkow. Odin. Tariq Qasim. Bioweapons. Four German double agents executed in a Stasi prison. Three Syrians blown up in Neukölln. Mark Jenkins followed and intimidated. Harry Vance murdered. What was all this?

Maybe the dead can speak. Maybe Harry was speaking to him now.

And maybe he was saying: *Get out while you can.*

CHAPTER 33

Brodie climbed the stairs to Anna's apartment. He saw that the door was still damaged from his forced entry, and he could see a chain lock across the narrow opening. He needed to pay for that. Actually, he already had.

He knocked, and after a minute Anna peered through the opening, slid the chain, and opened the door. She gave him a half-smile, which he returned.

Brodie could usually judge the chances of a successful evening with a lady by how she dressed and how much paint had been applied. Anna wore dark slacks and a loose white blouse, and the makeup was light. Not a promising signal. But this was another country.

He said, "You need to get the door fixed."

"You'd just kick it in anyway." Anna ushered him into the apartment and slid the chain lock shut, then took his soaking-wet coat and put it on a hook and led him into the kitchen.

At the kitchen table was an open bottle of red wine and an empty glass.

Anna said, "It's a German Cab. Tastes like shit."

"Nice label." Brodie filled his glass and tried it. It was acidic, with subtle notes of sauerkraut.

Anna took her wineglass from the counter and sat at the table. Brodie took a seat as well.

She regarded him. "Are you drunk?"

"I've had a few."

She nodded.

Ms. Albrecht herself looked a bit glassy-eyed. Also, it looked like she'd been crying. Maybe this was a mistake. Brodie asked, "How are you?"

She drank some wine. "It's been a fucking day." She looked at him. "You hear about that explosion in Neukölln? It was two blocks from Körnerpark."

Brodie nodded.

Anna eyed him, trying to feel it out. "It's not . . . related?"

"Don't ask me questions I can't answer." He lifted his glass. "A toast to Harry."

"Not with this shit." She got up and located a bottle of scotch whiskey and poured two glasses. "Balvenie. Harry's favorite." She returned to the table and slid a glass to him, then raised hers. "To Harry."

They drank.

She set her glass down and stared at the whiskey. After a moment she said, "It's hard . . . to know that someone that you cared about died this way. My father. Harry. They did not just die. Someone took their life."

Brodie nodded. "I served in the infantry in Iraq. I lost friends. And losing them like that, it hurts in a different way. It's a different kind of grief."

Anna's look darkened. "Did you kill the people who killed your friends?"

"In battle it's hard to know. But at least one time, yes."

"Did it make you feel better?"

"For a moment."

Anna nodded. "I see them sometimes. The Stasi men. Well, less now. But five years ago. Ten years ago. If you went to certain bars, you'd see them. Usually alone."

"How would you know?"

Her face soured. "They had a bad, retro look about them. Cheap polyester suits. Too much hair gel. Like they were stuck in time. And they had this kind of air of self-importance that was a joke because they had no power and most of the time they had no money. They were like . . ." She thought a moment. "Captains without ships."

Brodie imagined these old Stasi men whiling away their twilight years in dim bars, nursing grudges, and remembering when they were wolves at the top of the food chain. The Nazi Gestapo in the postwar years must have had the same experience. Lonely, maybe haunted men who'd gone from swaggering to staggering, without power and without pensions, hoping someone would buy them a drink.

Brodie recalled his new friend Friedrich, who probably wasn't ex-Stasi, but could have been an informant, and was definitely frozen in time.

Anna continued, "I've had a fantasy of somehow . . . finding the man who ended my father's life."

Well, the man responsible for ending her father's life was the American military officer code-named Odin. But absent any justice on that front, Anna must have imagined a more tangible villain — the Stasi executioner who had pulled the trigger. He was probably some low-level thug, the type of interchangeable functionary who did the dirty work of every oppressive regime in history. Not an important man in any real sense, but important to Anna Albrecht. Or at least, a stand-in for the real and more elusive enemy. Brodie asked her, "And what would you do if you found him?"

She thought a moment. "I would make him talk to me. This man . . . saw my father in his last moments. It is almost like he has secret knowledge."

Brodie looked at her. "It's terrible knowledge, Anna. It haunts him and it doesn't need to haunt you too."

She nodded as if she already knew that.

He added, "Maybe one of these days, that old file will be taped back together, and you'll get a phone call. You'll get a name."

She waved her hand dismissively. "Bullshit. The Odin report was lucky. Like a strike of lightning. Or maybe someone knew just where to look for it. I'll never know. But I heard a number once, of how many people work at the Stasi Records Agency doing this work, the puzzle women. Now about forty people. It was even fewer in the past. And each person can reconstruct about one sack of paper shreds per year. You know how many bags of this shit they have? Over fourteen thousand. It will take three hundred and fifty years to put it all together." She poured more whiskey and knocked it back, then looked him in the eyes. "The government is not trying to finish the puzzle, Scott. They are just trying to *look* like they are."

So, forty additional government employees would shave one hundred and seventy-five years off that task. Not too much to ask for in a rich country like Germany. Of course, the inefficiency was by design. Not everyone wanted to see the finished puzzle.

On that subject, Anna asked, "Did you read the Stasi report?"

Brodie nodded.

"And?"

"It's disturbing that Odin was never found and never faced justice." He added, "Your father was very brave to risk his life to work for the West."

"Enough smoke up my ass. What can you tell me?"

"That I passed the report on to my colleagues in the FBI."

She stared at him. "I didn't give it to you to pass it on. I gave it to you to do something about it."

"I understand."

"Yes. And so?"

"And so, I don't tell you how to run your art gallery."

She didn't like that. "You seemed like a man of action."

He was, in fact, a man of action, so he got up. "Thanks for the whiskey."

"You're leaving?"

"I am."

"Why?"

"You'll figure it out."

He walked to the hallway, and he could hear her following. He grabbed his coat off the hook, and she said, "Scott."

He turned to her.

She put her hand on his shoulder. "Don't." She looked up at him with her big brown eyes. She appeared open; vulnerable in a way he hadn't seen.

"I'm not your answer, Anna."

"I don't expect answers."

Well, this was wrong for about half a dozen reasons. But he already knew he wasn't leaving.

He dropped his coat on the floor, took her in his arms, and kissed her. She wrapped her arms around him and pulled him closer. They fumbled their way into the darkened bedroom.

The faint glow of the streetlight through the bedroom windows cast shadows from the rain onto her white blouse. Brodie kissed her again and began undoing the buttons.

Anna closed her eyes. Was she thinking about Harry? Were they both just two lonely, fucked-up people using each other? Did it matter?

He kissed her neck and down along her collarbone, finishing the last of the buttons and pulling away her blouse. She wasn't wearing a bra and her creamy skin seemed to glow in the dimly lit room. He brushed across one of her nipples and she sucked in a quick breath.

Anna threaded her fingers into his hair and pulled him back up into another deep kiss. She let go of his hair and grabbed the fabric of his shirt and pulled him down onto the bed.

Brodie kissed her breasts and stomach. His fingers worked their way down her body and

made it to the button on her pants. She nodded, and he undid the zipper and pulled her
pants off while she played with her own
breasts. Then he undid his belt and removed
his pants and threw off his shirt. Anna pulled
him back on top of her. Brodie buried his
head in the crook of her neck as he pressed
himself in between her soft thighs. She
gasped out choppy, throaty breaths. He
worked his way back up her neck in between
thrusts. They tried to kiss at the same time
and traded small smiles and gasps for breath.

Outside, the thunder rolled, and the wind
picked up. In the distance a faint ambulance
siren wailed as it sped through the rain.

Brodie sensed Anna's energy changing. He
could see her retreating into herself. He
changed positions and his pace. She moaned,
then looked at him with those open, glassy
brown eyes and kissed him deeply. Then she
dug her nails into his back and made enough
noise to compete with the thunderstorm rag-
ing outside.

Suddenly she arched her back and tensed
up, her head barely touching the bed, crying
out something unintelligible. Then she collapsed in a messy, breathy pile, and he joined
her in release.

Afterward, they lay naked next to each
other in the dark, listening to the rain and
thunder. Anna sat up against a pillow and
pulled a comforter over her lap, then reached

for a pack of cigarettes on the end table. "Want one?"

Brodie sat up. The postcoital cigarette felt like a ritual lost to time in America, but in Germany apparently not so. "Sure."

She passed him a cigarette and lit him up, then herself. She blew out a long trail of smoke.

Brodie turned to her. She looked sad. He asked, "Would you like me to leave now?"

"I just gave you a cigarette."

"After the cigarette."

"Do you want to leave?"

"No."

"Then don't." She added, "You sense my pain. It makes you uncomfortable."

He took a drag, thought a moment. "No, not uncomfortable."

"It is always interesting, this time just after. Drained of sexual energy. You are left with the things that never go away. For me, the things that never go away are not so good."

He looked at her in the light of the street-lamps streaming through the rain-streaked windows. "Time helps, Anna. It doesn't heal, but it helps."

She had no response.

Brodie thought a moment, then said, "The Stasi men. If you'd somehow found the one you were looking for . . . you weren't just looking to talk, were you?"

Anna looked at him, weighing what to say.

Then she replied, "No."

Brodie nodded.

She seemed uncomfortable with this subject but continued, "I would usually keep my father's hunting knife in my purse. One time, one of the sons of bitches hit on me. I thought about . . . right there in the bar. Just pretend he was the one, put all the blame and hate on him, and be done with it. Thank God one of my friends was with me, she knew what I was thinking and got me the hell out of there." She took another drag and said, "You must think I am crazy."

Well, yes, but who isn't? He said, "It's understandable. But you're only punishing yourself with these thoughts."

She didn't respond.

After a moment, Brodie asked, "If Odin was caught and punished, would you . . . let this go?"

She replied, as if she'd been asked that question many times, "I would also want to see the Stasi bastards who arrested, tried, and executed my father — and did the same to many others — swing from a noose."

Germany had no death penalty, so that wasn't going to happen. And the German government wanted a happy reunification — not an ugly reckoning. So it looked like Anna was not going to get all she wanted, and never would. But Odin, if he was still alive, could face American justice — if anyone ever

518

discovered who he was.

Well, maybe Harry Vance really thought he could find Odin. And maybe, if someone hadn't prematurely ended his investigation and his life, he would have.

And where did that leave Scott Brodie? He could tell himself that the German Feds, the FBI, and his and Taylor's CID replacements would understand that there was more to the Vance homicide case than an Islamic terrorist hit. But the truth was, in a couple of days they'd put a bow on it and call a press conference. And Odin, the spy who got away, would remain unknown and unpunished. Maybe forever.

Anna stubbed out her cigarette and moved closer to Brodie. He put his arm around her, and she rested her head on his chest. She asked, "Can you stay?"

"A little while." He added, "I have an early meeting."

"And your colleague? Will she be jealous? Are you two . . . ?"

"No. It's not like that. But it's unprofessional to sleep with a witness on the case you're working and I don't need a lecture from her."

Anna thought that was funny.

"She tries to keep me out of trouble. Professionally."

"Good. She cares about you."

"Professionally." He suggested, "Let's

change the subject."

"Let's not talk anymore. Just be here. As long as you can."

"Okay."

He finished his cigarette and stubbed it out in an ashtray on the end table. Anna kept her head on his chest and closed her eyes. They sat in silence, and Brodie listened as the rainfall grew lighter and the storm dissipated. After a few minutes he could tell that she was asleep.

He checked his watch: 10:30 P.M. It felt much later, which is what happens when you start drinking too early and have sex before dinner.

Brodie listened to Anna's breathing and tried to quiet his mind. Why was he pretending he was still on this case? Why couldn't he tell her that he was flying out of Berlin tomorrow? Maybe because he was having a hard time believing it himself. Or maybe because Anna Albrecht thought she'd found the man who would take Harry's place in her bed and her heart. Forget heart — in her obsession with seeking revenge for what she'd lost. And he didn't want to disappoint her. Also, revenge was not justice.

He pictured himself with Maggie Taylor on the flight home, and then without her in Colonel Dombroski's office at Quantico, delivering their report. The colonel would give Brodie what he'd said he wanted — a better partner and better cases. His old career.

He'd go back to his shithole house and in the following days he'd hear about the official resolution of the Vance homicide investigation. He would never again see or hear from the woman now sleeping naked next to him. He was sorry he couldn't help her and sorry to be leaving an unsolved homicide, but that feeling would fade with time, and eventually go into the deep repository of things that Scott Brodie tried not to think about.

He drifted in and out of sleep. At one point he woke up and checked his watch again: 3:06 A.M. He needed to leave. He gently separated himself from her, and she rolled toward him and whispered, "Stay . . ."

He pulled the comforter up over her chest and said, "I'll be back."

"Promise . . ."

"I promise."

CHAPTER 34

The rain turned to a drizzle as Brodie walked alone through the dark streets of Prenzlauer Berg. The bars were all shuttered, and whoever was still looking to party on a Thursday morning at oh-dark-thirty had moved on to the clubs.

He passed under the elevated tracks of the U-Bahn with no particular destination in mind. He needed to wander, clear his head, and put some distance — physical and emotional — between himself and what had just happened at Anna's apartment.

Promise.

Promise what? To stay? To solve the case? To fill the void left by a dead man? He wasn't sure he was up for any of that. More importantly, he had orders to return to his duty station, so it really didn't matter what Scott Brodie wanted. The military sometimes made your decisions easier by not letting you make them.

Brodie meandered through the side streets

until he found himself on a main road. He spotted the lit-up Alexanderplatz TV Tower looming in the distance and headed toward it, passing a few pockets of young people and a couple of solitary drunks. He turned down a wide, desolate boulevard lined with modern residential housing blocks. A few cars and delivery trucks glided along the wet road.

He skirted the northern side of Alexanderplatz, then approached a bridge that crossed the Spree River onto what was known as Museum Island. On his right was the lit-up Berlin Cathedral, a handsome Baroque-style domed church that had either survived the war and the Communists or been rebuilt.

On his left was another Baroque building, massive with an even larger dome, which he assumed was the rebuilt Berlin Palace that their driver, Ulrich, had mentioned, the onetime home to the Hohenzollern royal dynasty. It had been damaged in the war and then razed by the Communists, who had built their own modernist "People's Palace" on the site to house the East German Volkskammer, the so-called parliament. That eyesore had still been standing when Brodie visited in 2000, though when he saw it, it had been abandoned, and a few years later was condemned for demolition because it was filled with asbestos and had attracted vagrants and drug addicts. A squalid end for a squalid nation.

Now the People's Palace was as obliterated from the cityscape as the original imperial palace, which had been reborn through careful recreation. The Cold War might have ended thirty years ago, but Berlin was still a battlefield.

Brodie had thought the walk would clear his head, but it was doing the opposite. Seeing Berlin like this, desolate and dark, reminded him of all the mysteries and unfinished business he was leaving to others.

After another thirty minutes he began to recognize the area and thought he was in the northern section of Neukölln. He spotted a sign for Karl-Marx Straße and turned onto it, heading south.

His detective instincts kicked in and he turned down a few side streets until he was on Richardstraße, the narrow residential road where the bombing had occurred. He kept walking until he saw the damaged building up ahead.

The top floor where the bomb had detonated was covered with a thick tarp, and a small perimeter of crime scene tape was still established around the building. Two Berlin Police officers in body armor stood in front of the building, holding assault rifles. The debris had all been cleared, and the road appeared open to traffic.

Brodie spotted a young Arab man crouched outside the police tape, lighting candles on the sidewalk. As Brodie got closer, he noticed piles of rain-soaked flowers around the candles. A memorial to the victims of the blast, who were also the perpetrators.

The man saw him approaching and quickly stood. He looked apprehensive.

Brodie said, "Guten Abend," then looked at the memorial. He noticed three pieces of cut-out plywood amidst the flowers and candles, painted white with black Arabic script — presumably the names of the three men who had died in the bombing. Two of the plywood pieces were shaped like Muslim crescent moons. The third was a Christian cross.

Brodie hadn't picked up much Arabic in Iraq, but he knew the word for "Christian." He pointed to the cross and asked the man, "Masihiun?"

The young man nodded. "Ja. Masihiun." He said something else in halting German.

"I don't speak German. Or Arabic. Were you" — he pointed to the man, and then to the memorial — "friends? Habibi?"

The man nodded. "Ashab. Naeam faela." He continued in Arabic, gesturing to the memorial.

Brodie interrupted, "Antazir. Law samaht," which he was pretty sure meant "please wait." His Arabic had sucked sixteen years ago and hadn't gotten any better since. But he knew someone with good Arabic, who kept her phone on at all hours when on assignment and who was duty-bound to indulge him. He pulled out his cell and dialed Maggie Taylor.

It rang a few times before she picked up. "Scott? What's up?" She sounded groggy and alert at the same time, which was impressive.

"I need your Arabic skills."

"Okay . . . should I come to your room?"

"I'm actually on Richardstraße, at the site of the blast. There's a young Arabic-speaking guy here that I need to talk to. I'll put us on speaker."

"No. I'm up now, and I need a jog. I'll be there in ten. Can you hold him there?"

"Just speak —"

"Put him on."

Brodie handed the phone to the man, who listened, nodded, and handed the phone back to Brodie, who put it to his ear and heard Taylor saying, "He's staying. See you soon."

Brodie replied, "Above and beyond."

"Put that in your report." She hung up, and he pictured her throwing on some jogging clothes to meet her partner before dawn on a cold, rainy morning, without even knowing exactly why. That was true dedication to duty. Or dedication to him. You never knew with Maggie Taylor.

The young man had returned to his task of lighting the candles, which must have been extinguished by the rain. Brodie wondered if this guy had been out here all night, keeping vigil at the scene of his friends' deaths, and possibly protecting the memorial from desecration — a task that he might not have trusted to law enforcement.

Brodie eyed the two Berlin Police officers. The nearest one was keeping an eye on the Arab man and on Brodie. Brodie moved down the road to give the young man space and to assure the cops that no altercation was going to happen between them.

In about fifteen minutes Brodie spotted a figure jogging up the street from the south. It was Maggie Taylor, wearing her thick winter coat, sweatpants, running shoes, and her wool beanie. She stopped a few feet from him, took a deep breath, and looked him over. She asked, "Have you been out all night?"

"I needed a walk."

She kept looking at him. "Drinking?"

"I made a few stops."

"I would have gone with you."

"Sorry. I needed to be alone."

"Okay. But thanks for calling when you needed me."

"Don't make me feel guilty."

"You can't even spell it, let alone feel it."

"You'd be surprised. Okay, so this guy —"

"His name is Kadeem."

"Right. So he was a friend of the three deceased."

"He said. Why do you need to talk to him?"

"I'll show you." He led her up the street.

Taylor greeted the young man by name and looked at the memorial. She said to Brodie, "There's a cross."

Brodie nodded. "You know any Christians in al Qaeda?"

Taylor had a brief exchange with the young man; then she said to Brodie, "Kadeem is from Syria and knew these three men there." She and Kadeem had another back-and-forth, and then Taylor continued, "They all grew up together in a village outside of Idlib. One of the dead men, Yosef Rahman, was a Christian. After the jihadis took over the province, Christians were in danger. So Kadeem and these other two men helped Yosef escape into Turkey. They all lived there together in Istanbul for a while and eventually took a boat to Greece, applied for asylum in Germany, and settled here in Neukölln. The three deceased rented this apartment together."

Kadeem said something in Arabic, and he seemed to be getting emotional.

Taylor said, "He says his friends are not terrorists."

Brodie looked again at the three name markers — the two crescents and the cross. He'd been to Syria once on CID assignment, about a year before the civil war began. Back then, Syrian Christians were a prominent minority community with full religious freedoms. Obviously, that changed once parts of the country fell to ISIS, al Qaeda, and other jihadi groups.

Taylor talked with Kadeem for a few more minutes, then offered him a twenty-euro note, which he politely refused. Taylor made the appropriate parting comments in Arabic, and led Brodie away, back toward the hotel. The two policemen watched them, and spoke to each other, probably wondering what was going on. And maybe thinking about asking. Or at least calling their superior. Indeed, Brodie thought, this was a city on edge.

Taylor said, as they walked, "Kadeem lives two blocks from here. He saw his friends the morning prior to the bombing and said they were not acting out of the ordinary. Kadeem relayed all of this to the Berlin Police officials who canvassed the neighborhood this evening looking for associates of the deceased men. He insisted to them that his friends had no terrorist links. The idea of it was absurd to him."

"And what do you think?"

"I . . . don't know." She added, "The German authorities know all this. Yet they say that these men were terrorists."

"It's the easy answer, which isn't always the right one."

She nodded, then thought a moment and asked, "What have you been doing all night?"

"I told you."

Taylor didn't press, and they kept walking.

She clearly could sense there was something he wasn't telling her. Or maybe she smelled Anna's perfume. Whatever. It was none of her business.

They saw Körnerpark up ahead, and Brodie headed toward the eastern entrance and Taylor followed. She said, "That cross screws up the narrative."

"Only if you want it to. All three men had secret lives. And in Yosef Rahman's case, a secret faith. The police will say they kept their radicalization to themselves. That's the narrative. It will be good enough for the press and the public, and probably good enough for a team of investigators who want this case to be over."

They reached the entrance to Körnerpark. Brodie and Taylor ducked under the chain and walked across the park toward the Art Hotel.

Taylor said, "The supposed link between the Vance homicide and the explosion on Richardstraße is not even public yet. Once it is, and the faces of those three Arab men are beamed all over the world . . ."

Right. Case closed. The dead guys had the murder weapon in their apartment and the victim's eye in their freezer, and a communication referencing a revenge plot that would make Harry Vance and Mark Jenkins logical targets. It all fit.

And yet . . .

Why were the men following Mark Jenkins being so obvious about it? To intimidate him? No. That had never made any sense. They wanted Jenkins to know they were following him so that he would report it, because that would fit the larger narrative. And that bomb was never meant for his car. It had gone off exactly where it was supposed to.

Obviously, the narrative was being manipulated, and the clues had been planted. But why? And by whom?

He stopped walking.

Taylor looked at him. "What?"

He reached into his jacket pocket and pulled out the small manila envelope that he had taken from Vance's jacket hanging in Anna Albrecht's wardrobe. He removed the microscope slide and held it up toward the light of a distant streetlamp, silhouetting the hazy purple splotches suspended in liquid. He said, "Black Harvest."

She didn't reply, but nodded slowly.

Harry had been researching Storkow and its unconventional-weapons program. Maybe he'd somehow gotten his hands on some of their research product. *Holy shit.*

He noticed that Taylor was pulling up a number on her phone. "Who are you calling?"

"Dombroski." She looked him in the eyes. "We're not leaving, Scott."

He looked closely at his partner. She had

531

that trademark manic look about her. Maggie Taylor was dedicated to her work like no one he'd ever seen. Yet she was also loyal to the institution of the Army and the chain of command, which was why her first reaction to this eureka moment was to call their commanding officer. But what happened when dedication to duty and deference to rank collided? They were about to find out.

Taylor hit the dial button and put the phone on speaker.

The colonel picked up. "Ms. Taylor. You're up early. Or late."

"Hello, sir. I'm with Scott. You're on speaker."

"What's up?"

Taylor said, "We have some new —"

Brodie interrupted and said, "Ms. Taylor and I would like to take some leave time here. Two weeks."

"Really?"

"Yes, sir. A road trip to Bavaria."

"Sounds like fun."

Brodie realized that Colonel Dombroski was wondering if his two agents were sleeping together. It would be useful if Dombroski thought they were, so he said, "Maggie and I have a lot of catching up to do. Plus, we got the rug pulled out from under us on this case and, frankly, we could both use a week or two to . . . commiserate." He added, "You would still have your report by Friday. I can e-mail an encrypted file."

Dombroski's bullshit detector must have been off the charts, and he said, "I can appreciate all that, Scott. But since this is an open case and you were the initial investigators, I need you on call in case anything arises. The Bavarian adventure will have to wait."

It sounded like the colonel was meeting Brodie's bullshit with a pile of his own. Raise or call?

Before he could decide, Taylor said, "Sir, we would like to stay in Germany until the conclusion of the investigation." She added, "On our time."

Dombroski was quiet a moment. Then he asked, "Why?"

"New information has come to light that directly contradicts the official narrative, and we have reason to believe that this case will be handled improperly." She added, "If we're to be on call, we'd prefer to stay in-country."

"You are no longer the agents on this case, Ms. Taylor. Whatever this new information is, I expect to hear it during the debrief, and you will pass it on to your very capable colleagues from the Fifth MP via the Legal Attaché's Office." He added, "As for your belief that this case will be handled improperly, tell me about it in person."

Brodie jumped in. "Colonel, the Germans, the FBI, and our own counterterrorism people are . . . mishandling this case. Harry Vance was onto something, and now he's dead, and whoever killed him is going to incredible lengths to see that this investigation concludes that Vance's murder was an act of Islamic terrorism."

"That seems to be the correct conclusion, based on the jihadis who blew themselves up and left Mr. Vance's eye in their freezer. Wouldn't you agree?"

"I . . . and Ms. Taylor believe another entity is manipulating the evidence to make it look like —"

"Like Tiny Tim killed JFK." He asked, "Do you hear yourself?"

"Sir —"

"Have you two been drinking?"

"Colonel —"

"Maybe you do need a vacation. But not now. I expect you in my office tomorrow. Tonight. Right from the airport."

Neither Brodie nor Taylor replied, and Colonel Dombroski shifted to a milder tone. "I appreciate your dedication to this case. That's why I wanted you both on this in the first place. But there are larger forces at play here, and you are being replaced by two of CID's best counterterrorism specialists."

Taylor said, "This is not a counterterrorism case, sir."

Dombroski was getting annoyed. "You will fly to DC tomorrow. You will be in my office tomorrow night for a debrief. Ms. Taylor, I will speak to your CO at Fort Campbell and have your connecting flight home rebooked, and you will also be present for this debrief. Is that all clear?"

Brodie and Taylor looked at each other, but neither responded.

Brodie looked around the park and realized they had stopped walking almost exactly where Harry Vance had been shot.

The dead can speak.

He looked toward the dark tree line along the eastern edge of the park, and imagined a figure there, a little over six feet tall, a skilled marksman. The Islamic terrorist who he'd imagined wasn't there anymore. Now he saw a U.S. Army traitor.

He looked at the microscope slide in his hand.

Unexploded ordnance.

The thing that was buried in the ruins, believed to be rendered inert by the passage of time. Harry Vance thought he was investigating something important but not dangerous. He was dead wrong.

Who still cared about the Stasi? No one. Well, almost no one. But what if the past is not past? Maybe in a place like Berlin, it never is.

"Mr. Brodie? Ms. Taylor? Do I make myself clear?"

Brodie and Taylor stood in silence, looking

535

at each other. Brodie thought about their last case together, about what they'd been asked to give. He didn't mind risking his life. That came with the territory, and maybe he kind of had a death wish anyway. But they'd been forced to compromise their integrity, their oath to duty, their commitment to justice. And for what? A bump in rank. A little extra pay.

He thought about Harry Vance, and about why the man had kept his investigation secret. The obvious reason was that it was outside his mandate. The less obvious reason was that he understood that the case was sensitive and did not know whom to trust. But Brodie suspected there was another reason, maybe present only in Harry's subconscious: He didn't think anyone other than himself and Anna would care about Anna's father, just another forgotten victim of an old war. As for Odin, the U.S. Army officially had no traitors in the Cold War, and they'd like to keep it that way.

Brodie looked at Taylor. As the senior partner, Scott Brodie had a responsibility to her. He knew that she'd follow him to the gates of Hell. In fact, she already had on their last assignment. But this time, Brodie didn't want Maggie Taylor to suffer collateral damage for his self-destructive choices.

Brodie said to Dombroski, "We understand, Colonel. See you tomorrow."

There was a long silence. Then Dombroski said, "It's different when it's a colleague. I understand that, and I appreciate the work you've done. Is there anything further?"

Brodie said, "Negative further."

"Safe travels." The colonel hung up.

Taylor stared at her phone a moment, then slipped it in her pocket and looked at Brodie. "That's it."

"Are you disappointed?"

"In him, yes. Which I guess means I'm still naïve."

"He was never going to go for it, Maggie. Sharon Whitmore and Chief Inspector Schröder want to know that we are truly off this case. Anything short of sending us back across the ocean communicates the wrong message."

Taylor nodded but did not respond.

Brodie looked toward the hotel. "Let's get inside."

They walked across the park and up the stairs, then crossed the street and entered the hotel lobby. A young Turkish woman they hadn't seen before was at the desk. She mumbled something in German as they walked past and up the stairs to their rooms.

Taylor paused at her door and turned to Brodie. She looked tired. "It's good that I will be there for the debrief."

Brodie nodded.

"The new CID team will be thorough,

Scott. Harry was their colleague. Their brother."

Ms. Taylor was trying to convince someone, but it wasn't him. He said, "I'm sure you're right. And we can contact the team and give them our thoughts and opinions on the case."

She replied, "I think we will be signing the same confidentiality statements we signed after Venezuela."

"Right. Also known as the don't-talk-about-shit-you're-not-supposed-to-talk-about statement."

She tried to smile.

"Okay," he said. "Get some rest. And good work, Maggie."

She nodded. "Likewise."

They each entered their rooms. Brodie did a quick sweep to see if any Lebanese gangsters, Islamic terrorists, American double agents, or former Stasi spies were lying in wait to kill him. He was alone, which was kind of disappointing.

Brodie took out his phone. He had decided what he was going to do and what he had to do. He dialed Colonel Dombroski, who picked up after one ring.

"Mr. Brodie. Did you forget something?"

"Yes, I did. I am calling to inform you that I am not leaving Berlin tomorrow, and I will not be present for the debrief at Quantico. I am resigning my commission, effective immediately."

"The hell you are."

"It has been an honor to serve under you, sir, and I will always respect you even if it is no longer reciprocated."

"Hold on, Scott —"

"Colonel, that is my final decision. I will e-mail you my resignation with copies to the appropriate —"

"*Scott.* Call me when you cool down."

Brodie turned the phone off and tossed it on the bedside table. He sat down on the bed.

That was not so hard. He'd had all the reasons he needed to do that before this Berlin assignment, and getting pulled from the case just as things were getting interesting was the last straw.

As for Chief Warrant Officer Taylor, if he'd resigned in front of her, she might have been tempted to do the same. But she had a bright career ahead of her, and he didn't want to be responsible for screwing it up.

He thought about Anna Albrecht, and whether he was doing this because of her. Was he really that stupid? He had to ponder that.

Promise.

Promise not to give up. Promise not to forget. Promise not to pretend the crimes of the past never happened.

That was Anna's demand, born out of decades of denied justice. But it was Berlin's demand as well, echoed in monuments and memorials and museums across this city that prosecuted its tragic past.

This happened. And this. And this. These are the names of the perpetrators. These are the names of the victims.

But Odin's story had not been told by anyone outside of an obscure Stasi report, and the names of his victims were lost to history.

As for poor Harry Vance, his name was not forgotten. It was screamed in every headline across the world. But he was about to be denied justice as well, by an investigation that either had gone wrong, or was being steered wrong. The three suspects, the Syrians, were themselves possible victims of something much larger and more sinister than anyone on this investigation could yet imagine. Something that was still formless, swirling in the dark, blotting out the truth.

I did this. I'm still here.

Odin's message, carved into Harry Vance's face. Right there for anyone willing to see it. But no one wanted to see.

And when the real perpetrators were unnamed, and the victims were unavenged, it was not enough to merely remember. That doesn't ask enough of you.

You must find the perpetrators. You must name them.

And you must make them pay.

■ ■ ■ ■

PART III

■ ■ ■ ■

CHAPTER 35

Scott Brodie sat on the bench ringing the central fountain of Alexanderplatz and watched a middle-aged street sweeper use his broom to dislodge debris from between the cable car tracks. The guy appeared indifferent as to whether the trash ended up in his dustpan or was blown across the square by the freezing gusts. The man's job was not to clean; it was to sweep. The wind was his accomplice.

Brodie had not turned on his phone since hanging up on Dombroski, after which he'd had a quick shower and change, then checked out of the Art Hotel, and left his bags with the indifferent Turkish teenager at the front desk.

He checked his watch: 7:26 A.M. Taylor would be looking for him. Calling him. Concerned but not yet frantic. She wouldn't board the plane without knowing where he was.

The city was waking up. Lights blinked on

in a supermarket across the square, and a few commuters began to emerge from the nearby U-Bahn station.

According to the metro timeline provided by the Berlin Police, Harry Vance had exited this particular metro station at 11:20 A.M. last Wednesday. On its own, that information wasn't very useful, as Alexanderplatz was centrally located, and Vance could have been going anywhere.

But he didn't go anywhere, he went somewhere. Two blocks from where Brodie was sitting was the headquarters of the Stasi Records Agency, which housed millions of files produced by the security service during its forty-year existence. Had Harry gone there? He wouldn't have been much of a detective if he hadn't.

This thought barely rose to the level of a lead — it was a hunch. But Brodie was a little desperate, and since he was now unemployed, with no oaths to keep, no constitution to defend, and no boss to bullshit, he could do what he wanted. And former warrant officer Scott Brodie, with the new rank of PFC — Private Fucking Civilian — wanted justice, and he wanted it soon, before anyone tried to arrest him, stop him, or kill him.

The Records Agency opened at 8 A.M., which meant Brodie had time for one unpleasant phone call. He turned his phone on, ignored all the pinging voice mails and text messages, and dialed Taylor.

She picked up immediately. "Scott, where the hell are you?"

"You need to get to the airport."

"Answer me."

"I'm watching the sunrise."

"Where? I'll have the cab swing by."

"I'm not leaving."

"Dombroski just called me to see if I could talk some sense into you. I can't believe you."

He had no response.

"You knew last night that you were going to do this. Why did you lie to me?"

"So I didn't have to listen to you argue with me."

"Well, you can listen now. Scott, we tried to stay on the case. And the colonel said no. A good soldier shows initiative and shows balls, but there are always limits. Even for you."

Brodie stood up from the fountain and started walking across the square. "I was always a lousy soldier, Maggie."

"I doubt your men in Iraq felt that way."

He didn't respond.

"This case is important, but there will always be more victims who deserve justice. And where will you be then?"

Home watching TV? Drunk on a beach in Florida? Dead in a back alley in Berlin? That all sounded better than going back to Quantico. He said, "I appreciate your concern for my future. You wouldn't be much of a partner

545

if you didn't try to change my mind. But it's over. I'm done."

"You're the one who told me that our CID colleagues could handle it. I guess you were just snowing me on that too."

"I was trying to convince myself. You have a different calculation to make, Maggie. You've got a long career ahead of you."

"Get down off your cross."

"I like the view up here."

There was a long silence. Then Taylor said, "Last night I thought about requesting a transfer to Quantico. I thought maybe we could . . ." She trailed off; then her tone shifted. "You're not the hero, Scott. Not on this. You're burning your life down and pretending it's something else. You've got an hour and a half to come to your fucking senses and get to the airport." She hung up.

Brodie kept walking and put his phone in his pocket. He'd expected Taylor to be angry, maybe disappointed. But she was more than that. She'd been looking toward a continued working relationship after this case, which came as a bit of a surprise to him. Maybe it shouldn't have. When it came to questionable and self-destructive choices, they were kindred spirits, and Brodie had upped the ante without looping her in. She felt betrayed. Rejected. And possibly resentful of the feeling that her partner was entering territory where she knew she couldn't or wouldn't follow.

Well, that was all the psychoanalysis Brodie could handle for the day, and it wasn't even sunrise. He grabbed a takeout coffee at a nearby café, then exited the square and turned onto Karl-Liebknecht Straße, a broad six-lane boulevard lined with large modern buildings. He crossed the street and continued until he reached a drab gray office building with a sign in front that read STASI-UNTERLAGEN-ARCHIV.

He looked at the wide eight-story building. Every level above the ground floor was lined with small square windows, most of them shuttered by opaque blinds. He assumed these floors held the stacks — the endless river of files produced by the Stasi over the course of four decades, their magnum opus, relating the lives and loyalties of East Germany's captive citizens.

A short flight of stairs led to a large entryway beneath a glass awning splattered with bird shit. Above the door was a security camera, the only one Brodie had seen outside of metro stations. Was this German irony?

He checked his watch: 7:58 A.M. He finished his coffee, and at precisely 8:00 A.M. fluorescent lights blinked on in the lobby.

Brodie tossed the paper cup in a nearby trash bin, then ascended the stairs and entered through the automatic glass doors, hoping that he was following in a dead man's footsteps.

CHAPTER 36

Brodie looked around the low-ceilinged lobby. In front of him was a row of turnstiles that led to a bank of elevators. To his right was an elevated security desk and to his left was a waiting area.

He approached the security desk where a hefty mid-fifties man in a dark suit with close-cropped blond hair sat near a computer monitor.

Brodie said, "Guten Morgen."

The security man, whose nametag identified him as "Lehmann," looked back at Brodie, blank-faced. "Haben Sie einen Termin?"

"Sprechen Sie Englisch?"

"Do you have an appointment?"

"No."

Herr Lehmann grabbed an English-language pamphlet from under his desk and slid it to Brodie. "Call the number on this."

Brodie looked at the pamphlet, which was labeled in large red letters: STASI REC-

ORDS ARCHIVE, along with a subheading: State Security: An Introduction. He asked, "Do you have a gift shop?"

"What?"

Brodie opened his cred case — badge and photo ID — and held it close to Lehmann's face. "Scott Brodie, U.S. Army Criminal Investigation Division. I am working with the Bundeskriminalamt, investigating the murder of my colleague Harry Vance. I'm sure you've seen that on the news."

Lehmann eyed the badge and ID, then slid his eyes back to Brodie, as if to ensure the photo was a match. He nodded.

"We have reason to believe that the deceased visited here in the days before his death. Were you working the desk last week?"

"I am here every weekday."

Brodie took out his phone, pulled up Harry Vance's military file photo, and showed it to Lehmann. "Has this man visited the archives?"

Lehmann looked at the photo for a moment, then picked up a phone on his desk, punched a couple of buttons, and had a brief conversation in German. He hung up and said to Brodie, "Passport."

Brodie pulled his passport from his sports jacket and placed it on the desk. Lehmann looked it over and entered some information on his computer, then jotted something down on a small white card. He returned the passport along with the card. "This is your visitor pass. Keep it with you. Wait over there." He gestured to the sitting area on the other side of the lobby.

"What am I waiting for?"

"Someone to help you."

"How long will it be?"

Lehmann looked at him as though that was a stupidly arrogant question. "Visitors often must make appointments months in advance."

"I am not a visitor. I am a criminal investigator."

"And this is why someone is coming down to see you without an appointment."

This guy could use a good schnapps or two. Brodie again held up the photo of Vance on his phone. "Have you seen this man, Herr Lehmann?"

Lehmann stared at Brodie. "I am not authorized to share the visitor logs with anyone, no matter their credentials."

"Thanks for your help."

Brodie walked across the room to the waiting area and sat on a boxy faux-leather armchair. He looked over at Lehmann, who was now busying himself — or pretending to busy himself — with something on his computer.

This man knew whether Harry Vance had been here. Was his refusal to answer the question evidence in the affirmative? Not necessarily. This was a German bureaucrat running security for the Stasi Archives. Only a Grade A tight-ass would want or get that gig.

Brodie observed his surroundings. In addition to a few armchairs there was a rack stuffed with pamphlets in a variety of languages, and at the far end of the room was a black door with a sign in German along with an English translation: ARCHIVE READING ROOM. NO ACCESS WITHOUT AUTHORIZATION. NO TALKING. NO PHONES OR RECORDING EQUIPMENT. The door handle had a fob-activated security plate.

The only other detail of note was the wall opposite him, which was wallpapered with what appeared to be a life-sized photograph of the archives' stacks — rows and rows of metal shelving lined with brown and yellow file folders stuffed with papers. It was a strange and vaguely ominous design choice.

In fact, this whole place was projecting a distinctly Germanic combo of mundane and sinister. The touristy pamphlets and the uptight bureaucrat on the one hand, and on the other the locked reading room, the creepy wallpaper, and the seven floors of Stasi files above — a monument to the most intrusive surveillance state in human history. This place was like a DMV with secrets. Or a lending library from Hell.

He waited about twenty minutes, during

which time an older man in a suit came in and pressed a keycard to the turnstiles before proceeding to the elevator, and an attractive woman in her fifties paid a visit to the fascist functionary at the security desk, then took a seat in the waiting area. Brodie wondered what she was there for. Maybe an academic conducting research. Or a former citizen of the GDR, who'd come to read her own file to discover if her nosy neighbor from thirty-five years ago had been a government rat.

"Mr. Brodie."

Brodie stood and turned toward the voice.

A woman in her mid-sixties stood with her hands clasped tightly in front of her. She wore a dark-blue suit and chunky black shoes. Her paper-white complexion was framed by shoulder-length dark-brown hair, and her small inquisitive eyes stared at him from behind oversize tortoiseshell glasses.

She said in a thick German accent, "I am Frau Ziegler, the chief archivist. You had an inquiry about our visitation logs."

Brodie flashed his badge again, committing his second crime of the morning by impersonating a law enforcement officer. "I am assisting your government in investigating the murder of my colleague, U.S. Army CID Special Agent Harry Vance. We have reason to believe he visited your archives in the days before his death."

She stared at him for a moment, then

asked, "What is the reason you believe this?"

"I'm not at liberty to say."

She nodded, considering that. "We take personal privacy very seriously here. If you wish to access our visitor logs, I will need a formal request from a German law enforcement agency."

"I don't wish to access your visitor logs. I just want to know if one man — now deceased — came here last week. In my work, the dead demand justice more than privacy."

"Well, in *my* work, Mr. Brodie, the violation of privacy is the injustice. And as for the dead, we must protect them most of all, for they are no longer able to protect themselves."

Actually, the dead had bigger problems. It was time for another approach: "Does this archive contain files related to the activities of the Stasi's foreign intelligence service, the HVA?"

Frau Ziegler paused. Then she answered, "Yes."

"Who is allowed to access those files?"

"Anyone who applies with a sufficient reason." She added, "Such files are often easier to access than most of our domestic surveillance archives. Matters of state, foreign relations, et cetera, do not generally name private East German citizens. As I said, our chief concern is for those whose privacy was so violated by the Stasi. We are less interested in guarding intelligence documents produced by an extinct nation."

That was interesting, though it also sounded a little like PR bullshit. Despite what Frau Ziegler just said, the report about Odin was never destined for this public archive, and only arrived in Anna's mother's hands because twenty years ago someone who worked here decided to steal the document and give it to her directly.

Brodie said, "I have a German friend whose father was involved with the Stasi. He is now deceased, and I know she was interested in finding out about his activities."

"Tell your friend to apply for an appointment. Direct relatives of deceased citizens may view their records, though depending on the circumstances, redactions may be necessary to protect others' identities, which can take some time." She asked, "Is there anything else I can help you with?"

Well, so far she hadn't helped him with anything. Time for a Hail Mary. "Just one more question. Outside of mythology, does the name Odin mean anything to you?"

Frau Ziegler stared at him for a long moment. She was a cool customer, but still couldn't hide being taken aback. She said, "We ought to continue this conversation in my office."

Well, it looked like his shot in the dark had hit something.

Brodie followed Frau Ziegler through the security turnstiles and into an elevator. They rode silently to the fourth floor.

The elevator doors opened, and they exited into a large room with countless rows of metal shelving reaching up to the ceiling. Each shelf was lined with dozens of folders stuffed with hundreds of documents.

Frau Ziegler led Brodie down one of the rows without speaking.

He asked, "Is every Stasi record kept in this building?"

"No. About half of what has been recovered. The remainder are spread among our twelve regional offices."

"I heard about the puzzle women."

"That is an outdated phrase. Men also work at Zirndorf."

"Puzzle people."

They turned and walked down a narrow corridor, passing a dozen aisles of shelves on either side, all packed with files. The amount of Stasi surveillance records in this one area of this one floor in this one archive was stunning. Frightening.

Brodie asked, "How long have you worked here?"

"I helped launch this project in 1990. I had been a librarian in East Berlin. After the Wall fell, I used my skills to assist in creating an organizational system."

"Wasn't it already organized by the last guys?"

Frau Ziegler threw him a look over her shoulder. "These records were created as tools of tyrants and are now a public resource. Form follows function. We had no use for their system."

Right. This archive must have represented the worst nightmare of the former Stasi spies and secret police — a catalogue of their perverse snooping, all here for any German citizen to access. In fact, the bastards had spent their last days in power shredding and burning everything they could, to try to prevent a place like this from ever existing.

They reached the end of the long aisle and approached a door with a frosted glass panel, and a plaque next to it that read: ELSA ZIE-GLER, CHEFARCHIVAR, STASI UNTER-LAGEN ARCHIV.

They entered a small office, which was spartan and orderly. A metal desk stood at one end, on which were a telephone and a closed laptop, and behind the desk was one of the many small square windows visible from the street. The only other things on the desk were a mug of coffee, a glass bowl of mixed fruit, and a half-peeled hard-boiled egg.

"You will excuse me," said Ziegler. "I was in the middle of my breakfast."

"Please."

Ziegler sat down and continued to peel her egg, dropping the shell fragments in a neat pile on a napkin. Brodie took a seat in the only other chair in the room, which was wedged next to a dying houseplant that apparently needed more sunlight than the small window could provide, and more love than Frau Ziegler was giving it.

Elsa Ziegler focused her attention on shelling her egg and asked, "Have you spoken to Anna?"

"Who's Anna?"

Ziegler shot him a look from behind her big glasses.

Brodie explained, "I cannot discuss the investigation, Frau Ziegler. Including anyone I may have interviewed." Or slept with.

She finished peeling her egg and looked at him. "Call me Elsa."

"Scott."

"Now that we are on a first-name basis, Scott, can we end the bullshit?"

"You first."

"Okay. I knew Anna's mother, Ursula. Difficult woman. Quite tortured."

Brodie nodded but said nothing.

Elsa bit into her egg, and asked between bites, "Why did you come here alone, without a German counterpart?"

"We have been given more work than we can do before we report in today, so we divided up the labor."

"Hm." She took a long sip of coffee.

"Tell me about Harry Vance's visit here."

"What does his murder have to do with the Stasi, or this archive?"

"Maybe nothing. We are exploring all avenues."

"There's the bullshit again."

"It's not the favored theory. But I have an interest in it."

"Ah. Striking out on your own, then. The American way."

Brodie did not reply, but if he'd had a cowboy hat, he would have waved it.

Ziegler thought a moment, then said, "He seemed like a good man. I was very sad to hear the news."

"Why did he come here, Elsa?"

She looked at him. "Spy hunting."

"I need details."

She nodded and seemed to be collecting her thoughts. "Mr. Vance had initially called here and spoken with one of my colleagues. He said he was looking for files pertaining to the Hauptverwaltung Aufklärung — the HVA — and their activities in the 1980s. My colleague told him this request was far too broad. Mr. Vance said the request pertained to a counterterrorism case he was working, and my colleague told him that he would need to submit an official request, in conjunction with a German law enforcement agency, and that this request needed to specify what records he was looking for based on dates, geographic location, and subject matter. Mr. Vance never got back to them."

This was the first Brodie was hearing of how Vance classified his own investigation into Odin — as a counterterrorism case. That was a convenient lie, given his official job title. Unless there was something Brodie was still not seeing . . .

Ziegler continued, "Instead, Mr. Vance accosted me, out front of this building. He knew who I was. He tells me his investigation is a matter of such secrecy and sensitivity that he cannot go through official channels. Now I think this man is maybe cuckoo, regardless of his credentials." She eyed Brodie. "I would have told him to go away, except he got more specific with me than he had with my colleague over the phone. He says he is trying to find information about an American military official who acted as a spy for the Stasi in the eighties. Someone who had never been discovered or prosecuted. And then I understand. Because I know who he is looking for."

"Odin."

She nodded.

"How did you know about Odin?"

"My position provides me a unique vantage point."

Of course. Elsa Ziegler, Chief Archivist. A woman with unlimited access who had been here since the beginning. Brodie said, "You are the person who originally intercepted the Stasi report on Odin and gave it to Anna's mother."

Ziegler stared at Brodie, blank-faced. "That would be a crime."

"Not one I'm investigating."

After a moment, Ziegler said, "I was familiar with the tragedy that befell the Albrecht family, and that they never got closure. Let us leave it at that."

Well, that was good enough for Scott Brodie. Especially since he was no longer actually on this case, and even if he had been, he had no jurisdictional authority to be interviewing Elsa Ziegler in the first place. In fact, he was pretty far out over his skis here, and should probably wrap this up soon, before Herr Lehmann decided to call the Bundeskriminalamt headquarters to confirm whether an American CID agent named Scott Brodie was involved with the Vance homicide investigation.

Brodie asked, "How many interactions did you have with Mr. Vance?"

"This single in-person encounter, which was quite brief."

"Have you told the German authorities about this encounter?"

"No."

"Why not?"

"I didn't think it was relevant."

"You had a conversation with a man in the

days preceding his murder, in which he was inquiring about an American double agent who was never discovered and who was responsible for the unmasking and execution of four Western intelligence assets, and you did not think that was relevant to report to the authorities investigating his homicide?"

She gave him an odd look. "My encounter with Mr. Vance occurred last *year*. Back in the spring."

What?

She added, "Early or mid-May, I believe. Yes. The cherry blossoms were all dropping their petals."

Brodie didn't respond. According to Anna, she and Harry hadn't even met until early July. *Unless . . .*

Something had been bothering Brodie ever since that first encounter with Anna, something that didn't sit right: What were the chances that an American military investigator just happens to stroll into an art gallery and meet a woman with a tragic family history involving an American military double agent? That was a hell of a coincidence. Unless it wasn't a coincidence at all.

Brodie said, "You told Harry Vance about Anna Albrecht."

She looked at Brodie as though that were obvious. "Yes. And that is all I told him. Her name, and that she might have the information he was seeking." She added, "It was something of a violation, I understood that. But Manfred's death . . . it ruined Ursula. And this investigator comes along, and I thought, maybe he could help Ursula's daughter find some answers."

Of course. Harry now had a name: Anna Albrecht. He looked her up, found her gallery. Came in to admire the art and chat up the gallery curator. Made it all seem like happenstance, as a way to build trust . . .

He asked Ziegler, "Why did Harry approach you in the first place? If you sent him to Anna, who or what sent him to you?"

"I was curious about that as well, and I asked him. He would not tell me."

"Right. Okay, is there anything else you can recall about your conversation that might offer a clue as to his motivation for searching for Odin? Something he may have mentioned or asked about?"

Ziegler thought a moment. "All I can say is that he seemed a very serious man, quite driven to find what he was looking for." She looked at Brodie. "I still fail to understand how my referring him to Ms. Albrecht last spring has anything to do with your case. His death was an act of Islamic terrorism. Was it not?"

Brodie had a feeling Elsa Ziegler was getting nervous that she'd possibly failed to report something of relevance to the German authorities investigating a homicide. Brodie said, "The timeline of your interaction with Mr. Vance is different than my assumptions. Given the context, there is little reason for you to have thought you needed to report a conversation from eight months ago."

Elsa Ziegler looked at Brodie. That was the answer she wanted, but it didn't explain why CID Agent Brodie had come to her Stasi Archives with questions that seemed to have nothing to do with the investigation of a homicide perpetrated by Islamic terrorists. She asked, "Is there anything else?"

"A few more things." He asked, "What can you tell me about the Stasi's plan to invade and occupy West Berlin? Day X."

Her eyes narrowed. "Are we still discussing your case?"

"I am a CID agent investigating a murder, not a history buff with time to waste." He added, "Please answer the question so I can report that you were very cooperative."

Ziegler nodded and replied, "All existing records pertaining to Day X — and there aren't many — are kept here and have been reviewed by academics and journalists, and their findings published in a number of news articles and journals that you can find on the Internet."

"Anything to add to the public record?"

"No." She hesitated, then added, "Though I do have one curiosity." She opened one of her desk drawers and removed a small mahogany box, then opened it and turned it toward Brodie.

He walked to the desk and picked up the box, which was lined with green felt and contained a star-shaped gold military medal hanging on a black-red-and-yellow ribbon.

Ziegler said, "The Stasi had these medals minted in anticipation of their successful paramilitary occupation of West Berlin. This one is the Combat Order of Merit for the Reunification of the Fatherland."

Brodie examined the medal, which featured the symbol of the Stasi — an arm hoisting a bayoneted rifle on which hung the flag of East Germany — along with German words ringing the symbol. It was bizarre — and chilling — to be holding a military medal created for a war that never happened.

He placed the box back on Ziegler's desk. "In retrospect, it looks like they suffered a crisis of overconfidence."

She took the box and looked at the medal. "They ruled with impunity over a small and terrified nation, and so they thought they were bigger than they were. I like to keep this here, as a reminder." She closed the box, returned it to her desk, and looked up at Brodie. "A reminder that they were not so big. And that their failed dreams now live in a little box in my drawer, next to the stapler." She checked her watch. "Now, I do have a meeting this morning that I need to prepare for."

"Just one more thing. Is there anything you can tell me about Operation Black Harvest?"

Ziegler looked surprised. "That's quite obscure. Where did you hear about that?"

"Turning over every rock, looking for maggots."

She said, "It was a rumored Stasi operation to develop biological and chemical weapons to kill livestock and crops in Western Europe. Degrade and destroy the food supply. I say rumored because no documentary evidence of its existence has ever been found. This evidence could have been destroyed in the Stasi's final days, or it could be sitting in shreds inside a bag at Zirndorf. Or the whole thing could have been made up."

"By whom?"

"By the only person who has made public mention of this operation. Stefan Richter. A former Stasi man. HVA. After the Wall came down, he began the rumors of agricultural weapons research being done by the Stasi in conjunction with the People's Army for this so-called Black Harvest." She added, "Many believed he was looking for his fifteen minutes, as you Americans say."

"What do you believe?"

Ziegler shrugged. "Anything is possible in the insane asylum that existed then."

"Where might I find Stefan Richter?"

"I have no idea if he is even alive. I spoke to him in person once, back in the nineties. We were hoping some of these old Stasi men had held on to some of the records of their work, and unlike most of them Herr Richter seemed to want to share his war stories. But he had no documentation. Nothing concrete. A lot of bluster. I'm not even convinced he was ever Stasi. I recall being unimpressed with the man."

Brodie nodded. Stefan Richter was likely the HVA official who had given the interview about Black Harvest that Taylor had read in a German foreign policy journal.

Ziegler seemed to remember something else. "The one thing Richter brought with him was a box of microscope slides. He claimed they were biological agents he'd taken from the lab as keepsakes. He wouldn't turn them over or allow anyone to analyze them." She smiled. "He probably bought them from a hobby store for ten marks." She looked at Brodie, and her smile dropped. "Mr. Brodie? Are you all right?"

Brodie stood. "Yes. Thank you. You have been very helpful."

She did not respond and remained seated as Brodie went to the door.

He added, "My German counterparts might be following up."

"Of course." She stood and made eye contact with him. "Tell me. Is this business with Odin connected to what happened to Mr. Vance?"

Brodie looked at her. "No." Elsa Ziegler deserved a more honest answer than that, so he added, "I don't know."

She broke eye contact, and in the dim light of her tiny office, Elsa Ziegler, the steward of millions of documents about a world she'd believed long dead, seemed worried.

And maybe she should be. Maybe she needed to watch her back. Maybe the past is not past. He advised her, "Take personal precautions. The police will further advise you."

Before she could respond, he left the office, made his way through the stacks, took the elevator down, and stepped outside into the cold, overcast day. He tried to order his thoughts. This case didn't begin with Anna Albrecht. And it didn't begin with Elsa Ziegler. Something had brought Harry here to these archives in May of last year. *But what?* The trail of breadcrumbs was getting reordered, and growing longer, and vanishing beyond the horizon in both directions.

He felt the inside pocket of his sports jacket, which still held the envelope with the microscope slide he'd taken from Harry's jacket.

Had Harry made contact with Stefan Richter? Was this guy even still alive? And if so, did Richter bullshit Vance the way Elsa Ziegler believed she had been bullshitted by Richter? And was Richter really a former HVA agent involved with a military biowarfare program — perhaps at Storkow — and was Scott Brodie carrying a sample of an East German bioweapon in his jacket pocket? That would be a more interesting souvenir than the overpriced chunk of Wall he got last time he was here.

And if Richter *had* worked at Storkow, was he there in 1988, on the day that Odin visited the facility? If he had been, and if Vance had recently spoken to Richter, Harry might have gotten a name — or at least a physical description — of Odin, and maybe wouldn't have traveled to a park in Neukölln in the middle of the night to acquire or cross-check that same Intel from Colonel Tariq Qasim, who could also have been at Storkow on that day.

Well, first things first — to figure out what actually had initiated Vance's search for Odin. Brodie took out his phone and dialed Taylor.

She picked up immediately. "Where are you?"

"The Stasi Archives."

"What? Why?"

"I'll tell you when I see you."

"When will that be?"

"Don't know. Are you at the airport?"

"No. Flight's delayed an hour. It's not too

569

late for you to fix a few of your many fuck-ups."

"So where are you now?"

"Unter den Linden. On my way to do the embassy drop-off."

"So you still have the Vance and Jenkins CID case files."

"For another five minutes."

"I need you to look in the files and find any CID investigations that occurred in April or May of last year."

"Are you serious?"

"Taylor, listen —"

"I already read them all, Scott. There was nothing pertinent to this case."

"Humor me."

"These are classified documents. I can't *read* —"

"This is an encrypted phone call. If the NSA eavesdroppers at the embassy want to hear us, they'll at least have to put in some effort."

He heard her sigh and then pull something out of her bag and begin riffling through papers. After a minute she said, "A lot of these cases are concurrent, ongoing investigations, there isn't a clear timeline at a quick glance."

"Just look for any cases that were initiated in April or May."

Another minute or two of silence; then Taylor said, "Two cases, one in April and one in

May." She flipped through some papers, then lowered her voice and said, "April thirteenth, some general signals intelligence chatter about Islamic extremist attacks against American facilities in Western Europe is passed on to CID and other interested American military agencies. Jenkins and Vance are put on the case . . ." She trailed off. "Nothing came of this, just wannabe terrorists boasting. The May one . . ." She was quiet a moment, then said, "Okay . . . May sixth, assault and battery. Joint American-German training exercises in Stuttgart. A retired German Army colonel, Karl Brandt, gets drunk late at night, encounters an American Army captain walking alone on base, pulls his service weapon, threatens to kill the American, who disarms him and calls the MPs." She added, "The American captain was black, and the attack was apparently racially motivated. Colonel Brandt was interviewed by American MPs and German military investigators, and he went off on a racist, white-supremacist rant."

Brodie asked, "Why were Vance and Jenkins brought in? What does this have to do with terrorism?"

"I'm pulling up to the embassy."

"There must be something."

Taylor said something to the driver, then to Brodie: "The German officer claimed he's part of a neo-Nazi group called NordFaust

— I guess, Northern Fist, Fist of the North, or something — and that they have agents everywhere. Refers to a 'secret army' within the German military. So, I guess that's why they called in the CID counterterror guys. Vance and Jenkins conducted their own interview, and by now the colonel has sobered up and also clammed up, and he does not repeat his statements. The Germans write it off as drunken boasting, and the Americans seem to concur. He is arrested for assault and a counterterrorism case is not opened."

"That's it?"

"That's it."

"How old is Colonel Brandt?"

"Gotta go."

"Maybe he was ex-Stasi."

"You're reaching. I'm hanging up." She added, "I wrote a very thorough report on our findings and analysis, which I am handing to Sharon Whitmore directly."

"Maybe you should leave it for General Kiernan at the Defense Attaché Office instead."

"What do you care?" She reminded him, "You don't work for the American government anymore." She added, "And I don't work for you."

"Right . . . okay. But I have no faith in the FBI to take our theories and findings seriously."

"Neither do I. But she is required to share the report with our replacements from Kaiserslautern. I'll make sure Colonel Trask has a copy as well." She thought of something and added, "You still have that slide you took from Harry's jacket?"

"I do."

"You need to turn it over."

"Right."

"I'm serious, Scott. It's evidence, and they'll need to have it analyzed. I'll call you after the debrief at Quantico." She added, "It doesn't have to be over. Listen to your own voice of reason. It's very faint and usually drowned out by your ego, but it's there."

"Thanks for that. Have a good flight." He hung up and slipped his phone in his pocket.

Taylor would turn in her case report. Whitmore would pretend to be grateful, Taylor would pretend she was leaving this case in good hands, and they would all pretend justice was done once Vance's murder was pinned on the three Syrians who were in fact homicide victims themselves, killed in an elaborate false flag operation.

Unless, of course, Scott Brodie was wrong about that — and everything else. He was at least open to the idea that he was completely losing his mind.

Well, better to leave that parsing for the after-action review. Or maybe, in his case, for the arresting officers' police report.

He thought about Elsa Ziegler, a sort of haunted look on her face when he left her office. When she first learned about Harry Vance's murder, she claimed to not think her brief conversation from eight months ago was relevant to the case. But a part of her feared that it was. The part that was buried deep, the old paranoia from the vanished East that she'd worked so hard to unlearn.

But history still had teeth in a place like this, and maybe the old divisions and old wounds remained, despite knocking down the Wall and selling the rubble to tourists, despite the cosmopolitan skyline that rose over the old death strip between East and West where guard dogs and snipers once patrolled, despite thirty years of trying to move on and willfully ignoring the forces that beat back against the current of history.

Brodie looked up at the gray hulk of the archives building. He'd come here on a whim and had struck pay dirt. Whether he was propelled by sheer luck, or brilliant intuition, or a guiding hand from beyond the grave, he knew he had to finish what Harry Vance had started.

CHAPTER 37

As Brodie walked, he called Mark Jenkins. "I need to meet you now."

"I thought you and Taylor were on your way home."

"I'm taking a later flight."

"Okay . . . sorry you got pulled."

"This is best handled by the Fifth MP."

"Yeah. But . . . not sure I'm supposed to talk to you."

"I'm mostly harmless. Where do you want to meet?"

"I'm in the Radisson lobby. Waiting for the two guys from Fifth MP who are replacing you and Taylor. So . . . maybe it would be awkward for you. And them."

"Let's pretend we're all professionals. See you in a few." He hung up.

As he walked toward Alexanderplatz, Brodie thought about his shaky status here in Berlin. Doors were closing. People weren't sure they should be talking to him. Ex–warrant officer Brodie's credit card and cell phone were somehow connected to his active-duty status, and he could imagine that both could be cut off, along with his PX card. In fact, by now Dombroski had definitely cut off his charging privileges at Officers' Clubs worldwide, and also had the lock changed on Brodie's office, along with the keypad code on the men's room door.

Well . . . when you say, "I quit," *they* quit you. There are consequences. He had an image of himself sleeping on a bench in the Tiergarten. But that was the least of his concerns.

Brodie crossed Alexanderplatz and entered the Radisson. He spotted Mark Jenkins, wearing a sports jacket, sitting in a club chair and dividing his attention between his cell phone and the lobby doors, looking for whoever showed up first — Brodie, or his colleagues from the 5th MP Battalion.

Jenkins saw Brodie coming toward him, managed a smile, and stood. They shook hands and both sat.

Jenkins said, "So, what can I do for you?"

Brodie thought that Jenkins looked more alert than last time he'd seen him. He must have skipped the morning schnapps. "I wanted to thank you for your help."

"That's not why you're here."

"Right." Brodie asked, "When are you leaving?"

"As soon as I meet and brief my colleagues." He asked, "When are *you* leaving?"

"I'm thinking of putting in for leave in place."

"Have you fallen in love with Berlin?"

"Maybe infatuated."

Jenkins looked at him. "When the script says exit left, that means you don't belong on the stage anymore."

"Right. I like backstage better."

Jenkins did not respond to that, but said, "So, as we all suspected, Harry had a fräulein here."

"Right."

"And you and Ms. Taylor found her."

"I'm glad no one else is taking credit for that."

Jenkins smiled. "Give it where it's due. May I ask how you found her?"

"Dumb luck."

"Don't be modest."

"I'm not."

Jenkins smiled again and asked, "So? Was she worth Harry's long commute from Kaiserslautern?"

"I'll leave that to your imagination, Mark."

"Was she at least grief-stricken? Did she love him?"

"I think so."

"Was she cooperative?"

"I . . . I would say very cooperative. And let's change the subject." He told Jenkins, "Taylor put all the details in her report."

Jenkins nodded, then said, "Ironic that your success in finding this woman seems to be the cause of you and Taylor being booted."

"One of many causes."

Jenkins nodded again. "Personally, I think your mandate was too narrow, and any display of initiative would get you in trouble."

"Everyone knew that. Especially me."

"Well, this was a very politically charged and sensitive case." He added, "It's not easy working in a foreign country. You really have to be a team player and not step outside the chalk lines."

"The Germans move the lines. And we let them."

"It's their country, Scott."

"I'll bet it was easier for the American military when we were an occupying force here."

Jenkins smiled. "Right. We won the war. But that's history. Now we are guests here, and the Germans are our allies and our equals. So we play by their rules."

"An American Army officer was murdered here. Your partner and friend."

"You don't need to remind me."

"Are you satisfied with the preliminary findings that indicate Harry Vance was murdered by Islamic terrorists?"

"I haven't been fully brought up to date." He added, "It's not my case."

"When you get back to Kaiserslautern, go

tell Harry's wife that."

"Should I also tell her about his fräulein?"

"Someone will. Might as well be you."

Jenkins glanced at his watch, obviously hoping the two CID guys showed up soon so he could say hello and good-bye. He said to Brodie, "You're welcome to brief your replacements."

"I have no instructions regarding briefing my replacements." He added, "It's not in the script."

"Okay. But it would be useful if you do that."

"Ms. Taylor has filed a full report of what we did here. The report is with Sharon Whitmore, the embassy legal attaché. Your colleagues should request a copy."

"Okay. I'll let them know." He added, "This case seems to be all but solved anyway." He looked at Brodie.

Brodie was tempted to say, "The fat lady ain't sung yet," but he said, "It would seem that way."

"Right. So . . . ?"

"So, I have a few questions for you, for *my* final report."

"Okay."

Brodie looked at him. "In May of last year, you and Harry were handed an assault case in Stuttgart."

Jenkins thought a moment. "The racist German colonel. That was a PR nightmare, which is someone else's problem. We were in and out in three hours. What about it?"

"Can you tell me anything about Nord-Faust?"

"What's that?"

"The neo-Nazi group that this colonel claimed membership in." He added, "It was mentioned in your report."

Jenkins nodded. "Right. There are a lot of those groups, or at least a lot of racist assholes claiming to be members of them. The German military has an issue with right-wing extremism, unfortunately. It's a problem, but not our problem."

"Until those extremists pose a threat to American military assets."

"But they haven't, and they won't. This is small-fry stuff, mostly. A handful of guys hoarding weapons, making up a name for their so-called group, fetishizing Adolf Hitler and posting anti-Semitic, anti-Muslim, and racist rants on social media. A lot of posturing, not much action." He added, "Lots of times grandpa was Wehrmacht or SS, and junior admired Opa, and got brainwashed by the old guy."

Brodie nodded. He could picture grandpa dragging out his combat medals, maybe even his Swastika armband. The sins of the grandfathers seemed to have skipped a generation and were visited on the grandkids, who were now all grown up and worked up about

Muslims and mosques and migrants.

History was prologue, and more so here than in most places.

Brodie returned to his questions. "Colonel Brandt claimed he was part of a secret army within the German military."

Jenkins rolled his eyes. "The whole thing smelled like bullshit before we even got to Stuttgart."

Brodie asked, "About how old was this colonel?"

"His exact age is in our report."

"Which is now back in the hands of the military attaché's office. Refresh my memory."

Jenkins thought a moment. "Mid-forties, if I had to guess."

Well, too young to be ex-Stasi. Unless he was in their youth group.

Brodie asked, "Anything about the interview you and Harry had with Colonel Brandt that might have caused Harry to pay a visit to the Stasi Archives in May of last year?"

Jenkins gave him a confused look. "I'm not following."

"Please think about what I'm asking."

"Okay . . ." Jenkins thought, then said, "The assistant legal attaché, what's-his-name . . ."

"Jason Butler."

Jenkins nodded. "He called me after they brought in Harry's girlfriend to BKA head-

581

quarters. Butler tells me this woman's father was Stasi, and a double agent for us, his cover got blown right before the Wall came down and he was executed by the Stasi, and Harry was supposedly helping her find the rat. Butler wanted to know if Harry had shared any of this with me. Which he didn't."

Brodie nodded. Jenkins did not seem to know that this rat was a member of the American military, code-named Odin, and he likely also didn't know about the three other double agents who were found and executed. Jason Butler had told Jenkins just enough to see if he had any relevant information about Vance's activities or statements leading up to his death. He said to Jenkins, "I just spoke with someone at the Stasi Archives who claims Harry visited there in May looking for information about an American military official who provided intelligence to the Stasi in the 1980s."

Jenkins thought a moment. "So, Harry was headed for divorce, met this hot number in Berlin, and followed his dick to the Stasi Archives to be her white knight. To me, this helps put his behavior in some context. What he was investigating was disconnected from his official CID duties, and also tied to an extramarital affair. Hence the secrecy."

"Right." Except that timeline was wrong, but Brodie wasn't sharing that.

Jenkins asked, "What the hell does any of

this have to do with this wannabe Nazi in Stuttgart? Or, for that matter, with Harry's murder by Syrian terrorists?"

Brodie wasn't sure himself, and if he expounded on his many theories, Jenkins would think he was nuts. And if Brodie heard himself say it all out loud, he might agree. "I just need to know if something happened in May, or possibly April, that might have gotten Harry suddenly interested in Stasi double agents."

Jenkins looked him in the eyes. "What are you doing? And where are you going?"

"Not sure, but what Jason Butler told you is not the whole story. In fact, he doesn't know the whole story, and his head is too far up his ass to even realize it. Same goes for his fellow FBI agents, along with the Berlin Police and the German Feds and, probably, your colleagues from Fifth MP being sent here to replace me."

"You're a bright light in a sea of idiots."

"I am."

"Actually, Scott, you're smug, vain, and insubordinate. That's your rep."

Brodie stared at him. "You ought to be as interested as I am in what sent Harry down this Stasi rabbit hole, because it wasn't Anna Albrecht, and whatever it was, it's directly or indirectly tied to his murder. Look into it. You owe it to Harry."

"Don't tell me what I owe Harry."

"Call me if you think of anything."

"If I think of anything helpful to this case, I'll pass it on to the people working this case."

"And tell my replacements that they can call me."

"Okay. And you can tell them why you just got booted off one of the biggest cases of your career."

"I'm here for justice. Not résumé-building."

"Justice is a group effort, Scott. Harry understood that — until, for some reason, he started behaving like you, and now he's dead."

"And I'm here to find out who killed him. Before someone gets away with murder."

"Jesus, Scott. It was the Syrians. Retribution for us killing Jibril Saleh in Tripoli. And they didn't exactly get away with it, did they?"

Brodie said, "So these three guys were, what? A sleeper cell posing as Syrian refugees who were activated because some wealthy corrupt businessman who was feeding Intel to the Americans got clipped in Libya?"

"That's where the evidence points."

"And then the al Qaeda handlers of these three terrorists waited for Harry to be in Berlin to kill him? Why Berlin? And they somehow knew you'd come to Berlin, and they'd kill you here as well? But before they whacked you, they were tailing you, and being very obvious about it, so you would report it? And how did they know you were at the Radisson? And why didn't they just whack you on the street? Instead, they over-complicate the hit and decide to rig a bomb to your car — that ended up exploding in their faces? Is that how they operate? Are they that stupid?"

Jenkins didn't respond.

Brodie continued, "I asked you what cases might have made you and Harry a target, and this Libyan case didn't even occur to you. Because it doesn't track, and you know it."

Jenkins hesitated, then said, "True, this isn't the typical modus operandi of Sunni extremist cells, but the evidence is obvious and indisputable."

"What if it was all a setup? A false flag op."

Jenkins looked at him for a moment. Then he said, "I think we're done here."

"Have you looked into the backgrounds of these three so-called terrorists?"

"No, Scott. Because this isn't my case." He added, "But I'm sure the BKA has, and regardless, your replacements from Kaiserslautern certainly will run their own background checks on the deceased Syrian suspects."

"That's a start." Brodie stood and looked at Jenkins. "May, April. The Stuttgart case, or maybe something else. Think about it. You have my number."

"I wish you'd lose mine."

Brodie walked out of the hotel and across

585

the square, confident that he'd at least planted a seed of doubt in Mark Jenkins' mind. More importantly, Brodie had pointed out inconsistencies and oddities in this case that didn't fit the forensics or the clues. And everything has to fit. And what made everything fit — including Harry's eyeball in the Syrians' freezer — was Brodie's belief that this was all an elaborate deception.

As he crossed Alexanderplatz, someone called his name. Brodie turned to see two men in suits and long dark coats approaching. The taller one, an African American guy in his early fifties with a shaved head and a square jaw, extended his hand as he got closer.

Brodie took it and they shook. "You lost again, George?"

The man smiled. "Same old shit. When are you gonna get serious?"

"When I grow up."

"Don't do that."

George Jones was a CW5, and Brodie had worked with him a few times over the years. He was capable and amiable, and had a good rep. Brodie knew that Jones was based in Kaiserslautern with the 5th MP, and apparently he was Scott Brodie's replacement.

Jones said, "This is my partner, Brad Mellman."

Brodie shook hands with Mellman, a rail-thin white guy in his mid-thirties who'd obviously been quick-briefed by Jones. Mellman said, "It's an honor to meet you."

"I just got booted back to Quantico, Mr. Mellman."

Jones smiled. "You laid the groundwork, Scott. That's not lost on anybody."

"I'm a headliner, George, not the opening act."

Jones shrugged. "The brass winds us up and says go, and we do our duty, right? Sometimes you're the hero and sometimes you're shoveling shit."

Mellman said, "We wanted this case from the start, but when word got out that it was going to be you, a lot of us were glad. You've got a reputation for getting results."

Brodie said, "So does the Fifth MP Battalion. I'm happy to turn this over to you."

Jones looked dubious, but said, "Harry Vance was the best of the best. Everyone loved that guy. We will get justice for him."

"I know you will." He told them, "My partner, Maggie Taylor, filed a report with the legat. Read it and take it seriously."

Jones nodded.

"And if you have any questions for me, Jenkins has my number." He added, "I'll be in Berlin for a few more days. Taking some leave time."

Jones, who knew how to interpret Brodie, advised, "Watch yourself, Scott."

"You too." He added, "The people who

killed Harry Vance are not dead. They are out there." He looked at them. "Good luck."

Brodie continued across the square.

Well, another seed of doubt planted. George Jones, like Mark Jenkins, probably thought he now had a pretty good handle on why Scott Brodie had gotten kicked off this homicide case. Jones would read Taylor's report, and he was professional enough to give it the attention it deserved. But ultimately, he'd run with the party line. That's what most people do, most of the time. Even the smart ones.

And that was why it was still up to Scott Brodie — a man with his career in the toilet, no hope on the horizon, and nothing left to lose — to see that justice was done.

CHAPTER 38

Brodie hailed a taxi and gave the driver the address of Stefan Richter on a street called Frankfurter Allee. If Taylor had been with him, he'd have told the driver it was near Hamburger Straße. But he was alone, though not yet lonely.

The address — which Brodie had found in the online white pages — was in the outer borough of Lichtenberg, in the former East Berlin, a thirty-minute drive from Alexanderplatz and a thirty-euro fare, which put a dent in his tightly budgeted Berlin adventure. According to the Internet, there was an U-Bahn station near his destination, but through experience he'd learned that taxis were the preferred method of transportation when you were trying to lose, spot, or avoid a tail. Which he always explained to the beancounters in Quantico when he turned in his expense sheet. This time, however, there would be no reimbursement; he was on his own. Which felt good, and not so good. Good because his hands were untied, and not so good because the Army and this job had become his life. And not a bad life, despite his complaints, which every soldier was entitled to. If nothing else, his work was interesting. And, now and then, dangerous, which was not a complaint.

On the subject of dangerous, he was still pissed off that he hadn't been issued a gun. They could have used guns at Proletariat, and maybe he could use a gun on Frankfurter Allee. "Hold the mustard or I shoot."

The driver glanced back over his shoulder. "Was?"

"I'm dictating a memo."

"Yes?" The driver, an older German man who, thank God, hadn't been a talker, became one and asked, "Why you go this place?"

"To see a friend."

"Yes? This place old . . . How you say . . . ? Bad people who work for GDR. You understand?"

"Insurance salesmen?"

"No. Wohnblock. House. Build for Polizei . . . Stasi. You understand?"

That was interesting. Sounded like a place where Stefan Richter, ex-Stasi, might live. "Government housing for government workers."

"Bastards."

"Right." He reminded the man, "It's over. Kaput."

"When they all kaput, then it is over. Like Nazis. All kaput."

"I'm sure there's a few old Nazis left."

"Ten years. All kaput."

"That's about right." The neo-Nazis, however, were mostly young. This place was more tortured and haunted than it appeared on the surface.

Brodie didn't feel like talking politics or history, but the driver did and said, "Stasi Hauptquartier in Lichtenberg. Museum now."

Brodie assumed it was a museum displaying the horrors of the Stasi — not their successes against the West or their own people. Well, in any case, that might be worth a visit.

The driver seemed to have exhausted his English, and Brodie sat back and watched the cityscape pass by.

This seemed to be a residential quarter of the city, dominated by huge, soulless, and decrepit apartment blocks, obviously built postwar by the Communist government, to replace what the Red Army had destroyed as they advanced into Berlin. A few of the older buildings had survived — traditional structures built on a more human scale than the monster monoliths that had risen from the rubble. Now and then there was an empty, weed-covered lot where a prewar building must have stood. As for commercial activity — stores, shops, restaurants — those were obviously not part of the Commie plan for the housing blocks. But it was only a matter of time before the Berlin real estate developers got interested in this wasteland. It usually starts with a Starbucks.

The taxi driver stopped in front of a grungy-looking slab-concrete, twelve-story apartment building that sat along the wide, windswept boulevard.

The driver seemed hesitant to abandon his American passenger here and asked, "This? Okay?"

"This is it. How much do you owe me for taking me here?"

The driver didn't get the joke, and pointed to his meter.

Brodie paid the fare and gave the driver a three-euro tip, which was three euros more than a Berliner would have given him.

The driver thanked him, hesitated, then said, "Have a good visit."

"Danke." Before Brodie got out, he asked the driver, "Is Richter a common name in Germany?"

"Richter? Yes. I hear this name." He asked, "This is your friend?"

"Yes. Heide Richter." He confided, "Her husband is out of town."

"Ah!" Which explained this American's trip to the outer borough of nowhere. The driver said something in German and laughed at what he'd said.

Brodie didn't need a translation and exited the taxi. He walked toward the entrance to the apartment building.

According to the white pages, this was the residence of the only Stefan Richter listed in Berlin. As per the taxi driver, Richter was not an uncommon name, and Brodie had seen a dozen more in the white pages. But only one Stefan Richter. Though like anywhere else, it wouldn't be too hard to keep your name unlisted for privacy reasons. So there could be another Stefan Richter.

On the other hand, the driver had given him the demographics of this neighborhood, and Stefan Richter seemed to fit the profile. Plus, the old Stasi headquarters was nearby, a short and convenient commute to work back in the GDR days when this shithole building must have been considered luxury housing. Right. Don't overanalyze it.

Brodie walked into the small outer foyer and scanned the directory, which had more than a hundred listings. Stefan Richter lived in Apartment 8F.

Brodie moved to the lobby door and reached for the handle in the belief that nothing built by the Commies worked. But the electronic lock worked, and the handle held fast. *Shit.*

Well, he could wait for someone to come in or go out and open the lobby door for him, but that could be a while in a place like this where half the residents were probably pensioners, and probably dead. And the other half were young squatters, whacked out on whatever was the magic of the moment.

He looked at the call box, and buzzed 8F. After a moment a man's voice came over the speaker. "Hallo?"

Brodie asked, "Ist das Herr Richter?"

"Wer sind Sie?" The man sounded elderly, and not very friendly, like the kind of guy who used to develop bioweapons for the Stasi. Well, maybe that was a stretch.

"Eine Lieferung," said Brodie, which according to the Internet was the German word for "delivery." He was suddenly back in Virginia, storming Private Hinckley's house in search of stolen meat loaf or whatever. Well, no matter what happened, Scott Brodie was never going back to that crap again.

Herr Richter did not reply, and then it sounded like he hung up.

Brodie started pressing call buttons, and someone who was too trusting or too lonely — or who was maybe expecting a lieferung — buzzed him in.

He entered a dim and dingy lobby that smelled of disinfectant. In front of him was a security desk that was unoccupied and, judging by the lack of a phone, computer, or even a chair, had probably been that way for thirty years.

There were only two elevators, one of which

had a sign taped to the door that said ACH-TUNG! followed by something in German that probably said "This one will kill you."

He pressed the button for the other one, thinking that maybe someone had switched the sign as a joke.

He got in the elevator and pressed eight, and the elevator ascended slowly, as though it worked for the government. He would definitely take the staircase down — if Herr Richter didn't shoot him on sight.

The doors opened and Brodie stepped into a very narrow hallway lit by fluorescent lights, many of which were burned out. A wall sign directed him to the left, and he passed between pools of light and located 8F in a dark section of the hallway. He rapped on the door. "Lieferung!"

He heard footsteps, and then the door slowly cracked opened.

A tall, elderly man with wispy white hair and a sour face stared at him through the crack in the doorway. The chain lock was still secured.

Herr Richter saw that the delivery man had no delivery and asked again, "Wer sind Sie?"

"Scott Brodie." He produced his badge and held it up. "U.S. Army Criminal Investigation Division."

The man's eyes widened.

Brodie asked, "Sprechen Sie Englisch?"

The man demonstrated his English by saying, "Go away," and slammed the door.

Brodie knocked again. "Herr Richter. I am working with your government on an investigation. You must open the door and speak to me. Or you will be subject to arrest."

The man did not respond. Should he kick the door in? What if this guy was the wrong Stefan Richter? Wouldn't be the first time that happened.

But . . . this guy's reaction . . . He knew what this was about. It was about the past that had caught up to him. It was about biological warfare, which Stefan Richter had blabbed about thirty years ago. But now Richter knew about Harry Vance's murder, and that must have changed his mind about having his fifteen minutes of fame. Therefore . . . there must be a connection. But was this enough for Brodie to kick down the door? Maybe he should try a different approach and call Captain Soliman, and get some Berlin cops here to take Stefan Richter in for questioning. That was SOP, but . . . Scott Brodie liked to keep what he found.

He banged on the door again and shouted, "Achtung, asshole! Polizei! Open the door!"

No response.

Brodie gave the door a kick above the handle, but it held fast. "You Stasi bastard! How do you like it when someone does to you what you used to do to other people?"

No response.

The direct, forceful approach wasn't working, so Brodie tapped on the door and called out, "Lieferung. Flowers for Mr. Richter." *Asshole.*

No response.

Well, Herr Richter might be calling the police himself, which was okay, but not likely. Or someone on this floor was calling the police, which was also okay. One way or the other, Stefan Richter was going to answer some questions.

Brodie put his ear to the door, to listen for Richter making a phone call, but what he heard was music. Classical music. Something very Germanic, like maybe a Wagner opera.

Well, thought Brodie, whatever calms your nerves when you learn that the Polizei are coming for you. Maybe a little schnapps with the music.

Then a loud, explosive sound blotted out the music for Brodie, who recognized that sound, spun away from the door, and put his back against the wall. The music continued. There was no second gunshot.

Brodie took a deep breath. Well . . . that's what people sometimes did. He'd had two of those in his last twenty years. This was number three. He didn't think the music was bad enough to put a bullet in your head, so Stefan Richter had other reasons to end his life. And Brodie could only guess at those reasons, and whatever they were, they were good enough for Herr Richter. But not good for this investigation.

Brodie reached for his phone to dial Captain Soliman's direct number, but then he caught a movement to his left and looked down the long hallway. Emerging from the fire stairs doorway was a tall guy, coming toward him. As the figure passed under a light, he saw that the man was dressed in black tactical clothes. As the guy got closer, Brodie also saw that he was wearing a ballistic vest with the word <u>POLIZEI</u> emblazoned across it. Well, that was fast. Actually, this guy had been here, in the stairwell for awhile, and he'd heard Brodie talking to the door. And Brodie had the feeling that something was wrong about that, and about this guy, who was not saying anything as he approached.

Brodie was about to ID himself, but then he heard a sound to his right and glanced down the hallway to see the elevator doors opening, and another guy stepping out. The elevator guy was dressed the same as the stairwell guy, and he had a walkie in his hand that he clipped on his belt as he continued toward Brodie.

They were both within thirty feet of him now, and neither man had IDed himself, though Brodie assumed that was procedure here as it was in most countries. Maybe one of them was going to point to the letters across his vest. Maybe not. The good news was that they were not going to kill him here. This was a snatch job.

The stairwell guy stopped about ten feet from him, but said nothing. The guy was about thirty with close-cropped blond hair and a nasty face to match the bad haircut.

Brodie glanced at the elevator guy. Same age as his accomplice, also tall, but very burly with buzz-cut brown hair. To Brodie's trained eye, they looked less like police and more like military. *A secret army.* The neo-Nazis in the police and military who had their own agenda.

Elevator guy also stopped, and the three of them stood there in silence. Brodie noticed that each of them had a holstered gun, and both holsters had the safety band unclipped.

Finally Blondie asked, in good English, "What are you doing here?"

"That's what I was going to ask you."

"Yes? Well, we are here to escort you to police headquarters."

"Why?"

"You don't need to know why. You just need to come with us."

Brodie now saw the handcuffs hanging from Blondie's belt. He said, "I assume you know who I am."

"Of course," said Blondie. "That's why we are here."

"Right. Well, I think the guy who lives in

this apartment — you know who that is — just shot himself. You need to call an ambulance."

Both guys exchanged glances, but neither of them reached for his walkie or cell. So, definitely not cops.

Blondie said, "That will be taken care of. Now you must come with us." He asked, "Are you armed?"

Brodie wanted to say, "If I was, you'd both be dead by now." But why give them ideas? He said, "Not armed."

Blondie nodded, then said something in German to elevator man, who hadn't spoken so far but now started toward Brodie while unclipping his handcuffs.

This was the moment, and Brodie knew there would be no more moments to turn this around.

Blondie said to Brodie, "Turn, hands behind your back." He put his hand on the butt of his gun to show Brodie he meant business.

Brodie nodded, turned his back toward elevator man, waited a second until the guy was close, then suddenly spun around and delivered a swift kick, under the guy's ballistic vest and into his non-ballistic balls.

Before Brodie had time to enjoy the moment, he spun again and saw Blondie going for his gun, but not backpedaling as he should have. Brodie was on him in a flash and aimed his fist at the second most pain-inducing spot on the human body — the nose. He connected and heard the crack of cartilage, and Blondie's hands flew up to his face, leaving Brodie to pluck the gun out of the guy's holster. Brodie put his back against the wall, surveying the scene of resisting arrest, or saving his ass. He wasn't a hundred percent sure it was the latter, but better safe than dead. If he'd screwed up, he could apologize to Captain Soliman and buy everyone a beer. Right.

Blondie was on his knees now, his hands still on his face and blood seeping between his fingers. Elevator man was rolling around on the floor, his hands clasped to his groin, probably feeling for his nuts. One . . . two . . .

Brodie glanced at the gun in his hand. It looked like an old Makarov, a 9mm semi-automatic, made in the Soviet Union and used by most Eastern Bloc countries. He'd seen a few of these in Iraq, and it wasn't a bad weapon, but not something a German policeman would carry. Nor would a German military man carry an old Soviet weapon. But it was something that would be used in a false flag job. There were plenty of Makarovs around since the end of the Cold War. He checked to see that there was a round in the chamber, and flipped off the safety.

What he needed to do now was cuff both these guys, take the other gun, then search them for ID. But a door opened across the hall, and an old woman stuck her head out to see what was happening. She saw the two guys in police gear rolling around, then looked at Brodie, who was standing there with a gun in his hand. She slammed the door shut, and presumably grabbed her phone to call the police. In fact, there were probably lots of those calls being made right now, and Brodie could almost hear police sirens approaching. Or was that the German opera from the late Stefan Richter's apartment? Well, the fat lady had sung, and it was time to leave. He definitely didn't want to deal with the police.

Brodie moved quickly toward the stairwell door, opened it, and started down the switch-back staircase, two at a time.

Well . . . what had he accomplished? A potential witness or informant had killed himself, two unidentified flaming assholes had tried to kill or kidnap him, and he was now on the run. But now he had a gun.

He got to the lobby level and cracked open the door. No one there. He shoved his gun in his waistband and walked casually but quickly toward the lobby exit and into the cold outside air.

He looked up and down the street for a police vehicle but didn't see one, confirming his deduction that these guys were either impostors or real cops who were pursuing an extracurricular activity.

Frankfurter Allee looked peaceful, and he continued walking as though out for a stroll. He checked his phone and located the U-Bahn station on Magdalenenstraße and headed that way.

Well, so much for his taxi ride to avoid or spot a tail. Those two guys had followed him, and he'd missed it. Or . . . they'd picked him up in Alexanderplatz, and when they saw that he was heading toward Lichtenberg, they guessed where he was going and took another route to Richter's apartment building. Brodie had done that himself many times. But that assumed some foreknowledge on the part of the tails.

The other possibility was that these guys had been scoping this building, watching to see if anyone — or perhaps Scott Brodie in particular — was following in Harry Vance's footsteps and paying a visit to Stefan Richter.

Brodie recalled how Tariq Qasim's apartment building had also been watched — by Rafeeq Nasir's people, but also possibly by . . . who? The old white guy Brodie had spotted getting into a car in Neukölln and then saw again in the Hotel Adlon lobby. Maybe someone was keeping an eye on the trail of Vance's investigation, to see if anyone picked up the scent. And what they found was a very persistent American investigator who wouldn't take the hint that the case was closed.

He continued quickly toward the U-Bahn station. Maybe it was the adrenaline, but the city felt suddenly different, like a veil had slipped, revealing its true self — or maybe its old self. He looked up at the looming Soviet-era apartment blocks lining the boulevard, each of their hundreds of identical windows providing a bird's-eye view of his movements.

Scott Brodie had learned a lot of lessons over the course of his military career, both in war and on screwed-up investigations in fucked-up places. And one of those lessons was, if the path you're on is full of people trying to kill you, you're probably going the right way.

CHAPTER 39

Maggie Taylor sat at the airport bar, drinking black coffee and trying to figure out how it all went wrong.

It's just a job.

That had been her mantra in the months since getting back from Venezuela. Stop making it personal, stop making it *everything*. Leave room for the rest of life.

Nothing focuses your attention more than being in a combat zone. You block everything else out to get through each day — and as a way to accept that you might not make it home. That's what Taylor and everyone around her had done in Afghanistan.

The CID was different. It was still military service, but you could clock out. It was about as close as you could get to being a civilian without being a civilian.

Scott Brodie didn't make that distinction. He'd never clocked out. He was on one long deployment, one unending war, and it wouldn't be over until he was dead. Taylor wondered what had happened to him in Iraq. But that was a question you don't ask.

Some soldiers say they left a part of themselves on the battlefield, but that had always sounded wrong to Taylor. She'd come home from Afghanistan with a lot more than she'd brought with her. And not good stuff.

That was one of the main draws of Scott Brodie, if she was being honest with herself. A license to be broken. To not move on. To embrace what war had done to you, and to turn that vulnerability into a weapon. But that method had its limits, and Taylor had just run into hers.

Scott, you idiot. She was worried about him. Probably more than she should be. Definitely more than he deserved.

She sipped the coffee. It was bad. Should she have a drink? She was already sitting at the bar. Well, maybe not in her state of mind. She didn't need to amplify these feelings.

She replayed the moment at the embassy when she'd submitted her report to Jason Butler, that smug look on his face when he glanced at it. Like he was going to wipe his ass with it, and he knew that Taylor knew that, and he was just fine with it. *Prick.*

Something caught her eye on the TV above the bar. It was the military file photo of Harry Vance, on some German news channel. Then it cut to a podium, where a man in a suit who Taylor didn't recognize, mid-sixties, was speaking. Standing behind him were Sharon Whitmore, Chief Inspector Schröder, and Captain Soliman, as well as two guys she didn't recognize wearing suits with American flag lapel pins. Must be their CID replacements from the 5th MP. They looked like good guys. Hopefully they were.

There was no English closed captioning, but Taylor didn't need it. She knew what this was. It was the beginning of the end.

She looked away from the TV, then flagged the bartender and ordered a Jack Daniel's, neat. A touch of Tennessee in a bottle. She was depressed. Might as well ride it all the way down.

Before her drink came, a man standing slightly behind her asked, "Seat taken?"

She didn't look at him and replied, "No." In fact, almost none of the seats at the bar were taken. Maggie Taylor was not in the mood for this shit. She stared down into the black coffee, which was burned and bitter, just like her. She pushed it away.

The man asked, "Can I get you a Tennessee whiskey?"

She turned and looked at the man and froze. He looked back at her, a kind of glint in his eye, and that obnoxious half-smile she remembered. He looked tan. Probably had just gotten back from somewhere tropical. He'd say it was vacation, but Trent Chilcott didn't take vacations. He traveled the world with purpose, breaking things.

Taylor recovered and asked, "What the hell are you doing here?"

Chilcott's smile did not crack. "Work. Same as you."

She wanted to ask how he knew she was here on assignment, but that was a stupid question to ask a CIA officer. "Small world."

"Big world. But the world we live in is small."

She didn't respond to that, but asked, "Are you coming or going?"

"I've been here. Got in about the same time as you — and your partner."

No use asking him how he knew that. Trent knew everything. Or pretended he did, which was part of the job. Or the act. And she was tired of his act. She asked, "What hotel was I staying at?"

Chilcott smiled. "The Art Hotel." He opined, "Shithole," then asked, "Where's your partner?"

"You tell me."

"All I know is that he's not here." He added, "Where he's supposed to be."

"People are not always where they're supposed to be, Trent. Get used to it."

"Thank you for that advice." He took a seat next to her. "We need to talk."

Taylor's whiskey came and Chilcott ordered the same. She left her drink untouched and waited for him to deliver the next line of his scripted walk-on.

"So," he said, "in this small world we live in, you and I have been assigned to related cases."

She thought about the Special Collection Service — the SCS — the joint CIA-NSA spy nest reportedly on the roof of the American Embassy. Had Trent been intercepting her and Brodie's communications? *Jesus . . .*

Taylor looked at Trent Chilcott in the bar mirror. He was still annoyingly handsome, with a full head of dark-brown hair despite being on the far side of fifty, and he had piercing blue eyes. Kind of a Paul Newman quality, but with a more muscular build and no kindness in his eyes.

He was dressed in his usual CIA-casual — blazer, khakis, a button-down shirt, and no tie. A nice breezy style for a callous man, who looked the same whether he was returning from a yacht club or a war crime.

Chilcott leaned in and said, "Our interests here are aligned."

"My interests are in having a drink alone and getting on my flight."

He shook his head. "That's not going to work."

"Works for me."

Some old feeling was bubbling up, a feeling Maggie Taylor hated, one of the bad souvenirs she'd brought home from the war. A kind of weakness . . . an unhealthy attraction to CIA

Officer Chilcott, amplified by fear. But it was some other person who was feeling that, some stupid girl from the Tennessee hills who'd let her Georgetown degree go to her head and who thought she was smarter than she was. She hadn't been prepared for this guy when she met him. And then that girl died somewhere in the craggy mountains outside Kabul.

Except a part of her was still there, and always would be. She asked, "What do you want?"

"Your help."

"Put it in writing."

He laughed. "I put nothing in writing, Magnolia." Which reminded him: "Did you get the flowers I sent? I did write a note."

"Get to the point. But understand that whatever you tell me is not in strict confidence."

"Okay . . ." He thought a moment, then said, "I'm not going to ask you to trust me, because that's a joke. But you know what else is a joke?" He pointed to the TV. "A fucking clown show."

Taylor looked at the television, where the man at the podium — who must have been a senior BKA official — was now pointing to a picture on an easel showing photos of the three Syrian men who had died in the Neukölln bombing.

Chilcott continued, "You and your partner, Mr. Brodie, are here to investigate the murder

610

of your CID colleague Harry Vance, and I'm here for a related reason."

"You're probably here for the wrong reason."

Chilcott ignored that. "Our respective lines of investigation don't coincide, but they might intersect."

She really wanted a sip of whiskey, but left the glass on the bar. "Trent, you are the master of cryptic talk. And it's not as good as you think. Say something that has a subject, verb, and maybe even a noun or two."

"All right . . . You and Mr. Brodie have inadvertently stirred up something much bigger than you realize. And because of that, he — and you — are in more danger than either of you can imagine."

She looked at him. Now and then she knew when this manipulative bastard was telling the truth. This was one of those rare times.

They made eye contact and he said, "I need your help, Maggie."

"No you don't. You need to seduce me again. And again. And again. Not this time, Trent." She added, "I'm leaving."

He moved closer to her. "If you go home now, you're leaving something behind."

Scott. That's not what Chilcott meant, but it's what Taylor was feeling. Except she wasn't leaving *him* behind, it was the other way around. He was the one who'd gone rogue and blown up his career. She needed to stop

611

blaming herself for the bad decisions of the psychotic men in her life.

As for Trent, he was right that it was a joke to trust him. But he knew just what to say. Scott Brodie was in danger. And if there was even a small chance that this historically deceptive man wasn't lying to her, she needed to stay.

Trent Chilcott, who knew Maggie Taylor well, could tell she'd made her choice. He stood and threw some cash on the bar. "There's a car waiting. If you checked a bag, they'll pull it off the plane and hold it."

She stood and they began walking out of the bar, then Taylor grabbed his arm and gripped it tight. She got close and said, "You've lied to me, you've betrayed me, and you've threatened me, and the worst things I've ever done in my life were at your bidding. And if you betray me again, or harm Scott in any way, I swear to God, Trent, I will kill you."

Chilcott looked at her, and for the first time since she'd known him, she saw a look of something like fear pass over his features. Good. Sometimes even the monsters need to fear the dark.

She let go of his arm and walked out of the bar. Trent Chilcott followed.

CHAPTER 40

Brodie heard the train's computerized voice: "Dies ist der Hauptbahnhof, die letzte Haltestelle des Zuges."

Berlin's central train station. Last stop on the line. Or first if you were leaving.

He exited the train and walked up a long flight of stairs into the station's main hall, a vast and airy space of glass and steel, buzzing with activity. There were a lot of Polizei around, armed with submachine guns, and if the two guys Brodie had mistreated in the hallway of Stefan Richter's building were real cops, there'd be the German equivalent of an APB out on him. If they weren't real cops, they'd be arrested when the real cops arrived, but there would still be an APB out for U.S. Army Warrant Officer Scott Brodie. And by now, the Berlin Police would have a photo of him, compliments of the U.S. Army. The only one having a worse day than Scott Brodie and the two guys he'd taken down was Stefan Richter.

He spotted a men's clothing store in the concourse and went inside, where he found a knit cap, a blue scarf, and a gray wool coat. His credit card was still working — and leaving a paper trail — and he purchased the items, left, and went into a men's room, where he altered his appearance. Just in case.

As Brodie continued through the station, he looked for security cameras, and spotted a few. But nowhere near as many as he expected in a station of this size, and it wasn't too difficult to avoid getting picked up on them.

He exited the station onto a large stone plaza that faced the Spree River. He crossed the street and took a set of stairs down to the riverbank, which was paved and lined with benches. No one else was down by the river on this cold winter day.

He sat on a bench, pulled out his phone, and dialed his contact at the FXD — the Forensic Exploitation Directorate — which was the entity within Army CID responsible for deploying forensic and biometric support teams worldwide. The FXD was based in Georgia, where it was almost five in the morning. But Brodie's guy, a twenty-something civilian forensic scientist by the name of Tyler McKinnon, would pick up.

"Hello?" He sounded groggy.

"Mr. McKinnon, it's Scott Brodie."

"Hey, Brodie . . . What important thing can I do for you at this hour?"

He liked this guy. No whining. Minimal attitude. "Sorry to wake you. I'm six hours later in Berlin. What I need is a sample analyzed ASAP, for a case I'm working here."

"All right . . . We have arrangements with a couple of labs there. What is it?"

"I don't know. That's why I need it analyzed. It's on a microscope slide."

"Organic?"

"No idea, Tyler. I need it IDed, and also a DNA analysis."

"Okay . . ." He thought a moment, then said, "Let me make a few calls and get back to you in twenty."

"Make fewer calls and get back to me in ten." He added, "This is *urgent*. And confidential."

McKinnon didn't respond.

"It's a matter of national security."

Those were the magic words, a kind of catchall phrase for whatever bullshit you were trying to sling. McKinnon said, "I'll call you back in ten." He hung up.

Well, that was one ball in the air. Next up, he dialed Claudia Barese, his contact at the National Personnel Records Center, which handled all records of American veterans. The NPRC was an important resource in Brodie's work, and Ms. Barese helped cut through some of the red tape. The NPRC was located in St. Louis, Missouri, which last time he checked was west of Georgia and therefore

615

even earlier in the morning. Ms. Barese was not used to handling national security matters related to disease outbreaks, bioterrorism, or other time-sensitive issues, so her phone was off and Brodie was sent right to voice mail. He left a message that she needed to call him back as soon as she was up, and that it was urgent.

He stood from the bench and looked out at the placid water. He had no official duties, no partner, no commanding officer, and no future — unless you counted Leavenworth Federal Penitentiary — but he did have a newly acquired 9mm Makarov with a full mag, along with a newfound sense of purpose, drive, and urgency thanks to the two gentlemen who had tried to kidnap or maybe kill him. That always gets your attention.

He checked his phone for messages and noticed a missed call from Anna, from 5:15 A.M., which would have been about two hours after he left her apartment. He played the voice mail:

"Hi, Scott. I'm glad you came over. It was nice. And . . . I don't know. It feels like I put a lot on you. Forget about my bullshit. Anyway, I can't sleep, probably headed to my gallery to do some work. I've got a new show coming up featuring refugee artists. Stop by and see it if you find free time in the middle of your homicide investigation. New Berlin Art Gallery. Twenty-

616

five Lindenstraße. In Kreuzberg. But call first.
Okay. Bye."

Brodie tried calling her, but it went to voice mail. He left a brief but warm postcoital message, then mapped the address and located the New Berlin Art Gallery on what appeared to be a small pedestrian path set back from Lindenstraße. It was south of Unter den Linden, and not far from Checkpoint Charlie, the infamous border crossing between East Berlin and the American-controlled sector of West Berlin that seemed to appear in every Cold War movie, and was now a top tourist attraction. That was where Brodie had bought an authentic piece of the Berlin Wall nineteen years ago, and he was sure the racket was still going strong. What was different was Scott Brodie, who had become less gullible.

He wanted to see Anna again, of course, but he couldn't keep up the lie that he was still on this investigation in any official capacity.

And what about the other lie? The one Harry Vance had told her, of just ambling in off the street with a genuine interest in the avant-garde gallery scene, and happening upon Ms. Albrecht? Anna had clearly loved Harry, and Brodie hoped the feeling was mutual and that the guy wasn't just using her. Brodie didn't want to tarnish Harry Vance's memory in the eyes of his former lover.

Besides, if you're going to burden someone with a painful truth, there needs to be some upside to it. And Brodie couldn't see one. Better to keep that one to himself.

His phone rang. It was McKinnon, coming in just under the wire at nine minutes.

Brodie answered. "What have you got?"

"You have the sample on you now?"

"Yes."

"Okay. There's a place called Hyperion Lab, Eighty-two Kürfürstendamm. You need me to spell that?"

Kürfürstendam, colloquially known as the Ku'damm, was one of the most famous streets in the city, and the former commercial and cultural heart of old West Berlin. "I can spell it with my eyes closed."

"Okay. The guy who runs the lab is an American. David Katz. I met him at a conference in London. Brilliant guy. As a favor to me, he'll help you. The lab isn't contracted with us, but they are highly regarded, cutting-edge, and, if we need to move this into official channels, easy enough to explain, given the urgency of your request."

In other words, "I'm buying your bullshit, Scott, but you own this." Should he tell McKinnon that he was no longer employed by the Army? Might be bad timing. He said, "I'm heading there now."

"Good luck."

Brodie hung up, then found a cab and gave

the driver the address. They headed west, through the Tiergarten and then south into the old heart of West Berlin. They drove down the Ku'damm, which was lined with trees and stately older buildings featuring high-end shops, cafés, and hotels.

The cab pulled up to a modern-looking office tower sandwiched between an old hotel and a nineteenth-century apartment building. Brodie paid the guy, hopped out, and entered a small lobby. There was no security, but he spotted a directory and found Hyperion Labs on the fourth floor and took the elevator up.

The doors opened into a small, carpeted anteroom leading to frosted glass double doors. He entered and announced himself to the receptionist, a middle-aged German woman, and in a minute a lanky man in his early thirties wearing a white lab coat emerged to greet him. The man extended a hand.

They shook, and Brodie said, "I appreciate you taking a look."

Katz nodded and held out his hand. "The slide."

Brodie took out the small manila envelope containing the slide and handed it to Katz, who pulled out the slide and held it to the light. "Okay . . . follow me."

Brodie followed Katz down a long hallway and into a large windowless lab room filled with equipment, and a few researchers hard at work. As Brodie walked through the room his eyes caught a machine that was holding about four dozen droppers on a motorized arm that were being rapidly dipped into tubes and then dropping their contents onto a large grid of what looked like brass-colored microchips. He asked, "What kind of work do you do here?"

"Mostly gene synthesis. Research and therapeutics. Where'd you get this?"

"That's classified."

"Hm."

"What is that machine doing?"

Katz eyed the large machine as the robotic arm rapidly moved over the grid of brass chips. "Oligonucleotide synthesizer."

"I thought it looked familiar."

"The oligonucleotide components will be assembled into fully synthetic genes."

"Does that mean you can create completely synthetic organisms?"

Katz looked at him, deadpan. "That's classified."

Funny. They approached a cluttered desk with a standard light microscope. Katz sat down, put the slide under the lens, and had a look. He worked the knobs for a moment, then said, "On a first look, it appears to be Yersinia pestis." Katz looked up at Brodie. "The bacterium that causes plague."

Brodie did not respond to that.

"I was told you wanted it sequenced."

"Yes."

"It would help if I knew the source of this sample."

A dead man's pocket. "Don't know." He asked, "If a bacterium has been genetically modified or manipulated, would you be able to tell?"

Katz nodded. "And beyond that, our lab is one of the leading pioneers in genetic engineering attribution. We can detect not only the genetic manipulation, but we can attempt to pinpoint what country or what lab was responsible."

"How is that possible?"

"It's complicated."

"I'm smarter than I look."

Katz smiled. "It involves machine-learning algorithms, programmed to understand all of the subtleties that go into the design choices behind genetic modification. What genes are chosen, what enzymes are used, patterns created by different software, et cetera."

"What if the sample is old? Like, thirty or forty years old?"

Katz furrowed his brow. "Is it?"

"Maybe."

"Well, genetic engineering was much more primitive back then. Our methodologies would not necessarily be able to be applied to this."

"If it is that old, what could you learn

621

through a gene sequence?"

"If it is modified, we could see how it was manipulated and deduce the application. Was it made more virulent? Less virulent? More contagious? Immune to antibiotics? Yersinia pestis in particular can have drastically different impacts on an infected organism based only on subtle changes to a single gene of the bacterium. Were engineers attempting to make something more targeted to a particular organ or bodily system, or to a particular species of animal? Gene sequencing might tell us some of that."

"Anything else?"

"Isn't that enough?"

David Katz had a personality better suited for working with pathogens than with people. Brodie said, "I'm a detective. You just told me you can do the genetic equivalent of lifting prints. And I'm asking, what if the fingerprints are very old?"

Katz nodded, thought a moment. "We have a large database of existing known Yersinia pestis strains. So, if this is one of those, we can likely trace its origins. If it is a novel strain, and if it has been genetically modified, as I said we can determine that, though if the modification was done decades ago using more primitive techniques, our algorithms will likely not be able to trace its specific origins." He took the slide from the microscope and looked at it. "It is strange to label a sample like this with just numbers. A research lab wouldn't do that. You are telling me this could date to the eighties . . . Is it possible it originated from a state actor?"

Brodie nodded. "Possibly from East Germany's unconventional-weapons program." He added, "That is classified information."

Katz stood and looked at him. "Where did you get this sample, Mr. Brodie?"

"From the pocket of a murder victim."

Katz did not respond to that.

Brodie wrote his phone number on a notepad on Katz's desk, then asked, "How quickly can you sequence this?"

Katz appeared disturbed now and looked around the lab at his fellow researchers, a few of whom had become interested in their visitor. He said in a low voice, "Once the equipment is available, it will take two to three hours. But there's a backlog."

Brodie looked him in the eyes. "You need to clear the queue, Mr. Katz."

CHAPTER 41

Brodie walked out of the lab onto the Ku'damm. Next stop, the New Berlin Art Gallery. Anna Albrecht needed to be re-interviewed.

As he looked for a taxi, he thought about plague, and why Harry Vance had a sample of it in his pocket. Was it part of Stefan Richter's collection? Possibly. The old guy might have been willing or even eager to talk about his exploits to someone — anyone — who cared to ask. When Richter had spoken to Elsa Ziegler twenty-some years ago, he wouldn't turn over any of his slides. Maybe by the time he spoke with Vance his attitude had changed, or Harry Vance — already going rogue on an unsanctioned investigation — simply stole it. Then Vance was murdered before he could have the sample analyzed to find out if Richter's stories about Black Harvest were true or bullshit. And then Stefan Richter complicated things further by blowing his brains out.

Brodie's phone rang, and he was surprised to see the call coming from Maggie Taylor. He picked up. "Flight delayed?"

"Where are you?" She sounded tense.

"Berlin. Where are you?"

"I'm in a car. Leaving the airport. I need you to meet me. I'm sending you an address."

"What's going on?"

"Not on the phone."

It's never good news when someone says that. He pulled up the encrypted text message: *33 Kinzigstraße. Apartment 5A. In Friedrichshain.*

She asked, "When can you be there?"

He punched in the address. "Twenty."

"Okay. We'll be there by then."

"Who's we?"

She paused. "Unlikely allies."

"Taylor, I don't like this cryptic shit. What am I walking into?"

She ignored the question and said, "Trust me."

This was sounding strange. He and Taylor had a prearranged signal — clearing their throat — if one of them was under duress. But she hadn't done that. "Okay . . . I trust you. But —"

"Scott, I have reason to believe you are in danger. So be aware —"

"I'm always aware, Maggie."

"Okay. See you soon." She added, "Be safe." She hung up.

He put the phone in his pocket. What the hell was that all about?

Unlikely allies.

Which was another way of saying untrustworthy allies. In any case, he'd know soon what this was about. And he was happy to have a gun in his pocket in case he didn't like what this was about.

He flagged a cab and gave the driver the address in Friedrichshain, and they headed back east through the Tiergarten.

Brodie's phone rang again. It was Claudia Barese from the National Personnel Records Center. He picked up. "Brodie."

"Hi, Scott. It's Claudia. Got your message. How can I help you?"

"Are you at the office?"

"No. At home. Coffee's not even done brewing. But you said it was important."

"I need you to pull personnel files for me, for officers who were stationed in West Berlin in the 1980s."

"Branch?"

"Every branch that had a presence in the city."

"Rank?"

He thought a moment. In order for Odin to have had the kind of access he apparently did, the guy must have been high-ranking. Then again, Brodie didn't really understand what the force structure or chain of command was like in such a unique theater as

West Berlin and he didn't want to make too many assumptions. He said, "O-three and above."

"Okay . . . This is going to be a long list unless you can give me some more parameters."

"I'm looking for an individual who I believe is still alive, who was stationed in Berlin by 1982 at the latest and remained there until at least October of 1989, and who was likely involved in intelligence work." He suggested, "Send me those first."

"Okay . . . male or female?"

"Good question." He'd always assumed that Odin was a man, but by the 1980s there were a significant number of female officers in the armed forces. "Don't know. Give me both."

"Okay. You want the whole DD-201 file?"

"I do." He added, "Just e-mail them to me."

"When do you need all this?"

"Yesterday."

"Why did I ask?" She said, "Can you share with me why this is urgent?"

"Not at liberty to say. Can you access these files from home?"

"Possibly."

Ms. Barese clearly needed more motivation, so he said, "This is related to an ongoing homicide investigation with potential national security implications." He added, "I'm in Berlin."

"Oh . . . okay. I'll see what I can do."

"Thanks, Claudia." He hoped she didn't access *his* file and see that he'd resigned his commission. "You're the best." He hung up and looked out the window as the cab exited the Tiergarten and approached the Brandenburg Gate, whose imperial colonnade had once stood behind a concrete wall lined with barbed wire and guard towers.

The U.S. Army presence in West Berlin had taken the form of the Berlin Brigade, which would have been a few thousand men broken up into about a dozen units, including a few infantry battalions, artillery batteries, MPs, engineers, aviation, probably some form of Special Ops. The Air Force would have had some sort of presence as well. He'd see what Claudia Barese came back to him with.

He wondered if Harry Vance had gone digging in the personnel files in his search for Odin. That would make sense, especially if Vance had more to go on to narrow the list down. But even if Vance — and Brodie — had a stack of personnel files of the officers in the Berlin Brigade from that time period, would there be anything in anyone's file that smelled off? Not likely. Unless you knew you were looking for a rat. That's when things like efficiency reports, duty stations, and other notations could be a clue.

Well, whatever Harry Vance had done, he'd gotten close enough to the truth to die for it.

And now Scott Brodie was following the same solitary and self-appointed path. Hopefully with better results. And a happier ending.

CHAPTER 42

The taxi stopped in front of a nondescript, postwar five-story apartment building on Kinzigstraße, a quiet residential street.

Brodie paid the driver from his dwindling supply of euros, got out, and walked quickly to the entrance, where the call box was located to the right of the recessed door. An overhead security camera covered the entranceway, so whoever was in 5A had seen him arrive. He pushed the button and was immediately buzzed in, which confirmed that he was being watched. He pushed the button again and a man's voice said impatiently, "Come in."

Brodie replied, "I want to hear Taylor's voice."

There was a moment of silence; then Maggie Taylor's voice came over the speaker. "It's okay, Scott. Come on up."

No indication of stress or duress. A few tradecraft precautions go a long way. So does a semi-automatic pistol.

He walked into a small, clean lobby with a polished floor, and a mirror that could be two-way. There was a single elevator and a staircase.

This building was well-suited for a safe house, which Apartment 5A probably was. But whose safe house? He was about to find out.

Brodie chose the staircase for his ascent, and as he climbed he drew his Makarov and took it off safety, then slid it into his coat pocket and kept his grip on it. Just as Harry Vance had done in Körnerpark.

Each floor had a landing with only two doors leading to apartments, so the units were big.

He reached the fifth floor and saw only one doorway — 5A, so whoever owned or rented this place had the whole top floor. He thought he knew who that could be.

There was an eyeball camera on the ceiling, and a fish-eye peephole on the door, which he noted was steel, and unsuitable for kicking in. So he'd have to knock, which he did, then moved to the side.

The door opened and Maggie Taylor looked at him, nodded, and said, "All good. Come in."

Brodie stepped into the apartment, and the spring-loaded door closed behind him.

Spread out before him was a very large, bright living room with an open kitchen and dining area, and street-facing windows. The apartment was modern and well-appointed, a contrast to this unobtrusive building on a nondescript street.

Standing in the living room were two men, one of whom he recognized as Howard Fensterman of the State Department, dressed in his rumpled suit.

The guy he didn't recognize wore a blue blazer, khaki pants, and a button-down shirt. He had a bright-red handkerchief flowing out of the breast pocket of his blazer, which whispered "stylish" and screamed "asshole!"

Brodie thought he knew who this guy could be. But that couldn't be.

Howard Fensterman said, "Welcome, Scott. And thank you for coming."

Brodie didn't respond, and Taylor took his arm and steered him into the room, saying, "Scott, this is Trent Chilcott."

She didn't add, "The guy I used to fuck," but everyone was saying it in their heads.

In fact, Chilcott said, "Ms. Taylor and I are old acquaintances, as you probably know."

Brodie looked at Trent Chilcott. He was tall, tanned, toned, and well-coiffed. Brodie wouldn't be surprised to learn that he got weekly pedicures.

More importantly, the only good thing about this case so far was that the CIA didn't seem to be involved. Now there was nothing good about this case. But when you saw the

CIA, that at least told you things about a case that you suspected but couldn't prove. I.e., there was more going on here than anyone was saying. But he already knew that.

Chilcott fixed his eyes on Brodie's right hand in his pocket, then looked at Brodie. "Is that a gun?"

"Show me yours, and I'll show you mine."

Chilcott pulled open the left side of his blazer, revealing a holstered gun clipped to his belt.

Brodie drew his pistol half out of his pocket, then shoved it back and kept his grip on it.

Chilcott said, "Howard is armed only with his intellect."

"So he's unarmed."

Chilcott smiled. Fensterman didn't, but asked Brodie, "Where did you get the gun?"

"Not from the embassy, which should have issued me and Ms. Taylor sidearms. For our personal safety."

Fensterman didn't respond and didn't pursue the question.

Brodie, of course, wondered what the hell this was about, but he wasn't going to ask. Because they would tell him. But he did say to Chilcott, "The last time I had to deal with the CIA, after Venezuela, I had the distinct feeling I was being threatened."

Chilcott replied, "I know nothing about that. And I'm sorry if you felt that."

Taylor chimed in, "You know all about that, Trent. And you're not at all sorry. Intimidation is what you do best." She added, "Stop the bullshit."

Chilcott, who'd probably heard something similar a few times, remained cool, then said, "Really sorry."

Well, thought Brodie, these two had a history. And he knew part of it. And it was interesting that Maggie Taylor was signaling to Scott Brodie that she was loyal to her partner, and not to her former lover. She'd also done that in Venezuela. Though that had turned out to be a lie. He wondered if Chilcott had asked Taylor about her relationship with Scott Brodie. Probably. He hoped Taylor had told him that she and Scott were burning up the bedsheets.

But, back to more important things. Brodie said, "I don't respond well to threats. I don't know why you want to talk to me, or to Taylor, but if you cross the line, Chilcott, or cross me, like you did in Venezuela, I swear you'll meet with a serious accident." He looked at Fensterman. "And you too, Howard, because anyone who works with this guy is guilty by association."

Fensterman looked a little pale and said, "Let's ratchet this down. All right?" He explained, "We're here to talk about the Vance case, not . . . whatever happened between you in the past."

"Let's start by you telling me who you are."

Fensterman glanced at Chilcott, then said, "I'm not actually with the State Department. I'm with the National Security Agency."

Brodie said, "I assume you work for the Special Collection Service. Correct?"

Fensterman seemed surprised that Brodie knew of his department. He replied, indirectly, "I monitor internal threats to the German government, as well as threats to U.S. national security."

Taylor said, "Actually you eavesdrop on everyone, including U.S. citizens."

Fensterman neither confirmed nor denied.

Brodie thought about his cell phone conversation with Taylor when he was in Alexanderplatz and she was in a taxi — near the embassy, and well within range of the alleged SCS listening station on the embassy rooftop. And there were other times when he and Taylor had spoken too close to the embassy, like their meeting with Kim at the Reichstag. He thought too of his calls to Dombroski. And Anna. How far could those listening devices actually reach? He and Taylor had depended on their encryption app, available to any schmuck with a smartphone, which probably wasn't good enough to overcome the National Security Agency's capabilities.

Brodie regarded Howard Fensterman. He wasn't supposed to listen to the calls or conversations of U.S. citizens — only non-

635

U.S. citizens. But Brodie had no doubt that he and his staff listened and recorded the calls, texts, and conversations of everyone in the embassy, up to and including the ambassador, and certainly Sharon Whitmore. And quite possibly CID Agents Brodie and Taylor. If information was power, then Howard Fensterman was Superman. Brodie said to him, "I assume this place is bugged."

Fensterman nodded, but assured him, "The devices are off, so we can speak freely." He added, "I wouldn't want anything I said or Trent said to be recorded or transmitted. This meeting never took place."

"When did this become a meeting?"

"Call it whatever you want, Mr. Brodie." He motioned to a seating area. "We can sit."

Brodie replied, "You can sit. Ms. Taylor and I will stand."

"As you wish." He looked at Brodie and asked, "Why are you still in Berlin?"

"I've taken leave here."

"You should come back in the spring when the weather is better."

"Get to the point, Howard."

"All right. First, as Trent has already informed Ms. Taylor, your life is in danger."

Brodie glanced at Taylor, who said, "That's why I wanted you to come here. To hear this."

A phone call would have sufficed, thought Brodie. And he wouldn't have had to meet Maggie Taylor's former lover. On the other hand, it was interesting to see what kind of asshole she was attracted to. Also, when a CIA guy tells you your life is in danger, he is usually the cause of the danger. Then he offers to help you. In exchange for a favor.

Fensterman asked, "Does this subject interest you, Mr. Brodie?"

He turned to Fensterman. The guy had a sense of humor. "I've already been made aware of that danger."

"By whom?"

"By two guys who tried to kill or kidnap me." He confessed, "That's where I got the gun."

Fensterman seemed speechless, Chilcott seemed skeptical, and Taylor said, "Oh my God. Scott . . . what happened?"

"I'll tell you later." He looked at Chilcott and Fensterman. "Since you both seem to know that my life is in danger, maybe you can tell me who put it there."

Chilcott replied, "I'm sure you have many people who'd like to terminate you, Mr. Brodie. Including your closest friends. But in this case, I'm fairly sure it is NordFaust." He asked, "Have you heard of them?"

Just recently, actually. The neo-Nazi group in which the retired German colonel, Brandt, had claimed membership during his drunken racist rant last spring — before being interrogated by Mark Jenkins and Harry Vance regarding Brandt's assault on the African

American Army officer in Stuttgart. Jenkins did not seem to have taken NordFaust seriously and hadn't even recalled the name when Brodie asked him about the incident.

"Mr. Brodie?"

"You know I've heard of them, or you wouldn't have asked."

Chilcott nodded and said, "We have good Intel that the two of you" — he looked at Taylor — "have gotten on NordFaust's radar. In fact, you were followed yesterday — though I'm sure you picked up your tail."

Chilcott was being patronizing, but in fact that explained the man in Neukölln who'd reappeared at the Hotel Adlon. It's somehow comforting to have your paranoia confirmed on a regular basis.

Taylor asked, "Why were we being followed?"

Chilcott replied, "I was going to ask *you* that. We don't know. But clearly your activities in Berlin have put you in their . . . gunsights."

Taylor asked him, "Who exactly are these people?"

"NordFaust," replied Chilcott, "is one of several far-right and neo-Nazi groups in Germany. They have a presence within the Bundeswehr — the German armed forces — as well as the national police and local police forces. They are also potentially the most dangerous of the far-right groups."

Brodie assumed that the two goons who'd tried to kidnap or kill him were NordFaust guys. They weren't particularly good at their job. On the other hand, they knew who he was and where he was going. So that indicated an Intel network of some sort, or informants in the right places. More disturbing was that they were willing to act on their information and had no hesitation about trying to ice an American Army officer. Brodie didn't know why he and Taylor had gotten on NordFaust's hit list, but he pictured a bunch of these Nazis sitting around drinking beer in a smoke-filled room, and one of them saying in German, with subtitles, "These nosy Americans know too much, goddammit, so they must . . ." Finger across the throat. Problem was, neither he nor Taylor knew too much. But if NordFaust thought they did, then maybe they did. Maybe they'd hit on something. In fact, maybe it was NordFaust who'd killed Harry Vance. But why?

Chilcott was going on: "NordFaust operates differently than most of these neo-Nazi groups. Most of the other groups hold meetings, which leaves them open to infiltration by German Intel. They have online chat groups that can be monitored, they show up at rallies, like at the American Embassy, and they commit one-off acts of violence that leave a trail of blood and evidence. Nord-Faust operates more like a Black Ops and espionage unit. Long-term planning, stockpiling weapons, building influence among high-level contacts in the officer corps of the Bundeswehr, and doing the same with the police and far-right politicians in the Bundestag and also in the government ministries." He looked at Brodie, then Taylor. "Now and then, when they feel threatened by the news media, or by left-wing groups or government inquiries, they eliminate the threat."

Brodie couldn't keep himself from saying, "Are we still talking about NordFaust? Or the CIA?"

Even Chilcott smiled at that. He really enjoyed the role of secret agent man with a license to eliminate.

Chilcott, for the record, said, "Don't believe all those things you hear about us, Mr. Brodie." Which meant the opposite, of course.

Brodie reminded him, "The Phoenix Program in Vietnam, Operation Flagstaff in Afghanistan. Not to mention the shit I saw the Agency do in Iraq."

Chilcott was not happy hearing those words spoken aloud, especially Flagstaff, which he had been deeply involved with — while also involved with Maggie Taylor, whom he'd seduced in more ways than one.

Chilcott stared at Brodie. He should have let that go, but he said, "Should I remind you, Sergeant Brodie, of what you and your unit did to 'liberate' Fallujah?" He added,

"The civilian dead stunk up the streets for a month. So don't get sanctimonious on me, Sergeant."

"Trent . . . can I call you Trent? Trent, go fuck yourself."

Maggie Taylor said, "Stop! Stop this!"

Brodie wanted to explain to her that this is what two alpha males do to compete for top dog. But she probably knew that. She probably also thought that Brodie's aggressive behavior toward Trent Chilcott had something to do with Trent having had sex with Maggie Taylor. Well, she was completely off base on that. Not even in the ballpark. Those thoughts never crossed his mind.

Howard Fensterman, playing peacemaker again, said, "Gentlemen. We need to move on."

"No," said Brodie, "first you need to tell me why I and Ms. Taylor are here."

Chilcott replied, "Two reasons. The first should be obvious. You're here in this safe house because your lives are in danger. You'll stay here for a day or two, then we will get you on a flight back to Washington." He let them know, "There are four bedrooms here — one for me, one for a security person, and one each for both of you." He smiled. "So you don't have to share a bedroom."

Brodie had already told Trent Chilcott to go fuck himself, so he moved on to: "I and Ms. Taylor are not staying here, and certainly not with you. We are leaving as soon as we're finished here, which will be soon."

Chilcott said, "I must insist."

"Me too. Okay, what's the other reason we're here?"

Chilcott seemed annoyed and frustrated that Brodie was not going along with the program and not grateful that Chilcott was offering them a safe place to stay and a ticket home. But he collected himself and said, "I need some information from you. Which I'm sure you'll share with me in exchange for me alerting you to the danger you're in and offering you a safe place and safe passage —"

"Trent, Maggie was on her way home before you waylaid her. And I don't need your safe house. If you need information from us, you need to pay for it with information."

Chilcott glanced at Fensterman, then replied, "Okay. We have information you can use in your criminal investigation."

Taylor said, "We're off the case, Trent. You know that."

"I'm fairly sure I can get you both reinstated. If that's what you want." He added, "It's my understanding that you are both at a . . . well, a career crossroads, and that —"

"Let us worry about our careers," said Brodie. "Worry about your own."

"There's nothing for me to worry about. I play the game. And I make the rules."

Asshole. Brodie was fairly certain that his

642

resignation hadn't progressed beyond Dombroski's desk, so a phone call would fix that. As for him and Taylor getting back on this case . . . He said, "You have no influence in the Army, Chilcott."

"You'd be surprised."

"I would be." But maybe Trent and his colleagues in the CIA did have some influence in the Pentagon. It certainly seemed that way when Brodie and Taylor were in Venezuela. And the reason for that was these joint Army/CIA Black Ops programs that were borderline illegal — or not so borderline. When people become co-conspirators, they have each other by the balls, and no favor is too great to ask. Brodie glanced at Taylor, who nodded. Brodie said, "All right. Let's talk." He looked at Chilcott. "What do you need to know?"

Chilcott asked, "First, why was Mark Jenkins and Harry Vance's brief encounter with Colonel Brandt — a supposed member of NordFaust — in Stuttgart last year of interest to you in the Vance homicide case? We don't understand the connection."

How did Chilcott even know about Brodie's interest in the Stuttgart case? Well, it was likely that Mark Jenkins had told Brodie and Taylor's CID replacements — Jones and Mellman — what Scott Brodie was bothering him about. And Jones and Mellman, in turn, could have passed that on to the legat and other embassy officials, and then one way or

643

another that Intel would find its way to Howard Fensterman and Trent Chilcott. The other possibility was that Brodie and Taylor's phone conversation — while Brodie was in Alexanderplatz and Taylor was in a cab near the embassy — had been intercepted by the SCS. And maybe the answer didn't matter. Chilcott and Fensterman were in the loop, and they wanted their two CID safe-house guests to know that. And yet, Chilcott and Fensterman were still missing some pieces of the puzzle.

Brodie replied, "We believe this Stuttgart case might be connected to the unsanctioned investigation that Mr. Vance was conducting here in Berlin before his murder."

Chilcott said, "We are aware of Mr. Vance's personal investigation into the identity of the American double agent Odin." He explained, "Jason Butler informed Howard about Anna Albrecht's interview with the BKA."

Brodie wondered if Jason Butler had informed Howard Fensterman knowingly, or via a phone tap. Brodie offered, "Vance's investigation of Odin began in May of last year, and I wanted to know if any part of his official CID business around that time might have been the catalyst for his interest in this double agent."

Fensterman asked, "And did you find a connection between Odin and the Stuttgart case?"

Brodie looked at him. "If I'd found anything, Howard, you'd be the first to know, but not because I told you."

Fensterman had no reply.

Chilcott stepped in. "Here's what we believe. Harry Vance was likely not killed by Islamic terrorists, and you two, in the process of investigating his murder and then continuing his search for Odin, have come to the attention of NordFaust and gotten on their hit list. Why?"

Brodie looked at him. "You're the spook. You tell me."

Chilcott stared back. "You know more than you're saying, Mr. Brodie."

"You too."

Chilcott couldn't hide his annoyance. Brodie pegged him as the kind of guy who projected the debonair affect pretty well, but had never gotten control of his inner demons enough to completely pull it off. Trent Chilcott practiced his smile in the mirror without looking too long into his own eyes.

Fensterman said, "We are privy to certain forensic evidence from the site of the explosion in Neukölln that casts serious doubt on the official narrative."

Taylor asked, "Such as?"

Fensterman and Chilcott shared a look; then Fensterman continued, "The IED that detonated in the apartment was radio-controlled. The radio receiver that was con-

645

nected to the electrical firing circuit survived the blast, as did the UHF radio transmitter that was intended to be used as a remote trigger. The problem is that the transmitter is not compatible with the receiver that was connected to the firing circuit. In other words, this bomb that was supposedly destined for Mr. Jenkins' vehicle could never have been detonated with the equipment found at the blast site. The German authorities can of course explain this as another example of incompetence on the part of our supposed Islamic terrorists. However, we believe that the real triggering device was outside of the apartment and operated by an unidentified individual. This was a setup, and those who placed the bomb in the apartment never expected the radio receiver to survive the blast, and perhaps made an oversight in planting the wrong type of transmitter in the apartment."

Also, thought Brodie, whoever set up the three Syrians didn't know that one of them was a Christian, and therefore not likely to be an Islamic terrorist. But Brodie didn't bother to share that and neither did Taylor.

As for improvised explosive devices, Brodie had seen his share of IEDs in Iraq — both intact bombs and detonated remnants. The receiver and firing circuit were attached directly to the explosives, and it was reasonable to assume the receiver would be obliterated in a blast. Except this time, it wasn't. And what was left behind was actual physical evidence of what Brodie had suspected: that this was an elaborate and violent misdirection. The three Syrian men were likely already dead — or drugged — when the bomb went off. And the cell phone that David Kim had described to them as containing the draft e-mail about the Tripoli operation had been purposely left somewhere in the apartment where it would survive the explosion and offer a reasonable motive for the assassination of Harry Vance and the planned assassination of Mark Jenkins.

What would it take to pull that off? How many people, how many resources, and what expertise? And what sort of person or persons would have had access to the information that Jenkins and Vance were the agents involved in the Tripoli operation in order to craft a coherent motive for them to be targets of Islamic terrorism?

Taylor must have been wondering the same thing; she asked, "Do you believe NordFaust was responsible for this explosion?"

Chilcott and Fensterman exchanged another look. Then Chilcott said, "We don't know. But we do believe they would have the capability."

Taylor added, "So if NordFaust is responsible for the blast, they are also responsible for killing Harry Vance."

Chilcott said, "They undoubtedly have skilled sharpshooters among their ranks."

"Then why," asked Brodie, "does this neo-Nazi group care about a former double agent for the Stasi, and Vance's attempt to find him?"

Fensterman replied, "That is what we are trying to understand. Is there a connection? Or was Mr. Vance targeted by NordFaust for an unrelated reason?"

Brodie said, "We believe Vance was in contact with Colonel Tariq Qasim — whom he knew as Abbas al-Hamdani — a former member of the Iraqi military who potentially could have identified Odin."

Fensterman nodded. "I was made aware of that finding by the legat's office."

Brodie continued, "We also believe Colonel Qasim is dead, and his killers used his phone to lure Vance to Körnerpark under false pretenses. So, the killer or killers were familiar with the details of Vance's investigation."

"That's a theory," said Chilcott.

"We're dancing around the obvious," said Taylor. "Odin is alive and working with Nord-Faust."

Chilcott looked at her. "That possibility had of course occurred to us, but we believe it highly unlikely."

"Why?" asked Brodie.

"I assure you," said Fensterman, "that if an American military or former military officer was a member of NordFaust, or any extremist group in Germany, we would know about it."

"Well," said Taylor, "an American military officer, code-named Odin, *was* a highly effective double agent for the Stasi for close to a decade, and apparently you people have never figured out who he is."

Neither Fensterman nor Chilcott had a reply to that.

The image of Harry Vance's hollowed-out eye socket flashed in Brodie's mind. And then he saw the self-mutilated visage of the Norse god of war and death.

I did this. I'm still here.

Brodie looked at Fensterman. "You sound a little too confident in your assessment, Howard."

Fensterman met his look. "If you had full knowledge of our capabilities, Scott, you would share my confidence."

"Right," said Brodie. "I'm sure that inside of your little rooftop spy shed you feel very smart, and your farts smell like flowers. But there's a world beyond what you can see and hear."

Fensterman did not respond, though he didn't look happy with that assessment.

Chilcott said, "Scott, we'd all like to know how you came into possession of that gun."

Brodie replied, "I borrowed it from a cop who didn't need it anymore." He briefly recounted what had occurred outside of Stefan Richter's apartment — including Herr Richter's early checkout from this life — and how he'd received Richter's name from Elsa Ziegler at the Stasi Archives. He added, "The microscope slide that I removed from Vance's jacket is currently being analyzed by a lab. The scientist I spoke with identified the sample by sight as Yersinia pestis — plague."

Taylor looked at him but didn't say anything.

Chilcott said to Brodie, "Let me see your pistol."

"I don't think so."

Chilcott smiled. "What will it take for us to trust each other?"

"For at least one of us to get a lobotomy."

"Just hold it up so I can see it."

Brodie pulled out the pistol and held it up. "It's a Makarov. Soviet-made."

Chilcott nodded. "The black market's flooded with those. Whether these men were genuine police officers or not, they were likely members of NordFaust. If you'd been detained by them, Mr. Brodie, you would have been taken someplace for a very unpleasant interrogation, and you'd probably be dead by now. You're a lucky man."

Brodie returned the pistol to his pocket. "I make my own luck."

Brodie noted that both Fensterman and Chilcott looked almost disappointed in what

Brodie had shared with them. So he reiterated, "Harry Vance was walking around with plague in his pocket, which he had likely acquired from Stefan Richter, a former Stasi foreign intelligence agent who was allegedly involved in East Germany's bioweapons program, and who responded to a knock on his door by an American CID agent by blowing his brains out." Brodie had another thought. "Or Richter had a NordFaust guest in his apartment who pulled the trigger."

Chilcott shrugged. "We can speculate all day. But I doubt NordFaust has much interest in an old Stasi Intel guy." He added, "This is all interesting history, but that's all it is. We are involved in trying to stop radical neo-Nazi groups who are operating *today* — that would be the twenty-first century — in a plot to bring down the modern German state. As for the plague sample, I can order a slide of that crap online for ten bucks. It's inert in that form, used for academic study."

Taylor looked annoyed. "Every step of the way in this investigation, we've had people try to explain away every connection we have found, every theory we have come up with. The German government just shared with the entire world its findings in this major homicide investigation, findings that everyone in this room has acknowledged are bullshit. And now you are dismissing out of hand any connection between NordFaust and

Odin, or Harry Vance's murder and an illicit bioweapons program that Vance himself was investigating."

Fensterman said, "We are not dismissing anything. But we have no indication of a bioterrorism or other unconventional weapons threat from NordFaust or any other extremist group. As Trent said, our job is to assess and neutralize the threats of today and tomorrow, and to leave the rest to historians."

The past is not past. But that wasn't something a technocrat like Howard Fensterman or an arrogant intelligence officer like Trent Chilcott would understand.

Brodie asked, "Why were these NordFaust guys watching Stefan Richter's apartment?"

Fensterman replied, "They weren't. They were watching *you,* Mr. Brodie. And they took their opportunity when they believed they had you cornered and alone in an isolated location." He added, "If they killed Mr. Vance, then you and Ms. Taylor became a threat to them the moment you stepped off the carefully constructed path that they were attempting to channel this investigation into. The motive for murdering Mr. Vance is as yet unclear, but the motive for attempting to silence you is easy to see." Fensterman checked his watch. "I need to get back to the embassy. Thank you both for your time, and for that information. I believe Trent still has something he needs to discuss with you."

Fensterman walked to the door and left.

Brodie looked at Chilcott, who looked back at him.

Brodie had no idea what Trent Chilcott was going to do for act two, but as they say in the theater, if you show a gun in act one, you have to use it in act three.

CHAPTER 43

Scott Brodie, Maggie Taylor, and Trent Chilcott stood in silence.

Without Howard Fensterman in the room, the dynamic had shifted, and it was now two against one. But which two? And which one? Brodie had no doubt that Maggie Taylor was on Team Brodie, but he also had no doubt that she was still somehow under the influence of her former lover, the sociopathic Trent Chilcott.

Chilcott, playing host in his company's safe house, asked, "Anyone want a drink? Coffee?"

Brodie and Taylor declined.

"Okay," said Chilcott. "What I am going to share with you now is highly privileged information. Within hours, German federal and local law enforcement will be conducting a series of raids against NordFaust and related groups in Berlin and other cities in Germany. The Germans are conducting these operations in part thanks to intelligence shared by American Intel agencies, and we have a degree of involvement in what is going to take place." Chilcott looked between Brodie and Taylor. "I'm offering you the opportunity to assist in this law enforcement operation, as American military advisers to American civilian intelligence officers in Germany."

Brodie replied, "We already have a job. And it's not with you."

Chilcott ignored that and asked Brodie, "If either of the men who tried to abduct you today is among those detained tonight, would you be able to identify him?"

"You can ID them. One has a broken nose, and the other has swollen nuts."

Chilcott looked at Brodie with some interest. "I'm impressed, Mr. Brodie."

"Coming from you, that don't mean a thing."

Chilcott kept his cool. "You both got screwed on this case despite being closer to the truth than anyone else. Scott, you set yourself on fire, which according to your reputation is something you do — or try to do — pretty often. It must work well on the ladies, who I imagine are always trying to fix you." Chilcott looked at Taylor and smiled.

Taylor stared at him, and his smile faded. Whatever game these two had played, Brodie could see that it was still playing out in the nonverbal language of ex-lovers.

Chilcott continued, "And you, Maggie, tried to tell yourself you were doing the right thing by following orders and leaving your findings with the FBI, despite knowing that nothing would come of it and that the wrong people — Muslims — would be implicated in the murder of Harry Vance. And that doesn't say much for your commitment to justice. I am now offering you both a chance to redeem yourselves."

Taylor said, "If anyone needs redemption, it's you, Trent. And as for justice, it's being delayed right now with your stupid offer. So, unless there's something else, I'm leaving here, calling my boss in Quantico, and making a very good argument for why he needs to get Scott and me back on this case. And we don't need your help in doing that."

Brodie added, "Based on past history, I'm sure you can understand why we might not completely trust you. In fact, every time the Army sleeps with the CIA, the CIA gets a good lay, and the Army gets fucked."

Chilcott stared at him. "Keep going down this road, Mr. Brodie, and you'll be lucky if you only end up in jail."

"Wherever I go — Leavenworth or Arlington — I'll be sure to take you and others with me."

Chilcott smiled. "There it is, that rogue spirit. You're like one of those little bottle rockets where you break off the stick before lighting the fuse. A hot flame shooting out your ass, going nowhere."

Brodie said, "We're done here."

Chilcott had a plan, but it didn't include Brodie having a gun, and clearly this was throwing him off. In fact, Brodie would not have been surprised to learn that it was the CIA station chief in the embassy who'd blocked him and Taylor from being issued sidearms. But Brodie had one now, so he didn't have to kick Chilcott in the balls to get out of there. "Good luck with the Nazi roundup."

Chilcott walked to one of the street-facing windows. "Before you both leave, come here and take a look."

Brodie and Taylor exchanged glances, then walked to the window where Chilcott was standing and looked down into the street.

A white-and-blue SUV labeled <u>POLIZEI</u> sat idling at the curb. A police officer in full tactical gear and holding an assault rifle stood next to the SUV, looking up at them.

Chilcott said, "Those are agents of the Bundespolizei. Federal Police." He eyed Brodie and Taylor. "They are here to ensure your safety. You two will remain in this apartment until the raids are concluded. We will require your participation in IDing any of the perps we sweep up in the raids, and in reviewing any evidence we obtain that might connect NordFaust to Mr. Vance's murder. And in return my agency will help you unfuck your lives. Get your careers back, or get better ones."

Neither Brodie nor Taylor responded.

Chilcott said, "Plus I have my own man in the lobby who will be up here shortly." He added, "You're not going anywhere. Unless or until I let you go."

Taylor said, "I'll be filing charges of kidnapping against you."

"You're under the protective custody of the German police. Don't make them bring charges against *you.*"

Brodie was thinking less legally, and more along the lines of punching Chilcott in the nuts and shoving his gun up his ass. But that was an option he could exercise later. He said, "Okay, we'll stay awhile. Do you know how to make a Negroni?"

Chilcott smiled and started to reply, but Brodie felt Taylor's hand on his coat, and quick as a cat she snatched his gun out of his pocket, and backpedaled as she brought the gun up and pointed it at Chilcott's chest, shouting, "Don't move, Trent! You move, you're dead. Hands up!"

Chilcott seemed incredulous; then, as he made eye contact with her, he slowly raised his hands.

She said, "Scott, stand behind him."

Brodie knew the drill and took up a position about five feet behind Chilcott, effectively limiting what Chilcott could do to turn this around.

Taylor said to her old friend and mentor, "Left hand. Very slowly, Trent. Slowly."

He brought his left hand under his blazer and slowly pulled his gun from his holster, holding the butt between his thumb and forefinger.

"Drop it."

He let the gun fall to the floor.

"Move away."

Chilcott moved away from his gun, and Brodie retrieved the 9mm Glock.

Chilcott, coming out of his shock, said, "I could walk out of here, and neither of you would shoot me."

Brodie suggested, "It's worth a try, Trent."

Taylor seemed to be in a weird zone and practically shouted, "*I told you.* I told you what I would do if you tried to betray me again."

"That's not what this is."

"You bastard. You used me as bait to get Scott here. You have always used me, lied to me, manipulated me . . ."

"If that's true, Maggie, you should pull the trigger."

"I'm thinking about it."

Brodie thought that Chilcott should not be goading Maggie Taylor, given her family history. You can take the girl out of Appalachia, but . . . Brodie pointed Chilcott's gun at him and said to Taylor, "I've got him covered, lower your gun. Chilcott, you sit down."

Taylor hesitated, then lowered her gun, but kept her eyes on Chilcott as though she reserved the right to resume her two-hand grip and paint Trent red.

Chilcott sat in an armchair and crossed his legs, acting like nothing out of the ordinary had taken place. Just another day of dealing with lesser beings.

Brodie said to him, "I don't like your pocket handkerchief."

"It was a gift from Maggie. That's why I wore it."

Brodie expected to hear Taylor emptying her magazine at Chilcott. He glanced at her and saw she'd calmed down, and was standing near the window, checking out the street. He and Taylor had control of the situation, but getting out of here was going to be a challenge.

Brodie took a seat opposite Chilcott, and Taylor put her back to the wall and held the Makarov at her chest in a two-hand grip.

Brodie tossed Chilcott's Glock on the coffee table between them. He said, "We all deserve to have choices in life. Now you have a choice. You can answer my questions, or you can go for your gun. You stonewalling is not one of your choices."

Chilcott eyed the gun on the table, less than five feet from him, calculating his odds.

Brodie said helpfully, "If it were me, I'd go for it."

Chilcott looked at him. "That's because you're an irrational idiot with more ego than brains."

"You've been reading my 201 file."

"I didn't have to. Maggie told me all I needed to know about you."

Taylor said, "That's not true."

Brodie didn't know if it was true — or partly true — but it pissed him off. So, rather than continuing down ex-lovers lane, he got down to business. "Trent, what are you actually doing in Berlin? Why are you here?"

Chilcott thought a moment, then said, "All right. I can share some of this with you. On a need-to-know basis."

"We don't need to know anything. We're off the case. But we *want* to know. Everything."

Chilcott settled back in his chair and said, "I was brought in to work with the SCS to collect and analyze signals intelligence about right-wing extremist plots in Germany. We zeroed in on NordFaust, who present a specific and imminent threat."

Brodie asked, "What is the specific threat?"

"NordFaust is planning a terrorist attack in Berlin. We believe the threat is imminent and is designed to catalyze a larger right-wing violent uprising against the German government."

Taylor asked, "What kind of attack?"

Chilcott hesitated, then said, "Last year German customs officers in Hamburg searched a shipping container arriving from St. Petersburg as part of a random security inspection and found over a dozen compact mortar-fired cluster bombs. We have since picked up intelligence that members of Nord-Faust were behind this attempted import, and that additional, identical munitions in another container slipped through security." He paused. "This intelligence also indicated that these weapons are to be used as part of a co-ordinated attack against the Arab immigrant community in Berlin." He added, "You're lucky you checked out of the Art Hotel."

Brodie heard Taylor say in almost a whisper, "Oh my God . . ."

Cluster bombs, as Brodie knew, were so destructive in part because of the large area a single bomb could blanket in deadly bomb-lets, which were inherently indiscriminate. These types of weapons were banned by many nations, including the United States and Germany, though they had allegedly been used to deadly effect recently by the Russian Air Force in Syria. Also, the American Air Force had used them in Vietnam. But not since.

Brodie asked, "Are these Russian weapons?"

Chilcott shook his head. "MAT-120s. Spanish-made. And hard to trace. These things are trafficked all over. Qaddafi used them during the civil war in Libya. They're relatively small, easy to transport and conceal. They have a limited range compared to larger rocket-propelled cluster bombs, but good enough for front-line infantry — or for a terrorist looking to hit an urban neighborhood from within the city limits."

Taylor said, "And you're trying to seize these weapons today."

"It's high on our shopping list."

The idea of a terrorist group deploying cluster bombs within a major European capital seemed almost inconceivable, but NordFaust sounded like the kind of psychotics who'd do it if they could.

Brodie asked, "Could the bomb's submunitions carry a biological agent?"

Chilcott looked at him. "We are talking about a conventional-weapons attack to kill and maim a large number of Arab immigrants in a concentrated area. Why the hell would a group of German white supremacists unleash biological agents inside their own city that would end up spreading everywhere?"

"Good question. And one worth asking."

Taylor asked, "Why were you trying to hold us here?"

"I told you. To protect you." Chilcott looked at Brodie. "Also, I don't need a rogue agent running around Berlin hours before this operation, especially someone who has managed to light a fire under the ass of Nord-Faust, who we've been methodically — and *quietly* — monitoring for months now." He added, "We've got enough turmoil already after the incident this morning in Neukölln. In fact, we're moving a few days sooner than planned because of it."

Taylor asked, "What incident in Neukölln?"

Chilcott looked at her. "Don't you read the news? It happened a few blocks from the Art Hotel. A young Arab guy was found dead in the middle of the street this morning. He'd been strangled to death, and a swastika was carved into his chest." He added, "His body was covered in pig's blood."

Taylor said, "My God . . . this is so sick. So evil."

Chilcott looked at her. "I thought you were in Afghanistan, Maggie. Didn't you see what the Taliban did to their fellow Muslims?" He added, "There's a bit of Taliban in all of us. And sometimes we have to go there ourselves — to fight the monsters. Moral judgments are not helpful or useful." He suggested, "You both need to get over yourselves. I'm not the bad guy. We're *all* bad guys. And we all call ourselves the good guys. The Taliban think they're good guys. So does ISIS. Nazis. Commies. The Stasi. Gestapo. Whatever. We are tribal. The only bad guys are the ones who betray the tribe." He concluded, "That would be Odin. Definitely a bad guy. A traitor to his country. His tribe."

Brodie saw some holes in Trent Chilcott's justifications for being a morally weightless prick, but the man made some valid points. Nonetheless, Brodie said, "Love is the answer. Okay —"

Taylor said to Chilcott, "You betrayed *me.* And I am a member of your tribe."

He looked at her. "I used you. There's a difference."

"Fuck you."

Brodie hated to interrupt what sounded like a long-overdue group therapy session, but he needed to get out of there — though beyond visiting Anna he wasn't sure where he was going, or what he needed to do after that. He said to Chilcott, "Anything else we need to know?"

Chilcott shook his head and told them, "I have things to do." He looked at Brodie. "I'm going to stand, take my gun, and walk out of here. You two will stay here."

Taylor said to him, "All right. Reach for your gun."

Chilcott seemed to be weighing his options.

Brodie took out his cell phone and began hitting the keys, saying to Chilcott, "I'm texting my boss, Colonel Dombroski . . . giving him a brief report of where we are, and who we're with . . . That's you, Trent Chilcott . . . And I'm telling him you threatened us, and if anything happens to us . . . Well, you know the rest." Brodie stopped typing, stood, and said to Taylor, "You do the same. Do not push 'send.' " He looked at Chilcott. "Thank you for the offer of protective custody. And for your briefing. Now, call your guy in the lobby and let him know we're leaving, and tell him to tell the Polizei that it's okay."

Chilcott hesitated, as though torn between wanting Brodie and Taylor gone, and keeping the two loose cannons in the safe house until the busts were complete. And, of course, there was always the possibility that CIA officer Chilcott had orders to terminate Brodie and Taylor with extreme prejudice. You never knew.

"Trent, don't make me beat the shit out of you in front of your old girlfriend."

Chilcott pulled out his cell phone, dialed, and said, "Peter, my guests are leaving . . . Yes. Please tell the police they can leave . . . All right." He hung up and said to Brodie, "The Agency has a long memory."

"And I have a short fuse. Walk us to the door."

Chilcott stood and eyed his gun on the coffee table, then glanced at Taylor to see if she had taken her eyes off him. Of course she hadn't. But he looked like he might go for the gun anyway . . .

Brodie delivered a powerful punch into Chilcott's solar plexus, and the man doubled over like a folding chair, then staggered a few steps and fell to his knees, unable to breathe or speak.

Brodie said, "That's for almost getting me and my partner killed in Venezuela. And you're getting off easy, because I'm a softie."

Brodie pulled Chilcott's phone from his breast pocket and punched in a random access code, then did it five more times and the phone was disabled. He threw the phone on the coffee table, took Chilcott's Glock, and shoved it in his pocket. He said to Taylor, "Let's go."

She stood motionless a second, looking at Trent Chilcott, who was still on his knees, his hands clasped to his abdomen, trying to breathe, saliva dripping from his mouth . . .

Brodie headed for the door. "Come on."

She followed quickly, and they exited into the hallway, drew their guns, and headed down the staircase.

On the way down, Taylor said, "He deserved worse."

"Do yourself a favor and call it even. I have."

"You don't know him," said Taylor. "There's more to come."

CHAPTER 44

Brodie and Taylor reached the lobby and pocketed their guns. There was a guy in a black coat standing there looking at them. Brodie said, "Peter?"

He nodded.

"Did you tell the police we needed a ride?"

"No . . . I thought . . . I told them they could go."

"Damn it."

"Sorry."

"No problem. Trent wants you to wait here until he calls." Which might be a while.

"Okay."

"See you upstairs later."

Brodie and Taylor exited the building, and Taylor said, "I must attract bullshit artists." She pulled up a map of the area. "There's a main road to the right . . . Bundesstraße. We can get a taxi there."

They turned right and began walking quickly.

Taylor said, "Okay . . . now what?"

Well, he'd been on his way to Anna's art gallery to re-interview her when he got diverted, but he wasn't sure if that was actually a good use of his time, or whether he just wanted to see her again. Either way, he hadn't pictured Maggie Taylor coming along with him.

"Scott? What's the move?"

"We'll figure it out. In the meantime we need to get out of the area before Trent can walk and talk again and tells his security guy what really happened."

They walked in silence toward Bundesstraße. Then Taylor said, "I spoke to Dombroski. We agreed that your resignation was an overreaction."

"I disagree. And please don't talk about me to —"

"He was very upset. He wanted to talk." She added, "People care about you."

"I feel the love every day."

"Asshole."

"On that subject, your CIA friend —"

"He's not my *friend.*"

"Did he say anything to you before I got there?"

"Nothing that he didn't say to you."

"Okay." Brodie wasn't sure why Chilcott went out of his way to lure him to the safe house. On the surface, it could be what it seemed: Chilcott plucked Taylor from the airport to use her for bait — to get Brodie in

669

the safe house to question him about what he knew, and also to put him in protective custody while the neo-Nazis were being rounded up. That was plausible.

But if Brodie factored in the Mercer case, and also the fact that the CIA — who liked to do the wet stuff overseas — wanted him and Taylor to take the Mercer case secrets to a very early grave, then it was also plausible that neither he nor Taylor would have left that apartment alive. How's that for paranoia?

"What are you thinking?"

"I'm thinking that we'll see Mr. Chilcott again."

They reached Bundesstraße and hailed a taxi. Brodie quickly checked the map on his phone, then told the driver to head to Treptower Park. The park was about a mile and a half to the southeast via major roads and would get them out of this neighborhood quickly while Brodie figured out whether his first postcoital visit with Anna should include Maggie Taylor. And crucially, this route would also keep them a good distance from the eavesdropping radius of the NSA's embassy surveillance station to the west.

As the driver navigated the midday Berlin traffic, Brodie's phone rang and he saw it was Mark Jenkins. He showed the screen to Taylor, put his finger to his lips, put it on speaker, and answered, "Brodie."

"Hey, Scott. It's Mark Jenkins."

"What's up?"

"Wanted to let you know that your and Taylor's replacements think you're God."

"They told me that. Anything else?"

Jenkins laughed, then got serious and said, "I'm driving back to Kaiserslautern. Before I left Berlin, I had a clerk in the Fifth MP pull up the translation of Colonel Brandt's initial interview, the one he gave while intoxicated before we arrived in Stuttgart, and there're a few interesting things there." He hesitated, then said, "You're off the case, but you and Taylor have to file a final report, so as a courtesy to you, I can forward this on to you. Or Taylor."

Taylor pointed to herself.

"You can forward it to her."

"Okay . . . I read this, and this guy, Brandt . . . I can pull over and read some of this to you."

"Thanks."

There was a pause. Then Jenkins continued: "Okay. Like I said, the interview was mostly a lot of rambling, but here's a quote . . . He said, 'We're everywhere. And we have important people . . . and an American officer who used to flush rats for the Stasi. But he's with us now.' "

Brodie glanced at Taylor, then said to Jenkins, "Okay. Sounds interesting. But apparently you didn't find it interesting at the time."

Jenkins replied, "Thinking back, I think Harry found some of Brandt's ravings more interesting than I did." He added, defensively, "It was mostly a lot of racist ranting, anti-Semitic, anti-Muslim shit. So this didn't exactly jump out at me as actionable intelligence."

"Right. Okay —"

Jenkins went on, "But Harry was a Cold War history buff, so I think he picked up on Brandt's saying that there was an American officer — presumably military — who worked for the Stasi, but who now worked for Brandt's neo-Nazi group. NordFaust."

"Right." Which would have sent Harry Vance to the Stasi Archives, and eventually to Anna Albrecht at her art gallery. And ultimately, that love affair sent Harry to his grave. "Well, thanks for revisiting this and calling. Send the transcript to Taylor."

Jenkins was silent. Then he said, "I wish Harry had told me what he was up to."

"Would your CO have sanctioned an investigation based on a vague, drunken claim from a German military officer who refused to repeat the claim when he was sober?"

"No."

"Harry must have thought the same. But he wanted to look into this supposed American military traitor, and he didn't want to make you complicit in his unsanctioned investigation."

There was a silence; then Jenkins said, "Right . . . Still, I'm sorry I missed it." He added, "Good work on finding this, Scott."

"Call me God."

"Arrogant asshole."

"Whatever works for you." Brodie added, "Don't be too hard on yourself. Pass this on to German Intel, and have them round up Brandt for further questioning."

"I already made that call."

"Good."

"Not so good. Brandt shot himself about a week ago."

The bodies kept piling up. "Assisted suicide?"

"The German authorities are not sharing that with me."

"Right. Okay, thanks again, Mark." He wanted to tell him to watch the schnapps, but he'd already told him, "Whatever works," and Brodie didn't want to contradict himself.

Jenkins said, "Sorry if I was a little shitty with you."

"You made me feel at home."

Jenkins managed a laugh, then said, "Good luck, Scott."

They hung up.

They rode in silence for a moment, then Taylor said, "Odin is working with or for Nord-Faust."

"That's a plausible conclusion."

"Do you think that this chance interrogation of Colonel Brandt, back in May of last year, is what got Vance started on his private investigation?"

"Probably. What we know for sure is that Harry Vance went to the Stasi Archives after the Brandt interrogation, where the chief archivist gave him the name of Anna Albrecht."

"Harry lied to Anna. I mean, he sought her out. He already knew who she was. Who her father was."

"Correct." He added, "He may have manipulated her, but he may also have loved her. People are complicated. Harry was no saint, but he must have believed that the end justified the means. Every cop believes that."

Taylor didn't respond and was perhaps feeling less generous toward a man who'd lied to his wife about an affair, and then lied to his lover about what drew him to her in the first place. After a moment she said, "Fucking men."

"Sexist comments on the job will not be tolerated."

"I'll sign myself up for sensitivity training when we get home."

The cabbie rolled through the slow-moving traffic as they crossed a bridge over the Spree River. The sky was a distinctive Berlin gray, and looked like it was considering more precipitation in the near future.

Taylor asked, "Where are we going?"

He still wasn't sure. Despite some new information, they didn't have a new direction. Brodie was waiting to hear back from David Katz of Hyperion Lab and Claudia Barese of the National Personnel Records Center, one or both of whom would hopefully provide something useful.

Brodie then remembered what Chilcott had said about the gruesome murder in Neukölln that morning, and he took out his phone and pulled up the news story. The victim was identified as an Iraqi immigrant named Hasan al-Kazimi, and the article featured a passport photo of the man.

It was Hasan, the young man who had followed Brodie after his visit to the Al Mahdi Islamic Center and had served as an informant for Rafeeq Nasir. He was also the one who had originally connected Nasir with Harry Vance, which had set Vance on his search for Colonel Tariq Qasim — a search that ended with Vance in Körnerpark on a cold winter night, hoping for answers but instead finding death.

Brodie turned his phone to Taylor. "The victim in Neukölln this morning was Hasan al-Kazimi."

She looked at the photo. "Oh . . . my God . . . That poor man. I can't believe it." She added, "And I can't understand it either."

Brodie thought about that. As far as the press was concerned, Hasan was a random

Arab victim of neo-Nazi terror. But Brodie and Taylor knew better.

But . . . *why?*

To silence him? That didn't make any sense. All that Hasan could do was connect Harry Vance to Rafeeq Nasir, and the police had already interviewed Nasir himself.

And then Brodie remembered something Vance had said all those years ago in his counterterrorism class: Terrorists are creators of spectacle, sometimes even to the detriment of their own tactical considerations, and that needed to be internalized by a successful counterterror agent. Never forget how much these sick assholes love a good show.

Clearly, the grisly murder and mutilation of Hasan was meant to terrorize the Muslim community. The swastika. The pig's blood. But . . . why *him?* Why kill one of Vance's only known contacts in Neukölln as he was investigating Odin?

And why Harry's eye?

That was another thing that had been nagging at Brodie. Taking a part of the victim and planting it as evidence at the bomb scene helped sell the ruse, but why not use a finger? Or an ear? If the entire point was to create a misdirect, why take an *eye,* the only thing that could symbolically tie the murder to Odin?

Well, Brodie knew the answer: It was another, hidden message, meant only for someone paying close attention. For someone who was on the right track.

We know that you know. And we don't care. Because you cannot stop us.

Which meant the audience for this message was now the only two people who were taking Harry Vance's investigation of Odin seriously and who had picked up where Harry left off: Scott Brodie and Maggie Taylor.

And that begged the question of whether these sick bastards would target someone else. Someone associated with the hunt for Odin. With Brodie and Taylor . . .

Brodie took out his phone and called Anna. Straight to voice mail. He checked the address on her voice message and said to the driver, "Zwei fünf Lindenstraße." He added, "Fast. Schnell."

The cabbie nodded and took the next turn.

Taylor asked, "Where are we going?"

"Anna Albrecht's art gallery."

"Why?"

He looked at her. "For nothing, I hope."

She looked into his eyes a moment, searching.

Brodie turned away and watched out the window as the cabbie drove. His heart was pounding, his mind racing, and for the first time since this investigation began, he hoped to God that he was wrong.

CHAPTER 45

Brodie and Taylor exited the cab on Linden-straße and approached a two-story building of white concrete and glass that was set back from the road.

They reached the building, which contained three storefronts. One was a travel agency that appeared closed, and another was vacant, its glass windows covered in brown paper.

In between them was number 25. A brushed-metal sign next to the door said: NEUE BERLINER KUNSTGALERIE. The street-facing window featured a large square painting on canvas depicting the smoldering ruins of a Middle Eastern city beneath a bright-blue sky. Dozens of children floated above the rubble holding on to bright red balloons. A sign on the window announced the title of the gallery show in German, Arabic, and then English: VOICES OF WAR. The metal front door was slightly ajar.

Brodie pushed on the door and stepped into a large, white-walled gallery with track lighting. Along the walls were several paintings, and most of them had been defaced. He drew his gun.

Taylor, behind him, said, "Oh my God . . . ," and drew her gun.

One painting, of a woman in a hijab looking up as the shadow of a jet fighter passed over her body, had been slashed. Another, of an Arab man holding a rifle in a field of flowers, was also slashed, and an abstract painting of children holding hands was covered with a spray-painted swastika.

They rounded a freestanding wall, where there was more defaced artwork, along with some German words spray-painted across the wall.

Toward the back of the room was a white door, half-open, and Brodie walked toward it. Taylor followed, scanning the spaces around them. Brodie pushed the door open with his foot, entered, and swept the small office.

Anna Albrecht lay on her back on the floor behind her desk. She had a large bullet wound in her chest, her white tank top red with blood, and a pool of blood around her.

Brodie stood there, frozen. He could hear Taylor's voice, but it sounded distant. He was staring at Anna's face. Her brown eyes were open. Vacant. The life drained out of them. Stolen out of them.

Taylor was on the phone now, and Brodie

slowly became aware of the surroundings. A red swastika was spray-painted on the wall above the desk, along with a German word written in large block letters that didn't need a translation:

HURE.

He felt Taylor's hand on his arm.

"Scott . . ."

He lowered his weapon and turned to her.

"I just called Whitmore. She is alerting Chief Inspector Schröder."

Brodie nodded but said nothing.

Taylor looked down at Anna's body. "Those . . . *fucking bastards.*"

Brodie shoved his pistol in his pocket and crouched next to Anna's body. He stared at her blank face, her pale skin, her lips turning purple. "I'm so sorry." He touched her face, then closed her eyelids and stood.

He turned to Taylor, who had watched him do that, and she looked like she wanted to say something, but didn't.

They walked out of the office into the main gallery space, and Brodie looked at the graffiti on the far wall: DER WOLF STEHT VOR DER TÜR.

Taylor ran the words through her phone translator, and said aloud, "The wolf is at the door."

He and Taylor stood in silence, looking at the graffiti and the desecrated artwork made by war refugees who thought they had finally

680

found a safe haven.

And Anna. A German woman who herself was haunted by the terrors of her past, just trying to bring a little light to a dark and war-torn world.

But now the war was no longer in a faraway land. The war was here.

The wolf is at the door.

Brodie felt a rage building inside of him. He needed to find who did this. And they needed to die.

Taylor said in a soft voice, "Scott . . ."

He turned to her.

She looked into his eyes, like she wanted to ask him something.

So he volunteered: "We spent last night together."

Taylor looked away. "Okay."

"It was . . . spontaneous."

She looked back at him. "You lied to me."

"I know. I'm sorry, Maggie."

Taylor nodded, though it wasn't clear if she was accepting the apology. She was probably questioning how much this had influenced Brodie's decision to stay in Berlin. And it was a good question.

He said, "We need to finish what Harry started. What Anna started. We need to find Odin."

"The German authorities will be conducting their raids on NordFaust —"

"Fuck the authorities. They're missing

something, and they've missed it for thirty years."

Taylor thought about that, though her mind was clearly still on the other subject. She looked toward the half-open door to Anna's office and said, "I understand now why you thought to come here."

Brodie didn't respond.

"We've been followed, Scott. This whole time. These bastards knew we spoke to Hasan, and they killed him. And Anna . . ." She hesitated, then looked at him and said, "Maybe they knew more about your activities last night than I did."

Brodie considered that, and it occurred to him that they were dealing with complete psychopaths. He said, "They are not worried about being caught. Not anymore. They put a lot of effort into throwing everyone off the trail with the Neukölln bombing. But it didn't work. And now something's changed."

Taylor looked around at the ruined artwork, at the screaming words across the walls and canvases, at the swastikas sprayed in thick red paint that dripped down the walls like bleeding gashes. She said, "Taking Harry's eye was a clue, but a relatively subtle one. It didn't make sense unless you understood *who* Harry was looking for."

"Right. There are murderers — like Odin — who see it as a game. They are arrogant and want to show that they are smarter than the law. So they leave a clue that has to be first identified as a clue, and then understood."

She nodded again. "Odin is telling us he's alive."

"And he's not living a quiet life in a retirement community. He is associated with a powerful group that has the resources to plan and execute the assassination of Harry Vance and the false flag bombing in Neukölln."

"And then," said Taylor, "they murdered Hasan, and they murdered Anna Albrecht. This is a new message, and it's not a subtle one. They know we are onto them, and they don't care."

Brodie looked at her. "An attack is coming. Soon. The cluster bombs."

Taylor considered that and shook her head. "The run-up to an attack would be the time to be the *most* cautious. NordFaust can't afford mistakes that might jeopardize their mission. You heard what Trent said. The authorities are actually accelerating their raids on NordFaust because of the murder of Hasan. And this . . ." She gestured around the gallery. "It's like they're shining a spotlight on themselves at the moment they can least afford to do so."

That was a good point. But maybe they were not dealing with a rational enemy. Or maybe there was something more that they were still not seeing.

As Brodie considered his next move, his phone rang. It was a German number. He picked up. "Brodie."

"Mr. Brodie. It's David Katz from Hyperion Lab. I had to really convince my colleagues to get priority for your sample, but I'm glad I did. This is some nasty stuff you brought me."

Brodie put the phone on speaker so Taylor could hear. "I'm listening."

Katz said, "This is an old strain of Yersinia pestis, first identified in 1979 in the Soviet Union after a lab leak from a secret biowarfare research facility in Siberia. Killed dozens of people and animals. This strain is not genetically modified, but a naturally occurring form of bubonic plague that happens to be particularly deadly. It was believed that the Russians were culturing it for potential deployment in a bioweapon. The only other documented incident of this specific strain was in 1996, when United Nations weapons inspectors found it, among other pathogens, in a biological weapons production facility in Iraq." He added, "The inspectors also discovered a mass grave of Iranian POWs, and a few of the corpses showed traces of this bacterium. The belief was that these prisoners were used by the Iraqis as human guinea pigs in experiments during the Iran-Iraq War."

This was beginning to fit. A plague strain first cultured in a Russian lab in the 1970s ends up in Iraq during the war with Iran in the 1980s. What was the link?

The East German biowarfare facility in Storkow. Stefan Richter. Colonel Tariq Qasim. Odin.

Brodie said, "This pathogen . . . could it have been part of East Germany's biowarfare program?"

Katz replied, "Could have been. The Soviets had a much larger and better-funded bio and chem warfare division than East Germany, and it would make sense that they'd share some of their research and maybe even specimens with their East German allies."

"Right."

Katz was silent a moment. "You know, this might be a long shot but . . . You said this sample is evidence in a homicide case?"

"Correct."

"There is a German genetic engineer named Reinhard Dorn, well-known in my circles. He used to work in biological and chemical weapons defense for East Germany before bringing his skills to the reunified country in the nineties. He's an expert on Yersinia pestis, and he also pioneered some of the earliest research into synthetic biology. He founded his own biotech firm here in Berlin maybe ten years ago. Titan Genetics. It's become a major firm. I'm sure he's a difficult man to get a sit-down with, but perhaps not for you and your colleagues, given that

685

this is a homicide investigation. And he might be able to give you a clearer background on this specimen."

"Titan Genetics. I'll look him up. Thank you for your help, Mr. Katz."

"Tyler McKinnon owes me a favor. Are you coming to retrieve the sample?"

"Someone will be in touch. Thanks again." He hung up.

Taylor looked at him. "Do we think Reinhard Dorn could have worked at Storkow?"

"We do."

"Would a man with that kind of background in biological warfare be welcome in the reunified German state?"

"We hired Nazi rocket scientists and all sorts of useful Nazis after World War II, so why wouldn't the new Germany bring in the old East German brain trust after the Cold War?" He added, "I think we need to talk to Reinhard Dorn."

"With what authority?"

"I don't know, Taylor, but we've been bullshitting our way through this investigation for days now."

"Talking to civilians, and a Lebanese mobster, and a librarian."

"Archivist."

"You're not getting an instant audience with the head of a large biotech firm just by flashing your badge, Scott."

"Watch me."

They heard sirens in the distance, and Brodie said, "We need to get out of here."

"We're the ones who called this in."

"And when Chief Inspector Schröder gets here, maybe he'll thank us, or maybe he'll detain us. Maybe both."

Taylor appeared conflicted.

"As your former senior partner, I need you to trust me on this."

She looked at him. "You get to use that exactly once."

They exited the gallery and ducked down a side street. This might not be a good lead, but you follow all leads — especially when you don't have a clue. What they did have was the name and place of work of an old geneticist who maybe worked at the Storkow facility thirty years ago. Odin had paid a visit to Storkow, according to the Stasi report. But only once, so what were the chances that Odin and Dorn had even crossed paths?

But why had Odin gone there in the first place? Because some of the intelligence he'd gotten from the Stasi moles was connected to that place — and to chemical or biological weapons. And then after Manfred Albrecht shared some Intel with Odin directly, one of Odin's first moves was to request East German citizenship. As if he had a feeling that something was going to drastically turn the tide of the Cold War.

Day X. Black Harvest.

HURE.

The image of that word flashed in his mind. And he saw Anna's body, lying there . . .

Brodie needed to find Odin. He pulled out his phone and dialed a number, then put it on speaker.

"Who are you calling?"

"I've got one last feeler out there."

Claudia Barese of the National Personnel Records Center picked up. "Hey, Scott."

"How's it coming?"

"It's coming. I need to comb through a few different databases, resolve any conflicting results, and then —"

"Have you gotten any hits for officers who might have been involved in unconventional weapons? Chemical, biological. Research or Intel or defense?"

"Yes. Hold on . . . I did pull up a guy who worked in the Army Chemical Corps, in their intelligence division. Colonel Charles Granger."

"He's alive?"

"According to my records. Born in August 1950."

"He was stationed in Berlin?"

"That's what you asked for. Berlin Brigade. Seventy-Sixth Chemical Detachment, 1981 to 1990. He retired in '94, but no duty station listed after 1990. But that's not uncommon for Intel guys."

"Last known address?"

"No address listed, but he fit your profile, so I searched his name, he's serving on the board of some biotech company in Berlin."

Brodie and Taylor exchanged a look. Brodie asked, "What is the name of the company?"

"Titan Genetics."

Holy shit.

Colonel Charles Granger of the United States Army Chemical Corps, Intelligence Division. Could he be Odin? Seemed like a good candidate. The kind of guy who would be tapped into the stream of Intel coming from assets within the Stasi, especially as it related to the Stasi and the East German Army's strategic posture, unconventional-weapons capabilities, and any planned enemy offensive operations — like Day X. Or Black Harvest.

Barese continued, "I have twelve other names so far that fit your profile, though no one else with a chem or bio background. I can e-mail everything over."

Brodie asked, "Are any of these other officers you've found living in Germany currently?"

"Not as far as I can tell. I'll keep looking, and I'll send what I have so far."

"Thank you, Claudia. This is a big help."

"Happy to hear."

Brodie hung up. He and Taylor stood in silence a moment.

Taylor said, "Colonel Charles Granger."

"It fits. He fits." He added, "Anna's father reached out to Odin directly, in March of 1989. The final months of the Cold War. Day X and Black Harvest were acts of desperation driven by hard-liners and crazies who saw their whole world coming apart, and Albrecht was desperate to warn someone."

Taylor thought about that. "According to the Stasi report, Manfred Albrecht had 'unique access' across divisions. Maybe he knew the fate of the last three guys who did what he was preparing to do. So he had to choose very carefully which American military officer he was going to approach. He needed someone high-ranking — an officer with an intelligence background who was specifically charged with collecting information about unconventional threats like Black Harvest. And that logic led Anna's father to Colonel Charles Granger — who was the wrong man to contact."

And then thirty years later, Harry Vance got too close to finding Odin, and paid the same price as Manfred Albrecht. As did Albrecht's daughter, Anna.

The Cold War had ended, but Odin's war had not. And now this man who had named himself after the god of battle and death was taking new victims, and Brodie was certain there were many more victims to come if he wasn't found. Soon.

CHAPTER 46

They rounded a corner and found themselves on a larger road. Brodie said, "Pull up the address for Titan Genetics."

Taylor looked on her phone. "It's about a ten-minute drive from here." After a moment she added, "Their website lists their board of directors and has a short bio on Granger." She read, " 'Charles Granger is a retired United States Army Colonel who served his country in West Berlin throughout the final decade of the Cold War. As an intelligence agent specializing in chemical, biological, and radiological defense, he played a critical role in maintaining the peaceful coexistence of a divided Germany. Following his years of military service, he utilized his broad technical and strategic knowledge as a consultant for the burgeoning biotech industry. Colonel Granger now contributes his considerable expertise as a senior director for Titan Genetics.' "

Brodie asked, "Is there a photo of Granger?"

Taylor shook her head.

"What does Titan Genetics actually do?"

"Let me see . . . Mostly research and development on genetically modified agriculture."

"Sounds pretty benign."

"Maybe it *is* benign." She pocketed her phone. "It sounds like Colonel Granger turned his specific expertise into a lucrative consulting career, as many retired military specialists do."

"Colonel Charles Granger is Odin."

"Maybe. But even if he is, his employer might have nothing to do with any of this. Maybe Colonel Granger has a cushy, overpaid position on their board because of his impressive biography. And in his off-hours, he's helping neo-Nazis plot against the German government."

"He's on the board of a company founded by a former East German military scientist, Reinhard Dorn, who worked with bubonic plague and God knows what else. And if Black Harvest was real, Reinhard Dorn could have been working on genetically engineered pathogens to destroy crops, and in his post-Communist life pivoted to making money off genetically engineered crops that resist pathogens. That makes sense. But it's also possible that Dorn and Granger are doing something on the side." He added, "They could have first gotten connected at Storkow."

Brodie hailed a cab and they climbed in. Taylor gave the cabbie the address for Titan Genetics, then said to Brodie, "I'll see if I can find any more info on Granger."

As the cab pulled out, Brodie checked his call log. He had four missed calls from Colonel Dombroski and one from General Kiernan, who had probably been asked by his old OCS classmate Stanley Dombroski to help corral his renegade CID agent. Scott Brodie was, in fact, in a world of shit. What else was new?

He saw he also had a text message from Dombroski: *Your resignation is not accepted. Call me.*

Apparently he was still in the Army. But at some point the colonel needed to cover his own ass, which meant not putting it on the line for an insubordinate warrant officer who had an uncomfortable relationship with the chain of command.

Well, the best way for Brodie to save his own ass and Taylor's ass and protect Dombroski's ass was to find Harry Vance's killer, who could be Charles Granger or someone Granger hired. And in the process Brodie needed to discover the identity of the traitor Odin, who was possibly also Charles Granger, and while Brodie was at it, he might be able to foil a neo-Nazi terrorist attack on

Berlin and possibly other German cities. That might all be more difficult than it sounded. Especially since he and Taylor had been taken off the case, and had no authority, power, or resources.

He recalled an old Army saying: "The difficult we do now, the impossible takes a little longer." The real problem here was that he didn't have much more time to do the impossible.

Taylor said, "I found something on Charles Granger, but it's not much. An *Army Times* article from May 1982, looks like a puff piece about commissioned officers who recently completed training at the U.S. Army Chemical Corps School at Fort McClellan." She read, " 'Among the graduates is Major Charles Granger of Greenwich, Connecticut, a Princeton graduate and Rhodes Scholar who told the *Times* he left his duty station at Camp Humphreys in South Korea in order to participate in the Army's recommitment to a robust chemical defense.' " She tapped out something else on her phone and said, "There is a hedge fund called Granger Capital based in Manhattan, founded by Sidney Granger of Greenwich in 1963 . . . Sidney has two children, Katherine and Charles." Taylor looked up. "That's quite a pedigree."

So, this guy had been born in one of the wealthiest towns in America, went to one of the country's top schools, then secured arguably the most prestigious scholarship in the world, joined the Army and became a commissioned officer, served in South Korea, then trained for the Chemical Corps and became an intelligence officer stationed in West Berlin through the final decade of the Cold War. That was the picture of a man who was born with a ton of advantages and leveraged them all into an extremely impressive career serving his country. In other words, Colonel Granger benefited from the system and had a hell of a lot to lose. Not the typical profile of a turncoat and traitor.

Then again, people surprise you, and you can't generalize whatever goes on in an individual's heart and mind. Brodie considered the timeline of Colonel Granger's military career and how that dovetailed with the Stasi report on Odin. Granger completed Chemical Corps training in May of 1982, and Odin was offering his services to the Stasi by March of 1983. Had Granger decided to aid the Stasi somewhere in that ten-month timeframe? Or was Charles Granger planning on treason long before he arrived in Germany?

Maybe something had embittered Colonel Granger, the kind of thing that wouldn't show up in an official bio or news article. Or maybe the guy had read too much Marxist theory at Princeton.

There was also the matter of money. Odin

made a point of not asking for money when he began his cooperation with the Stasi. That fit the profile of Charles Granger, who came from money and didn't need more of it. But then in July 1989, in exchange for turning over Manfred Albrecht, Odin demanded four million deutsche marks. Maybe Granger had been cut off from the family fortune in those intervening years, or had simply become disillusioned with the Communist cause and figured he might as well do a cynical cash grab before the whole East German system came crashing down.

Or maybe Charles Granger was not Odin after all. Maybe he was a patriot who'd stood at the front lines of a global conflict and helped defend the West against the threat of unconventional warfare. And the fact that he now consulted for a firm run by Reinhard Dorn, a man who used to be his Cold War rival, was simply an interesting footnote. Or maybe they had this completely backward, and Reinhard Dorn had been a mole for the Americans and West Germans and had fed intelligence to Colonel Granger, which was how the men knew each other and came to work together in later years.

Taylor asked, "What are you thinking?"

"That maybe we're hurtling toward the wrong conclusions."

"Funny. I was just thinking the opposite."

"Tell me."

She thought a moment. "What kind of man would betray his country to help the Communists, to the point that he risks his freedom and his life, and gets four pro-Western assets within the Stasi executed, and then, decades later, allies himself with NordFaust, arguably the most dangerous neo-Nazi organization in Europe?"

"Someone who's confused."

Taylor shook her head. "An active, intelligent mind searching for meaning. Someone who dislikes the world as it is and is trying to reshape it. Charles Granger did not have to climb his way to the top. He was born there. He feels secure, so secure that maybe he starts to question the foundations he's standing on. This is a man who wants to be in the center of things, a hand on the lever, working to shape the world. We don't know what he did between the end of the Cold War and working for Titan Genetics, but imagine he was in the wilderness. No direction. Looking for a new cause. It's not a coincidence that the center of right-wing white nationalism in this country is in the former Communist East Germany. Part of that's from a lagging economy and the resentment of immigrants. But there's something else. The idea of a lost cause. Like parts of the American South. You can't have the thing you were fighting for, but you also can't accept what's taken its place — liberal democracy, globalization, im-

697

migration. The whole modern world."

Brodie added, "So you reach further back in history. For another lost cause."

Taylor nodded. "And that cause, fascism, has unfortunately got a lot of gas in the tank these days. If you're a committed white nationalist, modern Germany offers you plenty of opportunity for grievance."

Brodie thought about that. It was an interesting psychological profile, and sort of made sense. Except, of course, that Brodie had every reason to want to believe that his partner was onto something, and that they'd found their man, and that they were possibly minutes away from confronting an American traitor who had evaded justice for thirty years.

Taylor looked again at her phone and said, "Here's something else. An obituary in the *Frederick News-Post* from December 1990 for a Rebecca Granger, aged thirty-seven years old, of Frederick, Maryland. She, quote, 'ended her life after a long battle with depression.' It mentions her loving husband, United States Army Colonel Charles Granger."

Brodie considered that, and tried to graft the little they knew about Odin's activities onto the even less they knew about the life of Colonel Granger. He said to Taylor, "Odin sought East German residence for himself and another person — probably his wife — around March of 1989. Odin had learned something that convinced him of an East German victory in the Cold War."

"Like the details of Black Harvest. And a planned invasion of West Berlin and West Germany. Day X."

"Right," said Brodie. "And he wanted to get himself and his wife out of West Germany before the bio attack and the invasion. But then, a few months later, he started to understand the folly of that assumption, and that perhaps his entire military career — along with his work as a double agent for the Stasi — might be ending soon due to the imminent collapse of Communist East Germany. So he demands money from the East Germans instead of sanctuary. And he probably intends to head back to the States. And then the Wall comes down and Germany is unified under a Western, capitalist government. Then what? He's lost. Rudderless. And maybe his marriage suffers because of this, and for some reason that we'll never know, his wife kills herself."

Taylor pondered that. "In the span of a year he lost his ideological purpose, his military career — or at least, the version of it that made him a valued and important intelligence officer in West Berlin — and then his wife."

Brodie nodded. That might screw anyone up. That might make you question everything. And on a long enough timeline, it might even draw you into the arms of right-wing crazies who, like you, do not like the world as it is, or what it is becoming.

Brodie looked out the window as they drove past a massive foundation pit dotted with construction equipment, and a large sign heralding the future site of some large commercial development project.

It felt, in a way, like this city was making up for lost time. Rushing toward the future. But not everyone liked the direction it was headed, and how fast it was headed there. And some of those people had access to weapons, and military training, and — perhaps — deadly biological agents.

Brodie pulled up the Titan Genetics website. He flicked through some promo images showing state-of-the-art labs and attractive scientists holding test tubes, operating equipment, and staring deeply into oranges, tomatoes, and other Frankenfoods that the company must have conjured through genetic wizardry. As far as biotech companies went, Titan Genetics appeared mundane, and also good for humanity. But appearances can be deceptive.

Brodie reminded himself that Harry Vance had discovered the Storkow connection and had sought out Stefan Richter, a man involved in the development of bioweapons, including plague. If Harry had missed his appointment with death in Körnerpark, he

700

might have traced that connection to Reinhard Dorn and Titan Genetics. Vance had been on the right path. Scott Brodie was also on the right path, but that path too could eventually lead to his untimely demise, though someplace a little farther along than Harry Vance had gotten. The trick now was to avoid a fatal mistake.

And in addition to NordFaust trying to kill him, Trent Chilcott of the Central Intelligence Agency was undoubtedly looking to exact his own revenge.

And on the subject of revenge, Anna Albrecht's death had to be avenged, along with the death of her lover, Harry Vance. There is justice, then there is rough justice. There is the law, and there is revenge. And when the crime becomes personal, revenge is the law.

CHAPTER 47

The cab stopped and Brodie turned over his last twenty-euro note to the driver, then he and Taylor got out.

They were standing on a wide boulevard on the north end of the neighborhood of Mitte, and the surrounding buildings all appeared to be newly developed. Across the street was the Titan Genetics headquarters, a soaring modernist high-rise of glass and steel with bizarre angles that gave the impression of an architect trying too hard. Large white text affixed to the building's façade featured the name of the company along with its logo — a flower whose stem was a DNA double helix.

The headquarters was set back about forty feet from the road, and in front was a stone plaza with some benches and tables, along with bare landscaped trees and bushes. There was no guard booth or other security visible on the outside of the building.

A voice said, "Good afternoon, Detectives."

Brodie and Taylor turned to where a man in a long black topcoat was approaching on foot. It was David Kim. He stopped about ten feet from them.

Brodie asked, "Are you lost, David?"

"I spoke with Sharon Whitmore. She told me about Anna Albrecht. Terrible."

Brodie spotted an idling Mercedes farther down the road. Ulrich was behind the wheel, watching them. The answer to how Agent Kim knew they were going to be here was that Anna's art gallery in Kreuzberg was probably just within the one-mile radius of the embassy's rooftop SCS listening station. So, Howard Fensterman and his colleagues had heard Brodie's call with David Katz of Hyperion Lab and Brodie's call to Claudia Barese of the National Personnel Records Center. Which meant his embassy pals knew a lot. But not everything.

David Kim said, "Let me give you a ride."

Brodie looked at the man. "Where to?"

"The embassy."

"No thanks."

"Then how about the headquarters of the Bundespolizei? Or the Bundeskriminalamt? Or we can take a long drive to Wiesbaden, where I know there are a few high-ranking officers at the U.S. Army Garrison who are interested in speaking with you."

"Is the FBI running errands for the Army now?"

"Everyone thinks we've bonded. So they sent me." He added, sincerely, "I do not want to be in this position."

Taylor said, "Yet here you are. Doing the wrong thing for the wrong reasons."

Kim looked up at the Titan Genetics building. "Whatever you think you're doing here, it is outside the mandate and jurisdiction of Army CID. Which is sort of beside the point since you're both off this case." Kim looked between his two erstwhile colleagues and added, "I am armed, though I'm sure I won't need to resort to that. I should also inform you that members of the BKA are staged nearby. They are more heavily armed than me, and less patient and understanding."

Brodie moved toward him. "I'm also armed, and pissed off, and not at all patient. So why don't you get the fuck out of here?"

Kim parted his jacket, revealing a pancake holster on his belt and the butt of an automatic pistol. "If I recall, you were bitching about not being issued a gun."

"I solved that problem." He pulled Chilcott's Glock half out of his coat pocket, and Kim stared at it.

Taylor said, "Look what I have."

Kim looked at her and saw the butt of the Makarov in her coat pocket.

Taylor said, "We are not going with you." She added, "You're being used, David."

"Don't insult me."

"Are you aware of the discrepancies in the fragments of the IED recovered at the blast site in Neukölln?"

He hesitated. "I am, but —"

"Are you also aware that one of the three Syrian supposed Islamic terrorists who died in the blast was a practicing Christian, and that none of the three men have any known extremist ties?"

Kim did not respond.

Taylor continued, "And I'm sure you're aware that the German authorities are executing raids within hours on a right-wing extremist group called NordFaust that our own intelligence agencies suspect might have been involved in the Vance homicide."

Kim looked uncomfortable. "Where did you get this information?"

"From our own inquiries and sources."

Kim did not respond.

Taylor continued, "This whole investigation has been a clusterfuck, and that presser this morning was extremely premature. You're a smart man, Agent Kim, but you got played on this one. We all did."

"No. I did my job."

Brodie said, "And your job was to put gold plating on a pile of bullshit. Well done."

"Fuck you, Scott."

Taylor's job always seemed to be keeping Brodie from making a bad situation worse. She asked Kim, in a soft voice, "Do you know why we are here, David?"

Kim looked at her. "You think a retired American army colonel, Charles Granger, who is on the board of this firm, is the Stasi spy Odin."

"Do you think we're right?"

"I don't know, but I know you have both crossed the line." He added, "This needs to be handled by the embassy and the Bundeskriminalamt." He nodded toward Ulrich in the idling Mercedes. "Last chance to come with me before I call the angry Germans with the assault rifles and arrest powers."

Brodie said, "This is your last chance to show some balls and either leave or come with us."

Kim did not reply.

Taylor said, "Scott and I have been tailed by members of this group NordFaust, and they attempted to detain and maybe kill Scott. They staged the bombing in Neukölln. They killed and mutilated a man there this morning, the same man who provided information to Harry Vance that led to his going to Körnerpark on the night of his murder. They also murdered Anna Albrecht. And they have gotten their hands on a dozen mortar-fired cluster bombs that they plan to use in this city in the very near future."

Kim did not respond, but he appeared taken aback.

Brodie said, "You are a counterterrorism agent, David, and we are telling you there is an imminent attack coming. The Germans are aware of this and are acting on it, but they are missing a big piece of the picture." He pointed to the Titan Genetics building. "An American traitor who has eluded justice for thirty years might be in this building. Or at least there might be a clue here to his whereabouts. Come with us and see if we're right. And then we'll go with you to the embassy, or a German jail, or wherever."

Kim hesitated, then said, "You really think you've found him?"

"That's why we're here."

Kim looked up at the Titan Genetics building. He actually seemed to be considering Brodie's invitation to do something crazy, and Brodie gave the guy credit for that. David Kim was a counterterrorism specialist brought in to assist on a homicide investigation that had now officially named the perps, who were Islamic terrorists. It was all bullshit, of course, but David Kim's career — not to mention his worldview — depended on him believing it.

After a few more moments of contemplation, Kim said, "You've earned about fifteen minutes of my time before I bring you in. Let's go." He signaled to Ulrich to stand by, and crossed the street with Brodie and Taylor.

The three of them entered the plaza in front of the Titan Genetics building. A few people wearing Titan ID badges sat at umbrella tables with heat lamps eating lunch. The Germans were weird. Brodie looked at the entrance, where a row of revolving glass doors led to a soaring atrium. Near the doors was a security camera pointed at the plaza. Through the glass frontage Brodie spotted a large reception desk in the lobby and a row of security turnstiles. He didn't see anything that looked like a metal detector or other security screening.

In addition to the security setup there were several pieces of modern sculpture and a few trees in large planters. The place appeared pretty high-end. Apparently there was good money in building a better banana, or whatever they did here.

They stopped near the revolving doors and Taylor asked, "Okay, what is the plan?"

Brodie replied, "We'll play it by ear."

"At least hum the tune."

Brodie said, "We ID ourselves and ask — or demand — to see Charles Granger on a matter of official business and extreme urgency."

Kim said, "Let's say that works. Now we're in Charles Granger's office. What do we want to say to him?"

"You're under arrest, asshole, on suspicion of espionage, treason, murder, and imperson-

708

ating a pagan god."

FBI Agent David Kim said, "Not sure about the last. Also, not sure I have arrest powers. I can call the Bundes —"

"We take him. And drag his ass to the embassy. I want him to face American justice."

"Okay, but —"

Brodie assured him, "If you do the wrong thing for the right reasons, and do it with enough speed and confidence, you can usually get away with it for just long enough to make it work."

Kim had no reply, but Taylor said to him, "When you work with Scott, you learn a lot."

FBI Special Agent Kim looked at them both as though he realized he'd fallen in with a bad crowd and wanted out.

Taylor continued, "If Ulrich remains on standby, from here we can be inside the embassy in less than fifteen minutes."

Brodie added, "If Granger isn't here, or they claim he isn't, we ask for Reinhard Dorn."

Kim said, "I doubt if Herr Dorn will see us, but if he does, what are we going to say to him?"

Brodie replied, "Depends on what he says to us." He added, "Reinhard Dorn is a person of interest."

Kim nodded. "Okay . . . but he's a German citizen, and we can't arrest him."

Brodie agreed, "We can't. But we can abduct him."

"I hope you're joking."

"Of course."

Kim turned to Taylor. "Your partner's brain-damaged, but there's still hope for you. Why are you doing this?"

She looked back at him stone-faced. "Because we've been deceived. Because good people are dead who have not been avenged. Because there is something very bad on the horizon, and we can't quite see it, and if we go a little farther out maybe we will."

Kim thought about that, then nodded. "You guys are out of your goddamn minds, but you commit."

Brodie asked, "Ready?"

Taylor and Kim nodded, and they pushed through the revolving doors of Titan Genetics.

CHAPTER 48

Brodie, Taylor, and Kim entered the lobby and walked toward the reception desk, where three individuals in dark-blue uniforms sat near phones, computers, and security monitors.

Brodie approached the youngest-looking security guard, an overweight man in his mid-twenties whose nametag identified him as "Vogel," and flashed his badge. Taylor and Kim did the same.

Brodie said, "I am Chief Warrant Officer Scott Brodie of the U.S. Army Criminal Investigation Division, here with Chief Warrant Officer Magnolia Taylor and Special Agent David Kim of the FBI. We are investigating the homicide of U.S. Army CID Special Agent Harry Vance, and we are here to see a member of the Titan Genetics Board of Directors, Charles Granger."

Herr Vogel looked overwhelmed by that mouthful. He thought a moment, then uttered the most dreaded words in Germany:

"Do you have an appointment?"

"No," replied Brodie. "We do not make appointments. We make visits." He added, "This is an urgent matter."

Vogel nodded. "One moment." He picked up his phone and dialed someone. He had a brief conversation in German, then set the phone down. "Can I see your identifications please?"

All three passed their cred cases to Vogel, who read the names to whoever was on the other end of the line. Then he waited in silence with the phone to his ear.

Brodie noticed that the other two security guards, a woman in her thirties and a man in his fifties, were watching their colleague. The older man, whose badge identified him as "Weber," asked them, "Why are you not accompanied by German law enforcement?"

Kim replied, "The FBI is the chief American law enforcement liaison to the Bundeskriminalamt. Our agents regularly conduct interviews and other inquiries without the accompaniment of German law enforcement, particularly when gathering information from cooperative individuals who are neither suspects nor persons of interest in our investigations."

Was that bullshit? Probably. But it sounded good.

Herr Weber did not seem completely satisfied with that answer but seemed disinclined to press it further.

Vogel finished his phone conversation, hung up, and said, "Mr. Granger is not in his office today. However, one of the executive assistants is coming down to speak with you." He gestured to a seating area. "Please sit."

Brodie said, "We would also like to speak with Dr. Reinhard Dorn."

"You may relay this request to the individual from the executive office." Vogel gestured again to the armchairs.

They walked over and sat on leather armchairs beneath a flowering cherry blossom tree, which was apparently genetically engineered to thrive in the German winter. Or it was made of plastic.

Brodie said, "They may be lying about Granger not being in. We will insist that the executive assistant take us to his office. Also, we will insist on seeing Dorn."

Kim said, "We're not getting past this lobby."

"Visualize success, David."

"They're going to call whoever they know at the BKA, and then they will call bullshit on us. In fact" — he pointed to the front entrance — "there's a better chance of armed federal agents coming through that door than anyone from Dorn's office coming down to see us."

"We are going up to the executive suites. One way or the other."

Taylor agreed, "I've never been given the boot by an executive assistant."

Kim had no response but was probably thinking that the Army CID was more Army than CID.

Brodie focused on a large flat-screen TV hanging in the lobby, which was showing a PR video about Titan Genetics. A montage of various microorganisms under high magnification was intercut with lab technicians at work, and the English closed captioning read: *"Titan Genetics is an industry-leading pioneer in the CRISPR-Cas9 gene editing protocol. With this groundbreaking technology, individual segments of the genome can be altered, augmented, or excised with unprecedented precision and scalability. The applications for this technology are as infinite as the human imagination, and have allowed Titan Genetics to produce safe, affordable, and resilient agricultural products to serve our growing and interconnected world."*

The video continued, talking about fighting world hunger with disease-resistant crops, and lauding the environmental sustainability of their methods.

Brodie tried not to be too judgmental of things he didn't understand — and he definitely didn't understand this shit — but he'd be lying if he said it didn't give him the creeps. He'd seen enough of what his fellow human beings were capable of to feel uneasy about them holding the keys to Creation.

David Kim, who was also watching the video and must have been thinking along the same lines, said, "This technology feels both inevitable and terrifying."

"Nothing is inevitable," said Brodie. "It just feels that way after we all let it happen."

Kim shook his head. "The only thing that stops human progress is human catastrophe." He gestured to the TV. "So, it's either this creepy shit, or blight, famine, and another dark age."

Well, that was a bummer. Brodie thought back to the bizarre machine he had observed at Hyperion Lab, and the kind of power it represented. Almost a century ago scientists split the atom, and it changed the world, with mixed results. Now they were splitting and rebuilding genes. He had a feeling the effects of that would be at least as profound.

Brodie's thoughts were interrupted as a fifty-something blond woman in a tan business suit approached them. She smiled and said, "Hello. I am Ida Zimmermann, executive assistant to Dr. Reinhard Dorn. I was told you wished to speak with one of our board members."

Frau Zimmermann was well put-together and had icy blue eyes and a kind of husky voice. Brodie, Taylor, and Kim stood, and Brodie said to her, "Thank you for coming down. We were hoping to speak with our compatriot Charles Granger about a case we are investigating."

Zimmermann nodded. "Unfortunately, he is not in the building. Our board members rarely are when there is not official business."

"In that case, we would like to speak with your boss, Dr. Dorn."

She nodded again. "Security has already informed me. The doctor is a busy man, but he has agreed to make time for law enforcement. We know about the tragic death of your countryman, and you have our sympathies." She gestured for them to follow her. "Please."

The three of them exchanged glances, as if to say, "Well, that was easy." They followed Frau Zimmermann toward the security turnstiles. She stopped before reaching them and handed each of them a gray wristband that appeared to be made of rubber or silicone. "Please put these on. They are your security passes."

Brodie looked at it. It was featureless except for an embossed Titan Genetics logo. "I had one of these at Disney World."

Frau Zimmermann said, "This is our mandatory security protocol within the building. Please make sure you wear it with the logo on the top of your wrist. The radio frequency chips can be temperamental." She held up her right wrist to show that she was also wearing a band, though hers was orange. "Your band has been temporarily coded with your ID. Every area of the building is equipped with sensors that allow for employees and visitors to access authorized areas."

Kim said, "And also track everyone's location at every moment."

Zimmermann gave a tight smile. "This campus contains valuable information and products that represent billions of euros in investment and decades of research and development. We would be remiss not to employ the best security system that technology offers."

Brodie was sure the Stasi would have issued one of these things to every citizen of East Germany. He slipped the band on, and Kim and Taylor did the same.

They followed Zimmermann through the security turnstiles, which opened automatically when they were a few feet away, then walked to a bank of elevators. They entered an elevator and Zimmermann pressed the top button. She checked her watch. "The doctor has a meeting in twenty minutes, I trust that will be enough time?"

Brodie said, "We have only a few questions for him." Such as: Did you develop weaponized plague for East Germany? And is an American double agent for the Stasi on your board of directors?

The elevator stopped at the top floor, the executive suites, and opened into a wide, brightly lit hallway. Zimmermann led them to the left and they turned into another hallway. Brodie noticed name placards next to the doors, though none that said Charles Granger.

They came to a set of double doors at the end of the hall, with no name placard. Zimmermann cracked a door and stuck her head in, said something in German, then swung both doors open for them and gestured them in.

They entered a large office that was sparsely appointed with modern furniture and artwork. The far wall featured floor-to-ceiling windows offering a panoramic view of Berlin, and in front of the windows was a wide glass desk covered with papers. Behind the desk stood a tall man wearing a dark suit. He said in a thick, harsh accent, "Thank you, Ida. You may go."

Zimmermann left and closed the doors behind her.

Dr. Reinhard Dorn looked at the three Americans. He appeared to be in his early seventies, with thinning gray hair, shiny skin, and a nose too small for his face. Maybe a genetic engineering experiment gone wrong. He also wore heavy black-framed glasses with thick lenses that magnified his gray eyes.

Brodie thought of Anna's description of the old Stasi men she would encounter in the bars. *They had a bad, retro look about them.*

Brodie said, "Dr. Dorn, my name is Scott Brodie, United States Army Criminal Investigation Division, and these are my colleagues, CID Special Agent Maggie Taylor and FBI Special Agent David Kim. We are in the process of concluding our homicide investigation into the murder of American CID Agent Harry Vance."

Dorn nodded, then gestured to three leather chairs across from his desk. "Sit. Please."

They all sat, and Dorn took a seat behind his desk. He moved aside some papers in front of him. "I heard on the news that you have identified the perpetrators. Congratulations."

Brodie said, "There are still a few loose ends."

Dorn did not respond.

"We see that Colonel Charles Granger is a member of your board of directors."

Dorn said, "Yes. He was a founding member."

Taylor asked, "Did you have a relationship with him before you founded this company?"

Dorn nodded. "Our relationship goes back many years." He added, "I was told you asked to speak with him first, before asking for me. What interest do you have in the colonel?"

Brodie looked him in the eyes. "In the months preceding his murder, Harry Vance was seeking the identity of an American traitor, a U.S. military officer who worked as an intelligence asset for the Stasi in the eighties. We have reason to believe that Colonel Granger might have information pertinent to the identity of this double agent."

Dorn's gray eyes blinked behind his oversize lenses. Then he said, "As I'm sure you know, the colonel himself was an intelligence officer, and served in Berlin at that time."

Kim asked, "Where is Colonel Granger now?"

"I really can't say."

"Meaning you don't know?"

Dorn did not respond.

Brodie said, "We understand that you worked with the Stasi around that same time."

Dorn adjusted his thick glasses. "I worked for the National People's Army."

"That's right," said Brodie. "At the facility in Storkow, correct?"

Dorn stared at him, expressionless. "For some of the time, yes."

Taylor asked, "Did you develop biological weapons at Storkow?"

Dorn hesitated, then replied, "Yes. As did the Soviets. As did your government. The existence of these programs is part of the historical record."

Taylor asked, "Was Stefan Richter a colleague of yours in this endeavor?"

Dorn looked at her and asked, "Where did you hear this name?"

"I read an interview with him in an old journal," replied Taylor. "He discussed Operation Black Harvest."

Dorn nodded. "I know this interview."

Brodie asked, "And do you know the man?"

"Not well."

Taylor asked, "Did you work alongside Stefan Richter at the Storkow facility?"

"You seem fixated on this particular place and this particular Stasi agent. Why?"

Taylor replied, "It is pertinent to our investigation."

Dorn paused, then said, "Herr Richter was present at the Storkow facility at the same time I was, though our interactions were very limited. I was a military scientist. He was a Stasi officer primarily concerned with the applications of our research."

Taylor asked, "Was Operation Black Harvest one of those applications?"

"It was."

"And Day X?" she pressed.

"That was a conventional military operation. Out of my area of responsibility. Our work with Black Harvest was designed to augment the conventional capabilities of the army. What the military calls a 'force multiplier.' "

"Were these plans hypothetical, or close to being operational and realized?"

Dorn thought a moment, then said, "We thought many things were real that turned

721

out to be illusions. Including our own strength and longevity."

The doctor said this last bit as if part of him still mourned his former East Germany. More surprisingly, the man had just verified the existence of Operation Black Harvest, heretofore just a rumor. That was breaking news to an interested journalist or historian, though maybe not relevant to their homicide case. Although Harry Vance had believed it was material to finding Odin. Time to brings things back to the present. Brodie asked, "Does Titan Genetics currently work with plague?"

Dorn did not respond. For a moment he seemed to be lost in thought, then eyed a bowl of apples on his desk. He picked one up and turned it in his hand. "These are wild apples from Kazakhstan. This variety is a direct descendant of the very first apples ever to grow on earth. They are dying from rising temperatures, deforestation. We are trying to save them. To modify their genetic code to make them thrive in a warming world, and to foster genetic diversity that is being decimated by a loss of habitat due to our species' rampant spread and ravenous consumption of resources." He set the apple down and looked at Brodie. "We humans are the pestilence, and yet we are also the cure. And the same might be said of some pathogens. Their destructive power might be harnessed to our benefit. So, yes, we do some experimental work. Anthrax. Ebola." He paused. "And plague."

Kim asked, "What possible benefit could those pathogens provide?"

Dorn looked at him. "Where are you from?"

"Los Angeles."

Dorn smiled. "I mean, originally. Your ancestry."

Kim looked like he'd had to entertain this question his whole life and was tired of it. "I was born in South Korea."

Dorn nodded. "So, you know of divided nations."

"I know I was lucky to be born on the right side of the dividing line. But we're getting off-topic. What kind of — ?"

Dorn interrupted. "I was in Beijing once. Impressive in some ways, but . . . dead, spiritually."

Kim looked annoyed. "Beijing is in *China,* Doctor, as I am sure you know."

Dorn smiled. "Yes."

Brodie couldn't read whether Reinhard Dorn was screwing with Agent Kim, or was just an out-of-touch old fart who didn't fully grasp the racist implications of what he was saying.

Brodie tried to refocus the conversation: "We believe that the American officer whom Mr. Vance was seeking had paid a visit to the Storkow research facility in 1988. It would have been at the same time as a visiting delegation of Iraqi Ba'athist military officials. Do you have any knowledge of this American's visit?"

Dorn looked at him. "Yes."

Brodie and Taylor shared a look. Brodie followed up: "Do you know the identity of this individual?"

"Yes. United States Army Colonel Charles Granger. Code name Odin. A highly effective asset, a brilliant strategic thinker, and a man who, like myself, dreams of a better world."

Brodie stood, as did Taylor and Kim.

Brodie said, "Dr. Dorn, we are taking you into custody. Stand up."

Reinhard Dorn looked at the three Americans and did not react. He thought a moment, then said, "For what it's worth, I did not advocate killing Mr. Vance. I thought it would bring unneeded attention, and that the man's chances of actually finding Charles were slim. But the colonel did not want to take any risks." He looked at his visitors. "It appears I was correct."

Brodie was trying to process all this. Why was this guy giving himself up? He said to Taylor, "Call the embassy. Get the legat on the line and tell her where we are, and that Reinhard Dorn has just confessed to being an accessory to the murder of Harry Vance."

"And Anna Albrecht," offered Dorn.

Brodie pulled his pistol and pointed it at

724

the doctor's head. "You piece of shit."

Kim said, "Brodie. *Stop.*"

Brodie gripped the gun as he stared into Dorn's eyes. He said to Kim, "I'll note your objections in the after-action report."

Taylor said, "*Scott.* Calm down." Then to Dorn: "Stand! Hands on your head."

Dorn remained seated, gazing down the barrel of the pistol. "You must understand, Mr. Brodie. We couldn't have Ms. Albrecht go seduce yet another American hero to avenge her fucking traitor of a father."

Brodie stared at the man, and suddenly saw him differently. His face without expression, his blank gray eyes like an ocean choked of light, the ridiculous glasses, severe and heavy, dragged from another era. Another world. This guy was a veteran of a lost war, but he hadn't surrendered. He'd just joined another army. NordFaust. Just like Colonel Charles Granger. The only open question was, what were these bastards up to now? Dorn was baiting him, and he was doing it because he'd rather make Brodie blow his brains out than answer that question.

Brodie lowered the pistol and asked Taylor, "Where are we with that phone call?"

"I can't get reception."

Reinhard Dorn kept his eyes locked on Brodie. "That's a problem in this building. When we want it to be."

Brodie looked at Dorn and an uneasy feeling came over him. "Stand up. *Now.*"

Dorn stood and calmly folded his hands in front of him. "What do you think is going to happen now?"

"We are going to perp-walk your ass out of this building."

Kim went to the office doors and opened them. "Let's go, Doctor."

Taylor took a step toward Dorn to pat him down, then stumbled and caught herself on the armchair.

Dorn checked his watch, then glanced at Taylor. "You weigh the least. So you're already feeling it."

Brodie looked at Taylor, who struggled to stay upright. "You okay?"

"I don't . . ." Taylor grasped the arm of the chair to steady herself.

Dorn said, "Have a seat, Ms. Taylor. I don't want you falling on the floor."

Brodie raised his pistol again. "What have you done to her!?"

Dorn looked into his eyes. "The same as I've done to you. On the underside of your wristbands is a dermal patch covered in hundreds of microscopic needles, presently delivering a powerful and fast-acting anesthetic into your bloodstream." He added, "Proprietary technology."

Brodie heard a thud behind him and looked over his shoulder to see Kim on the floor, struggling to get back on his feet. Taylor slumped into the armchair. She said, "Scott . . ." She tried to keep her eyes open.

Brodie could feel it now. A kind of heaviness taking hold . . . He looked at Dorn, who had gone blurry.

Dorn glared at him and said, "The Wall fell, and the world cheered. And then the world forgot. But we did not rejoice, and we did not forget. We toiled. And soon everyone will see the fruits of our labor."

Brodie looked at the blurry gray panorama of Berlin out the window behind the doctor. The sun was almost down, and he could see the illuminated Alexanderplatz TV Tower in the distance.

He tried to refocus. "Let's . . . go."

Dorn shook his head. "I don't think so."

Brodie was losing his balance and gripped the desk. His gun slipped from his hand and clattered off the glass desk onto the floor. Brodie heard people approach from behind him, and someone shut the office doors. A female voice said something in German. Dorn replied to Frau Zimmermann, and they shared a laugh.

Brodie fell to the floor. He watched Dorn round his desk, and the man's shiny black dress shoes stopped in front of him and kicked the pistol away.

Brodie looked up at Reinhard Dorn, who peered back at him and said, "The wolf is at the door."

CHAPTER 49

Scott Brodie opened his eyes and stared up at the moon and the gray sky. But it wasn't the moon, and it wasn't the sky. It was a round lighting fixture mounted on a high concrete ceiling.

He became aware that he was lying on his back, on a hard, cold surface. He took a deep breath to clear his head, then slowly sat up.

Against the opposite wall he saw a man lying on his side, and it took him a few seconds to recognize David Kim, who was wearing only his pants, undershirt, and socks. Brodie realized that he too had been stripped down to the same clothing. Brodie checked his pockets for his cred case and wallet, but they were gone. So was his phone.

Taylor.

He became suddenly alert and looked around the small room. Behind him, lying on the floor, was Maggie Taylor, dressed in the same jeans and black pullover that she'd worn for her flight home. Which, he realized, she might never make.

He tried to stand, but he felt wobbly, so he slid along the floor to her and put his ear to her chest. Her breathing was shallow but steady, and he could feel her heart beating regularly. Her pulse was good, and her skin felt cool, but not clammy. He saw that her wristband was gone, as was his. He patted her cheek. "Maggie . . ."

Her eyes fluttered but didn't stay open. He noticed there was a butterfly needle taped to her right arm.

Brodie slid to the wall nearby and propped his back against the concrete. He noticed now that he also had a butterfly needle taped between his right forearm and biceps. "What the hell . . . ?" He ripped out the needle and a line of blood ran down his arm. Instinctively he knew this was the least of his problems.

He looked around the dimly lit space. It was a windowless room, all concrete, measuring about twenty feet on each side, and he had the sense that the room was underground. In fact, it was a bunker.

The walls were spotted with a black stain that was probably mold. To his left was a rusted metal door with a latch handle that would open it, except he was certain that the door was locked from the other side.

Brodie had no idea how long they'd been there, but he had the feeling that it had been a few hours since he and his posse had been arresting Chief Executive Officer Herr Doktor Reinhard Dorn in his own office. That had gone sideways real quick.

Looking back on all that, maybe he'd acted too impulsively. Anna's murder had made him angry, and what Trent Chilcott had told him and Taylor had given them a sense of urgency that led to their reckless behavior. Well . . . *his* reckless behavior. He was surprised, in retrospect, that Taylor, then David Kim, went along with his version of police procedures. Well, it seemed like a good idea at the time.

Regarding time, he ran his hand over his face to check his stubble. It was maybe five o'clock. Time for a drink. Maybe water.

Brodie glanced up at the lighting fixture and saw an electrical conduit pipe running from the fixture to the wall above the door where it disappeared.

There wasn't much here in the way of clues to figure out where they were, but the lighting fixture and the door and latch looked retro, and he was reasonably sure that he, Taylor, and Kim were in a World War II bunker, maybe an air raid shelter. Hopefully they were still in Berlin, so when they broke out of here, they could hail a cab to the embassy. Or maybe the airport would be better. He laughed at his own stupid, dark Army humor; the GI's coping mechanism for when the world was exploding around you, and things were going to shit faster than you could process it. And some asshole would yell out, "Hey, Sarge, is this a training exercise? Or for real?" Then someone would yell, "Medic!" and that was no joke.

He refocused on his surroundings. There was one thing in this bunker that was not retro: a surveillance camera mounted high in the far corner, and it was alive, sweeping the room. Brodie flashed his middle finger at it, and on the assumption that the camera had a listening device, he shouted, "Fuck you!"

There was no reply.

He now spotted something he hadn't noticed before. In the center of the room, sitting on the floor, was what looked like an oversize coffee can. The piss bucket. Or maybe water. He slid toward it, and saw it had no lid; it was empty, but it had a slight odor that he couldn't identify. On closer inspection it appeared to be a container for some kind of powdered drink, with a label featuring chocolate bars, a jug of milk, and a smiling cartoon pig.

He inverted the can and put it back on the floor.

He stood slowly, got his balance, took a deep breath, and moved toward Kim, whose breathing sounded labored. He crouched beside the man and saw that his face was pallid and covered with sweat. There was a small puddle of vomit on the floor near his mouth.

Brodie checked his pulse, which was weak and erratic.

Brodie yelled toward the surveillance camera, "This man is very sick! Get a doctor here! Now! Assholes!"

No reply.

Brodie noticed that Kim, too, had a butterfly needle bandaged on his arm, and Brodie decided to leave it. Maybe someone would come and administer whatever Kim needed through the needle port. Maybe not.

Brodie then realized that Kim was awake. The man said in a weak voice, "Scott . . ." Then his chest heaved, and he coughed.

Brodie propped Kim against the wall so he wouldn't choke if he vomited again. "You're going to be okay." Which was what you say to soldiers who've been hit, and who are going to be okay. But it's also what you say to soldiers who are dying. They don't need to know that.

"Water . . ."

"None here. But I'll get some." He shouted at the surveillance camera, "Water! Wasser! Schnell!" He then said to Kim, "Hang in there."

He moved back to Taylor, who seemed to be looking better, with more color in her face and deeper breathing. He felt her pulse, which was stronger.

Taylor opened her eyes, and her head turned toward him. "What happened . . . ?"

"Dr. Dipshit slipped us a mickey through our wristbands."

She nodded, remembering her last seconds of consciousness. Brodie helped her sit up and propped her against the wall. She looked around and said in a weak voice, "Where are we?"

"Not sure." But it's not the executive suite.

Taylor was slowly becoming more alert and noticed the butterfly needle on her arm. "That son of a bitch . . ." She pulled it out and put pressure on her arm for a moment to stanch the bleeding. Then she spotted David Kim across the room. "David . . ."

Kim looked at her. Sweat was dripping down his face. He gave her a thumbs-up and then coughed.

Taylor managed to get to her feet, then went over to Kim as Brodie walked to the door and examined it. The door was not sheet metal, but armor-plated, blast-proof, and it swung outward, confirming that they were in an air raid shelter, or more likely a munitions storage room. He grabbed the steel latch handle, pulled it upward, and it swiveled to the open position. He put his shoulder to the door and pressed, but it wouldn't budge, nor did he expect it to. Locked from the outside. That's life.

He examined the latch handle, which would make a lethal weapon, but the mechanism was secured with heavy bolts that were rusted shut. *Shit.* He gave the door a kick with his stockinged foot.

Brodie looked at Taylor, who was tending to Kim. Then Brodie took a deep breath, got his head on straight, and stood at the hinged side of the door. Eventually, someone would come for them, and whoever it was needed to meet his fist.

A voice, coming from the direction of the surveillance camera, said in accented English, "Step away from the door."

"Fuck you."

The light suddenly went out, and the voice said, "I see you on infrared. Step away from the door, or you will all die a slow death from thirst and starvation, in the dark."

"If you wanted us dead, asshole, you'd have already killed us."

"There are things worse than death, Mr. Brodie. And you're about to find out what they are."

Brodie knew he should move away from the door, because there was no tactical advantage in standing there. And yet . . . This was the kind of situation where his ego and pigheaded tendencies came out in full bloom.

"Go fuck yourself."

"When the first of you dies, will the other two turn to cannibalism?"

Brodie could hear Taylor's voice in the dark. "Scott . . . come over here."

He didn't reply.

The voice said, "Listen to the lady." He added, "You have five seconds before you never see the light again." He counted, "One."

Brodie got himself — or the other guy deep inside him — under control and moved in the dark toward Taylor and Kim.

The light came on and the voice said, "Sit."

Brodie sat near Taylor, who had her hand on Kim's wrist, checking his pulse. She looked at Brodie and shook her head.

The voice said, "Do not move from there."

Brodie shouted, "Get a doctor here!"

The voice replied, "Mr. Kim has already seen a doctor — Dr. Dorn." There was a laugh, and the speaker was silent.

Kim went into a violent coughing fit and blood foamed up on his lips.

Brodie pulled a handkerchief from his pocket and gave it to Kim, who wiped his mouth.

Taylor said, "We've been exposed to something."

Which, thought Brodie, was not too hard to believe. Harry Vance hadn't been carrying that microscope slide of plague around as a good luck charm. Also in that slideshow were Stefan Richter, Storkow, David Katz's lab report, and Reinhard Dorn's cool, clinical lecture. *Plague.*

He looked at David Kim, who was in pulmonary distress. Brodie took a deep breath. His lungs were clear. He looked at

Taylor, who also seemed to be breathing normally.

Taylor said to Kim, "David, you may have been injected with something."

David Kim, who had been thinking about all of this and apparently had some acquired knowledge of the subject, shook his head and said, "It's . . . airborne. Probably . . . pneumonic plague."

Brodie looked at the canister in the middle of the room. Was this possible?

Kim continued, "Not like bubonic . . . attacks the lungs . . . and it's probably delivered as an aerosol . . . or . . ." — he nodded toward the empty canister — ". . . crystal form that vaporizes in the air . . ." He had another coughing fit and wiped his mouth with Brodie's handkerchief.

Taylor said to Kim, "But we — Scott and I — we feel okay."

Kim caught his breath, then looked at Taylor and Brodie, who seemed in much better shape than he was. "What's the difference . . . between me . . . and the two of you?"

Brodie and Taylor looked at each other. Taylor appeared shaken. "That's . . . Is that possible?"

David Kim, who had spent his career imagining and planning for all the horrifying weapons a terrorist might invent or acquire, nodded. He was silent a moment, then said, "Biogenetic weapon. Targets gene profiles.

736

Like . . . ethnic markers. In theory. No one thought it was possible. But if anyone could pull it off . . . it would be these bastards." He went into another coughing fit, and leaned over as blood ran out of his mouth and pooled on the floor between his legs. He stared at the splatter of blood-red sputum and said, "Genocide . . ."

Brodie and Taylor were silent. Brodie thought again about the specimen slide that Harry Vance had had in his pocket and about the Stasi bio and chemical facility at Storkow. And he also thought about Reinhard Dorn asking David Kim about his ancestry. But most of all, he thought about neo-Nazis — they could drop the "neo" — and about the multicultural society that Berlin and Germany — and Europe — had become. *Muslims Out.* And, while they were at it, everyone else out too, except the white race. He looked at David Kim, who was clearly very sick — and he and Taylor were not.

Brodie tried to wrap his mind around all this. An ethnic bioweapon — a genetically engineered bacteria that was only pathogenic to people with a specific gene signature. Or . . . the other way around — it was pathogenic to everyone *except* people who had certain genetic markers that were common to the Caucasian race . . . Was that really possible? Well . . . in an age when the genetic code could be manipulated down to the fin-

737

est detail — or even printed into existence from base components using the kinds of laboratory machines that Brodie had seen at Hyperion Lab — then, yes, maybe it was possible. In fact, such techniques were used every day for good purposes: cures for disease in humans, animals, and plant life . . . Brodie thought of the bowl of apples on Dorn's desk. He thought, too, of the Nazis and their Aryan racial programs, which were bogus science, and dependent on breeding, which was unreliable, and also dependent on genocide by bullets and poison gas, which were messy, inefficient, and time- and resource-consuming. The new Nazis, however, had gene-splicing. He recalled the Titan Genetics PR video: *The applications for this technology are as infinite as the human imagination.*

Holy shit.

He looked at FBI Special Agent David Kim, who was now a live specimen in a grotesque laboratory experiment. Brodie had no doubt that Dorn and his mad scientists had already used human beings to see if their bioengineering worked. But live human specimens were not that easy to come by, so these experiments must have been limited and maybe the results were not conclusive. But then along come Scott Brodie, Maggie Taylor, and David Kim, wanting to see Herr Doktor Reinhard Dorn, and lucky them, they're admitted to the sanctum of the head

738

honcho, who sees an opportunity to kill two birds with one stone: getting rid of three nosy American criminal investigators, and logging in another experiment.

Reinhard Dorn was out of his fucking mind. A total head case. But . . . never underestimate the insane; they may be crazy, but they're not stupid.

Another thought was that Dorn must know that the authorities were getting close to him. Brodie, Taylor, and Kim hadn't shown up at Titan Genetics on a hunch or a whim. And the three Americans must have told their supervisors where they were going. They hadn't, actually, but Dorn didn't know that.

The only conclusion Brodie could come to was that something was going to happen. Soon. And whatever that was, it would be big enough and bad enough to give Dorn and his co-conspirators all the cover they needed to avoid the consequences of their lunatic plans.

A sound came from the door, and it swung open.

A man in his twenties stepped into the room. He wore green camo fatigues and boots and carried an assault rifle. He stepped to his left and stationed himself next to the door, holding his rifle across his chest. After him came a woman, also in her twenties and in full camo, pushing a metal cart with equipment. She was attractive, but dead-faced, and wore a white armband with the red cross of a medic. The door shut behind her, and Brodie heard someone slide a bolt lock.

The woman seemed annoyed to see Brodie and Taylor sitting near Kim. She pointed to the opposite wall and said in a German accent, "Go there. Sit."

Neither of them moved. The woman said something in German to the young man, who pointed his rifle at Brodie.

The woman repeated, "Go there. Sit."

Brodie had never heard of a medic giving a shoot-to-kill order, but he had a feeling this was not the German Army here to save them.

They complied and returned to their places against the opposite wall and sat. Brodie watched as Nurse Ratched wheeled her cart to David Kim and began taking his vitals — pulse, blood pressure, temperature — and recording it with a pad and pen. Kim stared at her while she did all this, but she would not meet his eyes.

The medic put a stethoscope in her ears, then lifted Kim's shirt and placed the diaphragm on his back. "Deep breath."

Kim stared straight ahead and did not change his breathing.

The medic slapped him across the face. "Deep breath!"

Kim attempted a deep breath, then started coughing.

Brodie eyed the guard. The guy was tall and

muscular, and held his rifle with his finger just outside the trigger guard. His eyes were fixed on Brodie and Taylor. Brodie noted that he wore no patches of any kind on his uniform — no flag, no insignia, no rank or nametag.

A secret army.

Brodie wondered if this soldier and the medic were past or present members of the German armed forces, and also members of NordFaust, turning their military training and equipment back against the German state they had sworn to defend. Brodie also wondered how many more people like them might be present in this facility, whatever and wherever it was.

The guard was about fifteen feet away from Brodie and Taylor. Brodie played out in his mind how it would go down if he charged the guy and slammed his head against the wall. He eyed the man's rifle. He didn't know the make by sight, but it was an assault rifle, with what looked like a thirty-round mag, and if it was military-issue, then it was also fully automatic. Attempting a rush would probably get Scott Brodie ventilated by fifteen rounds within a second. And that still left half the mag for Taylor.

And even if he beat the odds, whoever was on the other end of that surveillance camera would have armed men in this room within seconds. Brodie noted that they were not

741

restrained, which said something about their captors' confidence that their prisoners had no hope of getting out of this place.

The medic drew two vials of Kim's blood via the butterfly needle, then placed the vials on her cart and wheeled it over to Brodie. She crouched and looked at his arm where the needle and tubing had been. "Why did you pull it out?"

"Why did you put it in?"

"No questions." She retrieved her blood pressure monitor from the cart. "Give me your arm."

Brodie stared at the woman and did not move.

"Arm!" she repeated.

"Say please."

The medic said something in German and the guard aimed his rifle at Taylor.

The medic said to Brodie, "Your lives have very little value here. Are you going to let your friend die to avoid having your blood pressure taken?"

Brodie raised his arm, and the woman applied the cuff and began to take a reading. The guard lowered his rifle.

The medic said to Brodie, "Your pressure is elevated."

"I wonder why."

She looked at him as she took off the cuff. "Are you a Jew?"

"Excuse me?"

The woman looked at him. "I asked, are you a Jew? A half-Jew? You don't look it, but some don't."

Brodie did not respond.

She kept staring at him. "We have already taken some blood, and a swab of your cheek, which is currently being sequenced. So if you lie, we will know. And they will shoot you for lying. They will also shoot you if you refuse to answer."

Brodie stared back at her. "I have no Jewish ancestry."

The medic turned toward Taylor, who glared at her and shook her head.

Brodie asked, "Why are you asking?"

She ignored his question as she produced a forehead thermometer and took Brodie's reading. Then she listened to his chest with her stethoscope and made notes on her pad.

She went over to Taylor and repeated her exam.

Brodie watched her and realized just how young she was. Twenty-two, twenty-three at the oldest. She had long brown hair tied up in a bun, and hazel eyes. But there was something so much older, and so much uglier, underneath her features. Some deep-rooted hatred that he could not understand.

He asked her, "Why are you doing this?"

She looked at him, surprised by the question. After a moment she said, "You have no right to that answer."

743

Brodie heard the door unlock, and as it swung open a man about Brodie's age walked in. He was tall, with a full head of brown hair, and he wore boots, black pants, and a button-down shirt with rolled-up sleeves. He said something in German to the medic, and she left the room with her cart and shut the door. The guard with the assault rifle stayed.

The man folded his arms and looked down at Brodie and Taylor. "You guys fucked up."

To Brodie's surprise, he spoke with an American accent. Brodie asked, "Who the hell are you?"

"You can call me Steve."

"Can I call you shithead?"

Steve laughed. "God, I miss American humor."

"Did you hear the one about the German tourist who drives to the French border?"

"No. Tell me."

"Later."

Steve crouched so they were eye-level. "So, who am I? I was a private military contractor in Germany for a few years, been with a group outside of Münster where I met some . . . like-minded individuals. Nord-Faust." He looked at Brodie and then Taylor and smiled. "My German friends thought an American would have better luck with you guys. But now that I'm here, you don't look happy to see a compatriot."

Neither Brodie nor Taylor responded.

744

Steve offered, "You're probably wondering where you are. It's a bunker. From the war. You'd be surprised how much of this shit still exists under Berlin." He paused. "I'm going to be straight with you. There's a chance both of you can get out of here alive, but you're going to need to cooperate."

Brodie was familiar with that line, and it was Grade A American bullshit. He said to Steve, "Get Agent Kim medical attention, and do it right fucking now, and then we can talk."

Steve looked over his shoulder at David Kim and scoffed. "Brother, he's a goner. You need to think about yourself. And your lady friend here."

"I'm not your brother."

"No?" Steve unbuttoned his shirt, revealing a large patch of red disfigured skin over his chest. "Two thousand six. North of Baghdad. My squad was told to dispose of an old, degraded Iraqi military weapons cache. Artillery shells. Except they were filled with mustard agent. Whoops. My buddy died and they lied about the cause. And I didn't even get a goddamn Purple Heart. I guess we found those weapons of mass destruction after all, huh, Scott?" He buttoned his shirt. "Except these were from 1985 and rotting in a fucking hole in the ground for twenty years, and probably made in America. Didn't fit the official narrative." He added, "Total bullshit."

Taylor said, "So the Army screwed you. Take a number. We don't all become Nazis. You are a disgrace to your country."

Steve stood and looked down at her. "My country is the disgrace, Maggie Taylor. A mongrelized shithole on the losing side of history." He paused and looked at them. "We could have separated you guys. Done the whole prisoner's dilemma thing, or tortured you, gotten you to talk." He gestured to the can in the middle of the room. "But the truth is, your main value to these people is as fuckin' lab rats. Besides, there's a *really* short shelf life on any intelligence you can give us. Like, a couple hours."

Brodie asked, "What happens in a couple hours?"

Steve smiled. "I promise I'll tell you once it's over, Scott. Sometime tonight. And then, depending on whether you were helpful, we'll either let you go or put a bullet in your head. Deal?"

"No deal."

Steve laughed. "You know, your German friends are making some headlines right now with their raids on NordFaust. Gun battle in Dresden. Seized explosives in Leipzig. Arrested a high-ranking Bundeswehr officer here in Berlin. They'll learn some things. But not the right things. And not enough things to stop what's coming." He added, "Nord-Faust and Titan Genetics are two sides of the same coin, as I'm sure you've figured out by now. But the Feds are looking at the wrong side of the coin."

Brodie recalled how sure Trent Chilcott and Howard Fensterman had been that Odin — whoever he was — had no affiliation with NordFaust, and that the threat NordFaust posed had nothing to do with biological or chemical weapons.

This thing was siloed. NordFaust on the one side, a conventional armed extremist group posing a conventional threat. And on the other side, the unconventional threat. Titan Genetics. Or at least, select members of that firm, along with select members of NordFaust to provide the muscle. Using engineering wizardry to concoct some sort of genocidal plague. The unexpected threat. The real threat. A threat so well hidden that even the CIA and NSA superspies were clueless.

And if Steve was to be believed, then whatever intelligence today's raids were able to net would reveal nothing about what was actually coming today. In a couple of hours.

Brodie looked at the canister and asked, "What has David been exposed to?"

"You already know, Scott." Steve gestured to the surveillance camera. "We heard Mr. Kim explain it all to you. Smart guy. Right on the money. It's an engineering marvel. Or so they tell me. I failed high school bio. But I know we're all mostly made of the same stuff, so precise targeting was tricky. Just a couple different genes here and there separate the races. But those small differences matter, and they always have, right? They determine slaves and masters." He turned and looked at David Kim. "He's lasting longer than that piece of garbage Qasim, who was old and fat, and on some level wanted to die."

Well, that answered one mystery. Tariq Qasim had met his death here, maybe in this very room, as a guinea pig for a biowarfare experiment — which was a fitting end for him, considering his former line of work.

Steve, who really liked the sound of his own voice, walked to the metal canister, picked it up, and tipped it toward them so they could see the empty bottom. "See that? Well, I guess you can't. But that's the end of the world right there. The end of *this* world, anyway. They call their new plague Götterdämmerung. You know, Wagner. Twilight of the Gods. The destruction and renewal of the world. Real kraut shit." Steve tossed the metal canister aside and it clattered across the floor. He stepped toward Brodie and Taylor and crouched again. "So. Here's your one and only chance to not die today. Who else knows about Reinhard Dorn and Charles Granger, and who knows that Titan Genetics is involved in any kind of association or conspiracy with NordFaust?"

"We don't know anything about that," said Brodie.

Steve looked at him. "Listen, Scott. I'm the good cop. Well, the best you're gonna get, anyway. You'll tell me voluntarily, or you'll tell someone else another way." He looked at Taylor. "And you won't like what happens to her."

Brodie nodded. "All right. Full disclosure. Everyone knows, Steve. The FBI, the BKA, the German military. They even know our current location. Luftwaffe's probably gearing up to drop a bunker buster on our ass any minute."

Steve looked pissed off. He stood again. "The Feds don't know shit. They showed up at Titan looking for you three. I guess they had a net on you. But not a very tight one. Dorn's people told them he gave you a tour of the lab and you left. No one knows you're here. You are up shit creek. And you just sank your only life raft."

Brodie became aware that David Kim was speaking softly, almost inaudibly. His words were muttered, raspy, and Brodie couldn't quite make them out. Then he realized that Kim was speaking Arabic.

Steve turned around to face Kim. "What the hell's this guy saying?"

Suddenly Taylor lurched forward and grabbed Steve's right ankle.

"Hey!"

Steve tried to yank his leg away from her, but Taylor shoved her hand under his pantleg, pulled out a small pistol from his ankle holster, and put a round through his mouth and out the back of his head, sending a splatter of blood, bone, and brains across the small room. Steve fell dead.

Before the guard could react, Taylor took aim and fired a round through his head, splattering brains and skull fragments across the door. The man crumpled to the floor.

Brodie dove forward and grabbed the guard's automatic rifle, put the selector switch on full auto, and aimed the rifle at the closed door.

For a moment, they were all still.

Brodie glanced at David Kim, who must have spotted the ankle holster when Steve was crouched with his back to him. Brodie looked Kim in the eyes and said, "Well done."

Taylor said, "They're coming."

Brodie heard heavy footfalls on the other side of the door.

Taylor raised the pistol toward the door.

Brodie said, "Agent Kim. Agent Taylor. It's been an honor."

Taylor kept her eyes on the door. "Same."

The footfalls stopped. The door swung open.

CHAPTER 50

The door swung outward, and Brodie fired a burst of rounds at the two guards, who reeled backward and crumpled to the floor.

Taylor rushed through the doorway and pulled an automatic rifle from the hands of one of the dying guards while Brodie retrieved a half dozen mags and shoved them in his pockets.

Taylor called back into the room, "David! We have to leave you. We'll get help."

They could hear Kim coughing; then he said, "Go . . . go . . ."

Taylor turned back to Brodie, who was now pulling the boots off the guards. He said, "Cover."

She dropped to one knee and aimed her rifle down the long corridor that ran from the bunker room for about forty feet, then seemed to T-intersect at another corridor running left and right.

The corridor was lit by celling fixtures connected by the electrical conduit that ran into the bunker room. Brodie knew he should fire a burst into the conduit and kill the lights, which would give him and Taylor the cover of darkness. But that would put Kim in total darkness, and Brodie couldn't do that. Or could he? The mission comes first, as they say, and the mission was to get the hell out of this underground labyrinth, then get help for Kim, which was the secondary mission. Bad enough leaving a man behind . . . but not in the dark.

As he was wrestling with this, Taylor fired a burst of rounds at the farthest lighting fixture, and Brodie could hear the bullets impacting the concrete and ricocheting before the lights in the corridor went out.

A few seconds later, two men carrying rifles appeared at the T-intersection of the corridors, which meant there were more people down here and they'd heard the gunfire. The two men turned into the darkened corridor, and they were backlit by the lights beyond where Taylor had severed the electricity. Taylor saw them and whispered, "Scott —"

"Got it." They both emptied their magazines downrange and both men fell.

Taylor quickly pulled on a pair of boots and Brodie did the same. Taylor grabbed the other rifle from the second man they'd killed at the doorway and ran back into the bunker room to give Kim the rifle and also give him some options that included not being taken alive.

Brodie checked both dead men for a walkie while keeping an eye on the lighted end of the corridor. No walkies, but each man had a cell phone that Brodie saw had no signal in the subterranean bunker. The phones were locked anyway, and therefore useless to Brodie and Taylor. Brodie left them in place in the event the phones could be tracked somehow, so whoever was doing the tracking would think these guards were at their post outside the bunker — which they were.

Taylor rejoined him and said, "We're good to go."

"Right. I got point. Twenty feet."

"Go."

Brodie held his rifle to his shoulder in the firing position and began walking quickly down the dark corridor, with Taylor twenty feet behind him.

They reached the T-intersection where the two guards lay on the floor, painted red, as they used to say, more dead than alive.

Brodie and Taylor retrieved the dying men's rifles. They were the same make as the ones Brodie and Taylor were carrying — Heckler & Koch G36s, the service rifle for the German Bundeswehr. They were made primarily out of polymer, which is a fancy word for plastic, though still more durable than they looked. But Brodie and Taylor were able to smash them against the concrete walls to deform the barrels and render them useless.

Brodie checked the men for comms devices. No walkies, but each had a cell phone that he checked. Locked and no reception. He left them.

Taylor gathered up another half dozen mags, which she shoved in her belt and whispered to Brodie, "I can see your T-shirt with my eyes closed."

He nodded, then knelt beside one of the guards who was half-lit by the lights in the intersecting corridor. The guy had taken three or four hits and his camo shirt was wet with blood, and definitely darker than Brodie's white T-shirt. Brodie unbuttoned the man's shirt and looked at his face. Young guy. Blond hair. Handsome. Dying for a cause. Wrong cause.

Brodie pulled off the man's blood-soaked shirt and put it on.

Taylor was crouched at the intersection, looking left and right down the long, empty corridor.

Brodie joined her and she whispered, "Which way?"

"I'm looking for a sign that says, 'Exit, Thank You for Coming.' "

"Not fucking funny."

"Right . . . Well, I thought I saw these two guys appear from the right."

"Okay . . . so maybe that's the exit."

"Which is also the entrance for any more assholes who are down here."

"It might be the only way out of here." She added, "The corridor to the left could dead-end."

He thought a moment, then said, "There are always two or more exits to an underground bunker complex, so people can get out if there's a collapse caused by bombs or artillery, or if one way is blocked by enemy soldiers coming in. So, either direction will eventually lead to a way out."

Taylor replied, "The war's over, Scott. Every entrance and exit except one could be blocked off by the authorities or by reconstruction."

"You make a point." He said, "These guys came in from the right, so we go to the right."

"Are you sure that's what you saw?"

He glanced at the two guards, who had stopped moving. No, he was not sure, and they couldn't tell him even if he spoke German. Maybe Taylor shouldn't have blown Steve's brains out so quickly. In any case, he needed to give Taylor — and himself — some confidence in the mission. "I'm sure."

"Okay . . . let's do it."

"Back-to-back. I'm front."

They moved into the lit corridor and Brodie went to the right with Taylor walking backward behind him to cover the rear.

The corridor was quiet, and the air was stagnant and damp. Up ahead was another T-intersection, and they advanced quickly.

Brodie'd had his share of training and real-life experience in urban combat, including clearing buildings, but it was a special kind of suck when you had no idea where you were, where you were going, how big the place was, or even a basic idea of the enemy's strength. In fact, it was a minor miracle they were still alive.

Suddenly a guard emerged from the left side of the cross-corridor and ran across, firing a pistol erratically. The shots went wide, and Brodie returned fire with a burst of bullets. The figure was thrown back and hit the wall.

Brodie advanced toward the body slumped against the wall. It was the female medic. She stared ahead, dead-eyed, still gripping her 9mm automatic pistol.

Brodie said to Taylor, "Check the left."

"Copy."

They entered the T-intersection, and Brodie spun to his right and Taylor to her left. They saw no one.

For a moment they both held their positions, looking down the empty corridors. Then Taylor crouched and took the medic's pistol, a spare mag, and a key ring that was clipped to the woman's belt, while Brodie checked both directions. He saw a door about thirty yards down where the medic had come from.

Taylor stood and they moved toward the

door, with Brodie backpedaling and covering Taylor's back.

They reached a red metal door. Taylor tried the knob. Locked. She tried the medic's keys one by one as Brodie kept eyes on both ends of the corridor.

The third key was the charm, and she turned the knob slightly, then kicked the door open.

The room was pitch-black, and they both dropped to one knee as a muzzle flashed in the dark and a single shot hit the wall. Brodie squeezed off a burst in the direction of the shot, heard someone cry out in pain, then raked automatic fire across the room, hitting metal and concrete and shattering glass.

He stopped firing, moved into the room to his left, and listened. "Clear." Taylor entered, located a light switch, and turned it on, then shut the door and locked it.

Directly ahead of them, a man sat dead in an office chair. He was in his fifties and wore a white lab coat covered in blood. A pistol lay on the ground near his feet.

They were inside a large room, about forty by thirty feet. An old, faded map of Berlin on the far wall indicated this might have been some sort of command room back in Adolf's day, but now it had been converted into a lab with long metal tables, computers, tubes, and beakers, and various pieces of high-tech equipment. There was shattered glass everywhere.

"Scott . . ."

Brodie turned to his right. Taylor had her rifle trained on another man in a lab coat who was crouched in the corner, his hands above his head.

"Bitte . . ."

Brodie said, "Up."

The man rose to his feet. "Bitte . . ."

"Shut up. Speak English?"

"Ja. Yes. Yes. I speak English."

The man appeared to be in his late forties, heavyset with thinning brown hair. Brodie asked, "What's your name?"

"T-Tomas. Tomas Stellmacher."

Taylor asked, "Are you a geneticist?"

He nodded.

Brodie, realizing he'd shot the place to shit, asked, "Are you producing the plague organism here?"

The man shook his head. "This is not — We are collecting data, analyzing samples, to understand how it works."

"How it kills," said Brodie.

Stellmacher did not respond.

Brodie said, "Give me your ID."

Stellmacher dug in his pocket for his wallet and handed Brodie his driver's license.

Brodie checked it, then put it in his coat pocket. He spotted a landline telephone on a nearby desk and picked up the receiver. No dial tone. Brodie pressed the space bar on a desktop computer to wake it up.

Stellmacher informed him, "No phone. No Internet. Someone turned them off."

Brodie noticed a small television on the desk and punched the power button. It turned on and displayed a German news channel. Weather report. Brodie raised his rifle again at Stellmacher. "What is happening in two hours?"

Stellmacher raised his hands defensively. "What?"

"Two hours! Answer me!"

"I don't know!"

"Do you want to die, Tomas?"

The man started crying. "Bitte. Ich weiß nichts! Ich weiß gar nichts!"

Brodie eyed the locked door. It was possible that he and Taylor had killed everyone down here other than Stellmacher. But it was also possible that more armed men were on their way. They had to get out of there, and fast.

Taylor asked the man, "Do you know Charles Granger?"

Stellmacher got hold of himself and looked at Taylor. He nodded.

"Have you seen him?"

"Ja. He — It was, maybe it was six hours ago."

"He was *here*?"

Stellmacher nodded again. "He came to see

759

Dr. Hausner."

She asked, "Who is that?"

"The chief genetic engineer. He comes to check our data sometimes."

"What were Hausner and Granger talking about?"

Stellmacher shook his head. "They do not involve me in these things."

"What things?"

"Anything. I collect and analyze data. That is all."

Brodie moved toward him. "Did you hear Granger say *anything*?"

Stellmacher looked desperate. "Just 'hello' and 'good-bye' when he comes and leaves." He thought of something. "Colonel Granger said to Dr. Hausner, 'I will see you later.'" He added, "'In the field. I will see you later in the field.'"

Brodie asked, "What field?"

The man looked at Brodie. "I do not know, sir."

"Shit!" Brodie lowered the rifle, and his eyes landed on a large metal table in the center of the room, where about four dozen blood vials were held in a rack. Each was labeled in black marker. He moved closer and spotted three vials that said: D. KIM.

He stared at the tubes, and at the few milliliters of blood that represented all that David Kim was worth to this whole evil enterprise. He looked at the other names on the blood vials. Dozens of names. A few of them were labeled T. QASIM. He spotted vials with his and Taylor's names as well. The rest of the names all looked non-European. Whoever these people were, they were probably dead now.

Brodie turned toward Stellmacher and gestured at the blood vials. "Who are these people?"

"Th-they are . . ."

"Are they alive?"

Stellmacher shook his head.

Brodie raised his rifle again toward Stellmacher. "One of them is still alive, and I'm going to kill you unless you help him. Do you understand?"

The man glanced at his dead colleague in the chair and nodded.

"Do you have a treatment for the plague?"

Stellmacher stared at the barrel of the rifle and nodded again. "The engineers developed a novel antibiotic."

"I hope you have the antibiotic here or you're dead."

"Yes. Here."

"Get it. Now."

Stellmacher ran to a small fridge.

Taylor said in a low voice, "We need to escort him back to David. To make sure he actually administers the antibiotic instead of escaping."

Well . . . maybe. But they had an obligation

761

to get out of this bunker alive to share the Intel they'd gathered. Not to mention that Scott Brodie had a very personal interest in finding Charles Granger . . . finding Odin.

Brodie said, "Stellmacher works here and if he runs into anyone, he can make up a legitimate reason for going to see Kim. We're a liability to him."

Taylor considered that as Stellmacher returned with two IV bags along with tubes and needles.

Brodie said, "Pack it. And you'll need a flashlight."

The man retrieved a large medical bag from a cabinet, and he pulled a flashlight off a wall-mounted bracket. He packed the medication and gear with trembling hands.

Brodie asked, "Do you have a map of this place?"

Stellmacher nodded.

"Get it. Quickly."

The man ran over to a filing cabinet and retrieved a map, and Brodie unfolded it on the table. The map showed a network of tunnels and rooms.

Brodie asked, "Where are we?"

Stellmacher pointed to a room toward the top center of the map.

Taylor asked, "Where are the exits?"

"One exit," said Stellmacher. He pointed to an X in one of the hallways toward the bottom left of the map. "This leads to a subbasement in the Titan Genetics building."

Brodie stared at the map. "Titan Genetics built their headquarters on top of a Nazi bunker?"

Stellmacher explained, "I was told that the bunker was discovered while digging the foundation." He added, to show he was cooperating, "Certain things and people go in and out through the building's subbasement."

Brodie asked, "Tomas, do you have a family?"

The scientist looked at him. "Yes."

"Children?"

"Yes."

Brodie took Stellmacher's driver's license out of his pocket and held it up. "If you do not save David Kim's life, I will go to your house and I will kill your family. Then I will find you and kill you."

Stellmacher's eyes widened.

Brodie asked the man, "Do you believe me, Tomas?"

Stellmacher nodded.

Brodie said to Stellmacher, "You need to get to David Kim quickly. If you run into anyone, you tell them you received orders to move the detainee. Mr. Kim is armed, so announce yourself before you enter the room, and tell him that you are now working for U.S. Army CID. After you administer the antibiotic, get him out of here and to a

763

hospital. Understand?"

"Yes."

Brodie unlocked the door and quickly swung it open. With his rifle out front he pivoted to his right into the hallway and Taylor took the left. The passage was empty except for the body of the medic.

Brodie turned to Stellmacher and said, "Clear. Go. Now!"

Stellmacher grabbed his medical bag, then looked at Brodie. He appeared to be mustering his courage to say something. "The plague was engineered to have an extremely accelerated incubation period. Mr. Kim was infected with the pathogen over three hours ago. His chances of survival are in no way guaranteed."

"Then you better hurry the hell up."

"My family —"

"Go!"

Stellmacher ran into the corridor.

Brodie shut the door and locked it. He saw that Taylor was staring at him and he said to her, "I'll say what I need to if it helps give David a chance."

She nodded. "I understand. As long as you didn't mean what you said to him."

"Taylor, this is the most evil shit I've ever seen in my life, and maybe I don't know the answer to that."

She did not respond.

Brodie looked again at the map of the

764

bunker and at the symbol showing the single exit. There was no way they could get out of this bunker without going through the Titan Genetics subbasement, where there were probably more armed guards.

He spotted an isolated rectangle at the top of the map near the room they were standing in. It was labeled with the letter "U" inside a circle, which was the logo for the U-Bahn system.

Brodie observed the old, peeling map of Berlin on the opposite wall. If this had been some sort of command room during the war, it would have made sense to have an alternate form of egress here. He looked around the room. On the right-hand wall was a three-foot-by-three-foot hinged metal door embedded in the concrete. He went to it and pulled it open, revealing a dark passage.

Taylor pulled a flashlight from a wall-mounted bracket next to where Stellmacher had retrieved his and handed it to Brodie.

He flicked it on and shined it down a dark, concrete-walled tunnel that ran about twenty yards and dead-ended at what looked like a series of metal ladder rungs embedded in the concrete.

Taylor peered into the tunnel. "With any luck, this leads to the U-Bahn."

Brodie knew that during the war the underground U-Bahn stations were used as civilian bomb shelters, in which case it would make sense for the German military to give themselves this type of escape hatch.

Taylor noticed two long topcoats on a coat tree. She gave one to Brodie and they each put one on. Both coats had bullet holes from Brodie's aggressive entry into the room, but these were less noticeable than his blood-soaked camo shirt. He put the flashlight in his coat pocket.

Taylor retrieved the pistol that had been fired by the dead scientist and handed it to Brodie. It was an HK 9mm, and he slipped it into his other coat pocket.

Taylor said, "Let's go. We'll get our hands on a phone and call the cavalry."

Brodie said, "We need to find Granger."

"We don't know where he is or what he's up to. But a police raid on Titan Genetics might tell us."

"Maybe. Maybe not. Something is going to happen in a couple hours, according to Steve."

"He could have been screwing with us."

"What if he wasn't?"

Taylor did not reply.

Brodie looked at the television. A helicopter shot showed thousands of people marching down a nighttime street in the middle of a snowfall, many carrying signs. On the German-language chyron was the word NEUKÖLLN. The image cut to a ground-level shot of the marchers, and Brodie recog-

766

nized the street as Karl-Marx Straße. Throngs of people carried signs in German and Arabic, while others held aloft flashlights, candles, lighters, and smartphones. Brodie also saw several people holding up photos of Hasan, the murdered Iraqi immigrant. It was a vigil, and a protest.

Brodie said, "They like a good show."

"Who?"

"Harry Vance's words, on terrorists. Ask yourself, why would Reinhard Dorn and his engineers make the pathogen have a shorter incubation period?"

"Because it's harder to treat. More deadly."

"On the individual level, yes. But it's also much harder to spread if the infected get sick and die quickly. You don't have asymptomatic carriers walking around spreading the disease."

"What are you getting at?"

"These bastards want to make a statement. They are planning a *terrorist attack,* not a covert dispersal of the plague pathogen. They want Armageddon. Götterdämmerung." Brodie pointed to the vigil on the TV. "They are going to launch their biological attack into the heart of Neukölln, into the middle of a march that they knew would happen tonight because of the murder of Hasan al-Kazimi that they themselves committed."

Taylor thought about that. "The cluster bombs."

Brodie nodded. "I'll bet the German authorities didn't find them in the NordFaust raids today. Because they are in the hands of a man no one suspects: retired U.S. Army Colonel Charles Granger — an esteemed Cold War intelligence officer who helped defend the West against the threat of unconventional weapons. Granger could have packed the cluster bombs' submunitions with the bacteria."

She looked again at the marchers on the TV.

"And then, who knows? Hold the country hostage with the threat of another bioweapon attack? Use NordFaust to storm the Reichstag? Demand that all Muslims leave the country? We don't know. And right now it doesn't matter. Because whatever their plan is, it starts here in Berlin, and it starts soon."

Taylor took all that in. "It's a real Day X and Black Harvest, but much worse."

"Right. And we are dealing with portable mortar-fired cluster bombs. They could be launched from anywhere."

Taylor thought a moment. "What is the maximum range of that type of mortar?"

He considered that. Some of the vehicles in the 3rd Stryker Brigade had carried 60mm and 81mm mortars for dismounted maneuvers, but he was never part of a crew that operated them. The MAT-120 cluster bombs that Trent Chilcott had claimed were in the hands of NordFaust were, per their name, 120mm, which were considered heavy mortars and generally had longer ranges because they were packed with more propellant. Though a mortar filled with cluster munitions might be even heavier than average . . .

"Brodie?"

"I'm going to guess somewhere north of three miles. Maybe a three-and-a-half-mile maximum effective range."

Taylor grabbed a marker off a desk and walked to the map of Berlin on the wall. She located Körnerpark, then moved her finger east to Karl-Marx Straße, which was named something else in the Berlin of the Third Reich. She tapped the street. "The vigil is around here." She referenced the distance scale at the bottom of the map, then drew a rough circle. "There is our potential attack radius."

Brodie looked at the map. The circle encompassed an area stretching south from Neukölln to the edge of the city, east into neighborhoods on the opposite bank of the Spree River, and north into parts of the central district of Mitte. In fact, this was completely useless information, even if his range calculation had been better than an educated guess.

Brodie then spotted a huge green expanse just west of Neukölln that appeared almost twice the size of the Tiergarten and was well within the radius. He looked closer and read aloud: "Tempelhofer Feld."

Taylor said, "Tempelhof Field. The site of the old Tempelhof Airport. Which Ulrich said is a public park now."

Brodie nodded. Tempelhof was famous as the focal point of the Berlin Airlift in the late 1940s, when the Soviets blockaded West Berlin and the Allies had to fly in massive amounts of supplies to the starving city. Brodie examined the expansive area on the map, whose perimeter must have been close to five miles. He repeated Colonel Granger's words: "I will see you later in the field."

Taylor said, "The field of operations. The field of combat."

"Or it's literal." Brodie pointed to Tempelhof Field. "This open expanse provides a unique tactical advantage for a covert mortar strike in the middle of a city. No obstructions, no public roads or private residences, restricted public access after nightfall, minimal security, little or no chance of a civilian or a police officer happening upon you, and the ability to surveil anyone making an approach from hundreds of yards in every direction. It's also a symbolic choice for Odin, a bitter old Cold Warrior who bet on the losing side. Spectacle. Symbolism." He added, "Revenge."

Taylor stared at the map. "You might be

right. Actually, we can't afford for you to be wrong."

"That rarely happens. Let's get out of here."

CHAPTER 51

Brodie crawled through the dark tunnel with Taylor close behind. His G36 rifle was slung on his back, and he held the flashlight in front of him. In a few minutes, they reached the end of the tunnel and climbed the metal rungs up a narrow thirty-foot shaft.

The rungs stopped at a flat ledge, and Brodie pulled himself up, followed by Taylor.

Brodie swept the flashlight around. They were in a passageway with walls made of the same degraded concrete as the bunker. The passage ran about fifty feet and ended at a concrete block wall with a steel door.

They walked to the wall, which appeared to be of newer construction than the surrounding passageway. The steel door also looked newer and was secured by a long sliding bolt.

Taylor asked, "You feel that?"

The whole passage felt like it was rumbling and was soon filled with the thunder of a fast-approaching train. They heard the train whip past them, then slow somewhere farther down, followed by the faint but familiar sound of the U-Bahn's PA system announcing the stop. Bernauer Straße.

Brodie slid the bolt and pulled open the heavy steel door. They exited onto a narrow walkway in a dark train tunnel. The walkway ran about twenty yards along the tunnel to a set of stairs and a security gate that led to the train platform.

The U-Bahn train was at the platform, and passengers were getting on and off. Brodie and Taylor took off their winter coats, slung their compact rifles along their right sides, and put the coats back on. This concealed their rifles, but created a bulge, though not enough to draw attention. They both held their pistols inside their right jacket pockets and walked quickly along the catwalk to the platform as the train pulled out.

Brodie climbed the stairs, then vaulted over the low security gate onto the platform. Taylor followed. A few people noticed them, and an older man started yelling at them in German. They walked quickly up the station stairs and out to the street.

It was nighttime. The city was covered in about an inch of snow, and dense flurries were coming down. Judging by how many people were on the street, and by the traffic, it was the middle of rush hour.

Taylor said, as if to herself, "Back in the land of the living."

Brodie had no reply, but thought of David Kim, stuck in the land between the living and the dead.

Taylor looked up and down the wide road at the slow-moving stream of cars rolling through the snow and slush. She said, "A taxi is going to take too long."

Brodie spotted a young guy in a hooded winter parka sitting on a Vespa at a red light. The man had an insulated food delivery bag strapped to the back of the Vespa and he was fiddling with a smartphone that was mounted between the handlebars.

Brodie approached the guy and pulled out his pistol. "Off."

The man looked at him. "Was?"

"Off." Brodie raised the pistol slightly so the guy could understand what was happening.

The man saw the gun and yelled, "Scheiße!" then jumped off the Vespa and ran.

Brodie grabbed the handlebar, pocketed his pistol, and jumped on. Taylor hopped on behind him and held on tight.

Brodie peeled out into the intersection and weaved between the cars and trucks. A few vehicles honked and someone yelled as he cut left and headed for the tram tracks that ran between the opposing lanes.

Taylor held tight to him and asked over the rushing wind, "Have you driven one of these?"

"It's been a while. But you never forget." He added, "Never in snow. Hang on." He cranked the throttle and sped down the tracks. There was no tram in sight, which made this a pretty good express lane.

Taylor asked, "Do you know how to get to Tempelhof?"

"No." He glanced at the smartphone, which was unlocked and running GPS. He took it off the cradle and passed it back to her.

Taylor let go of him with her right hand and took the phone.

Brodie struggled to see as they whipped through the dense flurries. He spotted a pedestrian about to cross the lane divider in front of him and pressed the horn as he sailed past the guy.

They were approaching a bend in the track, and he saw a single headlight curve around the bend — a tram heading straight at them. The tram rang its bell.

"Hang on!"

Brodie cut hard right onto the parallel track, and the tram shot past them. He spotted a side street to his right with no traffic and peeled off the tracks and down the road. So far, the tires had not skidded out on the turns, but a patch of ice could send them sliding.

Taylor called out, "Make a right at the next major road you see. Otto-Braun Straße. That will take you across the Spree and through

Museum Island. You'll cross two bridges and then make your first left."

"Copy." He added, "See what kind of food this guy was delivering."

"What is wrong with you?"

"I'm hungry." There was traffic up ahead. Brodie swerved up onto the sidewalk and beeped his horn. He suggested to Taylor, "Pocket the phone so you can hold on better."

"I'm calling backup."

"Who?"

"Trent." She explained, "One of the few numbers I've memorized."

"I disabled his phone. But leave a detailed message." Well, they could use the backup. And someone else needed to know what they knew in case they got flattened by a truck in the next few minutes.

He was approaching a cross street with a stop sign. He leaned on the horn and sailed through, staying on the sidewalk to bypass the traffic. Twenty feet ahead a man emerged from a building. Brodie hit the horn and swerved as the man jumped back just in time.

He saw the major road up ahead. They had the green and the road was clear, so Brodie drove off the sidewalk into the street and cranked the throttle as he turned right. He could barely hear Taylor behind him yelling something over the wind. It sounded like she was actually having a conversation, so Chilcott must have gotten his phone working again. Brodie made out "Charles Granger," as well as "bioweapon," and "Tempelhof Field."

She hung up, pocketed the phone, and grabbed onto Brodie again, yelling through the wind, "They didn't find the mortars in the NordFaust raids."

Well, that was because the mortars were in the hands of Colonel Granger, probably at Tempelhof Field, which was why he was risking their lives to get there.

They were approaching a large intersection and had the red. Six lanes of cross traffic cut through the intersection. He said to Taylor, "Hang on!"

He felt her arms tighten around him and her face pressed into his neck.

He blew through the red and cut between a sedan and a truck coming from the left, then weaved through the next two lanes, where a truck barreled toward them from the right. Brodie cut left and revved the throttle to outrun the truck and cut in front of it, then zagged to the right and flew between lanes of oncoming vehicles. People honked their horns as he zipped past. He spotted a break in the cars and cut left across the remaining lanes, then careened down the middle of Otto-Braun Straße.

He checked the speedometer. He was pushing a hundred kilometers an hour, which felt

777

like the limits of what the Vespa could do. He peered through the flurries and saw a bridge up ahead. Bridges freeze before roads and he looked to see if there was ice on the pavement, but he couldn't tell. The area was choked with traffic. Brodie veered back onto the sidewalk, which was wide and mostly empty, and shot past the cars and over the Spree River.

They sped through what must have been the southern end of Museum Island, and then over another bridge. Brodie kept his eyes out for the turn as they approached a light that had just turned green. He shot across the road and blared his horn as he cut in front of three lanes of approaching traffic and onto a small two-lane road.

They hurtled down the narrow road, weaving between lanes to get around the cars. He hit a patch of traffic and zipped between the lanes. There weren't a lot of cross streets here, and no large roads, and he blew through every intersection while blaring his horn.

After a few minutes they were in what looked like a more residential area of small apartment buildings and parks. Taylor called out, "Tempelhof should be coming up soon!"

Up ahead the road ended at a T-intersection. On the far side of the intersection was a long chain-link fence topped by razor wire. Tempelhof Airport — now a park.

Taylor said, "It looks deserted."

Brodie crossed the intersection and drove onto the sidewalk, then turned left and sped along the length of the fence, looking for an opening.

Thirty yards ahead was an entrance. He slowed the Vespa.

It was a pedestrian access path blocked by a ten-foot-high sliding metal gate that was padlocked. There was no razor wire atop the gate.

Brodie turned off the Vespa. The area looked desolate, and the road was quiet except for an occasional passing truck or car. Streetlights illuminated the road, but the area on the opposite side of the fence was hard to make out through the gloom and the swirling snow.

Brodie and Taylor got off the Vespa, then scrambled up the gate and over it.

They surveyed their surroundings. They were in a snow-covered park dotted with trees and picnic tables. There were no lampposts around to light the area, but he could see a path leading toward a distant tree line. They appeared to be alone.

The unslung their G36s and did an ammo check. Brodie had only three rounds left in his rifle's mag, so he swapped it with a full mag in his pocket, then checked his pistol. One round in the chamber, six in the mag. He returned it to his pocket. Taylor also popped a fresh mag in her rifle.

Brodie signaled Taylor, and they sprinted through the snow toward the tree line. They reached it and looked out. Beyond the trees was a flat, seemingly endless white expanse beneath a washed-out sky. It was like a moonscape, vast and alien, diffused through the veil of a steady snowfall.

Brodie scanned the snowy expanse. It was hard to see much of anything, but if Granger and his people were here, they'd have a lookout, equipped with night vision surveillance. It occurred to him that he could also be completely wrong about Granger's whereabouts, and the whereabouts of the mortars, in which case he and Taylor were running around an empty park after hours with automatic weapons while the opening act of NordFaust's Götterdämmerung unfolded elsewhere.

Far off to their right Brodie saw LED lampposts amidst a large, empty parking lot. Beyond it was the vague silhouette of a wide, low building.

Taylor said, "That must be the old airport terminal."

Brodie scanned the distant building. On the northern end of it, which was closest to them, was a tall tower with a white radar dome. The air traffic control tower. He pointed to it and said, "If they are here, and if they know their stuff, there'll be a lookout or a sniper up there. Probably both."

Taylor nodded. "But even with a night vision scope or binoculars, their visibility will be crap in this weather."

"Better than ours."

"Look."

Brodie looked where Taylor was pointing. Off to their left he could see the impression of tire marks in the snow, running from an opening in the tree line twenty yards away and cutting across the field.

Brodie gestured for Taylor to follow him along the tree line. They reached the break in the trees, where there was a narrow asphalt path barely visible. The tire marks originated somewhere farther to the east and ran through the tree line out into the snowy field. Brodie thought he could see the faint red glow of taillights somewhere beyond.

He said to Taylor, "I'm going to follow these tire tracks. Count to fifteen and follow."

She looked at the distant air traffic control tower, which was designed to have a view of everything above and below. "Okay . . . but that tower —"

"Then stay here and cover me."

Brodie broke out of the tree line and ran across the field, following the tire marks. He didn't hear any gunshots, and in a few seconds he saw the taillights of a stationary vehicle ahead of him. He aimed his rifle toward the vehicle as he ran closer.

It was a small white sedan with some sort

781

of logo painted on the side. The car was still running, and the driver's-side door was open.

He rounded the driver's side of the car and got low with his rifle trained on the windows. The back seat was empty, and there was no one in the front. Then he spotted a single bullet hole in the middle of the windshield.

The crack of a rifle rang out somewhere behind him. He dropped behind the car and spun around as Taylor ran across the field. She dove behind the car as another shot shattered a car window.

She caught her breath. "I saw the muzzle flash. He's in the tower. Just at the base of the radar dome."

Another shot hit the body of the car.

Brodie spotted a dark object in the snow, about twenty feet ahead of them. It was a body, lying face down. Maybe park security. The guy must have been doing his rounds or maybe responding to something he saw or heard. The sniper put a round through the windshield, the man panicked and fled the car, and then he caught one in the back.

Taylor said, "I guess we're in the right place."

"That's the good news." Brodie relayed the bad news: "The sniper will radio our location to his friends. We have to move. Now."

Taylor nodded.

Brodie looked out at the snowy field. A charge through the snow under sniper fire with limited ammo was not exactly a good plan, but it was the only plan. Backup from the German police might be minutes away, or hours away. Would Trent Chilcott have immediately contacted the German authorities? Or would he delay that phone call, and allow time for two renegade CID agents to go out in a blaze of glory before the cavalry arrived? Brodie could make a good case for either. So could Trent Chilcott.

Brodie gestured out to the field and said to Taylor, "We don't know where they have set up the mortars, but tactically speaking, the dead center of the field is the most isolated position and would allow them the most time to surveil anyone approaching. So let's assume that is where they are. Due south. Vary your speed and your direction as much as you can. Try not to be a predictable target." He added, "The snowfall gives us some concealment at this distance."

Taylor looked him in the eyes and did not respond.

He continued, "I will go first. If I fall, you do not stop. And if we don't see anyone, we keep going until we reach the far perimeter fence, then move left, to the east. That puts more distance between us and the sniper tower, and also puts us closer to the end of the field that is nearest the suspected target in Neukölln."

Taylor nodded, then took his hand and

squeezed it.

Brodie looked in her eyes. "See you on the other side." He got to his feet and took off across the snowfield.

CHAPTER 52

Brodie sprinted across the white expanse with his rifle across his chest. Within two seconds he heard a gunshot. And then another. He slowed down, then cut left and sped up, trying to avoid a straight line or a constant speed, to make the sniper work for his kill.

In the snowy haze ahead of him he thought he saw a vehicle. Two more shots rang out from the distant air traffic control tower as he ran toward the vehicle, which Brodie realized was speeding toward him. The vehicle flicked on its headlights, momentarily blinding him.

He kept running as he fired his rifle above the headlights, at the windshield, sending tracer rounds streaking toward the approaching vehicle. It kept coming.

He pivoted to his left as another sniper shot rang out from the control tower. He looked over his shoulder and saw Taylor behind him, still running and peeling off to the right.

The vehicle swung toward Brodie, gunned

the engine, and sped straight at him. Brodie fired another burst at the oncoming vehicle, which he could now see was a four-wheeled military personnel carrier, which would be armored, and the windshield and tires would be bullet-resistant, and nothing he was carrying was going to put a dent in that thing.

The personnel carrier was getting closer, and Brodie pivoted right again to force the vehicle into another sharp turn to stay on him.

Taylor was ahead of him now, and beyond her Brodie could see men running. Someone barked orders in German. A piece of equipment was being pushed across the snow.

The armored vehicle swung around again and was bearing down on Brodie, and the headlights illuminated what he and Taylor were charging toward.

Brodie had only seconds to take in what he was seeing — two men in camo were setting up a large mortar tube on a wheeled base and bipod, and another two held a long, finned mortar round. Three men with assault rifles were standing in front of a military utility truck with their rifles trained on the approaching silhouettes.

The headlights of the armored truck momentarily blinded the armed men, and they fired wide, just missing Brodie and Taylor and pinging off the front of the truck. Brodie and Taylor returned fire, and one of the men fell.

The mortar team dropped their equipment and scrambled for weapons as the armored vehicle screeched to a halt behind them and flicked off its headlights as two men jumped out.

Brodie slammed full-speed into a soldier holding a rifle and they fell back into the snow. Brodie got on top of the guy and pressed his rifle barrel across the man's throat, choking him. The guy punched Brodie in the gut and rolled away, then stood and raised his rifle, but Brodie put two rounds in his chest before the man could fire. A second later, he heard Taylor cry out.

He turned toward where he'd heard the cry, but he could barely see anything now in the dark field amidst the swirling snow.

Someone fired in Brodie's direction, and he saw a tracer round streak past his head. He dove for cover behind the utility truck. The rear of the truck was a large flatbed with metal sides and a canvas cover. The truck contained long metal ammunition cans that probably held additional mortar rounds. He got low as he heard two bullets impact off the side of the truck.

The shooting stopped for a moment, and then another shot rang out and hit the truck a few inches to Brodie's right. The soldiers were limiting their fire, wary of hitting the mortars through the canvas flatbed cover and blowing them all to hell. That would actually be a pretty good outcome, all things considered, as they were in the middle of nowhere and the heavy snowfall would probably limit the bioagent's spread. But when the best you can hope for is getting yourself blown up, you're not having a good day.

Brodie stayed low near the rear of the truck's flatbed with his rifle in a firing position, sweeping the area and trying to get a visual on anything around him. He quickly evaluated the situation. There were at least six or seven armed men still standing, Taylor was down, but hopefully not out.

I will see you in the field.

Colonel Granger and chief geneticist Dr. Hausner were planning to be here, to witness the launch of Titan Genetics' latest product.

So, where were they? Maybe they'd decided it was too risky. Or maybe they'd departed after the first gunshots.

Brodie eyed the canisters of biologically weaponized mortar rounds. He'd momentarily interrupted the attack, but they would begin firing into Neukölln as soon as he was dead or captured. Meanwhile, where were the German police? Brodie had to buy time, and the way to do that was to stay alive long enough for the cavalry to arrive.

Brodie dashed around the passenger side of the truck with his rifle trained ahead of him. He heard someone shouting orders in German and more gunfire. Then someone off to his right started pumping rounds in his direction. They missed and hit the side of the utility truck, but didn't detonate the mortar rounds. So maybe he'd have to do that.

Brodie returned fire until his mag was empty. He checked his pockets for another mag but realized he was out. He tossed the rifle and pulled his pistol as a soldier came running around the truck toward him.

Brodie squeezed off two rounds and dropped the guy, then pressed his back against the truck and swept his pistol across the snowy field. He was exposed at all angles, with almost no visibility and nothing but a sidearm with limited ammo. In fact, he was as good as dead as soon as more men came around the truck and got a visual on him, so maybe the time had come for him to empty his pistol into the boxes of mortar rounds . . .

Time seemed to slow down. Scott Brodie looked out at the expanse before him, but it wasn't snow. It was sand, stretching to the horizon on both sides of the road, and filling the air from the powerful winds blowing across the hot desert wastes and blotting out the midday sun.

He smelled the acrid stench of burning fuel and rubber. And flesh. The Stryker at the head of their convoy had been disabled by a roadside bomb and was now a burning wreckage blocking the road. Another explosive device had taken out the vehicle directly behind theirs. They were on a highway cutting across the desert west of Ramadi, which meant they were isolated, with no one around except the people trying to kill them.

Sergeant Brodie's machine gunner had been killed, so he manned his Stryker vehicle's mounted gun, pumping .50-caliber rounds into the sand dunes on both sides of the road where the enemy had taken positions for their ambush. Bullets pinged off the gun shield and both sides of the armored vehicle. His remaining men had left the Stryker to engage, and he heard a guy get hit. And then another. Someone yelled for the medic, but the medic did not respond.

As Brodie swiveled between both sides of the road unloading heavy rounds into the swirling sandstorm, he made his peace. He'd die here. He'd die young. Shit happens.

He heard the beating of helicopter blades overhead. The air cavalry had arrived. Maybe this was not his day after all.

A chopper flicked on a searchlight as it streaked across the sky, and he was back at Tempelhof, in the swirling, freezing night. A loudspeaker blasted orders in German.

Some of the men started firing at the chopper and took return fire. In the confusion a soldier rushed around the truck right into Brodie's line of fire and Brodie shot him in the chest. Then Brodie ran back around the utility truck toward where he thought he'd heard Taylor.

He found her lying face down in the snow near the armored personnel truck and dragged her under it as bullets from the helicopter rained down around them. The helicopter descended onto the field and SWAT police poured out of the chopper and exchanged fire with the remaining soldiers who'd taken cover behind the utility truck. Then he saw another chopper — the command and control craft — which remained airborne and swept the field with its searchlight.

Brodie turned Taylor onto her back and looked at her. Her eyes were open and she was breathing normally. He told her, "SWAT team's here. We'll get you medevaced."

Taylor nodded.

Brodie saw a bullet hole in her winter coat on her left side above the waist. He put his hand under her coat and sweater to find the wound. The jagged flesh and warm blood was on her far left side, and felt to him like a grazing wound, with no penetration. He grabbed a fistful of snow and packed it on the wound, then placed her left hand over it. Taylor shuddered. Brodie said, "Hang in, soldier."

He located her pistol in the snow and put it in her right hand. He looked her in the eyes and said, "You've been hit before, and worse than this."

"Thanks for the memories."

Suddenly a vehicle door opened, and someone jumped out of the personnel carrier and ran. From beneath the vehicle Brodie could make out a civilian winter coat and dark pants.

He looked back at Taylor. "I think I see Granger. Running."

"You need to pursue."

Brodie didn't move.

"Scott . . . Don't let him get away."

He looked at her. "Okay. Be right back."

"You better . . ."

Brodie rolled out from under the personnel carrier and stood. The SWAT police were still engaged in a firefight with the remaining NordFaust soldiers, and the C&C chopper was sweeping the southern end of the field with its searchlight.

Brodie ran toward the fleeing figure, who was headed away from the choppers and toward the southeastern corner of Tempelhof Field, where there was a long chain-link fence topped with razor wire.

Brodie shouted, "Army CID! Halt! Or I shoot!"

The man kept running. Brodie fired a shot in the air.

The man stopped, but did not turn around.

"Put your hands on your head!" He added, "Asshole!"

The man slowly complied.

Brodie approached with his pistol trained

on the man's back. As he got closer, he saw that the man was gray-haired and balding, and wearing a black wool coat. "Turn around!"

The man turned, hands on his head. He appeared to be in his mid-fifties. Not Granger. He looked Brodie in the eyes with an expression filled with contempt.

"What is your name?"

"I am Dr. Martin Hausner. And you must be Mr. Brodie."

"I must be. And where is Colonel Granger?"

Hausner didn't answer.

Brodie aimed the pistol at the man's heart. "Where is Charles Granger?"

Hausner stared at him and said, "I have no idea." He added, "Even if I knew, I wouldn't tell you."

Brodie lowered his pistol to the man's right knee and pulled the trigger.

Hausner screamed and fell.

Brodie pressed the pistol to the man's other knee while he writhed on the ground. "I've got four more rounds and I'll make sure none of them kill you. Get it?"

The man was hyperventilating. After a moment he got control of himself and said, "He . . . ran ahead of me . . . to the gate . . ."

"Where is he going?"

The man closed his eyes, but didn't answer.

Brodie fired another round, this one into

Hausner's left ankle. The man screamed again.

"Where is he going?"

"The . . . march . . . Please . . ."

"Does he have your plague with him?"

The man hesitated, then nodded.

Brodie looked at Hausner writhing on the ground. This bastard deserved a round to the head, but he was worth more alive. Also, Brodie couldn't spare any more bullets. He pocketed his pistol and took off across the field toward the gate, praying there was still time to stop the unthinkable.

CHAPTER 53

Brodie stuck his pistol in his belt and scaled the gate leading out of the park. He dropped to the sidewalk and ran onto a narrow residential street.

He was in Neukölln now, and Karl-Marx Straße was a few blocks east of him. He could make out the faint sounds of the protest march in the distance.

He ran through the empty street, passing a middle-aged Arab man on the sidewalk. He saw no one else. Everyone was at the march.

Brodie crossed the street and looked down the next block, which was lined with trees and a few streetlamps. In the distance he saw a tall figure in a long coat walking away briskly, passing under the white light of a streetlamp. The figure's right hand was in his pocket. In his left he held a bag or briefcase at his side. Instinct, training, and experience told him this guy — like Brodie himself — did not belong in this neighborhood.

Brodie could hear the marchers more

clearly now, and through the snow he glimpsed the stream of people on the cross-road farther ahead.

A block away to his right, Brodie noticed an idling police car, and on another corner were two police officers in full tactical gear with assault rifles. Berlin PD was out in full force tonight to control the march. They would know that something was happening at Tempelhof, and that it was probably related to threats against this protest march. If Brodie had his CID creds, he'd enlist these guys' help. But there was no time to convince them of who he was, or who he was looking for. Or why.

Brodie slowed his pace as he passed the police so as not to attract unwanted attention, but he felt their eyes on him.

He cleared the intersection and looked around, but did not see any other police, so he sprinted ahead, trying to keep his eyes on the tall man in the distance. Just as he started running the man reached the march and slipped into the crowd.

Brodie darted around a barricade at the next intersection and kept running.

He reached Karl-Marx Straße, where a sea of people, mostly Middle Eastern–looking, marched slowly down the blocked-off road through the steady snowfall. Some held signs written in German and Arabic; others held up candles or the bright screens of their smartphones. A few carried photos of Hasan al-Kazimi, the murdered Iraqi man. Some were angry, shouting a spirited call-and-response chant in Arabic. Most were silent and somber.

Brodie slowed down and slipped into the stream of people. He scanned the crowd but could not find the man in the long coat.

Then in a break in the crowd, Brodie saw him. The man was unzipping a black nylon bag and making his way to the outer edge of the march.

Brodie pushed his way through the marchers. "Move! Move!"

Some people got out of his way as he pushed forward, but the crowd around Brodie was too dense. He saw now where the man was headed — toward a trash receptacle on the sidewalk about ten yards away from him. The man had dropped the nylon bag and was holding a canister in his hands. Brodie pulled his gun. "Stop!"

Someone caught sight of Brodie's gun and yelled. People started screaming. The crowd surged. They spilled onto the sidewalks where they could, running between or climbing over the parked cars that lined the street.

Brodie charged forward, shoving people to the side as he fought his way through.

He lost sight of the man for a moment, and then in another break in the crowd he saw him. The man was facing him now. He held a pistol in his hand pointed at Brodie, who saw the muzzle flash, followed by the sound of the discharge.

A searing pain shot up Brodie's right thigh. He squeezed off two rounds in the direction of the man, who returned fire. There was screaming all around him. Brodie looked down and saw his blood on his leg and on the snow and brown slush. He took a step forward, then found himself lying in the snow.

Brodie looked up and saw the man lying on his right side toward the edge of the street. Next to him was the canister, which Brodie saw was an innocuous-looking, commercial-sized coffee can.

Brodie tried to stand but couldn't. He shut out the pain and forced himself forward, crawling and dragging himself along the snowy road toward the man, his pistol still in hand. He called out, "Charles Granger!"

Granger was alive, and looked at him. He was in his sixties, with pale skin and wispy white hair. He had a long, prominent nose, bushy gray eyebrows, and deep-set gray eyes. He wore a long black coat and a white dress shirt stained with blood on the right side of his chest. The man's pistol lay a few feet in front of him, and the canister was a few feet to his left. Brodie saw that a small device was attached to the coffee canister — explosives and a detonator. It was a mini bio-bomb, filled with genetically modified pathogens that would kill every non-Caucasian in Neukölln — maybe all of Berlin. Men, women, and children. And once that happened, there would be a stampede of Arabs, Turks, East Asians, and others out of Germany, and maybe out of Europe. And maybe that was just the beginning . . .

Brodie stopped crawling about ten feet from the man and aimed his gun.

A small smile cut across Granger's lips. Brodie now spotted an old Nokia cell phone in the snow about four feet from Granger, which Brodie knew from his time in Iraq was used as a remote trigger device for bombs. Four feet was not an easy reach in Granger's current state but not impossible, and they both knew it.

Brodie said, "I got you . . . you son of a bitch."

Charles Granger managed a weak laugh. Then he began to cough up frothy blood, indicating a punctured lung. He looked up at the black sky and the falling snow. After a moment he said, "I got you too, Mr. Brodie."

Suddenly Brodie heard shouting in German. He saw that a few Berlin Police officers had taken up defensive positions behind the parked cars, and they were aiming their rifles at Brodie over the hoods of the cars.

"Waffe weg und Händ hoch! Oder du wirst erschossen!"

Granger looked at Brodie again. "They're

going to shoot you if you don't put the gun down."

That was good to know. But if Brodie dropped his gun, Granger would go for the bomb trigger. These cops probably had no idea who Scott Brodie was, or who Charles Granger was. But only one of them had a gun pointed at the other.

Well, whether Berlin PD knew it or not, Scott Brodie was still a cop, so he said to Granger, "You're under arrest, asshole. Put your hands on top of your head and keep them there."

Granger stared at Brodie. "You're young . . . too young . . . to understand any of this."

"I understand enough. I understand you are a traitor to your country and a murderer."

Granger coughed again, and a ribbon of blood ran from his lips into the snow. He said, "I . . . am a dreamer. But my dream died. And . . . I found a new dream. You . . ." Granger took a long breath and wheezed. "You . . . fight for nothing. For absolutely . . . nothing. This world is already dead. You . . . just don't realize it . . ."

"Waffe runter!" A few more police had taken position behind the cars, and two officers were now advancing on the road toward Brodie, pistols drawn.

Brodie felt the rage building inside him. "Don't patronize me, you prick. You killed Harry. You killed Anna."

Granger said, "Collateral damage. The real target was these . . . these . . . vermin. Scum. Why don't you understand?"

"You're . . . a sick piece of shit."

Brodie was feeling light-headed and his heart was pounding in his ears. He was losing a lot of blood, and realized that his femoral artery had probably been hit, which meant he'd bleed out in a few more minutes. He also realized that Granger must have noticed this, and was talking to run down the clock on Scott Brodie's life. And then Granger would complete his last mission.

Brodie kept his finger on the trigger of his pistol. This was it. He had to do it. Before he couldn't . . .

"Scott Brodie! Drop your weapon!"

He recognized that voice. It was Captain Omar Soliman of the Berlin Police Department. The voice sounded like it was coming from his left. Brodie did not take his eyes off Granger, but sensed movement in his peripheral vision. Soliman was standing in the road, about fifteen feet away.

Soliman said, "Drop it, now! We need to get both of you immediate medical assistance."

Granger stared at Brodie, and now his eyes were full of fury. He said, "Go ahead . . . listen to the Arab."

Granger's arm slid slowly across the snow, toward the cell phone. "I just . . . need to make a phone call."

Brodie said, "Captain . . . that's . . ."

Soliman pointed his pistol at Brodie. "Drop the weapon, Mr. Brodie. I will not ask again."

Brodie looked at Granger, whose hand was moving, almost imperceptibly, toward the cell phone trigger device. Granger looked at Brodie, as if daring the man to stop him.

Brodie could feel the edges of his vision begin to cloud, as if he were entering a dark tunnel. He kept his eyes on Charles Granger. On the man's face. On his eyes. And in those eyes . . . those eyes . . .

There was too much life left in those eyes.

Do what has to be done.

Brodie steadied his aim, squeezed the trigger, and put a round through Granger's left eye. The man's head snapped back and he went slack and still.

Odin was dead.

Brodie expected the next shot to come from Captain Soliman, but it didn't. Brodie dropped his pistol. Captain Soliman looked down at him in a moment of shock, then immediately crouched and applied pressure to Brodie's thigh as he began shouting orders in German.

Brodie stared at Colonel Charles Granger as the world began to fade. Blood ran from Granger's shattered eye socket.

Scott Brodie wasn't religious, but he found himself saying aloud, "I hope you're in Hell."

Brodie was vaguely aware of what was happening around him. A lot of commotion and people speaking urgently. He heard the wail of an ambulance. His eyes landed on the canister that stood next to Granger's corpse.

He looked up at Soliman, who was still applying pressure to his thigh as he looked around and waved someone over.

Brodie said to Soliman, "That . . . canister . . ."

Soliman looked at him. "What?"

"Hazmat . . . Explosives . . . Airborne plague . . ."

Soliman looked at the can, then immediately started issuing orders to people around him, likely to seal the area and get a biocontainment team and a bomb squad on-site.

Brodie looked again at the corpse of Colonel Charles Granger. Snowflakes settled on his dark coat and melted in the blood around his chest. Brodie now noticed a wedding band on Granger's left ring finger. He wondered if the man had remarried or had kept it as a remembrance of his dead wife. He wondered how anyone could be capable of loving another person and still do what this man had done.

Brodie still had no real sense of this man, of what had turned him against his own country, and what had happened in the years between the Cold War and now to embitter him against the entire world order, to turn him into an avowed white supremacist. There probably wasn't an answer — at least, not a single one, or a simple one. Colonel Granger had been on a four-decade road to Hell that began before Scott Brodie was even born. There were probably lots of twists and turns along the way, and maybe even a few off-ramps, but Granger hadn't taken them. And maybe it didn't matter anymore how Charles Granger's soul had been poisoned. All that mattered now was that the son of a bitch was dead.

We got him, Harry. We got him, Anna.

Brodie realized at some point that Captain Soliman had left, and someone was applying a tourniquet around his upper thigh, and he was lifted onto a stretcher and loaded into an ambulance. Someone put an oxygen mask to his face, and someone put a blood pressure cuff on his arm. The sirens wailed and the ambulance sped down the road, and he heard rapid-fire German among the EMTs surrounding him as someone placed an IV line in his arm and began administering fluids.

He thought of Taylor. He hoped she was okay. And David Kim.

He thought of the people who were not okay and never would be. Harry Vance. Anna Albrecht. Anna's father, Manfred. The three other executed Stasi informants. The three murdered Syrian immigrants. The young Iraqi man, Hasan al-Kazimi. And the dead whose names were written on those blood vials.

Brodie pictured Odin's corpse in the road, lying in the blood-drenched snow. The bastard was dead, but death was too easy an end for him.

He said through the oxygen mask, "He . . . deserved worse . . ."

An EMT put a hand on his shoulder and said, "You are going to be all right."

Brodie assumed he meant physically. Mentally, maybe not so all right. Why else would he be doing this for a living? Justice. And there was enough injustice in the world to keep him employed for a long time. But that came with a cost.

He recalled a famous line from the German philosopher Friedrich Nietzsche: "Whoever fights monsters should see to it that in the process he does not become a monster."

That was the big trick.

CHAPTER 54

Scott Brodie sat alone in a hospital bed in a dimly lit room. Through the window he could see the hazy sky of nighttime Berlin. He listened to the white noise of the IV infusion pump and the occasional footsteps of doctors, nurses, and orderlies in the hallway outside the closed door.

Brodie — along with Maggie Taylor and David Kim — had spent the last forty-eight hours in a biocontainment facility on the outskirts of the city. For Brodie and Taylor, it was a precautionary measure. For David Kim, it was to save his life.

Brodie looked at the empty hospital bed at the other end of the room. Taylor should have been transferred by now, and a nurse had told Brodie they would bring her here. Maybe by morning.

As for Special Agent David Kim, Tomas Stellmacher had taken Brodie's threats seriously — or Stellmacher had had a talk with his better angels — and he'd administered the antibiotic to Kim and gotten him out of the bunker and into an ambulance. And because Stellmacher played with plague, he knew exactly where to have David Kim taken for treatment and biocontainment. Brodie had demanded and gotten a full report on Kim's condition from a doctor at the facility who told Brodie that his colleague, Mr. Kim, had been close to death, but was expected to make a full recovery. A lot of bad things happen in this broken world, but miracles happen too.

The door opened and a tall man stepped in. By the dim night-lights, Brodie could make out a long object in his gloved hand.

Brodie said, "Visiting hours are over."

Trent Chilcott replied, "That's why I'm here."

Brodie tried to see what Chilcott had in his hand. Gun? Hand grenade? "Is that for me?"

Chilcott lifted the object. It was a small bouquet of flowers wrapped in brown paper. "For Maggie." He eyed the empty bed. "But I guess she's not here yet."

"She doesn't want anything from you."

Chilcott dropped the bouquet on a nearby table, then walked into the room and stopped a few feet from Brodie's bedside. "I wanted to congratulate you. And thank you."

"You're welcome." He added, "How's your solar plexus?"

Chilcott ignored that and said, "Reinhard

807

Dorn is dead."

Brodie didn't respond.

"He got hold of something sharp in his cell and slashed his wrists."

"Good."

"The German investigators don't feel that way."

"There's nothing they could offer a man like that to get him to cooperate."

Chilcott nodded. "The BKA's still sorting out who knew what among the detained Titan staff and NordFaust members. But they think only a few people within both organizations knew the full details of the biological attack plan." He added, "Fortunately, Titan Genetics kept meticulous records, even of the secret operations that were siloed from the legitimate side of the company. Titan has a count of every bacterial colony on every pour plate in their labs, and they recorded how much was deployed in each of their experiments. They even catalogued the bacterial concentration of each of the submunitions in each of the mortar warheads. Reinhard Dorn's obsessive need for control over his creation will be an Intel bonanza."

Well, those were the kinds of habits you picked up after years of working in a police state. Brodie asked, "Do I have a need to know this?"

Chilcott stared at him. "I know that once

you're out of here you're going to try to hunt down the truth, and I thought I'd save you the time. And demonstrate to you that things are under control and need to stay that way."

There it was. Brodie thought he'd at least be stateside before he got this talk. He said, "I helped bury your shit once and I'm not doing it again."

"This is not my shit, to be clear."

"The answer's the same."

Chilcott took a step closer. "I'm not asking."

"Hey, Trent, my leg is fucked up but the rest of me is fine. Come any closer and I'll show you."

Chilcott paused a moment and looked like he was trying to keep his temper in check. Then he said, "Let me explain something to you, Scott. Sometimes our best protection against bad actors is their own limited imaginations. Outside of a small circle of people, no one knows that a biogenetic weapon such as the Götterdämmerung plague is even possible. And if it becomes common knowledge that it is not only possible, but feasible, and that there is in fact an *existing strain* capable of killing eighty fucking percent of the world's population . . ." He trailed off. "This isn't the Mercer case, Mr. Brodie. This isn't about protecting people from embarrassment or accountability. This is much, much bigger. Neither of us sets the rules on this one — or

809

has the luxury of breaking them."

Brodie didn't respond. Chilcott had dropped his aloof affect and actually looked a little worried. This threat of biological Armageddon really was bigger than all of them, and maybe it dwarfed considerations of pride, ego, or even principles. That was a disturbing thought.

Brodie thought about the late Colonel Charles Granger, who was currently dominating headlines. The American Army traitor who had evaded justice for decades, and who had spent his later years plotting with the most dangerous white supremacist group in Europe to launch attacks against Arab immigrants.

The news had reported on the seized cluster bombs but said nothing about the plague inside of them, and made only a passing mention of Charles Granger's status as a board member of Titan Genetics, a biotech firm that coincidentally had just been raided by federal police for reasons unknown. The public might theorize about a connection between those two events — or three events now, with the prison suicide of the Titan Genetics founder Reinhard Dorn — but there was not yet enough information to draw any real conclusions. And if Trent Chilcott and his Intel colleagues got their way, there never would be.

Brodie looked at Chilcott. "I'll see how this

plays out."

Chilcott stared back at him. "That's not the answer I need from you, Scott."

"It's the best you're going to get."

"Do you have a hero complex, or a martyr complex?"

"My shrink says both, with high paranoia."

"Paranoia is good. Watch yourself."

Brodie looked at him. "The doctors told me I need rest, and you're pissing me off."

Chilcott turned and walked to the door, and was about to leave when Brodie asked, "Why were you in Berlin?"

Chilcott turned to him. "I told you. I was working with the Special Collection Service to monitor NordFaust."

"Yeah, you told me. I didn't believe you then, and I don't believe you now."

Chilcott did not respond.

"You came here to whack us, you sick fuck. But then you realized our homicide investigation was dovetailing with the NordFaust plot that your colleagues were monitoring, so you decided to bring us in and under your control, to see what we knew."

Chilcott was silent. Then he said, "You're right, Scott. You need your rest." He gestured to the flowers on the table. "Get those in some water or they'll die."

"Stay away from Maggie Taylor. Or *you'll* die."

Chilcott locked eyes with Brodie. "I'll

remember you said that, Scott. And you might come to regret it." He added, "I owe you one." Trent Chilcott walked out of the room and shut the door.

Brodie knew he was right about Chilcott's presence in Berlin. He'd seen it in the man's eyes. And Brodie knew he and Taylor weren't done with this treacherous psycho.

He checked the time on the phone he'd been lent by the U.S. Embassy: 9:20 P.M. Then he looked at his call log. Nothing from Taylor, who might or might not have been given his temporary phone number, but he saw the five missed calls from Colonel Dombroski over the last two days, all with corresponding voice mails that he hadn't listened to. He couldn't deal with a phone call at the moment, but maybe a text would do:

Good evening, Colonel. You've heard the bad news by now that I'm alive and mostly well. Good news is Taylor is the same. I'll call tomorrow.

Dombroski replied almost immediately: *Yes, General Kiernan has kept me briefed. Rest up. You earned it.* There was a pause, and then he sent another message: *Your office at Quantico is ready for you when you return. The Army needs you and your country needs you.*

Brodie looked at that guilt-trip message. He'd broken every rule in the book, and a few unwritten ones, but apparently there was some forgiveness when you help stop a genocidal mass murder. Maybe this case would earn him a promotion. Or maybe it was enough to be spared a court-martial.

Brodie wrote back: *I'm under sedation for an enema. Call you tomorrow,* then set his phone down on the table next to the bed and reclined, letting his mind go where it wanted . . .

Anna.

When he tried to think of nothing, he thought of her. And he wondered if there was something he could have done differently to prevent what had happened.

But that wasn't fair. He had done what he could, which was to finish what Harry Vance had started. Vance himself had picked up the trail from Anna's mother, Ursula, who had in turn been seeking justice for her murdered husband, Manfred. And what had inspired Manfred Albrecht to risk his life by passing on Stasi secrets to the West? Probably his own day-to-day work inside Stasi headquarters, where he'd seen thousands of innocent people spied on, harassed, threatened, and arrested, their lives slowly ground to dust. Some people have a sense of justice, a sense of right and wrong, and the balls to act on that. Most of those people were dead. But new ones came along.

Brodie drifted in and out of sleep, and eventually he woke to early morning light streaming in through the window. A new day.

The door opened, and Maggie Taylor rolled in on a wheelchair being pushed by a male orderly who flicked on the lights.

Brodie sat up. "Good morning."

Taylor smiled. "Good morning. I am officially not a biohazard."

"Congratulations. You look great."

She wore a hospital gown, and actually looked pale, unkempt, and exhausted. But there was life and light in her eyes, like she knew she'd been through Hell and survived. Again.

The orderly helped Taylor out of the wheelchair and into the hospital bed. She winced in pain as she eased into the bed. The bullet she'd taken had not hit any organs, but it had nicked a rib and caused extensive soft tissue damage that would take a while to heal.

Taylor thanked the orderly and he left with the wheelchair.

She raised the bed so she was sitting upright, then turned to Brodie. "You look good."

"I feel great."

"Ready to return to duty?"

"Maybe tomorrow."

"I probably shouldn't be surprised that a case I work with you ends in a hospital."

"Better than a three-volley salute and taps."

She had no reply, and they sat in silence awhile. Then Taylor said, "I spoke to David,

814

over video. He's still very weak but doing a little better every day."

"Good."

Taylor looked across the room at the bouquet of flowers, which had wilted. "Who are those from?"

Brodie didn't reply.

Taylor nodded. She knew who they were from.

Brodie swung his legs over the side of the bed, then eased himself off.

"Are you supposed to be walking?"

"Let's find out." He shuffled over with his IV pole and sat in a chair next to Taylor's bed.

They looked at each other. Taylor said, "I spoke to Colonel Dombroski. He told me that he considered your resignation a rash decision, made under the stress of a tough assignment."

"I'll put it in writing."

"Scott . . ."

"This job doesn't suit me."

Taylor laughed.

Brodie said, "I'm serious."

"I know. That's why it's funny." She suggested, "Take your medical leave in the Caribbean." She added, "That's what I'm going to do."

He didn't reply.

They were both quiet for a moment. Then Taylor said, "I'm putting in for a transfer back to Quantico."

Brodie looked at her. "Good."

Taylor was waiting for him to say something more, so he added, "Don't partner with Brad Evans."

"I'm partnering with you."

Brodie did not respond.

She continued, "You had your reasons for resigning. But the fact is you stayed on the case on your terms."

"Which is why I can't go back to theirs."

Taylor thought a moment, then said, "You want to know what Colonel Dombroski said to me? He said that he dreaded to think about what would have happened if he had assigned a different team to this case. He'd never say that to you, but he said it to me, and I'm telling you."

Or, she'd learned how to bullshit from Scott Brodie. "Thank you for that."

"War changes you, Scott. It changed me, and it changed you. This job changes you in another way. In either case, we're not fit for duty in the civilian world." She looked at him. "This is it, buddy. This is us."

He knew that, but said, "Worst re-up pitch I've ever heard."

She smiled, then said, "The truth hurts, but bullshitting yourself hurts more."

Brodie looked at his partner, who, despite loss of blood, lack of sleep, and days inside windowless rooms eating bad hospital food, looked . . . vibrant. Almost radiant. He pictured her all those years ago on her first government-paid trip to Germany — in a hospital bed at the Landstuhl Regional Medical Center recovering from the IED blast in Afghanistan that almost killed her.

Maggie Taylor wanted to live on the edge, but it wasn't because of the adrenaline rush. It was because that's where she found the meaning. That's where she thought she could tip the scales of justice.

Maybe Harry Vance had felt that way too. Or at least he came to feel that way toward the end of his life, when he found a cause worth fighting for. And dying for. The thing about being on the edge is sometimes you fall off. And the people who don't fall are supposed to carry on.

He said to Taylor, "All right."

"All right?"

"We'll be a train wreck together. Mutually assured destruction."

She held out her hand. "We'll split the blame and share the glory."

He took her hand and looked in her eyes. "Deal."

ACKNOWLEDGMENTS

We would like to thank Alex's friend Matthew Longo, an assistant professor of political science at Leiden University, Holland, for sharing some of his research and insights on the Stasi. We had the good fortune of writing this book while Matt was researching and writing his nonfiction book titled *The Picnic,* about the first breach in the Iron Curtain along the Austro-Hungarian border.

We would also like to thank Alex's friend Milena Pastreich, along with her mother, Ingrid Eggers, for their assistance with the German dialogue.

Alex also wishes to thank his wife, Dagmar Weaver-Madsen, for her immense patience, support, and creative insights during the long process of writing this book, and also his daughter, Margot, age five, who tolerated long stretches without her papa. Alex would also like to thank his mother, Ellen, and his sister, Lauren, for doing close and careful reads and — despite obvious bias — giving honest and detailed feedback.

Alex also extends a special thanks to his in-laws, Carol and Anton Weaver-Madsen, for their generosity and hospitality in offering their beautiful home in New York's Hudson Valley as a writing refuge. Much of this book was written there.

We would also like to thank our editor at Scribner Books, Colin Harrison, for his expert editorial input and his generally calm demeanor as we blew past several deadlines. And much gratitude to our agents at CAA, Jennifer Joel and Sloan Harris, for their excellent guidance and encouragement.

Last but certainly not least, many thanks to Nelson's hardworking assistants Patricia Chichester and Dianne Francis for managing the at times complicated workflow of a coauthored novel.

The following people or their families have made generous contributions to charities in return for having their name used as a character in this novel: **David Katz** — The Crohn's & Colitis Foundation (CCFA); **Howard Fensterman** — The Crohn's & Colitis Foundation (CCFA); **Frank Kiernan** — The Crohn's & Colitis Foundation (CCFA); and **Tyler McKinnon** — various charities.

We hope all these individuals enjoy their

fictitious alter egos and that they continue their good work for worthy causes.

ABOUT THE AUTHORS

Nelson DeMille is the author of twenty-three novels, seven of which were #1 *New York Times* bestsellers. His novels include *The Maze, The Deserter* (written with Alex De-Mille), *The Cuban Affair, Word of Honor, Plum Island, The Charm School, The Gold Coast,* and *The General's Daughter,* which was made into a major motion picture starring John Travolta and Madeleine Stowe. He has written short stories, book reviews, and articles for magazines and newspapers. Nelson De-Mille is a combat-decorated U.S. Army veteran, a member of Mensa, Poets & Writers, and the Authors Guild, and past president of the Mystery Writers of America. He is also a member of the International Thriller Writers, who honored him as 2015 Thriller-Master of the Year. He lives on Long Island with his family.

Alex DeMille is a director, film editor, and author of the *New York Times* bestselling novel *The Deserter* (written with Nelson De-Mille). He grew up on Long Island and received a BA from Yale University and an MFA in film directing from UCLA. He has won multiple awards and fellowships for his screenplays and films. He lives in Brooklyn with his wife and daughter.

The employees of Thorndike Press hope you have enjoyed this Large Print book. All our Thorndike Large Print titles are designed for easy reading, and all our books are made to last. Other Thorndike Press Large Print books are available at your library, through selected bookstores, or directly from us.

For information about titles, please call:
(800) 223-1244

or visit our website at:
gale.com/thorndike